THE AMERICAN ZONE

THE AMERICAN ZONE

L. NEIL SMITH

A TOM DOHERTY ASSOCIATES BOOK
NEW YORK

THE AMERICAN ZONE

Copyright © 2001 by L. Neil Smith

This book is printed on acid-free paper.

Edited by James Frenkel

A Tor Book
Published by Tom Doherty Associates, LLC
175 Fifth Avenue
New York, NY 10010

www.tor.com

Tor® is a registered trademark of Tom Doherty Associates, LLC.

ISBN 0-312-87369-7

First Edition: December 2001

Printed in the United States of America

0 9 8 7 6 5 4 3 2 1

FOR KEN FLURCHICK

(and all of you others who wanted another
straightforward, no nonsense novel about Win Bear in the
North American Confederacy).

Hey, Kenny, we're goin' home!

ACKNOWLEDGMENTS

THERE'S AN AWFUL LOT in this book that I owe to the late, great Robert LeFevre. I'd also like to acknowledge the groundbreaking brainwork of David F. Nolan, founder of the Libertarian Party, and Marshall Fritz, founder of Advocates for Self-Government and the Separation of School and State Foundation, in devising the political diamond Lucy describes in Chapter 17. My conclusion with regard to what lurks at the bottom corner of the diamond differs from theirs.

MANY THANKS to European American Armory of Cocoa, Florida, to Crimson Trace Corporation of Beaverton, Oregon, and to Chris Reeve Knives of Boise, Idaho, for their valuable assistance in making this a more interesting book than it might otherwise have been.

CONTENTS

THE AMERICAN ZONE

Of all the animals in creation, only human beings have civilization, because only human beings have *buttocks* on which they can be beaten to instill it into them.

—Bennett Williams, *The Seat of All Virtues*

1: A YANKEE DOODLE DANDY

The great secret of life lies in choosing the right woman.
It's a *mother's* job to tell you not to play with fire. Marry
the girl who tells you, "Go ahead."
                    —*Memoirs of Lucille G. Kropotkin*

Whoooooosh . . . Bang!

The pop-bottle rocket, fired past me from across the street,
damn near singed my eyebrows.

Offering some unseen neighbor the middle-finger salute, I
backed off the balcony, through the sliding transparent doors,
and into the relative security of my living room. Even if things
got out of hand and something made it through the doors, the
glass would heal itself by morning—which was more than could
be said for me.

Sometime tomorrow I'd remind myself to have a word with
an overly zealous patriot.

On second thought, he (or she) could hardly be blamed for
his (or her) enthusiasm. I'd probably just remind myself to skip
the whole thing. Nearly having my beezer Francis-Scott-Keyed
off was certainly no more than I deserved for having foolishly
poked it outdoors on this night of nights.

After all, it was July Second, 220 A.L., and across the vast,
twilit metropolis that was Greater LaPorte, sprawled from the
Cache la Poudre River to Pistol Sight Mountain between the toes
of the Rocky Mountain foothills (in a region many another culture labels "northern Colorado"), hundreds of city neighbor-
hoods had already begun twinkling, sparkling, and sputtering,
snapping, crackling, and *popping!* in blissful commemoration of
the signing of a certain illegal document that had made young

Tommy Jefferson and his little playmates terrorists in the eyes of the British Crown.

Yes indeed, it was high summer once again on the High Plains, and—perhaps just a little high themselves by now—the good ladies and gentlemen of the North American Confederacy were celebrating their favorite occasion: Independence Day. Here in the Confederacy, it actually still meant something. And it probably helped that there wasn't a building in all of Greater LaPorte that would burn any longer than thirty seconds, even if you dropped napalm on it.

For the first time in a long while, I glanced down at my left hand where I had a place-keeping finger stuck between the pages of a freshly imported hardcover I'd just brought home that afternoon: *Al Franken Is a Pathetic Little Wannabe* by Rush H. Limbaugh. I hadn't gotten past the introduction so far. Turning my back to the colorful display outside, crossing a living room carpet the size of a small basketball court to the wet bar, I poured myself a scotch and scotch, adding a dash of scotch for flavor.

It smelled wonderful. I'd tried Irish whiskey once, Bushmill's. It smells even better, but it tastes too damned good, and for someone who has a little trouble in that direction already, it's a gold-plated invitation to alcoholism.

The fact is, I'd have enjoyed celebrating, too, especially here, in the heart of one of the Confederacy's great cities. But my heart's companion (and the most luscious female I've ever met), Healer Clarissa MacDougall Olson-Bear, was busy making housecalls—as she always was on July Second—attending to such seasonal calamities as scorched fingers, ruptured eardrums, and dittoed eyeballs. For what is there worthwhile in life that *doesn't* involve some hazard?

Back where I came from originally, such a ruggedly Darwinistic sentiment would likely have soiled the lace unmentionables of the whole Volvo-driving, wine-and-cheese gobbling, no-sparrow-shall-hiccup set of what the author I was reading called "lifestyle Nazis." But I ask you, what's left of the meaning of Independence Day, if you let some jumped-up city council, some upstart county commission, or some state legislature that doesn't know its place, confiscate your Roman candles, your M-80s, or your pop-bottle rockets? North American Confederates would laugh out loud at such a contradiction—once the gunsmoke had cleared and the politicians' bleeding carcasses had been hauled away.

Leaving the book facedown on the bar, I found a comfy chair to sit in near the big glass doors and started to offer a lonely toast to my sad reflection. But just as you're really beginning to enjoy feeling sorry for yourself, there's always somebody who comes along and spoils it for you. This time it was my wife's cat Silvertip—now where had she come from?—who hopped up into my lap and settled down, purring like a contented meatloaf. I say my wife's cat. From the moment Clarissa had brought the little gray and white feline home, she'd decided she was mine—or rather, I was hers. Okay, then, happy July Second, kittycat. And happy July Second, private detective Edward William "Win" Bear. What the hell. Clarissa would be back sometime during the wee, small hours, and she'd be here tomorrow, and the day after that, and the day after that . . . What more can a middle-aged fat man ask for?

Silvertip wasn't any help; she looked up at me and asked, "Eww?"

As if in answer to my unasked question, the doorbell chose that moment to ring. Silvertip jumped off my lap, leaving poke-marks in my trousers—not to mention the flesh inside them—and headed upstairs. She doesn't really like anybody but Clarissa and me.

Grudgingly, I rose to answer the door, not even bothering to glance at the monitor on my way over to the half-flight of steps that led down to the front door. I'd seriously considered not answering it at all, but only for a moment. My guess was that I was about to have some Independence Day customers, myself.

Understand that it had taken me *years* to acquire any kind of professional reputation in the virtually crime-free Confederacy, where Captain Sam Colt had made everybody equal and President Albert Gallatin had kept 'em that way (not necessarily in that order). People tend to mind their own business as a consequence, and have very little use for detectives, private or otherwise. If I wanted to hold on to that living room that you could land small aircraft in, and all the rest of 626 Geñet Place that went with it (not to mention my own self-respect in a culture where absolutely nobody rushes to protect you from feeling ashamed of being a bum), I couldn't afford to lose any live ones—even if it meant going to work on the Glorious Second.

I did make sure that my trusty old .41 Magnum Model 58 Military & Police revolver was still hanging where it was supposed to be, from beneath my left armpit, underneath my tunic. I'd made one or two—hundred—folks a bit unhappy with me over the nine years since I'd come to the Confederacy. Now was not the time—with my personal physician out of the house—to get careless.

The front hall monitor was considerably less easy to ignore than its upstairs equivalent; it took up the whole front door. Turned out there were two of them, standing out there in the fireworks-light; I could see them (with the technology behind that monitor I could have seen them if it'd been a pitch-black overcast night and Mount Colfax was filling the air with volcanic ash) but they couldn't see me. Which may be the reason I gasped and stumbled on the last step, fetching up against the wall of the

·stairwell and damn near spilling the drink I'd forgotten I was holding.

Mindful of making a good first impression on new clients, I opened the coat closet at the bottom of the stairs, stuck the drink on the top shelf between a couple of hats, shut the closet door with one hand, summoned up my Grade-Two Professional Smile, and opened the front door with the other.

The monitor hadn't lied.

The couple apparently seeking my services this holiday evening had seemed familiar from the first moment I'd seen their images at the top of the stairs. No less so now. He was perpetually fiftyish-looking and of medium height, with a uniquely textured voice, broad shoulders, compelling eyes, a bristly salt-and-pepper mustache, and rather conspicuous ears. Several strands of his hair fell sort of boyishly across his forehead and into his eyes.

She was a thin, not-quite-pretty, fortyish platinum blond ("Better living through chemistry," I quoted to myself before I could stop me) with nervous mannerisms and what I was soon to discover was an exceptionally sharp tongue.

Together they informed me they'd been referred by an old mutual friend, one Lucille Gallegos Kropotkin—a former neighbor of mine who was presently out exploring the Asteroid Belt—and introduced themselves as Carole and Clark.

As in Carole Lombard.

And Clark Gable.

Whah, Ah do beeleeve, ef Ah'd been Scarlett O'Hara, Ah would hev jist *swooned.*

You-all, honeychile.

2: SMOKE GETS IN YOUR EYES

> There are two kinds of people in the world, those who
> say, "There are two kinds of people in the world," and
> those who don't.
>
> —*Memoirs of Lucille G. Kropotkin*

"Well, do you plan to let us in or just go on standing there, dribbling on your shoes?"

The blond rolled her eyes impatiently under the front porch-light I'd turned on, not quite tapping a high-heeled toe on my colorful doorstep. It wouldn't have done her much good in any case: the surface beneath her feet was rubberized concrete and the whole block echoed with the *ratatatat* of long strings of fire-crackers going off. A faint, marvelous aroma of black gunpowder drifted in on the evening breeze.

"Janie!" her husband objected.

"Hush, Pappy, Mama knows best. Can't you see the poor dope is starstruck?" He peered at me clinically as she went on; I felt like crawling underneath the doormat. "We have to *unstrike* him right away, if we're going to deal with this mess!"

"I, er . . . uh," the poor dope replied after deep reflection. "Please come in, please?" You'd think I'd be used to this kind of stuff by now, wouldn't you?

Nevertheless I was nothing short of breathtaken to recognize my prospective clients as the otherworld counterparts of famous movie stars, both of whom had been dead for decades in the version of reality I hailed from. The husband had died of a heart attack in 1960 (I looked it up later), the wife a generation earlier in a military air crash during a Second World War that had never happened here. The pair were well-known entertainment person-alities in the North American Confederacy, as well, and both owed plenty to its advanced geriatric and cosmetic technologies, since it was 1996 by the pre–Confederate European calendar, and Gable was ninety-five years old.

Somehow I gathered my wits enough (of course there weren't that many left to gather) to invite them in. I tried to retrieve my drink discreetly as I hung her wrap up in the hall closet, but she caught me with an understanding *Lost Weekend* kind of wink. Takes one to know one, I guess.

Shrugging, I led them up the half-flight of stairs into the living room, where I offered them a place to sit and a drink. Together, they opted for a sofa only slightly smaller than the U.S.S. *Missouri*. It was one of my favorite places, in any world you care to name, for an afternoon nap. She took a double-dessicated vodka Martini, he a bourbon and bourbon, with a dash of bourbon for flavor. All in all, it was turning out to be a pretty high-octane evening.

"Now where did you come from, sweetie?"

Silvertip was suddenly present in the room. She stropped herself across Lombard's decorative ankles a couple of times—I'd seen that cat shear around other people's extremities like a mechanical apple peeler, and with about the same results—then levitated up and into the woman's lap, landing lightly as a blown kiss.

I started to warn Lombard about Silvertip's temperamental nature, but gave it up as pointless. The animal was obviously perfectly content in the lap she'd discovered, getting cat hair all over a dress worth more than my car.

Somehow, I felt a little betrayed.

Both Gables lit cigarettes—Silvertip tolerated even that—and I followed suit with a nice Belizian Jolly Roger. Unlike other places, smoking hasn't fallen out of fashion in a continuum with effective cures for cancer, emphysema, and political correctness, although one negative aspect to Confederate technology is that it's impossible—unless you pull the house breakers—to fill a room full of the wonderful aroma of cigar smoke.

Outside, the heavens went on sparkling and coruscating with colorful explosions.

Gable turned out to be a pacer. The minute I started to ask him, "What can I do you for?" the man was up and stomping around in circles like a caged cliché, his Tony Lamas or Dan Posts or whatever they were threatening to wear a rut straight through the living-room carpet into the hardwood and polymer floor underneath it. Then he stopped abruptly, took a long drink and a longer drag on his cigarette, and regarded me with that famous sideways squint of his. I started looking around again for that doormat. "On my own time, Mr. Bear, I'm a man of few words!"

Tweed. That's what the texture of his voice reminded me of, rough tweed. I don't know what it was about this guy that made me want him to like me—and took it as a failure of character on my part if he didn't. Maybe that's the definition of charisma or something. If it is, you and Judy Garland can have it.

From the bar, where I was pretending to be busy freshening my own glass, I turned and replied, "Let's make that 'Win,' Mr. Gable—'Mr. Bear' was my father." Actually, Sergeant Bear was my father. A waistgunner, he'd died aboard a B-17 in Germany when I was too young to know anything about it.

"Fair enough." Gable nodded and grimaced in the famous way I'd seen a thousand times on the giant silver screen (as well as the nasty little plastic one that superseded it). "Then I'll be Clark to you. The point I was going to make is that I flatter myself that you know our work, Janie's and mine. We do drama—a little Shakespeare, an occasional thriller for the right author or director, even some intelligent comedy."

I nodded because the customer is always right except sometimes. Pulling around the chair I'd occupied earlier, I sat down,
ignoring my drink. The unfortunate truth was, having grown up
in an entirely different universe, I'd found this world's Gable
and Lombard a little difficult to fathom. They'd made only one
picture together where I'd come from, nothing special, early in
their respective careers. It'd been *offscreen* that they'd been a
national sensation, or a scandal, depending on who was writing
the memoirs. But here in the North American Confederacy, they
were a legendary theatrical couple, like Tracy and Hepburn, Rohan and Rohan, or Branagh and Thompson.

Gable shrugged angrily. "Now, suddenly, there's all of this . . .
this *crap* flooding the Telecom! *It Happened One Night* and, by
Gallatin, Janie, what did they call it?"

Sipping delicately at the vodka to which I'd added not more
than fourteen molecules of vermouth, Carole Lombard wrinkled
up her not-quite-pretty nose. *"Gone with the Wind."*

He shuddered. *"Gone with the Wind,* by Gallatin!"

"By Margaret Mitchell, actually," I offered unhelpfully. There
hadn't been a War between the States here, either, and the "Gallatin" he'd mentioned—Albert Gallatin, second president of the
Confederacy—was foremost among the reasons. So the film I
personally regarded as the greatest movie ever made must have
seemed to them like bad skiffy, something like the 1950s *War of
the Worlds,* maybe, or *Creation of the Humanoids.* "Just wait'll
you see *Teacher's Pet.*"

"We have!" they both wailed miserably. Hell, I never liked
Doris Day, either.

Eventually they managed to come to what faintly resembled
the point of their visit. The Gables wanted me to do *something*
(they weren't exactly sure what, and neither was I) about certain
recordings in various media being imported, apparently, from

some parallel world or worlds unknown, featuring strangers who looked and sounded an awful lot like them, but who *weren't* them, in some fundamental and disturbing ways.

Miss Lombard seemed most concerned for their careers—not to mention that they weren't being *paid* whenever these "movies" were offered on the 'Com, an all-embracing Confederate improvement on the Internet back home—and maybe the fact that she wasn't quite as big a star, wherever these entertainments were coming from, as she was accustomed to being here. To be fair, most of her otherworld counterparts hadn't lived long enough to become big stars. Cosmically speaking, World War Two had been a very popular war.

For her husband, it was more personal: he intensely disliked what he'd seen of these other versions of himself. "He simpers!" Gable complained.

To make things even worse, some versions of the Gable and/or Lombard films that were rapidly becoming classics here didn't even have Gable and/or Lombard in them! There was a version of *Gone with the Wind*, for godsake, starring Robert Cummings (remember him?) as Rhett Butler and Bette Davis as Scarlett O'Hara.

Well, hesh mah mouth.

Apparently unaware of what universe I came from—the first historically alternative universe to be discovered by Confederate scientists—Gable blamed it all on immigrants to the Confederacy. "If only those blasted bluebacks . . ."

"Don't talk dirty, Pappy," Lombard snapped.

Gable grumbled, "Aw, Janie . . ."

In the end, I warned them that there probably wasn't any way to stop the vile traffic they complained of, or even to collect royalties on the performances of individuals who merely looked like them. (I happen to have a lookalike myself here—I'd bought this house from him and he'd gone out to explore the Asteroid Belt with Lucy Kropotkin—we even have the same fingerprints!) I did agree to try and find out who was marketing these other-world flicks and see whether some reasonable accommodation could be reached about embarrassing the "real" Gable and Lombard.

At that, my clients seemed relieved, if only to have placed their problem in somebody else's hands. They finished their drinks and let me show them to the door, having offered me a retainer fully in keeping with their lofty status as stars of stage, screen, and (whether they welcomed it or not) Telecom. One of the things I like best about the North American Confederacy is that said retainer now lay heavy in my pocket, and *jingled*.

As we said good-bye, I was mentally composing a smug message for the answering machine in Clarissa's hovervan—and even planning some interplanetary C-mail to Lucy to thank her for the referral. At least I *think* I meant to thank her. I was feeling happy, and the Bear Curse hadn't stricken yet.

The Bear Curse? Something I'd never even told Clarissa about. All my life, when things seem to be going best, just when I realize I'm happy, it's suddenly spoiled by a feeling of certainty that it can't last, that some unnamed disaster is about to strike, almost as a punishment for the happiness I'm feeling. That dark, horrible cloud had lowered over me as long as I could remember—even as a kid. As an adult, I'd come to understand that it was partly from living in a culture where every popular religion holds that the only reason we're alive is to suffer, and the purpose of government is to take your happiness away and give it to somebody else. But mostly, I believe, it was from hundreds of thousands of books, movies, and television programs where it's a standard plot device—and an extremely unfortunate one. Here's the hero, going along, fat, dumb, and happy, when all of a sudden the bad guys maim and murder his wife, his children, his dog, his hamster, and the neighbor's parakeet—and that's just to get the story started. From sheer repetition, that damned scenario has crept deep into the human soul and soured it, possibly beyond repair. Now I lived in a free country with a beautiful, sexy woman who adored me—and still there was nothing I wanted more than to be able to experience happiness without dread.

Enough of that. I'd taken a few notes and accepted the assignment they'd offered me with a resigned sigh, knowing without a doubt that tomorrow morning I wouldn't be able to avoid visiting the one section of Greater LaPorte that never fails to depress me: the several impoverished, dirty, crowded square blocks that Confederates have come to call the "American Zone." That was where new immigrants tended to settle when they first arrived, and it was where the imported movies were most likely coming from.

I watched my brand-new clients walk across the driveway to their waiting hovercraft. I don't know what I'd expected them to be driving. I guess some ostentatious kind of gold-plated, diamond-encrusted chauffeur-driven limousine, or a tiny but expensive little sport hoverer, maybe. What they climbed into— Gable inserting himself happily behind the controls—was the Confederate equivalent of a United States of American four-wheel-drive "sport utility vehicle." Except, of course, that wheels were optional on this baby. It *was* big—maybe a Suburban and a half. And it was new, a 220 Taylor Off-Roader, powered by huge turbofans capable of pushing it up a 45-degree incline, and as fully at home hovering over ocean water, swamp-grass, or quicksand, as over *Terra firma*.

I'd momentarily forgotten that Clark Gable was an inveterate trout fisherman and hunter. As I watched their taillights whisk away down the drive, the car suddenly swerved and slid to a shuddering stop. In what seemed like the same instant, a blinding flash filled the evening darkness. I was picked up off of my big flat feet and slammed down hard on my big fat ass, bouncing on the rubberized concrete amidst an all-enveloping, thunderous Kettledrum-Roll-of-the-Gods that became my whole universe for an eternal moment and left my ears ringing afterward for hours. Trees swayed in the blast-shattered air; the ground heaved like an ocean swell. And speaking of heaving and swelling, I knew I'd soon be following its example. The Bear Curse had struck again.

3: JOSHUA FIT DE BATTLE

> Not many women will admit it, but the only thing wrong with men, from their viewpoint, is that they're not women. If you try to make them into women, it will only annoy most of them. And the few you succeed with, you won't like.
>
> —*Memoirs of Lucille G. Kropotkin*

I was up on my knees in an instant, the carry-worn muzzle of my big .41 sniffing back and forth for something to bite. My first thought was that the Gables' Off-Roader had exploded. But there the hovercraft still sat, taillights aglow, one hundred metric yards down my absurdly palatial driveway, amid the trees of my miniature national forest. The driver's door swung up as my client, gun in hand, climbed out to see what the hell was going on. This was not some movie cream puff who talked big and tough on camera and then let himself get buggered on the street. I remembered a grieving Clark Gable from my world flying bona fide bombing missions, just like my dad, over Germany during World War Two.

So exactly what *had* blown up? Eyes, ears, and nostrils wide open. There wasn't a trace of smoke or fire in the immediate vicinity. Even the celebratory Second of July pyrotechnics had died off exactly as if somebody had turned a tap. Then, from a long way off, I began hearing sirens wail—a sound surpassingly rare in Greater LaPorte—as multiple volunteer fire companies raced across the city, presumably to the scene of whatever disaster had just occurred. " 'Com!" I issued the command into thin air as the Gables came trudging back up the driveway, she levering a shiny silver roscoe back into her tiny purse. His gun was still in his hand. In the same thin air (over a patch of rubberized concrete almost as smart as it was resilient) a colorful transparent three-dimensionsal image formed of a menu screen, which I promptly ignored.

"Local news—explosion in West Central!" We were rewarded with an aerial view of one of the many sections of Greater LaPorte that pass for "downtown." There's never been a real center to the city: as Dorothy Parker once observed of my home-world's Los Angeles, "there isn't any *there* there."

"Pappy, it's the Old Endicott Building!" Lombard exclaimed. "Why, I was shopping on the three-hundredth floor there, just this afternoon!" Gable shook his head ruefully, but said nothing. The outlandish shape and scale of North American Confederate cities takes a little getting used to. Half of working LaPorte is actually underground, covered in private residential holdings that run to aromatic forest and restored High Plains. (Good thing Confederate medicine has better allergy remedies than Benadryl or Sudafed.)

Individual lots are huge, eight to ten times the size I'd grown up accustomed to. One of my neighbors maintains a stand of the type of prairie grass that overtopped a mounted man's head in pioneer days. Back home, the neighborhood Nazis and municipal lawn fascists would have been after him with torches and pitchforks. Here and there, architectural structures that would make Howard Roark whimper jealously arise from the golden breast of the Grand Prairie, clawing their way a mile into the clear, dry semi-Colorado air. My clients and I were looking at one now, hanging holographically before our eyes, cross-lit at the moment by the emergency beams of half a hundred hovering aerocraft—like the one whose viewpoint we happened to be sharing—flown by firefighting companies, various militiae, civilian gawkers, and the ubiquitous and useless media.

The Old Endicott Building was a pretty silly name for something that had been designed in a popular style known here as "NeoEgyptian." It was a glassy-sided pyramid, the uppermost half of which had just been raggedly removed and dumped into the streets below or blasted into the flanks of neighboring sky-scrapers which, luckily, were more trajectile-resistant and farther off than they would have been in any comparable United State-sian city.

The noise was absolutely unimaginable, straight out of Dante—or John Cage. Even this high above it, vicariously speaking, we could hear the screams of injured or frightened individuals—thousands and thousands of them—the roar of at least a dozen types of aerocraft, the caterwaul of emergency ground vehicles, the earth-shaking rumble and crash as more pieces of the build-ing slid off in huge slabs and plummeted into the helpless crowd half a mile below.

At the smoking apex of the ruin, a secondary explosion sud-denly engulfed a little sport dirigible in flames—it had been gal-lantly trying to rescue survivors—and sent the wreckage hurtling into the street. I realized that this wasn't the U.S.A. in another sense. There could be no hope of it being after hours, with the building blessedly empty: LaPorte is a twenty-four-hour-a-day kind of town. A lot of people were going to be dead, and a lot more badly hurt. No doubt about it, this was the worst disaster the city had seen, even probably the worst in Confederate history since the Peshtigo-Chicago Meteor Fires.

And all I could think about was—*"Win?"* Clarissa was okay! Her voice cut through the chaos as a "window" opened Micro-softly in a corner of the scene we were viewing. It showed me the face I most like to look at in a million universes, that of a pretty honey blond more natural than my latest client, with merry hazel eyes, and what's customarily called a "smattering" of freck-les across her cheeks and the bridge of her uptilted nose.

She also has long, graceful legs, ample apples, and is half a head taller than I am. She once offered kindly to add six inches to my legs if it bothered me. It doesn't.

Just presently she sat behind the wheel of her powerful medical van. Judging by the way the scenery was whizzing into the distance behind her, she was doing at least three times the usual city speed. I sure hoped her lights and sirens were going. Her 'Com software would be cancelling out the latter, so we could talk.

"Right here, baby!" I replied, trying hard and failing not to let pathetic gratitude show in my voice. Looking down, I realized I still held my revolver in my hand. I wiggled it into the holster under my arm. "What the hell is going on?"

She brushed a strand of hair from her eyes. "I've no idea, dear. I was on a housecall—oops!"

Hard to tell, but I thought she'd swerved to avoid some obstacle, most likely vehicular. Ordinary traffic would appear to be standing still to her as she sped by. It gave me the yammering jim-jams to watch my beloved driving like that, several miles a minute on a pillow of compressed air down the middle emergency lane of what I recognized as the city's busiest thoroughfare, Confederation Boulevard. "I no sooner heard an explosion, than I had C-mail from three fire captains and the city militia commander!" That would be Will Sanders, voted the neighbor most likely to have fired that bottle rocket at me, what now seemed like a year ago.

I nodded. "So you're going to help. Take your phone with you when you leave the car; I'm coming down, too. I'll want to find you." I'd been a cop—Denver City and County Homicide—back in the bad old days before the Confederacy and I had discovered one another. I could probably make myself useful at the disaster scene.

Gable and Lombard looked at each other and then at me.

"Planning to get your own car out," Clark asked me, putting away his heavy autopistol, a Greener .720, "or just ride with us?"

IN THE END, I opted to go with them, grabbing a few useful items from the house and planning to return with my spouse whenever. It could be hours or days. Confederate emergency services—usually run and funded by insurance companies, augmented by every kind of volunteer association imaginable—were generally excellent. But who in Great Lysander's name had ever expected them to cope with a calamity like this one? A calamity that already looked suspiciously artificial to me.

The Gables and I didn't speak much on the way "downtown." They didn't speak much to each other, for that matter. The streets were hellish, noisy, full of lights that confused, rather than illuminated—people rushing toward disaster, others running away—and getting there took an incredibly long time. Each of us was wrapped completely in his own thoughts. And by a reflex I'd discovered was peculiar to immigrants like me, my thoughts all seemed to be political.

In the States I came from, politicians view any catastrophe like this as a career opportunity. By now they'd all be trampling over one another looking for TV cameras, demanding that everybody and his kid sister be locked in belly chains and leg irons for the duration of the emergency—for which read "forever." Nine times out of ten, the public would obligingly let themselves be stampeded by that kind of dumbassedness. There aren't that many politicians in the Confederacy—the climate isn't healthy for them—individuals here value their freedom above all things, and there isn't anything to vote on. So I wondered what the political fallout would be like from this unprecedented mess. Mostly I considered Confederate history—very different from the history I'd been taught in school—a history that allowed more room than mine did for optimism about America, about Americans, and maybe even about the human race in general . . .

TENSCORE AND BUT a pair of years earlier—1794, for those with fewer than two-hundred fingers to count on—and with the ink just freshly sanded on the brand-new shiny U.S. Constitution, President George "If I ever tell a lie, may I be bled to death by leeches" Washington, and his Secretary of the Treasury, Alexander Hamilton, decided it was high time they tried out their brand-new shiny powers of taxation. Their first victims were to be western Pennsylvania farmers, long accustomed to converting their corn crops into a less perishable, more profitable high-octane liquid form.

Unfortunately (for George *et* Al), many of these rustics, especially those in the vicinity of the frontier municipality of Pittsburgh, were also accustomed to reading books, speaking in words of more than two syllables, and holding meetings where they formally debated the myriad aspects of living in a limited-government republic. They also placed a somewhat different emphasis (than high school teachers do today, for instance) on Revolutionary slogans regarding taxation without representation. In their view, they'd fought the bloody Brits from '75 to '85 to abolish taxation altogether, and they weren't interested now in having representation *or* taxation imposed on them by that gaggle of fops in Philadelphia, at that time, the nation's capital. This they proceeded to make manifest by tarring and feathering Mr. Hamilton's tax collectors, burning said officials' houses to the ground, and filling the stills of anybody who willingly paid the hated tribute with large-caliber muzzle-loading bullet holes.

Feeling their authority challenged, Washington and Hamilton dispatched westward a body of fifteen thousand conscripted troops equal to half the population of America's largest city (Phil-

adelphia once again, which would later become famous for dropping high explosives from police helicopters on miscreants
charged with disturbing the peace), the equivalent of sending in
five million National Guardsmen to quell the Rodney King riots.
A mere four hundred Whiskey Rebels, properly impressed by
this host of fifteen-thousand, subsided, and the all-too-familiar
political miracle by which the private transgression of robbery is
somehow transubstantiated into a public virtue was firmly established. Pay or die. The inevitable consequences—poverty and
unemployment, endless foreign wars, the Branch Davidian Massacre, and reruns on television—are still with us today.

Meanwhile, in another Pennsylvania far, far away, one Albert
Gallatin, recent Swiss immigrant, Harvard professor, and gentle-
man farmer, decided *not* to talk his whiskey-making friends and
neighbors out of an uprising that might get them all killed (as
he'd done in my version of history) but to organize and lead
them instead, inspired by the ethical and political implications of
a single word ("*unanimous* consent of the governed") that somehow got blue-penciled out of my copy of the Declaration of Independence. An erudite and persuasive fellow (in my world he
was among the first to study Indian languages academically, invented the science of ethnology, and became Alexander Hamilton's counterpart in Thomas Jefferson's cabinet), Gallatin
somehow shamed the fifteen thousand conscripts into reversing
themselves and marching with him, against the City of Botherly
Love.

The rest, to coin a phrase, is alternative history. Shown a suitable backstop, President George was duly ventilated for his
counter-Revolutionary transgressions, while Secretary Al bolted
for Europe, where he met a fate surprisingly similar to that which
befell him in my world, although at the hands of a Polish count
named Coveleskie, rather than those of Aaron Burr. The Con-

stitution—the vile document that had emboldened them—was replaced with the Revised Articles of Confederation it was supposed to have been all along, fitted with a "Covenant of Unanimous Consent" rather than the weaker "Bill of Rights."

Government—at least that of the United States—forever deprived of its looting privileges, grew smaller and less significant in the lives of Americans every day thereafter, guaranteeing the survival of individual liberty, and giving rise to unprecedented peace, prosperity, and progress.

Albert Gallatin became the second President (at his insistence they went on counting George) of what would someday become known as the North American Confederacy.

THE REMAINDER OF the next three days is pretty blurry. I lost track of both Gables right away, although I spent a long while working shoulder to shoulder with Will Sanders. The lighting and noise were still like something straight out of Classical Hell, victims screaming and moaning, rescuers shouting at one another, heavy machinery rasping and whining as it tried to pull half a building off of bodies, living and dead. I'm a former homicide detective, and I can't even begin to describe the smells.

Will had a big black heavy blade he'd brought from his car and was using it as shovel and crowbar as much as a knife. I've a vague memory of the man hacking away, trying desperately to cut through a titanium concrete reinforcement rod with it, to rescue a terrified and injured little girl, cursing blue blazes with every stroke. In the end, we covered the little girl with our coats and shirts and fragments of plywood. Then Will pulled out a great big pistol and shot the rebar right out of the concrete it was set in. Two minutes later, we had the little girl out and in the arms of her mother. Will and I laughed and wept and danced around each other, both of us covered from head to toe with concrete dust and looking like a negative of an old-time minstrel show.

I didn't catch up with my darling Clarissa for hours after that, not until the very end of the nightmare, when I suddenly became aware that I was lying on my back, peering up through a shock-induced haze. She was standing over me like some kind of angel, strapping Bassett coils on me in an emergency tent.

"We gotta stop meeting like this," I remember telling her. She smiled wearily, crinkling around the eyes in that way I've always felt was so sexy. The first time I'd seen her lovely face, nine years ago, she'd been patching up a whole bunch of bullet holes that the badguys had blasted through my carcass—I'd felt like Fearless Fosdick. While she was doing that, she'd incidentally cured me of what would eventually have been cancer.

This time, I'd "merely" broken my left forearm, radius and ulna both, compound fracture. Lemme tell you, there's nothing quite like seeing the ends of shattered bones poking out through your own skin. I'd been helping forty other sentimental idiots lift a room-sized slab of reinforced concrete and more of that titanium rebar in order to rescue an orange tiger-stripe and her litter of four kittens. I guess my fingers—or somebody's—had slipped.

At that point, there hadn't been many left to save. Happily, the Old Endicott Building (I've always wondered who Old Endicott was) turned out to have been partially empty after all: renovation underway on several dozen floors. Partially empty or not, it was still the size of a small city. The death toll was 1,198, by a horrid coincidence only I was in a position to notice ('cause it hadn't happened here), the same number of people who had died aboard the *Lusitania*. Clarissa and I showered together, not from any romantic urge in the beginning, but simply to hold each other up. She hadn't broken anything, but she was nearly as beat-up as I was. She'd left her well-equipped medical van downtown to be used by the colleagues who'd relieved her. To this day I can't remember how we got home.

Eventually, however, that old black magic had us in its spell. I have a serious sexual problem where my lithe and lively Clarissa is concerned. I just can't seem to get it . . . down. She noticed.

"Well," she observed, as hot, soapy water sluiced over both of us and steam rose to fill what little space was between us, "I know that isn't a pistol in your pocket, because you're not wearing any pants."

She confirmed her diagnosis by Braille. I put my hands on her. "Doctor, I seem to have this terrible swelling. Can you do something?"

"Why yes, Mr. Bear," she grinned, "I believe I can."

"Nnnngh! I believe you just made it worse."

"Well, then," she asked, "how about this?" The distance between us disappeared. I lifted her up a little, felt her smooth, wet flesh against mine, wrapped my arms around her slender waist, let her down again and held her tight. Sometimes it's good, her being a little taller than me.

"Perfect," I replied. "But I warn you, in my condition, I'm likely to fall asleep on the forty-ninth stroke."

"Fine. That'll be forty-nine more than I've had the last three days."

"Okay, if we can just avoid slipping on the tile and killing each other . . ." The shower heads hissed on for a few moments.

"Oh! My! Goodness!" Clarissa exclaimed, breathing hard. "Aaaah . . . it wouldn't be a bad way to die, at that, would it!"

I didn't answer her, I was busy—and too dignified to scream, "Oh! My! Goodness!"

The last thing I remember, between the time we let the bathroom dry us and my right ear hit the pillow with Clarissa curled up behind me and Silvertip sleeping between my feet, was hearing my old friend Buckley F. Williams of the Franklinite Faction on the 'Com, screaming for martial law.

4: TABERNA EST IN OPPIDUM

> The function of government is to provide us with service;
> the function of the media is to supply the Vaseline.
> —*Memoirs of Lucille G. Kropotkin*

Early morning—well, midmorning, anyway—found me headed the opposite way the Gables and I had taken three nights ago, northeast, driving the shiny red turbocharged Neova HoverSport I'd "inherited" with the house from the guy who took my name, face, fingerprints, and next-door neighbor with him to the asteroids. Already the traffic had begun to slow from its usual ninety miles an hour to a sluggish, confused crawl that betrayed the drivers in the area as new to the Confederate rules of the road and scared half to death.

I know a conservative radio talk show host back home who avoids thinking about real freedom with a sort of mantra. "You're the people who don't want there to be any traffic signs," he always prattles at libertarians as if it meant something. I've tried to tell him that libertarians just want the traffic signs to be private property, but he never listens. Maybe somebody else will get through to him.

As I drove the 'Com blatted, something about immigrants, as usual. Interworld travel, mostly the one-way kind being done by hundreds of thousands of political and economic refugees these days, was *the* hot topic with Confederate natives and immigrants alike. Weird alternate histories had seized everyone's imaginations just as unlikely stories in the *National Inquirer* or *People* magazine do elsewhere. The folks in this uniquely wonderful world were discovering that they loved to shudder deliciously over versions of America that had taken a wildly different (and almost invariably worse) turn than their own.

A typical headline might read, COMES FROM WORLD WHERE AMERICA STAYED BRITISH! Lost in thought, I found I'd passed the corner of Farah and Bock where the Zone unofficially begins and, to a dismaying degree, the Confederacy, for all practical purposes, ends. My onboard computer was talking to our machinery at home and the 'Com system in general (Confederates have had what we call the Internet for seventy-five years, they just named it something else), compiling a list of folks it might be useful for me to talk to. With my attention divided—and trying to avoid the embarrassment of a slow-motion collision—I didn't actually hear the phone until the answering machine kicked in. "This is Win Bear. I'm not in my car right now, so if you'll leave a mess—" Swerving to avoid a genuine four-wheeled Toyota Land Cruiser, that big, gray, friendly elephant of a car (and how the hell had they gotten *that* through the broach?) I jabbed a button on the dashboard. "Sorry about that—hello?"

"Hello, yourself!" A rugged and familiar face appeared on the screen. "I expected to see you languishing on a bed of pain, not racketing about town in your little red hovercraft like a teenager! How y'doing?"

It was my neighbor-across-the street, Captain Will Sanders of the Greater LaPorte Militia. Since the horror of July second, he'd obviously showered, shaved, and put on clean, undamaged clothes. About ten years my junior, Will had curly dishwater-blond hair, a recently acquired handlebar mustache, a pair of drop-dead-gorgeous wives (both of them more than a little pregnant at the moment), and the sleepy eyes of a natural-born killer. He was a good man to have at your back in a fight, as I'd discovered several times. "Almost perfectly well, my dear Sanders . . ." I arranged my features into an expression of high dudgeon (whatever that means—I've always meant to look it up). "No thanks to you—I didn't mention it the other night, but I'm thinking seriously of putting up barrage balloons around the property!"

That sonofabitch actually laughed heartily, and grinned that I'm-Errol-Flynn-Forgive-Me-Anything grin of his. "The bottle tipped over as the rocket went off—next year we'll make it RPGs! I was referring to your arm—you were pretty damned lucky not to have sheared it off!" I could still hear the sound that giant concrete slab had made when the whole thing fell through two floors, taking a mortgage company with it, and two marijuana brokers. A short section of rebar had casually slapped me on the arm as it went by.

Just now I had to steer around some kids—humans and chimps—playing in the street with a ball and bat. It was unusual to see simians at all in the Zone and a good sign as far as I was concerned. It reminded me: the LaPorte Patriots were playing the Mexico City Aztecs this afternoon. I split the screen (Will could share) and sent the system channel-hopping, looking for the game. I also switched to a heads-up display I'd had installed, so I could see traffic while I talked on the 'Com.

Three days after, the so-called news media were still wallowing in the Old Endicott Building disaster, "dancing in the blood" as my darling Clarissa had put it, every second, every minute, every hour, shoving mikes and cameras in people's faces, asking everybody and his aardvark how they felt (never what they thought, mind you) about what had happened. There had even been talk, for no reason that made any sense, of postponing the ballgame. I switched off their half of the 'Com and ignored them.

"There's nothing wrong with me that enough time than the elecromagnetic Force won't cure. I thought you'd be back at Old Endicott still digging for bodies." I would have been, too, in spite of the damned media, except that I had a job.

Will grimaced. "No bodies left to dig for, according to the

dogs and our instruments. The toll officially stands at 1198, and there were more injuries among the rescue gang than the few survivors we found in the collapsed parts of the building."

A surprising number of people had lived—several thousand—proving that tort law does a hell of a lot more for the advance of architectural science than building codes do.

I interrupted him. "Tell me about that hunk of iron you were using that night. I've got a working knife, but it's too big and heavy and I don't carry it." Will was familiar with the toadsticker I'd taken off Tricky Dick Milhouse, during my first days here in LaPorte.

"An import," he explained, "from one of our native worlds, yours and mine. It's a Chris Reeve Project I, made by a guy from Montana—by way of South Africa—not the guy who played Superman. I got mine at Daggett's Wonderful World of Sharp Pointy Things, on North Snowflake."

Here in the Zone. I refrained from telling him that in my world, most recently (I have an unfortunate habit of keeping track of such things), Superman had been played by *Keanu* Reeves. I was about to inquire after Fran and Mary-Beth, Will's pretty young wives, when he interrupted himself. "What's that you're carrying? You look naked and it isn't a pretty sight!" A burglary dick for another City and County of Denver than mine, Will had worked as a gunsmith when he arrived here the year after I did.

My arm was in a sling, bone-healing Bassett coils wired to power cells that not only made it awkward to drive, but impractical to wear a shoulder holster. Lacking a hip holster for my .41, I'd settled on a Browning "High-Power" pistol that I'd field-confiscated amidst all the ruckus associated with my having moved here, from a federal agent of the type—known better now than then—who delights in burning children to death or shooting mommies in the head while they hold their babies in their arms.

"My old P-35," I replied, referring to the Browning by another of its many names, "with the new barrel." Will shared my interest in exotic cartridges. I'd equipped the pistol with a brand-new tube, custom-made for a cartridge I'd invented myself one evening, after perusing *Cartridges of the World*, my all-time favorite bathroom reading material. I'd christened it ".375×19 Win-Bear," enjoying the combination of English and so-called "metric" designations. It had started as an obscure Japanese military item, 8mm Nambu, "blown out," as they say, and shortened a trifle. Its rim had been turned—"rebated" is the technical term—to match that of the 9mm cartridge the gun had originally been made for. With a 145-grain ⅜" bullet traveling 1180 feet a second, it was no magnum, but better than the European popgun fodder I'd been feeding it for years.

Will shook his head. For him (as for the overwhelming majority of Confederate gun-toters), decent-sized guns begin at .40. But instead of giving me a hard time about it as he usually did, he asked what I was up to today.

"Acting on behalf of some new clients." I suppose, to any outside observer, after what had happened three nights ago, the Gables' case may have seemed trivial. But I was pretty sure it didn't seem that way to them. In any event, moping around, pretending to mourn twelve hundred strangers the way everybody had been forced to do when Kennedy got shot—which Kennedy, of course, depending on what world you're from—sure wouldn't do the victims any good, and it was just plain crazy (or counterfeit as a zinc penny) to believe or act otherwise. The point was, I'd taken the Gables' money, and, as they probably observed themselves from time to time, "The show must go on."

I said as much to Will, not mentioning my clients' names. He was from a line of alternate probability similar—but not identical—to mine and probably wouldn't have believed me, anyway. Clark Gable. Carole Lombard. Right. By now my house and car computers had assembled a list of a dozen individuals in this part of the city who were generally associated with crossworld imports. I thought I knew already where at least half of them would be hanging out.

"My system says you're in the Zone," Will told me. As usual, I'd forgotten to block the locator. "I'm organizing an investigation of the Old Endicott Building blast, and some fingers seem to point in that direction. So don't be surprised if you bump into me over there, okay?"

I answered him: "I'm glad that somebody's looking into it. I don't know anything about explosions, but it didn't smell, taste, or feel like any accident to me." Will gave me a neutral grunt that told me he agreed but was too professional to say so. We exchanged good-byes and hung up.

THE HANGING JUDGE, at the corner of Mason and Rodney, did not refer to Roy Bean (a Supreme Court justice in this particular branch of surreality) or to those like Roy with an inclination to judicial severity. No, the sign outside, over the entryway, consisted of a white-wigged dummy in long black robes swinging from a gibbet by a length of looped hemp with the thirteen traditional coils above the knot. At the bottom was a legend: "*Sic semper tyrannis!*"

Aside from that, the double doors and bay windows with stained glass were pretty much like those of any "brass and fern" tavern you might happen across. A card suction-cupped on the left half of the door proclaimed, SORRY, WE'RE OPEN. I swung the doors aside and strode into the dark interior as if I owned it—which I did, along with my not-so-silent partners, Yolanda and Maximillian (a.k.a. "the Wizard") Parker-Frost.

In the benign absence of any law prohibiting it, the Hanging Judge opened up in the morning so that Yolanda (if you see her, better call her "Lan") and her husband, who fancied themselves gourmet chefs (and more often than not demonstrated it with aplomb) could serve a late breakfast. At the moment the place was empty but it wouldn't stay that way. The bar itself was at one side, to the left, tables and chairs at the other. The proprietors stood behind the bar, backs to the doors, Lan's arm draped over the Wizard's shoulders. discussing whatever they were cooking on the grill. It smelled wonderful. I recognized it as an apple-cinnamon-vanilla omelette, a recipe they'd gotten from my very own Clarissa, who makes breakfast almost as nicely as she showers.

On the wall facing them, where you'd expect to see a business permit or a license from the Board of Health (just not happening in the Confederacy) was an animated sign:

2230 DAYS WITHOUT POISONING A CUSTOMER

I happened to know it was the number of days, exactly, since they'd opened the place. There was another joint down the block with a similar sign except the number was only two—in their case a selling point. They sold those little Japanese puffer-fish that make eating sushi such an adventure.

Lan was average-sized, I guess, tall compared to her husband, substantial, sort of like Kathleen Turner in *Romancing the Stone*. She wore neatly pressed blue denim bib overalls this morning, a dashing red silk blouse puffed at the wrists, dangly earrings, and high heels. Her eyes were made up and she'd chosen extra-long eyelashes. Her straight ash-blond hair fell to her waist. On a narrow belt slanted across her hips, she carried an elegantly designed Whitney autopistol. The Wizard wasn't more than five-

feet-two or-three inches tall. The expanse of his scalp, exposed
in front, was shiny pink. His sandy hair at the back and sides
was long like Benjamin Franklin's and caught in a ponytail. He
affected a full beard and mustache somewhat redder than his
hair and thick glasses medically unnecessary in the Confederacy,
which had developed laser eye surgery about the time of our
Spanish–American War. My guess was that he was just busy and
hadn't gotten around to getting himself repaired yet.

They cure baldness here, too.

The Wizard's shoulders and arms, broad and powerful like
those of a bear, ended in broad hands with stubby, competent
fingers. Watching him use them was like watching a Muppet,
especially since (like most Muppets) he was left-handed. Barrel-
chested, he had a narrow waist. His legs were short and slightly
bowed. His feet were small, like those of a child. He wore a
white dress shirt, a suit vest (with a calculator sticking out of the
pocket), and a pair of bell-bottom jeans. He carried a well-worn
Colt Delta Elite 10mm automatic tucked into his waistband. Both
guns—hers was a .22, believe it or not—were pure United Statesian items, held by all the locals here to be ridiculously under-
powered, although Yolanda and the Wizard both shot
competitively and I wouldn't care to be on the receiving end of
anything they fired in my direction.

"Yo, Wiz!" I announced myself. "Yo, Lan!"

"Duh," she finished the pronunciation of her name. "Come to
collect your piece of the action, or just slumming?" I liked Lan's
voice when she was being sarcastic. It reminded me of . . . napalm
in the morning.

I shook my head. "Just information," I waggled a printout of
my list at her, "and some of that omelette!"

"Fine," the Wizard replied in a voice textured suitably for

telling tales to little children. Naughty children. Tales about can-
nibals. "You want coffee with that?"

"The Real Thing," I replied, congratulating myself for perhaps
the millionth time on one of the best R&R—rescue and reloca-
tion—jobs I'd ever pulled off for the Confederacy: three Atlanta
corporate types from my homeworld who knew the formula for
Coca-Cola and had been jailed for refusing to divulge it to a
socialist government that had just outlawed trade secrets.

At one end of the bar, lying open and facedown, was a plas-
tiback copy of *The Steamcoach Pillagers* by Ted van Roosevelt. It
was a particular favorite of mine, as Confederate fiction goes.
The Wizard noticed me noticing and winked. "Made a hell of a
lot better novelist than he did a president, didn't he?"

I nodded. Most people where I come from still don't realize
that socialism in America—started by Abraham Lincoln, who
suspended the Constitution (and undid the Revolution) during
what he called a civil war—got shoved along a whole lot further
by another chief executive who desperately despised the free-
market economy that had made his family rich, and stomped and
shredded the Constitution himself, if only by pushing the concept
of public lands.

"Just bully," I replied.

The Wizard grinned, the corners of his eyes crinkling behind
his spectacles in a way that made you think his beard should
have been snow-white and smelled faintly of reindeer. He cut the
enormous omelette he was working on in half and slapped it on
a plate. Adding a couple of outsized country sausage patties, he
garnished the whole thing with a sprig of mint and handed it
over. The corners of my jaws twinged painfully, like they do
sometimes when you're hungry and about to eat something so
delicious it should be outlawed. Lan was apparently going to

chitchat with me, where I sat down at the bar, but just then a dozen or so customers came in all at once—the brunch hour was beginning in the Zone—and she and her husband got real busy. So instead of chit-chat, I sat and ate and thought.

THE MAJOR CONSEQUENCE of the historical events that resulted in the creation of the Confederacy is that the inhabitants of this world—unlike others I might mention—are completely in charge of their own individual destinies. Another was that, without government "help," science and technology have progressed more rapidly than elsewhere. The nineteenth century west was explored and populated by steam-driven off-road vehicles, rather than by covered wagon, railroad, or stagecoach. People first walked on the Moon—where they'd come to build a permanent settlement—in 1949. And travel between alternate realties, through a "probability broach" invented by a scientific porpoise, became possible in 1987. Or make that 211 Anno Liberatis, since these folks reckon their dates from July 2, 1776, when the Declaration of Independence was really signed. And now, in the Confederacy's third century, hundreds of thousands of former "United Statesians" like me, fleeing numerous alternative versions of a government becoming more bloated, rapacious, and violent every day, were making a new start alongside refugees from hundreds of similar nations in dozens of similar continua. Newcomers to the Confederacy, a culture that uses private coinages of precious metals, typically arrive with their pockets full of worthless government paper money. With little in the way of resources besides their hands and their minds, they all hope that the "American Zone"—the seedy LaPorte neighborhood they settle in—will turn out to be only a temporary jumping-off place in this land of unimpeded opportunity.

• • •

"YOLANDA PARKER-FROST, something has to be done about this!"

I glanced up from breakfast as a gaggle of indignant citizen-types heretofore generally unknown in the Confederacy pushed through the door, led by a puffy faced, prematurely middle-aged guy with hair so blond it was white. He was wearing the first necktie I'd seen in five years and held a great big roll of paper aloft like a semaphore flag, swinging it back and forth.

"Problems with your arm again?" Lan asked. The Wizard grinned to himself and turned over a crepe.

Above the necktie, which didn't even redeem itself with an interesting color or pattern, the guy's face swelled and reddened. A little bald-headed fellow who'd followed him in let a tiny giggle escape, but the blond guy pounded him back into place using only his nearly invisible blond eyebrows. It must be a gift.

"You know perfectly well what I mean!" He unrolled his paper on the bar three feet from my left elbow. I gave it a casual perusal. "This is a chart of every vending machine within a five-block radius that sells drugs or alcohol or ammunition to anyone who has the money! Even children!"

"And?" Lan asked blandly.

"And we've formed a committee to have them all removed!"

"Even children!" an idiot in a brass-buttoned blue blazer echoed, nodding his head and making his preppie bangs bob absurdly. If I were forming a committee, it would be to prevent guys over fifty from getting Moe Howard haircuts. "For pennies!" These chumps were complaining about something I'd always thought was rather charming about the Confederacy. In a free-market system, competition always forces prices down, while driving progress that keeps quality high. The result? A box of pistol ammunition even children can buy for pennies from a vending machine. An armed schoolyard is a polite schoolyard.

While the Wizard continued apparently ignoring them, Lan shook her head at the blond guy and his companions. There were four of them, the bald guy, the preppie, an extremely tall and skinny guy with bad skin, and somebody in a Spiderman costume. Go figure. "Look, Douglas," Lan took them all in with a contemptuous glare from beneath her eyelashes. "Most immigrants to the Confederacy considered themselves libertarians— even anarchists—where they came from in the 'Land of the Fee and the Home of the Slave.' To them, the Confederacy is their every dream fulfilled. They're grateful just to be here." The blond guy started to splutter but Lan cut him off before it came to anything. "Still, there's always someone like you, having personal trouble—"

"The technical term is 'acculturation,' my dear," said the Wizard.

"—personal trouble adjusting to full ownership of their own lives, along with everything that implies, trouble that they somehow think they have a right to pass along to everybody else! Well you don't have such a right, Douglas! Nobody ever promised you that being free would be easy!"

The Wizard added in his best Shel Silverstein voice, "You can't child-proof the world. If you try, you end up with a mess like we all escaped from." He lifted his spatula in emphasis. "The best you can do is world-proof your children. That's hard work, undeniably. But nobody here is going to let you fob it off on someone else."

"How dare you—!" Shaking with fury, the blond guy opened his mouth again, but an all-too-familiar voice from a storeroom behind the bar chopped him off in mid-harangue.

"Blow it out your ass, Dougie! Those vendin' machines're private property, standin' in locations that're private property, too, most of which're protected by Griswold's Security! Now, y'wanna go an' tangle with *them*?"

Everybody in the room shook their heads and said, "*Brrrr!*" simultaneously, including yours truly. At least these newbies knew about Griswold's. A huge plastic carton wiggled through the narrow door, held up and propelled by a little old lady. "Lan, where y'want this stuff, honey?"

"Lucy!" I yelled. The voice alone told me it was Lucille Gallegos Kropotkin, my former neighbor and second favorite Confederate. "I thought you were—"

"Out Beltside, Winnie? Not on your carbonaceous chondrite! I mean t'find the assholes who knocked down the Old Endicott Building, whoever they are—I was the majority stockholder—or know the reason why!"

5: EASY WINNERS

As much as "sunshine soldiers" or "summer patriots," beware an ally—more common than you know—whose fear of the uncertainties of success moves him to surrender at the very moment of victory.

—*Memoirs of Lucille G. Kropotkin*

"Now if y'don't want any breakfast or beer," the little old lady told Douglas and his crew, "you can all get your baldheaded backsides outa here!" I'd have applauded if my arm hadn't been in a cast. She can be plenty spirited when the situation calls for it, but that was about the strongest language I'd ever heard Lucy use directly on anyone. For just a moment, the guy in the Spiderman outfit thought he was going to talk back. He got out a mere handful of United Statesian cusswords—much nastier than is customary here, something that included "bitch"—before Lucy laid a hand on her pistol grip and he shut off with a sort of gurgle.

"Your mommy know you talk like that?" she asked with deceptive mildness.

The Wizard looked up briefly from where he was performing culinary miracles at the sizzling grill. "He didn't have a mommy, he had a village."

Not that Lucy wasn't sufficiently hot-tempered and salty-tongued in her own way. But Confederate profanity includes neither religious nor sexual references, the former, I guess, because everybody figures that religion is a very personal business and they tend to keep it in their pants. The latter because sex is too nice. It isn't politically incorrect here and never was. The American epithet "Get fucked!," for example, is likely to elicit an astonished grin and, "Thanks, friend, I'll certainly try." All of

Douglas's delegation seemed well-enough acquainted with Lucy, and obeyed the heavily armed old lady without a moment's further hesitation. They departed the Hanging Judge, no doubt to hold another committee meeting somewhere. I wondered if they'd ever realize that they were becoming exactly what they'd come here to escape.

Except for the little bald guy, who unabashedly bellied up to the bar for one of the Wizard's fabulous apple omelettes. Looking down at my plate, I couldn't blame him.

"Hey, Douglas left his chart!" Lucy observed. "Somebody staple it up over there by the door so people'll know where to find those vending machines!"

The little bald guy was soon joined by two dozen others drifting in through the double doors, attired in everything from workman's clothes to the more formal bolero jacket and serape of a Confederate businessman. I was wearing one of the striped and colorful blankets, myself, thankful that local fashion made it easier on somebody with his arm in a tube of rigid plastic. This was a popular spot in the Zone and attracted all kinds of characters from all kinds of worlds. I kept expecting to see a Wookkie or— what were those lizard people called in *Babylon 5*? Oh yeah, the Narn. And maybe a Klingon or two, as well. They'd like the cooking.

Way at the back, behind the pool and *mah jong* tables, somebody put some money in the Copperodeon, and we began to hear music, music, music. It was the only place I knew of in several universes where the jukebox played Scott Joplin.

Lucy Kropotkin was, let me see, now, 145 years old, born Lucille Conchita Gallegos, "in the shadow of the Alamo," as she often put it. One of the feistiest, kindliest individuals I've ever known. Lucy had once been married to a Russian prince with whom she'd helped colonize Antarctica and fight a war against the Czar in 1957. She didn't look a day over a hundred. Think of Thelma Ritter (Debbie Reynolds' traveling companion in *How the West Was Won*) only wirier and tougher, Mexican instead of Jewish, with a San Antonio accent instead of something strictly from Brooklyn, and an enormous .50 caliber Gabbet-Fairfax "Mars" automatic pistol strapped about her tiny waist.

Looking back now, I don't think I've ever seen Lucy without that goddamned gun. (I shot it once; it was an experience I'll never forget—neither will my carpal tunnels—or ever willingly repeat.) The first time I laid eyes on her, she was wearing hair curlers and that pistol belted around a faded chenille bathrobe. No, it was hanging dangerously from one of its pockets. Don't blame me, I was only just semiconscious at the time, shot to pieces and bleeding profusely on her next-door neighbor's garage floor. Today Lucy had selected a colorful "broomstick" skirt and one of those white Mexican peasant blouses with a little colored ribbon woven into the lace at the neckline. She may even have been a full five feet tall in those expensive high-heeled Lucchese dung-displacers she had on under the skirt.

Lucy turned to me, spreading her spindly arms as wide as she could for a hug. "Ain't you a sight for sore eyes, Edward William Bear Mark Two—but then who wants sore eyes?"

"I like to think of myself as Edward William Bear Mark One," I told her. We were joking, of course, about her husband, my counterpart in this continuum.

"I'm sure you do, Winnie, I'm sure you do." She looked up at a clock above the bar. "The sun's down over the yardarm somewhere on the planet—probably Bulgaria about now! Wanna drink?"

Dangerous, but warranted, given the occasion. I gave her a jaunty, what-the-hell shrug and took the Cuba Libra she offered me, "since you already got started on that brown, bubbly, Atlanta stuff." Having a rather difficult time with the cast, I managed to pick up my plate with about a quarter of the wonderful omelette left on it and one precious sausage patty—I could have ordered more, but that way, as someone said, lay fatness—and moved with her to a great big, comfortable booth across the room under the wall-sized picture of a naked lady traditional to better saloons everywhere and everywhen. The jukebox in the back finished "The Entertainer" and began my favorite, "Ragtime Dance."

Somebody in the big room—the tobacco totalitarians would have gasped in horror back where I came from—had lit up a pipe. Cherry Blend, I think. I could just barely smell it, but the aroma went perfectly with my sausage and omelette.

"Well, there ain't nothin', however attractive," Lucy observed, nodding toward the bald guy at the bar as she settled in behind her drink—a tequila sunrise almost as big as she was—and a big sopapilla overflowing with green chili and chorizo, "that's entirely without its blemishes, is there?"

"I'm extremely sorry you feel that way about me," I complained melodramatically around a mouthful of egg and apple. I'll confess here and now that I deeply envied her the chorizo. Deeply. It's unspeakably delicious but I'm deathly allergic to the stuff. One bite equals about two days running to the toilet spewing at one end or the other or both. I took a big swig of rum and Coke, instead. "I always liked you well enough, I guess."

Waiting for her reaction, I looked up at the naked lady picture, pretending to examine it minutely. It was new to the place, very nice to look at, and about twenty feet long. I suddenly realized that it was Bettie Page. In my world, she was a 1950s pinup model with an enormous cult following, mostly on the Internet, who'd failed to make it in Hollywood because she'd dared to bring her personal morality with her from Tennessee. In this world—where demanding a session on the casting-couch could

get a producer's or director's *cojones* shot off for his trouble—
she was every bit as big a movie star as Gable or Lombard, and
her soft southern accent, like everything else about her, was completely genuine.

Lucy shook her head and grinned. "You'll clown at your fu-
neral, Winnie! You know perfectly well I was talkin' about little
Dougie and his friends. If I hadn't seen too much of 'em already
this mornin', I'd ask 'em who they thought was gonna enforce that
idiot edict of theirs, the governments they jumped headlong
through the broach t'get away from?"

I laughed, but I didn't mean it cruelly. Well, not very cruelly,
anyway. The sad, simple truth was that I'd suffered many of the
same cultural shocks, gone through many of the same personal
adjustments that these poor saps still had ahead of them. For me
at least, it was always the little things that had been the hardest.
The window glass that grew back by itself. The number and
shape of the holes in the electrical outlets. No driver's licenses
in anybody's billfolds. No license plates on their cars. No wheels
on their cars, either, as far as that goes, but that's a whole different story. It hadn't been fun, but it had sure been worth it. I
said as much to Lucy.

"I never doubted you for a minute, Winnie!" One of the
things I liked best about Lucy was that, even at her age, her hair
wasn't blue. This morning it was fiery red. "You were born for
this world! These blasted newcomers, though . . ."

I laughed out loud. "Next thing you know they'll be talking
about banning tobacco!"

She peered at me, wondering if I was serious. "There's more
to it than that, even! Thanks to a lifetime spent in one welfare
state or another, somewhere at the back of his beady little mind,
even the noisiest anarchist among 'em expects some official program t'handle his little dissatisfactions—these morons an' their

vending machine vendetta for instance—or t'keep his family eatin' while he looks for work."

I felt my eyebrows rise and I was suddenly perfectly serious.
"You know, I think you may be onto something, at that."

"You bet I am, Winnie. He's always stunned by the truth—
that nobody cares if they don't like the vendin' machines. (I'm
surprised they didn't mention the Porn-O-Mats!) That he's expected t'raise his own kids and leave everybody else's alone. That
we've got charities in the Confederacy, but they're all totally private—an' reserved exclusively for a miniscule minority legitimately incapable of feedin' themselves."

"Yeah," I agreed. "And even worse, there are those who used
to be doctors, lawyers, engineers, scientists, or technicians Stateside. They soon discover that they have more than a century of
professional catching up to do (or that they aren't needed at all;
hell, it almost happened to me)—and have to start all over again
as busboys, janitors, or . . ."

"Fry-cooks." I looked up to see the Wizard standing beside
me, wiping his hands on his apron. I shoved over in the booth,
but he waved me off and pulled up a chair. Lan squeezed in with
Lucy. They'd brought plates with them and drinks of their own.
The Wizard was famous for the size and potency of his margaritas, sometimes known around here as "Mexican martinis." I
briefly regretted settling for rum and Coke. "On the other hand,"
he went on, taking a swig of his fabled lime and tequila elixir,
"they get paid in real money while they're catching up—copper,
nickel, silver, gold, platinum, palladium—not a single grain of
which is ever subject to income, sales, excise, or self-employment
taxes."

"Or ever confiscated," his wife added, "using the excuse of
some worthless government insurance pyramid scheme." General
nodding all around. Given everything that went on within its

walls, the Hanging Judge as we knew it wouldn't have been al-lowed to exist in any of the regimes we'd variously and severally left behind, and the dozen or so individuals it employed would have been on food stamps. Or in prison.

"Tell me something," Lan asked. "We've been so busy, Max and I, getting restarted in life, that we haven't paid much atten-tion to what passes for politics in the Confederacy. Until now, we felt pretty safe doing that, but maybe we were wrong. Who are these Franklinites that seem to be monopolizing the 'Com ever since the Old Endicott Building disaster?"

Lucy grinned. This was her meat. She had degrees, I'd been told, in engineering and the law. She'd even been a judge once upon a time. But this was her thing. Someone had once described her to me as an individual who hated government and loved politics.

She opened her mouth, but I interrupted her. "They're a bunch of sore losers, free-market rejects, who want some kind of government—any kind of government—established, not from any high-minded (if wrongheaded) principle, but so it can issue lucrative contracts that they and their cronies can get rich on."

I smiled brightly at Lucy.

She frowned, torn between annoyance and approval. She'd been my mentor on this and many other topics, and it was funny to watch her deciding what attitude to take about being upstaged by her pupil. I hurried on before she could make up her mind. "They'd be plain old Republicans where I come from. Buckley F. Williams ramrods them and, rumor has it, bankrolls them. It's practically a family business. His little brother, well-known philosopher-thug Bennett Williams, runs their online journal, *The Postman.*"

I'd actually met older brother Buckley the first year I'd arrived here in the Confederacy, although not under the most auspicious

of circumstances. Very funny kinda guy. Lan wrinkled her forehead at me. "*The Postman?*"

"I get it!" her husband answered.

"I'll bet you do at that," I replied. "Good old Benjamin Franklin, author, inventor, the Williams brothers' hero, and the Franklinites' namesake. Most people don't realize he was the father of
corporate socialism—or of state capitalism, if there's a difference—in Revolutionary America. It was his intention that the
government would accomplish everything it undertook by grant-
ing monopolies to certain 'deserving' parties. That's how, in most
worlds, he wound up in charge of the government postal monopoly."

" 'Neither rain, nor sleet, nor dark of night,' " Lan misquoted,
" 'nor threat of competition will stay these messengers from their
appointed rounds.' I get it now, too: *The Postman.* And darling,
it's called mercantilism. Corporate socialism and state capitalism
hadn't been invented yet. I wonder if Ben Franklin ever met its
nemesis, his contemporary, Adam Smith."

"They're sure as shootin' tryin' t'set up some kinda government now!" Lucy remarked. "Call it mercantilism, corporate socialism, state capitalism, or Ring Around the Rosie, they don't
give a hoot as long as they get a piece of the action!"

"Ragtime Dance" finished up, and something else began,
maybe it was "The Cascades." I wished Clarissa could be here
to share the talk. Simply to learn that Lucy was visiting Earth
would delight her. But she was busy this morning with a client.
One of the services she offers is "time therapy." Clarissa didn't
invent it, but she was one of its first practitioners. The course of
treatment is often compared to humans first learning to walk
erect, or to the discovery of fire, because it deals with such a
fundamental problem. What it does, by various means, is alter
an individual's perception of the passage of time, so that it

doesn't seem to go by more quickly the more fun he's having or the older he gets (one of the greatest tragedies, otherwise, of living a long time). I never thought anything could actually make sex *better*, but I was wrong.

Lan chuckled softly. "You know, boys and girls, they could get away with it, these Franklinites. Most native-born Confederates have no experience of government whatever. They simply refuse to believe the horror stories we immigrants have to tell them about the brutal and corrupt police states we escaped from, the crazy and stupid regulations we were expected to obey, the life-crippling taxes we were expected to pay. 'Five times the tribute a medieval serf owed his master? You've got to be pulling my leg.' Try to explain that we were prisoners of the majority, in a system where our votes didn't count for anything, and they just shake their heads."

"Or slap their holsters and wink!" her husband added. Back at the bar, somebody started to complain loudly about the lack of service. Lucy and Lan started to get up, but the Wizard held out a hand and shook his head. "You know the drill as well as I do!" he hollered back at his customers over his shoulder. "Punch your orders into the bartop, and I'll get right to them!" Remaining at the end of the table, he flipped a panel open at its edge, pressed a button, and closed the flap. Instantly, the third of the tabletop closest to him glowed to life, becoming a virtualized replica of the grill he'd just been slaving over. (It could have been anything else he wanted, including chess, checkers, Trivial Pursuit, or this afternoon's Patriots–Aztecs game.) Touching the image of this or that ingredient, that or this utensil, he began preparing several exotic omelettes at once, an order of emu eggs over easy, bacon, sausage, chorizo, fried tomatoes, and a personal favorite of mine, grilled parsnips.

Maybe, I thought, I should stay for lunch.

I glanced in the direction of the grill, always tickled to see what was happening there in the Wizard's virtual absence. A pair of mechanical arms—covered with cheerfully red- and white-striped fabric so they could be called "waldos" with double accuracy—were mimicking every move he made here at the table, to the vast amusement of the formerly dissatisfied customers at the bar, who were whistling and cheering them on.

The arms flipped food onto plates, placed them on the counter before the now-mollified patrons, and served them the drinks they wanted. A hundred years behind Confederate technology or not, the Wizard was catching up fast. He'd designed and constructed the system he'd just put to good use. It wouldn't be long before he'd acquired the polish required to be a fully practicing crosstime engineer.

"I know what you mean," I told Lan, continuing our conversation. "With no taxes to stand in the way of a newcomer acquiring a home or other property, no government to drain him at the rate of half of everything he earns and half of everything he spends, he doesn't need to work more than four or five hours a week to maintain the relatively modest standard of living he was already used to, working forty hours a week back home."

The Wizard nodded, swallowing a bite of spiced apple omelette. "And those willing to work harder usually do better. If they decide to start a business, they just start it—that's what we did! All they need is an idea and capital, since there are no permits to buy, no phony safety standards to meet, no environmental impact statements to file, no bureaucracies to satisfy, no inspectors to bribe—"

"All such impediments," his wife finished for him, "having been legislated in our world by corrupt politicians working for those they were supposed to regulate, to prevent fresh market entries and new competition. But it's the same old story as it was back home. America was vastly better than anything the world had ever seen before because it was vastly *freer* than anything the world had ever seen before. But Americans forgot that, somehow. In the same way, people born here in the Confederacy may not appreciate it, and they're all too likely to listen to parasitic creatures like the Franklinites."

"Public schools, that's what happened to America, to Americans. They didn't forget; they were never taught." I slid out of the booth, stood up, and stretched as much as I could, retrieving my hat and poncho. "Well, as much as I've enjoyed our little seminar this morning," I told Lan, the Wizard, and Lucy, "and as sincerely as I'd like to stay and have another meal or two, I have work to do."

They all groaned soulfully on my behalf and rhetorically begged me to reconsider such foolishness, but I could see that they had work on their minds, as well. People tend to be that way when they get to keep everything they earn.

With difficulty, I pulled out my increasingly wrinkled sheet of paper again. Now it even had a grease spot on it, from the sausage, I think. "I originally stopped by to show you this list of Zoners connected with interworld importing one way or another, and to ask if you had any idea who's responsible for bringing in otherworld movie titles like *Gone with the Wind* and *It Happened One Night*."

"Why not ask the 'Com channels that show them?" the Wizard asked.

"Because the Hanging Judge is Alternate World Central—anything going on in the Zone is usually heard about here, first. Besides, I did, first thing this morning, and they told me to fribble off. And anyway, I needed breakfast." I reached into one of my pants pockets and extracted the proper amount in copper coins to cover the meal and a tip. Neither of them refused my money. And I wouldn't have let them. After all, I was a partner in this establishment, and I'd be expecting my cut at the end of the month.

I got a cigar out and lit it—the perfect finish to a perfect meal. The Confederacy had another thing we didn't have in the States besides cures for cancer, heart disease, and emphysema: adequate ventilation. Come to think of it, I was surprised friend Doug hadn't complained about cigar and cigarette machines, which were plentiful.

"I would have told you to fribble off, too," said the Wizard. "Private business is private business. Anything you're looking for in particular?"

"In addition to these people? Yeah, but I'm not sure how to put it. Tell me: who played Rhett Butler in the version of *Gone with the Wind* that you grew up with?"

"Clark Gable," he replied. Yolanda nodded agreement. "Who else would it be?"

"Me, too. But somebody's imported another version, starring Robert Cummings—featuring Bette Davis as Scarlett O'Hara. Of course that might seem perfectly normal to some of these immigrants—although I doubt they'd actually remember any movie that resulted from that particular casting."

Lan raised her eyebrows. "So what do you want us to do, Win?"

The usual. Talk to people. Listen to them. Tell these folks I'd like to talk with them. Keep your eye out for anything really bizarre like . . . well, Bob Cummings and Bette Davis. I know, it's a hard thing to judge. But keep an open mind and let me know."

They were about to tell me they would, when the floor began to tremble under our feet, the way it had the night of the Old Endicott explosion. The Wizard wiped an arm across the table, clearing it of the stovetop images—the Copperodeon halted right in the middle of "Solace"—bringing up a news service. It was the animated, cheerful, interactive, image of InstaNews' bottle-nosed dolphin, Lightning, one of the Confederacy's historic contributions to mass media. Not.

". . . apparently hit a deliberately set obstruction at eighteen thousand miles an hour, vaporizing itself and blasting out a mile-wide crater." Lightning took an absolutely unnecessary breath. "To repeat, an ultrahighspeed underground train bound from LaPorte to Mexico City has apparently hit a deliberately set obstruction at 18,000 miles an hour, vaporizing itself and blasting out a mile-wide crater. No reliable word yet on casualties, but we'll let you know as soon as we hear."

Okay, my fault: I'd just had a great breakfast and felt as contented as a Canadian. I was a perfect mark for the Bear Curse.

6: HELL IN A BUCKET

> Want to understand why politicians do what they do?
> Simple: when you're a big, gray, greasy rat, walking
> around on two hind legs, you have a lot to gain by turn-
> ing the world into a garbage heap.
> —*Memoirs of Lucille G. Kropotkin*

I don't think five minutes passed before the Franklinites were on
the 'Com again, demanding—as they had for more than two centuries—that *something* be done. This time (surprise!), they had
something specific in mind.

"What this unspeakable tragedy teaches us, Jerry," their
spokesman intoned hypersincerely, egged on by the sleaziest dirt-
grubber in all the Confederate media, "is that we must begin keeping better track of one another. People must be required to carry
cards with holographic likenesses and other vital information on
them. Fingerprint or retinal pattern records must be established
and maintained—or perhaps both fingerprint *and* retinal patterns—
and everyone must be fingerprinted and scanned."

"Frogsnot!" a furious Lucy exclaimed. Bereft of handy sexual
or religious epithets, Confederate profanity approaches the Dalí-
esque—although the fine old expression, "Shit!" is well thought
of and often used.

"Why, that fatherless villain!" I heard a voice say. I looked up
and was rewarded with the vision of a huge heavyset man with
long gray hair and a big gray beard looking over my shoulder.
He was wearing patched and faded jeans and the first tie-dyed
T-shirt I'd seen in almost a decade.

"Hullo, Lucy. The man's addressing what happened as if it
were some sort of natural disaster, ignoring the criminals who
did it, and trying to punish the survivors!"

"Hush, Papa!" Lucy responded in a whisper everyone could hear. The tie-dyed fellow looked very familiar somehow, but I couldn't place him immediately. We were all looking down at that multitalented tabletop in the booth in the Hanging Judge, although by now there were half a hundred other surfaces around the room—most of them vertical—displaying the same disgraceful performance that held our attention captive in the booth. Some things never change from continuum to continuum.

Onscreen we saw the regrettably wealthy and famous Jerry Rivers, a specimen of *H. journalismus* whom the denizens of any number of different universes would have recognized, although not always by the same name, and never with any genuine enthusiasm. Where I came from, he'd dumped the ethnic names that he'd been born with, then taken them back when they became fashionable. He was a Latino, dark and slight of build, with a big mustache of the kind that were once called "soup strainers." The broad-lapeled, pin-striped, double-breasted suit he was wearing—an American import with a white turtleneck sweater— probably cost more than my first house.

In any world, the man was a professional tearduct and syndicated hairsprayhead even the networks had avoided for twenty years. For him, no act of dishonesty, depravity, or simple bad taste was too low in the pursuit of ratings. Pretending to uphold the downtrodden (a difficult class to find in the Confederacy), his strategy was always to set one group against another, so that he could cash in on whatever conflict that generated. "Y'know, Winnie," Lucy offered, as if she'd been reading my mind, "That pile of hyena dung—"

"Meaning Rivers?" I asked, discovering an itch inside my cast.

"Meaning Rivers—he once pushed a crackpot theory that cetaceans aren't actually sapient—their intelligence is faked by humans as part of some kinda gigantic an' horrendous plot against the simians: gorillas, chimpanzees, orangutans, and gibbons!"

The Wizard laughed. "I remember that! He never explained who or what or when or where or why—after all, it was the same humans who 'elevated' simians in the first place and offered them full partnership in Confederate society."

"This lack of sapience sure must have come as a surprise to Ooloorie Eckickeck P'wheet." I chuckled. She was the porpoise who invented the probability broach that had brought me and thousands of others to the Confederacy.

Now that I'd noticed it, the itch was getting worse. Lucy began writing something in a notepad in her spidery, almost microscopic hand, Lan looking over her shoulder, offering comments. I knew it meant somebody was in for a heap of trouble.

I was surprised not to recognize the guy Rivers was interviewing. It wasn't Buckley F. Williams, who usually did the talking for this bunch. Words scrolling across the screen bottom labled him Allard Wayne, junior associate director of the Franklinite Faction of the Gallatinist Party. The man was colorless and characterless, as if he'd been put through the washing machine too many times and dried at too high a temperature. If the expression, "Those are my principles, and if you don't like them—I'll change them!" hadn't already been tacked onto George Bush's New England carpetbagger backside, it would have fit this guy perfectly.

Lucy looked up from her notepad. "I wonder where Buckley is about now, and what he's thinkin'."

"I usually disagree with him about nearly everything," Lan said, "but this seems kind of over-the-top even for him. He strikes me as a basically decent guy."

"Decent if a litle misguided," I agreed. "He even invited me for a ride on his "yacht" once, a two hundred-foot dirigible where we could relax and smoke some Sonoran Sillyweed he was bragging about. I declined with regret."

"And that's why they call him 'dope,' " said the Wizard.

Meaning me, not Buckley. I meant to ask if he had a pickle fork or something that could get at the itch in my cast, but got distracted by the 'Com.

Just now, Jerry was pretending to be "fair" in his own inimitable fashion: "Is it true, Mr. Wayne—may I call you Allard?— that some opponents of these reasonable, commonsense reforms you Franklinites advocate object; that they compare it to being 'ear-tagged like cattle'? I've heard some call it 'pre-incrimination' and others point out that it would be unconstitutional even in most versions of the Old United States."

That's what they called the pre-Confederate nation that had merged with Mexico and Canada in 120 A.L. Sometimes the name was applied—by morons like Jerry Rivers, ignorant of history—to otherworld counterparts that hadn't ever merged with their neighbors to the north and south.

"Well, Jerry," the junior associate director responded to Rivers's softball question, "the Confederacy's Founding Fathers, however wise they happened to have been, couldn't possibly have conceived of something like this overwhelming tidal wave of *aliens* under which our beloved traditional Confederate values are beginning to break down. If for no other reason than for the sake of our children, the naive eighteenth century notions of Thomas Paine and Thomas Jefferson and Albert Gallatin must be set aside—at least temporarily—in favor of peace, order, and security."

The stained glass windows of the Hanging Judge rattled with a unanimous "Boooo!" erupting from its several dozen occupants. Lucy pounded on the table with her pistol butt, threatening to crack its image-generating surface. Always it's the children who serve as a handy excuse for whatever atrocities those in power want to justify. These people had had a belly full of it already—that's why they were here—and so had I.

"You know," said Lucy as she began to calm down, "this character is relatively clever—"

"Or whoever wrote his script for him," Lan observed.

"And coached him with the big words," the Wizard added.

"Well he's clever in at least one respect." Lucy looked around, daring anyone else to interrupt. "In only two sentences, he's blamed both of these catastrophes on you immigrants. He's branded you as Martians or Venusians or something. He's established the Founding Fathers as a bunch of hopeless nut cases. And he's asserted that the Franklinite Faction knows better than anybody else what's good for everybody concerned!"

I, too, looked around, and saw a bunch of grim faces. "All these people," I told Lucy, "these immigrants to the Confederacy, are all too well accustomed to dog-and-pony shows like this one. Most of them, given the chance, leaped through the probability broach to escape exactly this kind of insanity."

Lan nodded. "And the ever-increasing restrictions on their lives that result from the fact that established authority never seems quite competent to ferret out the guilty and so instead, invariably punishes the much handier innocent."

"That seems to me," Lucy suggested, "like a good reason not to establish any authority at all!"

The Wizard slapped a broad palm down on the tabletop. "I just realized how clever these Franklinites really are. Lan's right. Native Confederates—with the exception of those like you, Lucy—might not appreciate what they have. They might even be willing to give it up, perhaps a little bit at a time, just to stop all of this carnage and destruction."

"And?" I asked, just to be helpful. Maybe a teriyaki stick . . .

"And Wayne and his buddies," the Wizard replied, "have now singled out the one and only group likeliest to oppose what amounts to their overnight takeover of the Confederacy—recent immigrants fleeing the kind of tyranny they want to impose—and made them the likeliest suspects for a pair of manmade disasters that renders such a takeover 'necessary.' "

"Shit," I said, and meant it.

"Shit, indeed. Everybody in this room knows exactly what comes next. Having broken the ice with this ID card scheme of theirs, next they'll demand that Congress be reconvened 'for the duration of the emergency.' "

"Meanin' 'til the sun burns out!" Lucy offered. She'd finished her own food and was helping the Wizard finish his.

"Until the sun burns out. Before we know it," the Wizard went on, ignoring the plundering of his plate, "for the first time in over two centuries, careful talk of taxes 'for increased security' will begin to be taken seriously by Rivers and his odiferous ilk, along with 'reasonable, commonsense' restrictions on immigration, and maybe even on the personal weapons you Confederates carry every waking minute of your lives—"

"Which happens to make the Confederacy the most crime-free society in this or any other world," I said.

The Wizard answered, "Right you are, Win. But when did a perfectly solved problem ever help a politician? I tell you, if we don't do something, the Confederacy could easily end up just like the places we all escaped from!"

"Sssssh!" There was a whole chorus of hissing shushes as the interview went on.

"On the other hand, Allard," Rivers was saying, "there are those who say the reforms you call for don't go nearly far enough—among them the political advocates Jerse Fahel and Howard Slaughterbush."

"Those gabbling too-farists?" Wayne pretended to be amused. "Well, Jerry, that just goes to show why the people of the North American Confederacy desperately need the Franklinite Faction to balance things out. Unlike Fahel and Slaughterbush, we're a part of the nation's history, a part of the Gallatinist Party. We're in favor of as much freedom as is possible and practicable. The purely temporary measures we recommend are minimal, but they're necessary if we wish to keep any freedom at all."

I'd only vaguely heard of Slaughterbush before now—some kind of political kook, exactly like Wayne and his masters—but for the first time since I'd gotten here, I began to have that old, helpless, hopeless feeling one experiences standing in the path of an oncoming legislative steamroller. I'd had that feeling all my life as an American. It was a feeling I'd almost forgotten here. I remembered it now. I hated it.

But for me, it was time to go to work. I'd suddenly remembered where I'd seen that big tie-dyed guy—or a reference to him, anyway. He was on the list that I'd compiled earlier in the car. Now, telling my friends good-bye for the third or fourth time, my hat, coat, broken arm, and I followed him out the double doors, onto the brightly sunlit multicolored sidewalk of the Zone.

"Hey, Papa!" I hollered after him, remembering that someone had called him that back in the bar. On my list, he had another name altogether. "You got a minute?"

A little old lady—and in this culture that meant *really* old—heavyset and stooped, approached me. She had a big hat with an almost opaque veil, and a small basket full of smaller change. "Contribute to the Spaceman's Fund?" she asked in a cracked and ancient-sounding voice. I looked down: she'd tugged at my serape.

There's no government welfare of any kind in the Confederacy, which is why I try, ordinarily, to be as generous as I can. But I was in a big hurry at the moment. "Not now," I told her, "maybe later," and rushed past her.

I yelled again, "Hey, Papa!"

The guy slowed and turned. He wore what we once called "granny glasses" and carried a big leather purse on a wide strap over one shoulder. There was a bulge under his shirt over his right hip. He looked at my left arm. "You're injured. How may I help?"

I grinned at him—an armed hippie. "I'm okay. You can tell me who played Rhett Butler in *Gone with the Wind*."

Nine out of ten people would have been annoyed or perplexed. Papa simply said, "Now let me guess—the cinema? I'm afraid I've never heard of a Rhett Butler, or *Gone with the Wind*. Is it something I should look for on the 'Com?"

I introduced myself and explained a bit of what I was up to. We'd reached my car, the little Neova shining candy-apple red in what was rapidly becoming the broiling afternoon sun. There were some places in the Confederacy where local merchants had thrown in together and air-conditioned the whole damned city. I wished Greater LaPorte were one of them. "Let me guess," I told the guy. "You come from a world where the United States never fought a civil war."

"As I understand it, the proper term is 'War Between the States.' " He grinned. "But I come from a world in which there never was a United States." He extended a big hand and a kindly smile. "Karl LeMat at your service, late, but not lamentably, of the Dominion of British North America."

"*That's* where I saw you!" I snapped my fingers . . . er, with him, not at him. This had nothing to do with my list. "You're the guy that story on the 'Com was about."

The big man sighed. "It's true enough. I suppose the notoriety has been good for business, though."

It was all coming back to me now. "Papa" Karl LeMat, age sixty-six, was a gentle, grandfatherly grassroots philosopher of great charisma and somewhat variable philosophical rigor. He was one of those types you like from the moment you see them, and was on my list because he had a small business importing some of the most remarkable coins and currency in the known universe.

"The Dominion of British North America was never witness to any revolution against the Crown, nor to a civil war, nor a war between the states." Papa told me, once we'd adjourned to my "office," parked at the curb down the street from the Hanging Judge. Even with two big men, it wasn't too cramped inside, and the air-conditioning was beginning to feel good.

It turned out that he'd come in for breakfast but never ordered any, so disgusted had he been with what he'd seen happening on the 'Com. I offered him coffee and had the Neova make it while we waited, nice and strong with that big dollop of chocolate Confederates are so fond of, and a pinch of cinnamon. Before we knew it, the air inside the car smelled wonderful.

He accepted a steaming cup. "I've read your history—at least one very close to it. I suspect that in my world the Crown found some way to bribe your Mr. Washington, as he became Sir George, and later Lord Washington, Governor General of as much of the North American continent as was under British authority at the time."

We both lit cigars, automatically kicking the car's ventilators up to Warp 10. I'd been putting it off, but finally I asked the inevitable American Zone question. "So how'd you wind up in the Confederacy?"

He took a long drag on his cigar, exhaled, then took a big drink of his coffee. "I'm afraid we British North Americans were never as sanguine about Manifest Destiny as you independents apparently were. Your America was carved out by ordinary individuals attempting to make something better of themselves. Mine was mostly settled by aristocratic second sons attempting to escape the beastly English climate. It is fair to say, though, that it's the American dominion that wags the British dog, these days. Even King Stephen spends more time at his residence in Boca Raton than he does in London."

King Stephen. No abdication in the 1930s, I'd be willing to bet, so this would probably be some royal clown I'd never seen or heard of—maybe even the kid that Wally Simpson was paid never to have. Suited me. "And?"

"And as a result of this history, I suppose, I found myself, somewhat late in life, a resident of the city of Trinidad in what you'd call southern Colorado, just this side of the Franco-Mexican border, and one of the leaders of a national movement to establish free trade with Russian California."

"I see." If you lived in the Confederacy, especially among its immigrants long enough, matters of geography—or rather of national borders—rapidly began to assume the solidity and importance of warm Jell-O. I'd met a guy once who claimed he was from a place where the United World capital was St. John's, Newfoundland.

He eyed me. "Perhaps you do, after all. We were beginning to enjoy some success politically. Rather too much, I suspect, as I was forced to escape—that is, to accept the refuge that was so kindly offered me by your Gallatinite Rescue Society—when I was suddenly accused of criminal sexual harrassment, for having winked at a female postal employee over the visiphone."

The GRS was only one of many groups here in LaPorte and

elsewhere throughout the Confederacy that made a practice of snatching freedom-loving people from unfree worlds. I'd worked for some of them, myself, including a really good one that made a happy specialty of exposing the nasty private habits of uptight public do-gooders. I still remember a certain Denver district attorney and his hidden walk-in closet full of rubber suits and whips and chains.

"For my own part, I wasn't certain what astonished me more," Papa went on, "that I was being watched by my own government—well, His Majesty's government, anyway—or by people from an alternate world I never suspected exists."

"Vast intellects, cool and dispassionate, or whatever it was H. G. Wells said. And now I understand you do a little rescuing yourself, a ha'penny here and a guinea there—"

"Dollars and centavos, actually, and only from government coffers, using a dirigible minibroach. Also, the occasional Mexican franc and Russian nickie. They're all reasonably popular among your Confederate numismatists—though not much of anyone else, since they're struck from base metals or aluminum." He pronounced it, "al-you-MIN-i-um," with the gratuitous British syllable. The guy looked so much like the late Jerry Garcia it was creepy to begin with, and it was even weirder hearing that plummy accent coming out of his mouth. I knew Trinidad pretty well, my mom had been born there. It was a sleepy little town, about half redbrick, three quarters Hispanic, and seven-eighths on welfare, built on steep hillsides and over coal mines. Windy as hell, too. I wondered what it would be like under British rule. Probably windier, with all those extra syllables.

"Not *my* numismatists, Papa. I'm just as much of a blueback here as you are, although I was the very first, back in 1987, reeled in by P'wheet and Thorens themselves."

His brow wrinkled. " 'Blueback'? I don't believe I've ever heard that expression before."

"You will," I grinned. "It's for 'the searing azure color of the broach-margin.' "

" 'Searing azure . . . I see—or rather, I didn't see. I was taken away in a passenger car with its windows painted black—I still don't know how, as private motor vehicles are forbidden in my native land—and brought over blindfold to preserve the other-side secrets of my rescuers." He blinked. "You're rather poetic for a detective, aren't you?"

"Actually," I grinned, "it was my lovely and talented mate who first described the broach that way. Go down to the Interworld Terminal sometime and have a look. It's really spectacular. But you wouldn't know who's importing Stateside movies?"

He shook his head regretfully. "Not my bailiwick, I'm sorry to say. Thanks ever so much for the coffee, Win, and good to meet you. I believe I'll go back in now and have that breakfast of which I deprived myself."

"Thanks, Papa, have some for me." We shook hands. He lifted the door and climbed out of the car, thoughtfully taking his empty cup with him. I caught myself thinking that if I'd had a microwave, we could have had hot doughnuts with our coffee. But there I was again, concentrating on my stomach, and zero for zero, informationwise. Oh well, I told myself, that's how they all start.

I consigned my empty cup to the Neova's trash disintegrator and leaned down to start the engine, when I heard a rapping coming from outside the big curved window at my left. I looked up to see Lucy demanding my attention. I signaled for her to step out of the way and swung the door up.

"You don't happen to have a knitting needle inside that

steamer trunk you're carrying?" The hotter it got the worse the itch.

" 'Fraid not, Winnie. I haven't knitted since the Kaiser War."

"Then what can I do for you this fine, sunny summer day, my dear Miz Kropotkin?" I was happy to see her again. She'd lost the apron, gained a huge leather purse, put her hair up in a bun—it made her look like Tweety Bird's granny—and wore her giant Gabbett-Fairfax belted around a jersey dress of green and yellow paisley.

"You can let me hire you, Winnie! If we don't get to the bottom of these disasters—an' find out who's behind 'em—we're gonna lose the Covenant!"

By which she meant the Covenant of Unanimous Consent, the document Gallatin had insisted upon once Washington—general and president, not sir and lord—had been duly ventilated. To Lucy, the Covenant was as sacred and worthy of defense as the American Bill of Rights.

And, at least until now, it was a hell of a lot better enforced.

7: LAWYERS, GUNS, AND MONEY

> The fact that nobody asks you to sing is *not* an indication
> that you should sing louder. This appears obvious until
> it's applied to matters like mass transportation. In the
> United States there are virtually *no* private mass transit
> companies and thousands of public ones. This does not
> represent the failure of the market to provide a needed
> service, it represents the failure of an unneeded service
> to *go away*!
>
> —*Memoirs of Lucille G. Kropotkin*

North American Confederates are as peculiar about knives as
they are about everything else. In the branch of history I grew
up in, when Colonel-by-courtesy James Bowie and his smarter
brother Rezin were dreaming up the fabled hand-wide, foot-long
sharp-edged slab of steel—meteoric nickel-iron in the Hollywood
version of the legend—that, in my homeworld, bears their family
name, defensive handguns were single-shot contraptions, cum-
bersome, finicky, loaded with loose powder and lead balls at the
muzzle, and often still ignited by a chunk of flint. A couple of
generations later, Buffalo Bill Cody, a little behind the times in
his choice of social cutlery, is reputed to have dragged around a
Bowie knife with a sixteen-inch blade. That's a scant two inches
shorter than a Roman legionnaire's regulation-issue *gladius*.

However in general, as pistols began to mutate into revolvers,
increasingly more powerful and reliable, the knives that gentlemen had been carrying around for personal defense started to
atrophy, inch by inch, until (except for the occasional street-
punk's switchblade or spouse-perforating kitchen knife), in my
time as a cop in the U.S.—the seventies and eighties—they'd
vanished altogether.

In the Confederacy, on the other hand, knives seem to have grown right along with the increasing power of handguns, as if everybody wanted a toadsticker that was somehow *worthy* of his primary weapon. A belligerent fashion statement, if you see what I mean.

In Greater LaPorte, you hardly ever see a pistol belt without a dirk or dagger of some kind hanging from the off-side. One of the first individuals I encountered when I arrived, entirely by accident, believe me, was a gray-haired old gent trailing a huge cavalry saber. To make matters even more confusing, he'd been a chimpanzee.

All this was on my mind as we drove to the place Will had told me about, Daggett's Wonderful World of Sharp Pointy Things, on North Snowflake, deep in the Zone. It was the only clean place on the block. I don't know what it is about the Zone that makes it seem . . . well, grimy. Objectively, the several dozen square blocks where American immigrants have decided to light—entirely on their own; no Confederate has the inclination or power to make them—are every bit as well-repaired and freshly scrubbed as anyplace else in LaPorte. Maybe attitude can permeate a place as much as dirt and grime.

Or maybe it was just me.

Lucy and I were actually on our way, at her insistence, to take a look at what was left at the site of that hypersonic train wreck, south of town. I'd already tried telling her, several times, that she couldn't hire me, as attractive as a little extra cash might be. I had another commission I'd already accepted payment to deal with. But each time I tried to explain myself, she didn't hear it. The whole thing was all very Lucy. Okay, I figured the trip out to the wreck that she wanted to make anyway might be just the thing to convince her that top men were already hard at work on the case.

Top. Men.

I'd also done a little insisting of my own, hence a brief detour to take a gander at some grownup toys. Thomas Daggett (the name seemed familiar, somehow) seemed to be another recent immigrant from some variation of the U.S. But unlike the delegation that had sent itself to the Hanging Judge, protesting the availability of objects and activities they considered naughty, he seemed happy to be here, a sentiment I could well appreciate. Daggett was a short, broad, tough-looking guy, sort of a low wall of muscle with a heavy black beard, a nose like the beak of a raptor, and shrewd, dangerous eyes. His hands reminded me of the Wizard's, although where Max resembled an oversized hobbit, this worthy looked to me like one of Tolkien's mining dwarves. Belying his appearance, his voice was a quick and lively tenor. I had a hard time placing his accent, which seemed to have bits of New York and Chicago in it, maybe even Boston. I learned later that he spoke fluent Korean.

"I was an attorney back in Beaverton, Oregon," he said. I perused the glass cases and wall displays in his shop (trying to picture him in a suit and tie—Beaverton: I'd often wondered why *Hustler* hadn't made its headquarters there). I'd admitted I'd never seen so many cutting tools and edged weapons in one location in my life. Lucy agreed. "Y'know, Tommy-John, from sheer weight of metal, this place must generate a magnetic anomaly identifiable from orbit!"

Daggett beamed at her words and said nothing. He and Lucy had greeted each other like old friends. That happens all the time with her. I guess in 145 years you get to know a lot of people.

As we inspected what he had, I'd figured it couldn't do any harm to ask him about *Gone with the Wind*—he was from another Clark Gable and Vivien Leigh–type world—and he'd ended up telling me something about himself. "I got sick and tired of trying to defend my clients with both hands tied behind my back. The cops and the prosecution were always wailing about 'revolving door justice,' but I wasn't allowed any of the basic necessities—like appealing to the Bill of Rights."

"What?" It was the first time I'd ever seen Lucy shocked.

Daggett put a solemn hand to his heart and nodded. "Absolutely true, Lucy. The Bill of Rights is only for 'higher intelligences' in the appeals courts to deliberate—well after the defendant's been properly terrified, exhausted, and financially destroyed. And the result? Well, if you shot somebody legitimately, in defense of your own life, it still cost you everything you had—your life savings, your house, your car, the braces on your children's teeth—just to get through the legal meatgrinder."

I added, "And you'd damned well better not get caught shooting somebody in defense of your *property*."

"Damn straight," the ex-lawyer declared. Proudhon rules the day in America's courts, where property—private property—is theft."

Here, except for duelling, shootings in defense of property were the commonest kind—and happened maybe twice a decade, because, well, who'd want to risk it? Lucy shook her head and sighed. "I see now, why Lan and the Wizard named their saloon the way they did."

I laughed.

"Hard as it may be to believe," Daggett wasn't through, "I wasn't even allowed to tell the jury of their thousand-year-old right and duty to reject an unjust, unconstitutional, or just plain stupid law. That was grounds for a mistrial—and maybe a little downtime in the pokey for the defense attorney. So if the law itself was illegal, and my client had broken it simply by exercising his rights, what could I do?"

"Emigrate!" Lucy replied.

I hadn't told him that I'd been one of those cops, Stateside. "It always seemed to me," I remarked, "that 'revolving door justice' was reserved for genuine criminal scumbags who knew how to work the wheels and levers, while members of the productive class, accidentally caught up in the gears of the machine—responsible individuals who'd never done anything illegal in their lives—"

"They were the ones got chewed up and spat out by the system?" Lucy finished. "If I were the religious type—which I'm not, thank God—I'd be feeling mighty grateful I was born here an' not there!"

"Well it wasn't as bad as I make it sound," Daggett answered. "It was worse. Most of the time the jury had been handpicked by the judge and his minions to favor the prosecution and police, through a process of interrogation called 'voir dire'—which a newspaper columnist friend of mine says is French for 'jury tampering.' "

That was good for a laugh until I realized we could be heading for a system just like that if the Franklinites got their way. I changed the subject. "A friend of mine said you import knives made by a guy named Chris Reeve. I'd like to see some, if you don't mind."

"This case here," Daggett said. "We get them in from half a dozen timelines; there're a lot of model variations—Bowies, bolos, spearpoints, tantos, even a *bat'leth*. Anything specific in mind?

"My friend had something called a Project I."

"That'd be Captain Sanders, of what we call the 'sharpened prybar' school. The Project I's a big, heavy, thick knife, all right."

"What's the little one at the back?" I pointed to a smaller knife. I don't know what it was about it that caught my eye, some combination of line and form and size—and in this case a curved, gleaming edge—not to mention a sexy voice you hear sometimes, whispering seductively, "I belong to you, Win. I'm your knife. Take me home." That's more or less how I'd acquired my .41 Magnum.

"The Chris Reeve Sable IV." Daggett bent down, reached into the case, and pulled it out, together with a heavy black leather scabbard. "Extra careful, Lieutenant Bear." He indicated the cast on my left arm. "You look accident-prone to me, and this thing is literally as sharp as a razor. Reeve knives are all that way."

I frowned, wondering how he knew my name. "You may not know it, Lieutenant, but you're famous in the Zone. A legend. The first individual to step through the broach, and the hero who saved the Confederacy from the Hamiltonians. Somehow it always reminds me of that famous painting of Daniel Boone crossing the mountains into Kentucky—or was it Moses into the Promised Land?"

"It was just some poor schmuck in a pasture," I lied, "trying not to walk in the cow patties. Anyway, I didn't step through the broach, Daggett, not intentionally. I was *blasted* through and fetched up on my head and parts south in that park over by Confederation Boulevard."

"Yeah," he said, "but it sounds better the other way—call it artistic license." He handed me the knife.

Papers in the box said, "Chris Reeve Knives, 11624 W. President Drive, #B, Boise, ID 83713, United States of America." Sure enough, one was a warning about how sharp the five and a half-inch single-edged blade was. It wasn't kidding. The trademark hollow handle was made from the same billet of steel as the blade, knurled so well you could almost use it for a file, topped with a threaded aluminum cap sealed with an O-ring. The whole length of skillfully worked metal was covered in a dark matte gray finish. I didn't know what I'd keep in that little compartment, most likely just some extra atmosphere, but it was nifty knowing it was there.

In shape, it was like a Finnish puukko knife, but what I liked best about the Sable IV was its size. Unlike my Rezin, it was a tool a man could live with every day. If he had to, he could fight with it, sure, but he was more likely to cut up vegetables and stir-fry meat, do camp chores, maybe whittle a toy for a kid. And more likely to need to, as well. That damned thing felt better in my hand than any knife I'd ever owned. And there was that sexy, seductive voice whispering, "I belong to you, Win. I'm your knife, take me home." Sighing because, even in the Confederacy there are so many toys and so little money, I reached deep into my pocket—no easy matter with my gimpy wing—in search of gold and silver coins.

"Whatcha got, Lieutenant, moths?" Daggett pointed at my left side.

"What are you talking ab—oh!" There it was, between my plastic-covered elbow and my left love handle, a small, round hole, about a quarter of an inch in diameter. That didn't bother me so much, except there was another hole just like it, where the fabric fell in a natural fold. And another in the back of the garment. When I stood up straight the holes all lined up.

The knife merchant clucked. "Looks like somebody doesn't like you, Lieutenant."

"Yeah," Lucy agreed, "Somebody who can't shoot worth sour owlshit."

Vaguely, I recalled a recent tugging at my poncho—it would have to have been a small-caliber weapon wearing a noise-suppressor, something almost unheard of in the Confederacy—although it took me a moment to place it. Had I almost been assassinated on the street by a little old lady collecting for the Spaceman's Fund?

Suddenly the itching in my cast got a whole lot worse. I'd been shot at before, but it wasn't something you ever got used to. Or *I* ever got used to, anyway. I left the cardboard box, plastic peanuts, and paper with Daggett, and fastened my new knife's scabbard onto my pistol belt.

"Come on, Lucy, let's go see a train wreck."

"*YAAAHOOOO!*" THAT WAS Lucy hollering, but she was hollering for both of us. My stomach gave me a sort of swooping sensation as the Neova tilted on its side and screamed its way around one of the few curves between LaPorte and what I thought of as the New Mexico border. We'd just emerged from a short tunnel bored under the Huerfano River, and it felt like being shot from a cannon.

Good thing I'm a passable one-hand driver.

Without a doubt, what I love best about the Confederacy, aside from my darling Clarissa and the general atmosphere of untrammeled liberty (about to become trammeled if we didn't do something to stop it) is the highway speed: as fast as you can go with the pedal mashed all the way to the firewall, roughly 350 miles an hour. There's a couple of production hovercars that'll do twice that, just shy of Mach 1, but I wouldn't trust myself behind the wheel, or you, either, as far as that goes.

Ironically, Greenway 200, down which we traveled, was a pair of big, wide, grass-covered ditches, the mound between them containing the earth-covered, normally vacuum-filled tube that, farther along down the track, had been sabotaged somehow. I also love the weather in this part of the world—almost no matter what universe you happen to be in. (There are alternative continua where the weather everywhere has been changed permanently, for the worse, usually by governments or terrorists—or government terrorists—altering the course of medium-sized asteroids in order to overstate a political point. That same kind of thinking cracked the Moon in one universe I know of.) Where we were, roaring down the Greenway at a speed that would have made Ralph Nader pee his pants, the sun was shining hot and bright, and the sky overhead was so blue that the sheer pleasure of looking at it hurt your eyes. I wasn't thinking about almost being killed more than every five minutes or so.

At the same time, only a few miles east of the Greenway, a huge and angry-looking thunderstorm was building itself up eight or nine miles in the sky. Colors in the clouds ranged from gray to purple to black—lightning flashed occasionally from layer to layer and toward the ground—and a shadow lay across the land beneath it. (Actually, I'm told that lightning travels from the ground into the clouds, but that isn't what it looks like to me.)

Before long, we began to see the first of several dirty-looking extrusions thrust down from the clouds overhead. Out on the prairie somewhere, farm wives were gathering up their chickens and shooing their kids into the root cellar. One particular funnel suddenly touched the ground and generated an enormous debris cloud at its base. I'd seen tornadoes closer than this, but not a whole lot closer. Then, without warning, the funnel and the cloud above it were lit from overhead by the most intense red light I've ever seen, pulsing about sixty beats a minute. I assumed that it was some kind of warning.

About then, the red light shut off, and a beam stabbed down from the heavens. I don't believe there's a word for the color of that beam. The funnel began to shrivel and sucked itself up into the cloud. The cloud itself began to shrink, spilling itself onto the land it had begun to demolish.

The storm was over, the eastern sky cleared, and we roared on.

"Tornado abatement!" Lucy explained at the top of her lungs. When she discovered that it wasn't necessary to yell, she quieted down. "Done from close Earth orbit, probably paid for by the farmers' insurance companies."

I nodded, but kept my eyes on the road. "I could see that and figure it out. But how the hell is it done, by some kind of laser?" Lucy was an engineer and Knew Things.

"Nope. Look inside your freezer when you get home."

"Oh, yeah." Confederate refrigeration systems work on a completely different principle than refrigeration does back home. Paratronics is the name they give it, and like the broach, it's based on subatomic physics of some kind, but it still seems like magic to this savage. It's sort of the reverse of a microwave oven. Stick your beer in the fridge, and it's cold in thirty or forty seconds. I'd gotten my big Bowie knife off the body of a burglar who'd tried hiding in a walk-in paratronic freezer for maybe fifteen minutes. His name was Tricky Dick Milhouse, but it should have been Clarence Birdseye.

With electronic guidance from beneath the road itself, and no more weather control to entertain us, we arrived at the wreckage site, about two-hundred miles south of LaPorte (just the other side of the highway from what would have been Walsenburg in the world I came from), in less than thirty-five minutes. In this world, it was called Gonzales.

Bumbling up out of Greenway 200 and onto the prairie flat, the Neova settled to a dusty stop just outside a fluorescent orange tape-line that flashed over and over and over:

DANGER—EMERGENCY WORKERS ONLY
PLEASE STAY OUTSIDE PERIMETER
GREATER LAPORTE MILITIA

As I raised the bright red gullwing door to step out and disobey the warning, every bit of loose paper in the car took wing noisily like a prairie hen and disappeared into the hot desert wind. I was overtaken by the strangest, strongest feeling I'd been here before. It was more than mere déjà vu; I'd been in this place, and more than once. Then I realized what it was. In many ways, this disaster site was like another I knew well, the famous Barringer Crater, roughly twenty miles west of what I grew up calling Winslow, in northern Arizona.

The wind was roaring across the flat just like it does in that part of Arizona, splashing down into the gigantic bowl. (Barringer's an airplane trap—they fly in but they don't fly out—you can see pieces of wreckage if you know what you're looking for.) The only thing missing was the scary observation platform hanging out over the hole. I'd been to Barringer many times. It was sort of a shrine to me, the destination of half a dozen boyhood vacations with my mom, and later on, my friends, a place where a part of the sky had touched the Earth—and scared the living crap out of a million jackrabbits and the local paleo-Folsom-types.

Now here I was again, give or take a few hundred miles and fifty thousand years, but where the Arizona crater was weathered and rounded, this one was still steaming in the afternoon sunlight and sharp around the edges. There would be technical differences, of course, between a crater made by a Volkswagen-sized meteorite and one made when a big thing going eighteen thousand miles an hour met a smaller thing—it could have been a pea or a marble—that was, for all intents and purposes, motionless, immovable. I didn't know enough to see any difference.

Whatever the deadly instrument was, it could have been as small as a BB, introduced somehow into the vacuum-filled, mirror-polished tube that stretches from somewhere around Baffin Island, via LaPorte, through Mexico City, and goes on from there, practically to the South Pole. It would have made an entry hole the size of a BB, and an exit hole . . . well, we were looking at it, a mile in diameter and three or four hundred feet deep. The Confederate equivalent of Winslow—Haggard, I believe the town is called here, maybe after an English adventure novelist who was popular at the time the town was settled (I hadn't read him until I was grown, somehow having gotten the notion, as a kid, that his most famous work was called *King Solomon's Mimes*) and these days the site of a neat little spaceport—would have to look to its laurels now. This act of sabotage had killed at least one thousand people, or so the 'Com had told us, horrible to contemplate the day afterward, but morbidly interesting given the perspective of distance or history—which was the only way you could look at it and stay sane. First, we had to climb a hundred-foot ridge that the explosion had thrown up all around ground zero. Fortunately, the militia had erected temporary scaffolding, flimsy-looking but indestructable, that took us and the Neova halfway around the site to the top of the crater. The first faces Lucy and I saw within the tapeline were the grime-covered, sweat-streaked features of my across-the-street neighbor Will Sanders, who would be supervising the investigation here, and Olongo Featherstone-Haugh (say "Fanshaw"), President of the North American Confederacy and an eight hundred-pound lowland gorilla. He and Will sat side by side in the bucket of a fusion-powered front-end loader, having some lunch out of brown plastic bags and thermos bottles.

"Yo, Will!" I shouted cheerfully as we approached the pair. I thought Olongo looked particularly jaunty in his great ape-sized yellow hardhat. Like everybody else in the known galaxy, he greeted Lucy warmly. "What's that you're eating?" My mind seemed to be on food today. I wondered why.

"Peanut butter and chutney sandwich." Will replied. He held it up. "Hiya, Lucy! Either of you want a bite?"

"Geez." My stomach gave a lurch, not at all like the one I'd felt making that three-hundred-mile-per-hour turn. It could have been a reaction to being shot at setting in, but it was probably the chutney. "No, thanks. What ever gave you the idea for a sandwich like that, anyway?"

"The girls got me started," he grinned, taking a gulp from his vacuum bottle. I didn't even want to ask about that. "Fran and Mary-Beth. About the only craving they've experienced—that and hot-and-sour soup by the gallon. Not such a bad idea, really. After all, what is Major Gray's but mango preserves with raisins and stuff? Like I said, they thought it up, I tried it, and the rest, as they say—"

"Is nausea." I shook my head and waved the thought away. "Okay, y'wanna tell us what happened here? Lucy's trying to talk me into investigating this and whatever happened at the Old Endicott Building, of which she's a partial owner."

"Was," the president corrected. Like everybody else here, I was accustomed to having conversations with furry individuals. In fact, Olongo's English was better than mine. He didn't talk in the normal sense. The first apes to communicate, a century ago, had used manual sign language. Later, somebody figured out how to detect microscopic wrist and forearm movements that accompany signing, and translate them electronically into synthesized speech—without actually making the signs themselves. "The insurance companies wrote it off this afternoon as a total loss; I saw the news on the way out here. Presumably, my dear Mrs. Kropotkin, your check is in the mail."

His voice didn't seem to come from his wrist. He was wearing a synthesizer on each arm—I'd seen others do that so they could carry on two different conversations—creating the illusion that his voice was coming from somewhere between them. His lips didn't move, so, being a politician, he may have been telling the truth.

Lucy snorted. "That's a comfort. I'd as lief have the building, given a choice." She turned to me. "I'm partial owner of this mess, too, Winnie. About point two-five percent, as I recall. Boys, what're we gonna do? Somebody's tryin' hard to put me outa business!"

8: ALONG CAME THE F.F.V.

> Ever notice how the folks who claim to believe in animal
> rights generally don't believe in *human* rights?
> —*Memoirs of Lucille G. Kropotkin*

I tried to take a moment and look over the crime-scene as I had
so many others during my career as a homicide detective in the
States. Apparently Lucy was looking me over at the same time.

"What's the matter, Winnie?" she asked. "You're appearin' a
mite green an' peaked."

It wasn't an easy thing to confess, even to her. "I gotta face
it, Lucy, I'm a city boy."

"Denver born and bred," she nodded, understanding intellec-
tually if not at the emotional level. There isn't any Denver in the
North American Confederacy, just two little towns on the South
Platte called St. Charles and Auraria.

It's a fairly common thing, but people don't talk about it often.
Some little something deep down inside me felt dangerously exposed and was suffering the yammering jim-jams. Blame the wide
open spaces all around me. As it is in my world, this stretch of
high plains is about as empty and deserted as anyplace could be
this side of Outer Mongolia or the Moon, roofed over with a
merciless, blue, blindingly cloudless sky (Mongolians fear the
open sky and worship it), carpeted from horizon to horizon with
dry yellow grasses, sagebrush, and a few gnarled scrub oaks or
pines. Aside from the occasional twister, nobody even made a
stab at weather control down here. I think that was okay with
me, actually. It's nice to think that there's something left in the
world that's wild and out of control, even by default. But between the 110-degree heat and the forty-mile-per-hour wind,

I realized it was a whole lot like standing in a convection oven. A broad pair of subtly curved wings, so high overhead they could hardly be seen—some kind of big predatory bird—screeched and circled, no doubt on the lookout for a rabbit or a prairie dog that was about to die of sunstroke or heat exhaustion. Far below the crater lip where we stood, on the breast of the dry golden sea, I heard the shockingly beautiful warble of a meadowlark.

Down inside the crater and up onto the rim opposite where we were perched, a hundred individuals of assorted sizes, ages, sexes, and species poked around, examining the freshly ravaged ground with all kinds of instruments I wouldn't have recognized close-up, let alone at this kind of distance. I've always been a hands-on kind of homicide detective; I try to leave the scientific stuff to the scientists.

I turned to Will and asked, "So where's the wreckage?"

"An' all the dead bodies?" Lucy echoed, although I believe she realized the answer at the moment she spoke, about half a heartbeat before I did.

Will's eyebrows went up, followed by his shoulders. He wore a LaPorte Patriots baseball cap, a tan epauletted workshirt with faded denims, a big, unfamiliar-looking, silver-colored autopistol in a custom high-ride on his right hip, and what I guessed were Tony Lama boots. Python, I think. There didn't seem to be anything like a Greater LaPorte Militia uniform, not so much as an armband, lapel pin, or secret decoder ring. They all just knew each other pretty well, and that he was the boss. All in all, it's probably the best way to run an outfit like that. Very hard to infiltrate, anyway.

"There isn't any wreckage, Win, nor any bodies, Lucy. The best my people down there can figure, someone set a big explosive charge about where the center of this hole is—they probably tamped it by leaving a car parked on top if it—and left it to be set off, most likely by a seismic sensor of some kind. Mind you, that's just our best guess. It's how I'd do it if I had to. There isn't any evidence, either, to speak of."

"Or to put it another way," Olongo offered, having observed the unsatisfied expressions on our faces, "what evidence there may be—whatever wreckage—is all around us, in the form of microscopic particles in the soil, of shocked quartz and tiny beads of vaporized and recondensed titanium, steel, and plastic—"

"Not t'mention the vaporized and recondensed remains of more'n a thousand souls," Lucy finished for the president, "who probably never even knew what hit 'em." Her thumbs were thrust in her gunbelt, and she was looking more pissed off than I'd ever seen her. This was proving to be an educational experience. "Or what they hit."

Will nodded grimly. "So far, we haven't found so much as an intact strand of DNA. The best we can hope for is to identify the explosive—if my forensic team is right and there was one—and compare it to what we know about the Old Endicott Building explosion." He looked toward the president. "As I told Olongo, just as you were arriving, I mistrust coincidences in general, professionally speaking. Frankly, after more than two centuries of nothing like this ever happening in the North American Confederacy, I don't believe that the two events can be unrelated."

Something whirred and chittered out on the prairie, some kind of grasshopper or locust, I supposed. Once it got dark, we'd be hearing coyotes. I'd been told that there were rattlesnakes out here, and big wooly wolf spiders the size of your hand. I agree with Eva Gabor: give me the city, with its rats, pigeons, and cockroaches, any time.

"They're very clearly related in at least one sense," said Olongo after what seemed like a long while. I had to scramble, mentally, to remember what we'd been talking about. "For the first time in decades, something resembling a political party—"

"The Franklinite Faction," Lucy and I both spoke at once.

"That never-to-be-sufficiently cursed Franklinite Faction." the president corrected us. "Those vile bounders have redoubled their demands that 'somebody do something' about these terrible occurrences. Something . . . well, frankly, *governmental*." He spat the word out as if he were disgusted by the taste it left in his mouth. Funny attitude for one of the Confederacy's few working politicians.

"Giving the Franklinites a chance to make that 'something' permanent," I offered.

"Precisely," Olongo nodded. "Believe me, my friends, I'm as aware as you are that, in the words of the revered sage (whoever he was), 'No man's life, liberty, or property are safe when the legislature's in session.' "

"You can say that, again!" Lucy agreed. Pointedly, she drew her outsized pistol, pulled the bolt back a quarter of an inch, and inspected the thumb-sized cartridge in the chamber. Mention of certain words like "government" or "taxes" seemed to trigger that reflex in her, and in a great many other Confederates of my acquaintance, as well.

"Dear me," Olongo sighed. It was a strange thing to hear, coming from a giant, hideously fanged lowland gorilla, especially one wearing a yellow plastic hard hat and nothing else but a broad leather pistol belt—this morning he favored a Hunter & Jordan .500—over a red and purple kilt. "As president, I continue to resist such demands, of course. But I'm afraid that I can hold out only so long. I came out today, officially, to inspect the damage here, but the sad truth is, I needed very badly to get away from my office. Somewhere that Buckley F. Williams and his little brother can't find me."

"His little brother?" Will asked. "That's a new one on me."

"Bennett Williams," I supplied, recalling my earlier conversation with Lan and the Wizard. "He runs the Franklinite Faction's online ragazine, *The Postman*. Big guy, pleasant enough looking, and he's got a really wonderful voice—until you make the mistake of paying attention to what he's saying."

"Right as usual, Win. I believe they're taking turns calling me," Olongo complained. "They're also sending me dozens of C-mails a day, and that creature of theirs, that Allard Wayne, has virtually set up camp in my outer office!"

"Then throw the slimy little flatworm out, Olongo!" advised Lucy, holstering her mighty weapon with a snap of the wrist. "I'll be glad to help you!"

The president gave her an appreciative grin—one of the most frightening sights I've ever witnessed. "I would enjoy that very much, my dear Lucille, and I thank you for the thought. But they'd simply send somebody else. Besides, I deeply fear that the situation is more complicated than that."

I shook my head and rolled my eyes. "Great."

"What in Tom Paine's name're you talkin' about, old friend?" Lucy asked, a suspicious look gradually beginning to appear on her face. I could tell that she was frustrated because she'd already checked her pistol chamber.

"Two things, really," Olongo answered after a moment's thought. "In the vulgar parlance, would you prefer to hear the bad news or the worse news first?"

"Oh, by all means," I answered sarcastically, "the bad news, if we have a choice, old bean."

"Very well, Win." For the first time since I'd met the gentle giant, I'd failed to get a rise out of him when I made fun of his

Oxford accent; the poor guy's sense of humor was gone completely. "The first—and I must ask you all to keep this to yourselves for the time being—"

"Oops, here we go down the slippery slope," Will interrupted the president, "inventing exactly what the North American Confederacy doesn't need most—government secrecy!"

Olongo looked severely pained but ignored him. "The first is that, apparently, this is only the start of a series of horrible acts that somebody intends to commit simply to terrify our once-crimeless civilization."

"Like . . . ?" I asked, already having a general idea what he would say.

"Like a bomb," Olongo replied, "set to explode at noon, day after tomorrow, that was discovered this morning aboard the fusion dirigible *City of Calgary*. As you know, she's just one of dozens of vessels carrying hundreds of thousands of passengers continually from the North Pole to the South Pole and to points between. Had it gone off over the center of a city, many times that number would probably have died."

I knew that kind of airship well, having taken a short ride on the huge and elegant *San Francisco Palace* the first few weeks I'd been in the Confederacy. I'd come to love traveling by fusion dirigible—especially compared to the Bulgarian dungeon tour that air travel in my native country had become—and I wanted to get my hands on the asshole (figuratively speaking) who was trying to make the former just as unpleasant as the latter.

But the president was going on. "There are also rumors, unconfirmed as yet, of products in stores being randomly poisoned. The worst part is that no demands of any kind are being made, monetary, political, or otherwise, so we must assume that these acts are being carried out for their own sake."

"And that's only the bad news?" Lucy asked Olongo with a

highly uncharacteristic gulp. It was admittedly an extremely odd moment.

I generally tend to think of Confederates as tougher than the people I grew up among. But they're completely unaccustomed to witnessing violent crime on this or practically any other scale. I suddenly realized that they needed *Americans* to deal with this mess for them. They were too busy, figuratively or literally, throwing up to deal with it themselves. Lucy and Olongo were in a funk over the sheer callous brutality of it all. Will and I, on the other hand, who'd both been born into cultures jaded by such acts of barbaric criminality—usually carried out by governments—were more or less untouched by it. I wondered which reaction was healthier.

"I'm afraid so, my dear," Olongo told her. "The worse news is that I'm beginning to get other calls and C-mails, as well. Hundreds and thousands of them. It would appear that, despite their basically kindly nature, and a long history of judging other individuals strictly on an individual basis, many of our own folk—ordinarily rational, decent Confederates—are starting to blame all that's happening on you newcomers." He looked to Will and me.

In that moment, an old, familiar knot began to tie itself, all over again, in my stomach. God damn these sons of bitches, whoever they were. I hadn't had any trouble with my ulcer for nine mostly wonderful years. But now, here it was again, just like some long lost relative you dislike and have so far managed to avoid.

"After all," Lucy suggested, "these things never used t'happen 'til there was an American Zone."

"Right," I replied. "I seem to recall there's a name for that particular logical fallacy."

"Yeah," said Will, "*Headus upassus.*"

"Heretofore," the president went on, "we Confederates have tended to feel nothing but compassion toward the immigrants fleeing societies less free than our own. We have welcomed them in, helped them where we could, and they have made a respectable place for themselves. But under the present stress, I fear, the fine line between compassion and contempt could begin to blur. Certain unfortunate tensions could begin to manifest themselves."

Lucy had a funny, sick expression on her face and I knew exactly how that expression felt from the inside. Was the golden dream we all shared, of peace, freedom, and prosperity, coming to an end? What Olongo was saying certainly didn't sound like the North American Confederacy any of us knew. But I didn't say anything. What the hell *was* there to say?

"Naturally, those immigrants who are aware of the situation are growing increasingly angry and perturbed," Olongo continued. "But there is good news . . . of a sort. I believe I have found at least a stop-gap solution."

"Well, that's . . . that's something, anyway," Lucy muttered, more to herself than to any of us. I hated this. This woman, my second closest friend, had fought for freedom and the Confederacy in more than one war. She'd been a pilot in the famous Thousand Airship Flight against the Kaiser. She'd stood against the Czar in Antarctica. Now she was beginning to look her age—a century and a half—and it wasn't a pretty sight.

The president replied, "Indeed. Before things get any worse, I have endeavored to persuade a few of the more financially successful among their number to seek an expatriate like them, a former police officer from one of the United Stateses, to get to the bottom of this mess if he can."

I threw my hands up. "Olongo, I'm flattered as hell, believe me I am. But damnit, I already have a case! That's what I've been trying to tell—!"

"My sincerest apologies, old bean," said Olongo. So he'd been paying attention, after all. "I was referring to Captain Sanders, here. I understand that his public safety experience in his native continuum parallels yours remarkably. His militia credentials and contacts should make the job a trifle easier for him than it might have been for you—and, as you say, you already have a case. Please give my warmest regards to Clark and Carole, will you?"

Will, that sonofabitch, superciliated at me, gazed complacently at his fingernails, and buffed them on his shirt.

Meanwhile, I felt myself blush, hot and deep. "Well, pardon me all to hell while I go find a hole to fall into. There oughta be a prairie dog burrow around here somewhere—or how about that big crater over there?"

LUCY AND I had a long talk on the ride back to LaPorte. Mostly, I talked, about what I'd found for myself, here in the Confederacy, and what I felt I stood to lose. "It's kind of funny," I observed to my oldest Confederate friend (in a couple of meanings of the phrase). "It hasn't been a free ride, by any means. There are plenty of hazards associated with untrammeled individual liberty. For example, those who won't work are perfectly welcome to starve."

Out of the corner of one eye, I could see Lucy nodding, so I went on. "But I've noticed that, despite a complete lack of any kind of government welfare system, starving is a pretty difficult thing to do here. This society is just too wealthy and casually generous. Look at the way that you and Ed took care of me when I first arrived."

"An' Clarissa," she insisted.

"How could I ever forget? Be that as it may, the fundamental human right to *fail* is as scrupulously defended in the North American Confederacy as any other right."

"Make that a basic *sapient* right," Lucy corrected me again. She did a lot of that. "Gorillas an' chimpanzees an' dolphins an' Orcas gotta right to fail, too, same as you and me."

It was interesting to me the way that recent American immigrants who'd thought themselves bias-free regarding human beings of other nations, religions, or races, were now struggling with prejudices they hadn't known they harbored, against creatures they'd perceived all their lives as inferior animals. It seemed that scientific doodling with intelligence and communication—a century earlier here than another place I knew of—had resulted in the education (with a little help from genetics and electronics) of certain simians and cetaceans: chimps, gorillas, gibbons, orangutans, several kinds of dolphins, and killer whales, who were now respected members of society taking full part in its everyday life. As I'd told the Wizard, the paratronic machinery that brought him and me and so many others here in the first place was invented by a physicist, Ooloorie Eckickeck P'wheet, a genuine *Tursiops truncatus*, or bottle-nosed dolphin. A lot of newcomers—especially, it seemed to me, the most fervent former advocates of "animal rights"—aren't up to seeing all these furry and finny folk as people. But I didn't want to change the subject. We'd been discussing the responsibilities that come with full ownership of your life.

"Meanwhile," I continued, "any unemployment, or health, or—I don't know—liability insurance people want, they have to decide on and purchase for themselves. No Social Security or Medicare. Without a legislature to protect them from their own stupidity or negligence, they're fully liable for any harm they may bring to anybody else's life, liberty, or property. And you know the thing that surprised me most? It's that payment may be demanded in gold—or on the field of honor."

Lucy chuckled. "Well there certainly aren't any anti-duellin' laws t'prohibit it."

"Tell me about it." I'd fought a duel myself, in my first weeks in the Confederacy. To this day, I had mixed feelings about the practice. But in this culture, the only right that nonparticipants have in such affairs is . . . well, not to participate. You aren't permitted to make laws about something that other people do among themselves. Sensible. If you don't play the game, you don't make the rules.

"No need to," Lucy observed. "You know from your own experience that the North American Confederacy is the first culture in history—and the only one in any universe that we know of—run of the adults, by the adults, and for the adults."

"That we know of, Mr. Lincoln. And some people might give you an argument about duelling being an adult occupation."

She snorted. "The same ones that'd have you believe that 'honor' is only a word—an outdated one, at that. Winnie, there's always a gap between what justice demands and what the law or custom provides. Speakin' statistically, duelling fills exactly fifty percent of that gap (though I could make an argument that the person in the right is likelier to be a better shot). Anyway, that's more'n you can claim for any other system."

Damn it, there I'd gone and changed the subject! Having fought a duel, I could attest to what she said. It sure hadn't been much fun at the time, but duelling did seem to make for a better, cleaner world in the long run.

And that's a good thing, because the North American Confederacy is not a culture inhabited exclusively by saints, believe me. There's no lobby here at all for anything resembling patriotism, altruism, or civic virtue. What most former United Statesians fail to comprehend when they're first informed of it, is that what makes the place tick isn't the kindliness, decency, or rationality Olongo had referred to (although I like to think he's right about all of that), or even the love of liberty for its own sake—leave that to us huddled masses—but pure, unvarnished greed.

Every Confederate child is taught at his mother's knee to avoid being taken advantage of, just as he's taught to check the chamber of his pistol or count his change or (sometimes the hard and final way, at the hands of his intended victim) that crime can be as dangerous to any would-be practitioner as juggling bottles of warm nitroglycerin. The time-honored expression, "There ain't no such thing as a free lunch," is more than just a slogan here, it's a statement of natural law, and a courteous warning.

Immigrants from a hundred thousand Americas, brought up foolishly dependent on the false comfort of a government's "protection," must learn all these lessons and more, rather late in life. Some of them accomplish it more readily than others. Without zoning laws, building codes, trade commissions, or professional licensure, some fall victim to loan sharks, snake-oil salesmen, and crooks of every sort except the political variety—most of whom are bluebacks like themselves, preying on their own kind. Many newcomers suffered from the same disorienting experiences often reported in the late-twentieth century of my world by Communist refugees to the relatively better-off United States. Unequipped to bear the noise, the color, and the velocity of Confederate life anymore—or simply exhausted by its limitless array of personal choices and opportunities—they finally decided they wanted to go home. Failing that, they tended to pile up like dirty snowdrifts in places like the American Zone and whimper for somebody to pass laws that would turn the Confederacy into the same kind of stagnant cesspool they escaped from.

"Always it's the kids," I rattled on at Lucy, who was bearing it with commendable stoicism, "who serve as an excuse to demand special rules—drug laws, tobacco and alcohol prohibition, censorship, gun control—(so far, thank Gallatin, without success) which would restrict the individual pursuit of happiness and destroy everything that made the Confederacy the haven of liberty they escaped to so gratefully, once upon a time.

Lucy nodded. "On the other hand, their kids tend t'learn pretty quick that Confederate children have a customary right to divorce their parents, and that opens up a whole 'nother can of worms!"

We laughed together—*Bamm!*—until a tremendous blast right behind us lifted the rear of my little red Neova, flipping it end over end over end until it crashed upside-down on the sloped embankment of the Greenway, leaving Lucy and me to hang in our four-points, the smell of smoke filling the tiny passenger compartment. Strangely enough, the last thing I thought of before I lost consciousness was that I'd forgotten to tell Will and Olongo about the hole in my cloak.

9: CUTS LIKE A KNIFE

> Choose your allies carefully: it's highly unlikely that
> you'll ever be held morally, legally, or historically ac-
> countable for the actions of your enemies.
> —*Memoirs of Lucille G. Kropotkin*

There's a problem with gullwing doors that I'd never thought
about before: It's kind of hard to get them open when the car's
lying on them, upside-down.

Maybe I never fully lost consciousness. I remembered counting
at least four times that the little Neova had flipped ass over tea-
kettle before it finally shuddered to a stop, but I'd missed something else, because we were now facing backward, the way we'd
come. Whoever did the lawnwork on Greenway 200 was gonna
be really annoyed with us. We'd bounced eight times, gouging
out huge, ugly divots, then slid a long way, maybe a hundred
yards, digging a long, curved furrow upward, exposing the un-
derlying steel and concrete at the bottom of the ditch, onto the
east-side berm.

I shouted, "Lucy!"

She hung next to me in her seat belt, unconscious beyond any
doubt, a little blood trickling from her open mouth. It could have
been from a serious internal injury, a split lip, or a broken tooth.
For that matter, she might have bitten her tongue. The smoke
inside was getting thicker by the second. Briefly, I wondered
where it could be coming from. My little supercharged Neova
ran on some of the less volatile petroleum fractions—what would
probably be sold as jet fuel back in the States. At least we weren't
going to wind up getting fricasseed in gasoline. Carefully, I
braced myself against the ceiling with my good arm—the other
was still useless in its sling, of course—punched the seat belt re-

lease at the center of my chest, and managed a controlled fall onto my head. The passenger compartment seemed even tinier than usual. Once I'd managed to right myself awkwardly, I found that I was sitting in extreme discomfort on a collection of knobs and buttons sticking out of what had been the overhead console. Next time, I thought, a sunroof.

Momentarily, I considered unlimbering the Browning and shooting a hole through the transparent door, just to get an escape route started. But then I thought better of it. For all I knew, the tough high-tech plastic would bounce my puny little .375 slug all over inside the cab, and Lucy and I would both end up looking like Swiss cheese smothered in raspberry jam. But there wasn't much time left to think. I was beginning to cough from all the smoke in the cabin, and so was Lucy.

"Win?" she managed to croak between bouts of coughing.

"Right here, Lucy," I told her, "and just about to get us out—I hope."

She replied, "Be sure an' simmer the tricycle doors."

"Right, Lucy," I replied. Now she was delirious. What else was I going to say?

With a surprising amount of difficulty, I reached around my ample rotundity and retrieved my Chris Reeve Sable IV from its heavy leather scabbard. It was one of those deep, molded, Scandinavian deals that cover half the handle and don't require a strap. Without realizing it, somewhere in the middle of the process, I worked my left arm out of its sling. It didn't seem to hurt. If I was injuring it further, I couldn't feel it, and it was nothing compared to the two of us dying of smoke inhalation.

The floor of the Neova was some sort of composite, a bit like fiberglass bonded to a sheet of stabilized magnesium-titanium—an alloy that could only be manufactured in the weightlessness of space, that made the lighter of the two metals stronger and less prone to going up like a box of kitchen matches at the slightest provocation. I reached up and pulled two levers that released my seat. Before it fell, I pushed it backward, into the comic-relief rear passenger compartment, pulled the mat away, and pushed the point of the knife into the floor.

Or tried to, anyway. The knife was sharp and strong, and it penetrated maybe a full thirty-second of an inch. This was going to take a long, long time. Then I got a fairly bright idea.

"Lucy!"

"If the pertwonkies call," she advised, "remermelize 'em!"

"Lucy," I insisted, "let me have your gun!"

"Over my dead—oh . . . okay, Winnie." She was coughing very badly now. So was I. But the demand to surrender her beloved elephant pistol was like smelling salts, and her mind seemed to be working once again. I still wondered what was burning. "Whatcha gonna do with it, put us outa our misery?"

It was an idea. "No, I'm gonna get us out of this fucking car!" I took the mighty Gabbet-Fairfax in both hands, pointed it upward at the floor, said good-bye to my hearing and wrist tendons, shut my eyes as tightly as I could, and hauled back on the trigger.

BRRRRAAAMMM!

"*Clonk!*" went the empty case against the windshield. We could have cleaned the damned thing out and used it as a shotglass. The noise of the weapon's discharge had been several times worse than the explosion that had wrecked the car. It not only hurt my ears, it hurt my eyes, my teeth, my testicles, the top of my head, and every axon and dendrite in my nervous system. Lucy stirred and groaned, regaining even more of her consciousness. Oddly, her .50 caliber hip-cannon hadn't hurt my hands.

The big fat slug had expanded even farther on impact, opening a three-quarter-inch hole in the belly of the Neova, exactly as I'd hoped it would. I imagined there was smoke billowing out of that hole, and I hoped that somebody would notice it. Greenway 200, for all that it looks like nothing more than a couple of big ditches, is actually a highly sophisticated transport system. Its powerful electronic brain should have noticed by now that something formerly zooming down the line at 350 miles an hour was suddenly doing zero. In fact it should be warning all the drivers as far south as Raton that there was an obstruction on the right side of the northbound lane.

Us. Dead us, if I didn't do something about it, soon.

For all of its strength, the floor was less than an eighth of an inch thick. As I'd planned, I pushed the Chris Reeve knife into the bullet hole until it stopped, and began to rock it, back and forth. Now the hole was an inch wide, from one side of the circle to the end of the slit I'd cut. Now it was two inches wide, now three, now four, and I was beginning to lose leverage. Still, the blade was hard and remained sharp, despite the nasty stuff it was cutting through. Hell on the finish, though. Every now and again I shoved it in to the hilt (to avoid breaking it off) and rocked the knife from side to side to widen the cut as well as lengthen it. The big knurled handle helped a lot (most knives don't have handles nearly big enough, in my experience) as did the little friction serrations at the rear of the blade where my thumb was pushing.

Pretty soon I was using one of Lucy's shoes—the first thing that came to hand—as a combination hammer and fulcrum to drive the Sable IV farther along the line of the cut. This was mistreatment many another knife might not have survived. Smoke was billowing out of the elongated bullet hole for sure now, and the air inside the car was getting a little clearer. Even better, fresh air was coming in and I began to feel healthier. When I was about eighteen inches along, I fired another shot, made a right-angle turn, and cut a foot and a half in another direction, completing two sides of a square I hoped would be big enough to escape through.

By the time I started the third side, Lucy was wide enough awake to start offering "helpful" suggestions about what I was trying to do. Fortunately, completely deafened by the roar of her gigantic and powerful pistol—three shots in a closed space the size of your average closet, I couldn't hear her. At least that's my story and I'm sticking to it.

I didn't bother cutting the fourth side, but lay on my back and kicked at the trapdoor I'd made until it bent outward. Then Lucy hit her belt release, I gave her back her gun and put my knife away, and we rearranged ourselves awkwardly inside the tiny cabin.

I was handing her out through the makeshift hatch I'd whittled, onto the underside of the Neova, when the ambulance arrived. *Poor little upside-down Neova, cares and woes you've got 'em*, I misquoted sadly to myself, *because, little upside-down Neova, your top is on your bottom.* I'd never peeked under the skirt of a hovercraft before—this one was a modern, ducted-fan model, rather than the older kind with propellors that Lucy drove—and under other circumstances it might have been interesting. The EMTs lifted Lucy clear of the wreckage and CAT-scanned her on the spot in the back of their van. Naturally, they both knew her from way back. Everybody does. I thought I recognized Francis, the chimpanzee Healer, from a weekend medical convention (and second honeymoon) I'd attended some time ago with Clarissa. His paramedic aide was a tough-looking, grizzled gorilla named Snodderly who had somehow managed to grow himself a ponytail (better living through recombinant genetics?). He was a stranger to me, but a welcome one.

By now, Lucy was sitting up cheerfully. "Well, that was certainly refreshin', boys," she told us. "How do I look, Doc—never mind, the question was rhetorical. By Albert, I think we're startin' t'have an adventure here, Winnie! It was gettin' a mite boring, out in the asteroids."

Maybe I should explain about the asteroids—and Ed Bear. Not me, the other one. In my world, some joker—I think it was my mother—noticed an accidental resemblance between the name she'd given me, Edward William Bear (for herself, Edna, and my father, Bill) and the formal monicker of a certain character created by A. A. Milne: Edward Bear. From earliest childhood, guess who got called "Winnie." At that, I suppose it was better than "Pooh."

Over here, there never was an A. A. Milne—or he never wrote all those stories about Christopher Robin and the 100 Acre Wood—so the guy with my fingerprints on this side of the broach was allowed his dignity. When he grew up, he became a private investigator, bought a huge, beautiful house at 626 Geñet Place in LaPorte, drove a little red Neova Hoversport, and eventually married his 136-year-old neighbor and moved out to the Asteroid Belt.

"Rhetorical shmetorical." The Healer shook his head. "How do you look? Like one of the oldest human beings I've ever examined, Lucy, and in remarkably good health. How many regenerations have you undergone, if I may ask?"

"Just the one," Lucy replied. "I started another a little while back, but got interrupted by those Hamiltonian dungflies, an' I never finished it."

"I see." He turned to me. "You, Mr. Bear, have a broken arm."

"I know, Francis." With my good hand, I held out my sling where it hung across my body. "I didn't exactly borrow this from William S. Hart. And it's 'Win.' "

"William S. Hart . . . William S. Hart . . . now where have I heard that—" He shook his head as if shooing away a bothersome insect. "You don't understand, Win. You've broken your arm *again*. I don't even know how you got out of that car. It must have been something like hysterical strength."

Just then my poor little Neova burst into flames.

"Hysterical . . . strength . . ." Suddenly it was taking an awful lot of effort to understand him. "If the pertwonkies simmer the tricycle doors," I remember telling him—somebody had thought it was important, but I couldn't remember who, "remermelize 'em!"

It all went black and this time I really passed out.

"THERE YOU ARE." My beloved Clarissa frowned down at me, but I could tell she wasn't serious. I recognized this dream as a rerun from the Old Endicott Building explosion, and intended to enjoy it for as long as it lasted. "Honestly, Edward William Bear, sometimes I don't know what to do with you!" Watch it when they use all three of your names. She'd just been scrubbing her fingers with a damp-wipe, which she now disposed of. I could smell the alcohol and began to suspect that this wasn't a dream, after all.

"Cut my porkchops for me for another few days?" I grinned up at my adorably freckled spouse. I couldn't do much else; my left arm was now in a double-sized cast and I was lying on the gurney in the back of her van. I could tell, because she had a dozen pictures of our cat up on the ceiling for her younger patients to look at and enjoy. Through the windows and the wide-open back doors, I could see that we hadn't left the crash site beside Greenway 200 yet. Somewhere, not very far away, I could hear several voices. One of them was Lucy's, strong and vigorous. I said, "I'm happy to see you, too, honey."

Clarissa's professional facade evaporated. She bent over me, wrapped her arms around me, and laid her smooth, pink cheek next to mine. A tear trickled between our faces; I wasn't sure whose it was. I wanted to pat her somewhere, but a drippy-tube in my good arm and the brand-new exoskeleton on my left precluded it. Perhaps unromantically, I found myself thinking that this was definitely going to cause some self-defense problems. "I'm just so glad that you're alive!" she exclaimed. "Will says he thinks they used something on you called a Stinger!"

The hair on the back of my neck stirred and stood on end. It's a very peculiar feeling, let me tell you. "Gee, I'm flattered all to hell, baby! The Mujahideen used those things in Afghanistan to shoot down Russian helicopters. I wonder how the Neova survived as well as it did."

She shook her head ruefully and said nothing.

I went on. "But the real question is, 'they' who—or more to the point, can I get up now?" Clarissa started blubbering all over my chest, so I guessed the answer was no.

I TURNED fifty-seven last May 12—happily, in a culture where years imply experience, not necessarily decrepitude. At my age, I have very few illusions remaining about myself. I'm a short, swarthy, slow-moving, heavyset man, clumsier of wit and tongue and trigger than I'd prefer, who stumbled onto the joys and terrors of absolute liberty rather late in life. I've long since made my adjustment to it—or at least I think I have—although I can still be surprised occasionally by things the average Confederate takes for granted. Home heating, water-heating, and electricity, for example, come from a little foot-locker sized box in your basement, and the guy with the coveralls and clipboard who comes to service it twice a year pays *you*, for the deuterium and tritium he takes away.

I arrived here in LaPorte, in the North American Confederacy, entirely by accident and considerably worse for the wear, because I pushed the wrong button, pulled the wrong lever, or sat on the wrong knob during a brief but endless pistol fight in a physics laboratory at Colorado State University in Fort Collins, Colorado. I'd been investigating government involvement in the downtown Denver drive-by machine-gunning of a scientist that the government didn't particularly want investigated. Shortly after landing here, I somehow won the heart of a brilliant and highly respected physician, Clarissa MacDougall Olson-Bear, who also happens to be a beautiful and voluptuous strawberry blond. To be absolutely truthful, I've never figured out exactly what Clarissa sees in me, and I've always been afraid to ask.

On the other hand, I've always known why I love Clarissa. She consistently remains the most interesting person I've ever known—the face I'm always surprised and delighted to wake up to—and a study in contrasting stereotypes.

To begin with, she's gorgeous, five feet six inches tall, maybe 115 or 120 pounds, with a slender waist I can almost get my hands around, and a full complement of all the assets that go with it. If you just think of Mathilda May as she appeared in *Lifeforce*—no drooling, now—with that turned-up nose and those wonderful—er, cheekbones, only a little taller, with shoulderblade-length reddish blond hair and a scattering of freckles, you've got the picture. When I first met her she was thirty-three years old, but Confederate medicine keeps her looking an eternal twenty-five.

On the other hand, Clarissa owns the equivalent of three or four Ph.D.s in various subjects related to Healing, and is continentally famous in her own profession as an innovative pharmacologist and surgeon. In my world, academic doctors and practicing physicians are separate populations. Here, those who do are regarded as the only ones fit to write and teach. And they also, miracle of miracles, make housecalls.

At need, Clarissa can be harder-edged and more businesslike than any Las Vegas blackjack dealer, but with me, she's more tender and sentimental than any female I've ever known. I bought her an imported copy of *Dirty Dancing* a few years ago (in some ways she also reminds me of Cynthia Rhodes), and it always makes her cry. She's dedicated her life *to* life, to relieving suffering and fighting off death, but every day she carries a lethal hypersonic electric pistol on her person and knows how to use it.

It's an .11 caliber Webley.

Up yours, Alan Alda.

Clarissa—

"Lookie what we found!"

My romantic reverie was interrupted, not by Lucy, who'd made that noise, but by another noise, the unmistakable velvety roar of the local equivalent of a helicopter. Picture a set of bedsprings, thirty feet long, twenty feet wide, and six feet thick, stripped of foam and fabric, and chrome-plated. In the middle, like the egg in a toasted "bird's nest," place a Volkswagen Beetle-sized cabin with as much clear plastic underfoot as overhead— and enough cold fusion generator to run a hundred cars the size of my Neova.

Make that my *former* Neova. I missed my car already.

The thing soon touched down on a dozen or so insectile six-foot legs, just a few yards from Clarissa's hovervan. The original medical squad, Francis and Snodderly, had been dismissed with many thanks and a reasonable gratuity when Lucy had amiably refused their further services and my personal physician had laid claim to me. Now the swirly bright red lights went out, indicating that the bedspring part of the flying machine was no longer charged with the several hundred thousand volts that kept it in the air. The underside canopy popped open, Will Sanders climbed down the folding steps, ducked beneath the structure, and emerged into the harsh prairie sunlight.

Holding on to her hairdo, Lucy met him halfway. He held his hands out to show her something. That's when she'd hollered at Clarissa and me. An instant later, I'd sat up and was butt-scooting my way to the end of the gurney, greatly resenting the needle in my arm. Clarissa pursed her lips—not quite making a little growl like Marge Simpson—but she knew me. More important, she knew that I knew her. She was a worse patient than I was, especially when the prospect for some kind of action presented itself. She pulled the tube out and helped me up and out of the van.

Meanwhile, the swirly red warning lights went on again as the much-helmeted and darkly visored pilot of Will's aerial taxi—giving Lucy an enthusiastic wave and receiving one in return—applied the megavoltage once again to its complicated-looking wireworks. Air molecules, ionized by contact with the upper elements of the machine's openwork structure, were drawn at an extremely high velocity to the oppositely charged elements below, bumbling along with them a whole lot of nonionized molecules that acted just like the propwash of a helicopter. The machine rose switly on the column of moving air it had created without any pesky moving parts, started moving forward, as well, and was gone.

Meanwhile, Will was proudly dangling a plastic baggie in front of my face.

"Hold it still, goddammit, will you?"

"Sorry, Win." I bent and squinted, thankful all over again for the corrective therapies that gave me vision that was as good as it had been in my teenage years, both up close and far away. "It's money," I said, and so it was, a silky-looking bill about midway in size between what I used to carry around in the States and the really big money people used in my nineteenth century. It wasn't just the size that was weird, or the colors—mostly gold and brown—but the engravings:

This is to certify that, on deposit in the Petroleum Bank of New Orleans, Federated States of Texas, payable to the bearer of this note upon demand, there is one gallon of AAA grade low-sulphur petroleum.

On the other side, where it says "One Dollar" on the U.S. notes I'm familiar with, it said "One Crockett d'Huile," instead, and there was a portrait of ol' Davy himself in the middle, holding on to ol' Betsy, but looking a whole lot more like ol' Ross Perot than ol' Fess Parker. By now Clarissa was behind me, her arms around me, peering over my shoulder.

"Do you think it might have anything to do with the train-wreck?" she asked.

"Do Gypsies wear do-rags?" Will asked picaresquely. "One of my people found it anchored down by a fist-sized rock about where we figure they parked their getaway car."

"Under a rock?" I shook my head—it was about all I could do. "Then how the hell did you find it?"

He grinned. "I thought you'd ask that. It was easy—we caught a bright flash of metal from the air. This was sitting on top of the rock, like a beacon." He held up another plastic baggie. Will and I had introduced a lot of revolutionary concepts to peace-keeping in the Confederacy, among them the idea that no two sets of fingerprints are alike, and that evidence of that nature should be preserved. This baggie contained a big gold coin. It was very slightly larger in diameter than a silver dollar, but a trifle thinner. On one side was a picture of a guy with the name "Houston" underneath, and on the other side, it proclaimed itself to be "One Gold Samoleon."

Money with a sense of humor.

On an unembossed flat space right beside the portrait (I assumed) of Sam Houston, someone had left—apparently on purpose—a big fat, perfect thumbprint.

10: BEAUTIFUL, BEAUTIFUL TEXAS

Choose your enemies carefully: you'll probably be known much better and far longer for who they were, than for anything else you ever managed to accomplish.
—*Memoirs of Lucille G. Kropotkin*

The flat, hot yellow countryside blurred past at more than three hundred miles per hour. Overhead, one of the mile-long dirigibles we'd talked about with Olongo was making the same speed on its way south to Mexico City.

"The Federated States of Texas," Lucy mused, examining the two evidence baggies for maybe the fortieth time. "A universe where New Orleans is a part of the Lone Star Republic an' the banks issue gold coins an' oil-based paper currency. Shucks, it sounds almost as good as the Confederacy!"

"With engraved portraits of good ol' Sam Houston and Davy Crockett themselves on the money, to boot," I added. "Anybody ever hear of anyplace like that?"

Nobody said anything. Then, just to be different, everybody said nothing. We all knew about lots of different alternate continua that had been stumbled across in this latterday Age of Discovery. It was *the* favorite subject of the Confederate media. And to be objective, these were entire universes being discovered, complete with billions of galaxies, trillions of star systems, quadrillions of planets, and zillions of people. The whole deal was a lot more important than anything Christopher Columbus or Neil Armstrong had done. They'd only found a couple of continents by accident, respectively, and set foot on a big, cold, useless ball of rock. But the number of new universes seemed to be rising every day, and nobody could know about all of them. Nevertheless, I thought that this might possibly be something new. Like almost everybody, I'd heard of various independent Texases being discovered here and there—in fact they seemed to be a little more common than Texases annexed by the United States or Mexico—but I'd never heard of a Texas that included the crescent city or issued oil certificates.

"I hope the cooking is still good there," I muttered absently. On one of our many second honeymoons, Clarissa and I had eaten red snapper, and flounder stuffed with some kind of crab and shrimp herb thing in Galveston. The memory still made my mouth water.

And at the same time, Will said, "You know, that's not a bad idea, is it?"

"The cooking in Texas?" Lucy asked. "I guarantee you won't find any better in the solar system!"

"No, Lucy," Will told her, "an oil-based currency. Hell, they sometimes call it 'black gold,' don't they?"

"That they do, Willy," Lucy replied. "An' you can purchase oil certificates, or wheat certificates or tuna certificates, or any other kinda certificates y'want, right here—in LaPorte, that is—at any bank, if y'know what to ask for."

I saw Will file away the mental note he'd made about that, and made a small bet with myself that one of his wives handled the family accounts. Most likely Mary-Beth. I'd learned about oil certificates my very first week in the Confederacy.

We were barrelling—no oil-based pun intended—up Greenway 200 again, this time in Clarissa's medical hovervan, toward LaPorte. I'd been allowed by my physician to sit upright beside her, feeling both ridiculous and helpless with my recast arm. From time to time she patted my knee reassuringly. In the back, along for the ride, were our friends Lucy and Will. He was officially in charge, but I decided where we were headed, simply by blurting it out.

"Why not give Deejay a jingle?" I asked my lovely bride. "Tell her we'll be seeing her in a few minutes and that we'll want to talk to her partner Ooloorie, as well. They've done a lot of poking around with that invention of theirs. Maybe they know about this Federated States of Texas."

I LOOKED AROUND. Somehow, the place felt like home. This was the very room, after all—this very paratronics laboratory—from which first contact with my homeworld had been made, in 1986. It was also the laboratory in which, only two years later, my first private professional case in the Confederacy had resolved itself, and the murderer of Seaton Mott had met his unspeakable fate. There should have been a bronze plaque hanging somewhere.

"The Federated States of Texas," Deejay Thorens mused. She peered intently at the plastic baggie she held before her highly decorative face. This was her lab, situated in a sunny, landscaped corner of the main campus of LaPorte University, Ltd., located just across good old Confederation Boulevard from the very first bit of LaPorte I'd ever seen, however blurrily, a mile-long private park I'm not even sure has a name. Deejay had gotten up from her regulation swivel chair when we'd come in, and politely offered it to Lucy who'd shaken her head, trying not to bridle at what she privately considered an insult. So we were all standing around or leaning against various pieces of scientific furniture, me remembering with a little trepidation that that was how I'd ended up in the Confederacy. "Crockett d'Huiles and gold Samoleons—quick, somebody call Roger Rabbit!" She handed both baggies back to Will. "It all sounds very interesting, Win, very intriguing, but I'm sorry. I've never heard of the place."

How could anybody make a simple, declarative sentence like that so damned sexy? You could practically feel the breeze from her eyelashes. Will and I had decided on the way up here to keep the evidence that had been left for his people out on the prairie a secret—as much as possible, anyway, given the nature of the investigation—and Deejay had agreed. He said, "Know anybody who's likely to know?"

She shrugged. As with everything else Deejay did, it was a pretty shrug. I glanced at Clarissa. It's a good thing my wife isn't the jealous type. The fact is, if she noticed that I wasn't admiring a glorious creature like Deejay, she'd feel for my pulse. "While you folks were getting here, I C-mailed LIT and I'm afraid they've never heard of this particular time/space/probability continuum, either. The Federated States of Texas. They have no record whatever of anyone entering the Confederacy from it."

She was referring to the recently constructed LaPorte InterWorld Terminal, a miles-long underground establishment where thousands upon thousands of immigrants were pouring through every day from worlds of alternity that offered them less personal and economic freedom—and maybe shorter, nastier lives—than this one did. "On the other hand . . ."

I always find it difficult describing Deejay to anyone who hasn't seen her. I just don't have the vocabulary for it. Hell, she'd make a professional lexicographer drop his jaw, drool on his Florsheims, and mumble "Wannawannawanna." Anyway, you wouldn't believe your own eyes, even if you saw her. She's always reminded me of Loni Anderson in a white labcoat, but others have mentioned Daryl Hannah, Kim Basinger (if you can imagine either of them with any brains), or Natasha Henstridge, in *Species*. My darling Clarissa once admitted to me—sheepishly—that Deejay is the only female who ever made her feel the least bit tempted to give the girl-on-girl thing a whirl. Fortunate for me, they're both flaming heterosexuals.

But Deejay was going on, moving those full, ripe, luscious lips and giving us flashes of her perfect white teeth. "We're not really explorers, here, you understand."

"Whattya mean, honey?" Lucy wanted to know. She liked Deejay, too, and they'd been friends for a long time. Intellectually, at least, I'm pretty sure that Deejay reminded Lucy of herself—about a century and a quarter ago.

"This is a physics lab, Lucy, a paratronics lab, to be specific. Our discovery of the broach was accidental—we were looking for a star drive, which we still don't have."

"An' more's the pity," Lucy observed.

Deejay agreed with a nod. "But, after all," she said, "we were the first to poke our noses into other worlds of probability, and we are making an attempt to keep an orderly record of the more than eleven thousand alternative realities that have been discovered here and by other investigators so far."

"Eleven thousand?" I mused, hardly able to believe it, although I'd heard the claim before. It shouldn't have surprised me. The logic of the alternate probability says the potential number is . . . well, numberless.

"And change," she told me.

"And . . . ?" Will, fundamentally a man of action—he thought he was both Starsky *and* Hutch—was starting to get impatient. I knew the signs well.

She shrugged again; I tried not to sigh. "And sometimes what we discover out there surprises us. There seem to be interesting patterns or . . . I don't know, certain rhythms among the infinite worlds of probability."

Lucy raised her eyebrows and asked, "Patterns such as?"

"Such as . . ." She laughed, suddenly. "Well, just in the continua most of us would recognize historically, you know about the worlds where, say, Jeffrey Hunter performed in seventy-nine

Star Trek episodes as Captain Christopher Pike? Or where Rory Calhoun got the lead in *The Wild, Wild West?*"

I knew the programs, all right, from the 1960s, but with different actors. But I nodded along with the others to keep from looking any stupider than I felt.

"Well recently," she went on, "we noticed that in those worlds where Robert Conrad played James T. Kirk instead of William Shatner, William Jefferson Blythe Clinton never rose any higher than the attorney-general of Arkansas. And where the circle was complete, where Shatner played James West instead of Conrad, Clinton died in prison, or of AIDS, or both."

My wife asked, "And this means something?" I'm pretty sure her question was sincere. There isn't a molecule of sarcasm in the girl. She has a powerful mind and it wants to know things.

Deejay blinked. "I don't know, Clarissa, I don't know. It hurts my head sometimes. I suppose that it may not mean anything at all—like the coincidence in some worlds between the stock market and women's hemlines. I do know that we've never found a world in which those Puerto Ricans succeeded in assassinating Harry Truman." Everybody laughed. She pointed to a rotund little redheaded guy I hadn't noticed before. (It certainly isn't Deejay's fault that she tends to monopolize everybody's retinas.) He was wearing a frayed white labcoat and sitting on a metal stool in the corner of the room, reading the "Classics Illustrated" edition of *Story of O.* "That's my assistant, Fred May, over there," she explained.

The guy looked up at the mention of his name. He sported a reddish mustache and Victorian sidewhiskers of a similar color. On his head was an odd hat, something like a beret, hunter green, but with a big fluffy black pom-pom on the top.

"R. Frederick May," she pronounced, "you know Lucy Kropotkin, of course. These are my old friends detective Win Bear, and Clarissa Olson-Bear. And this is Captain Will Sanders of the Greater LaPorte Militia." She turned back to me again. "Fred here has just discovered a whole sheaf of worlds where, after losing the Battle of Tours in the eighth century, the forces of Islam hung a left, crossed the English Channel, and conquered the British Isles, producing a very strange history full of Celtic Moslems. In most of those worlds, they even beat the Norman invasion back in the eleventh century."

"*Erin go bragh, inshallah!*" I offered, but there weren't any takers.

"Hello, Lucy, how nice to see you again!" Fred put his comic book down—I made a mental note to borrow it from him when he was through with it—doffed his peculiar hat, and opened his mouth to say more, but he was interrupted.

"*My old friends, as well,*" insisted an extremely familiar voice as a wall-sized 'Com screen lit up at the other side of the room. We were suddenly being given a full-length, life-size view of a porpoise—*Tursiops truncatus*, the famous "bottlenose dolphin"— who, with a little help from friends with fingers, like Deejay, had invented the probability broach. Ooloorie Eckickeck P'wheet was calling from her own laboratory at the Emperor Joshua Norton University in San Francisco. It was like a scene straight out of *Johnny Mnemonic*, only her water was a lot cleaner than Jones's.

When I first met Ooloorie, she was an obnoxious snob, supercilious (if you can say that about somebody who doesn't have any eyebrows), and a bit of a racist—or would it be "speciesist"? She was only grudgingly willing to make exceptions—clearly her partner Deejay was one of them—to a general view that primates are inferior organisms whose ridiculous claim to sapience she only acknowledged because she needed the use of their hands.

Somewhere during the past eight or nine years, Deejay or Lucy or somebody else had somehow begun to straighten her out—I can't imagine how they'd accomplished it—because she was much easier to get along with these days.

"Greetings, landlings! I presume to interfere in the sanctity of your private deliberations," she continued, thrashing around in what must have felt to her like a confined space—sort of a fishy phone booth—*"only to remind my associate of the recent isotopic studies we discussed last week."*

"Highly speculative," her associate replied cautiously, sounding a bit like the porpoise herself, "and so far entirely uncorroborated." They would have made a swell vaudeville team—Marlin and Lewis . . . or Halibut and Costello.

"That is true, as far as it goes," Ooloorie acknowleged. *"However, we are not attempting to prove anything scientifically here, Deejay, merely to establish a direction in which our friends might pursue their investigation."*

"Would you mind telling me what the hell you're talking about?" Will asked. He'd only beaten me by a fraction of a second. Lucy, on the other hand, looked tolerantly amused. It wasn't an expression you saw often on her face. She'd been following them perfectly, jane-of-all-trades that she happens to be, and it gave me a distinct pain in the *tochis*.

Deejay turned to the frustrated militia captain. "There's a new theory," she began, clearly groping around for words that might mean something to a collection of underprivileged non-physicists, "that the distribution of isotopes varies slightly, but measurably—and, we hope, predictably—from continuum to continuum. You do know about isotopes, Captain Sanders?"

He nodded. "Make that Will. And yes—variations in atomic weight that don't change what element a given atom basically is. Uranium two hundred and thirty-five and two hundred and thirty-eight, for example."

"Carbon twelve and fourteen," I chimed in, not to be outdone.

"Very good." Deejay smiled and would have given us gold stars for our foreheads if she'd had any. "Now the idea is that someday we'll be able to identify the world of alternative probability that any given artifact comes from by the distribution of isotopes it contains. More U235 than this world maybe, and less C14. The theory is controversial and as yet to be demonstrated to everybody's satisfaction. But we have acquired the equipment to record and analyze data from these items you found, if you wish."

"What will it do to them?" Will wanted to know. I wanted to know, too. It was the only evidence we had.

"Nothing at all, landling," Ooloorie assured him. *"It's a simple matter of scanning the items in question under a kind of paratronic microscope, that's all. And then some computer time will be expended to analyze the data."*

"So it couldn't hurt?" he persisted.

Deejay laughed. "No more than chicken soup."

They both laughed. It was a good thing that Will was a happily married man—twice over—or that might have been the beginning of too beautiful a friendship. I wonder if there's such a word as "trigamy."

"THE GREATER LAPORTE Militia doesn't keep fingerprint records," Will informed us as we rolled up to our next stop, a low concrete structure with steel doors and angled walls. It only helped a little that the walls were painted a cheerfully clashing plaid, with blues and greens predominating. "In fact, we're forbidden to do so by our bylaws—it was my predecessor's last official act." I found that fairly interesting. Will's immediate predecessor as Captain-Commander of the GLPM had been one Scipio Africanus Kendall, an imposing figure of a man (although there was a persistent rumor that his wife called him "Skippy"), the father of both of Will's two wives, Mary-Beth and Fran, now retired to what used to be referred to as a "shooting estate" on the newly terraformed asteroid Pallas.

The sign outside what amounted to the only bunker in the North American Confederacy said:

GRISWOLD'S SECURITY

It should have also said, "Brrrrr." Inside—once the heavy steel doors had slowly ground open, the portcullis raised, and the tank traps grudgingly retracted—we entered an exercise in paranoia that reminded me of the local IRS office back in Denver. The anteroom was glaringly lit, steel gray, and stark, without furniture or any hint of decoration. By contrast, the receptionist, a young female chimpanzee, wore a hot pink go-go dress, white vinyl boots to go with it, a double shoulder holster rig, and a pair of high-capacity .475 Casasent Magnums. She was separated from us by a floor-to-ceiling transparent barrier at least four inches thick. Greeting Lucy as an old friend—the way everybody seems to—she leaned into an intercom and summoned a tall young human attired in a double pistol belt, military-looking blouse, and a kilt displaying the same color-scheme as outside, the company tartan. His hair was parted in the middle, and he had long mustaches that drooped to below his chin. He came through a door that had been invisible a moment before and met us on our side of the barrier.

"Why, hello, Lucy! It's wonderful to see you again! Dad'll be happy to hear of it, too! I'd heard you were out in the Belt." He turned to Will, while giving the rest of us the lookover. "Please forgive all of these security formalities; they're more advertising than anything else, I'm afraid. I'm Liam Griswold IX. What can

I do for you, Captain?" Will introduced Clarissa and me and explained about the Greater LaPorte Militia not collecting fingerprint records. What made S. A. Kendall's decision interesting to me was that, as far as he knew, his son-in-law-to-be was the guy who'd brought the whole idea of fingerprints into this world. Actually, it was me, but I wasn't particularly proud of it.

"But I understand that Griswold's Security does—" he told the proprietor.

The young man chuckled—nervously, I thought—making the ends of his long mustaches wiggle. "Well, yes, we do—two hundred whole sets, out of the more than two million individuals who live in this city alone. Please understand, Captain, we only take those prints that are offered to us voluntarily. And of course we only retain them on the same basis."

"For the time being," I said, but everyone ignored me except Clarissa, who dug me in the ribs with an elbow. I don't know what it is about this outfit that inspires such awe. I wasn't much impressed with Griswold the Ninth, a skinny kid with silly face-fur and a dress, whose guns—they looked like a pair of AutoMags, but probably weren't—seemed to be wearing him, rather than the other way around.

Will handed young Griswold a dataplaque, something like a floppy diskette, only a lot smaller. It was a bright, cheery yellow and about an inch on a side, with no moving parts, and contained the results of the paratronic scan Deejay had conducted, including several greatly magnified and enhanced images of the thumbprint. Her own computers, back at LaPorte University, Ltd., were juggling the same information now, trying to find an isotopic match with one of the eleven googleplex worlds, or however many it was, that had recently been discovered.

Griswold inserted the dataplaque in a slot in the side of a 'Com pad he was carrying. Confederates don't have much use for data-

plaques. Even in my own home world, when you transfer information by carrying a floppy from one computer to another, it's
referred to as using the "sneakernet" and sort of sneered at. In
this case, we hadn't wanted to trust these data to that vast equivalent to the Internet we referred to as the Telecom, not really
knowing how private it is.

To everyone's surprise, Griswold's results were much quicker
in arriving than Deejay's. "By Gallatin, we *do* have the thumbprint in question! It was acquired ethically—at the insistence of
its owner—during the routine investigation of some minor office
pilferage."

Will asked, "And it belongs to . . . ?"

The young man sniffed behind his mustaches and looked
down his long nose at Will. "There is the matter, here, Captain
Sanders, of client confidentiality."

Will glared up at him. "There is a matter, here, Mr. Griswold,
of two thousand extremely violent deaths in the past week and
possibly many more to come!

Griswold sputtered, "But I—"

"Look at it this way, friend," Will went on. "Would you rather
be sued by a single client whose confidentiality you may have
violated, or by the families of thousands whose deaths you could
be preventing right now? I'd be happy to arrange for the latter
personally!"

Young Griswold replied without hesitation. "Very well, it belongs to Bennett Williams, the editor of the Franklinite Faction's
online journal *The Postman*."

Will looked satisfied, but I felt the customary privacy and freedom of the Confederacy melting out from under my feet like a
well-salted ice floe.

> Hell hath no fury like the well-nursed resentments of a
> younger sibling.
>
> —*Memoirs of Lucille G. Kropotkin*

"The thumbprint belongs to Bennett Williams," young Griswold
had informed us, "editor of the Franklinite Faction's online journal *The Postman*." And that pretty much established where we
were headed next. If I'd had two fully operational arms, I might
have taken off on my own at this point. I was still working for
"Pappy" and "Janie," and nobody was paying me to look for the
Polybomber, or whatever he planned to call himself when he
wrote his bestselling autobiography. Okay, so Lucy *had* offered
to pay me. The figure she'd mentioned was significant. It would
have replaced my poor little broken car with a spiffy new cold
fusion-powered model if the insurance company got sticky about
it. But ethics were ethics. Lucy (and my poor little broken car)
were just going to have to wait their turn.

"Hey, Winnie, lookit this!"

I jumped, startled out of my thoughts. Using the van's computer, Lucy had logged onto Williams's comsite to get a feel for
the man's thinking. In her own inimitable manner, she read me
the heading that every edition of the Franklinites' online magazine carried, dating from the day Bennett had taken over and
changed the title from the stodgy, if more informative *North
American Franklinite*.

" 'This publication's dedicated to all of those, regardless of
label or party affiliation, who know that what they want can only
be achieved by *governin'*.' "

"There's an open confession for you." I observed.

"Or a warning," Will agreed, "like a rattlesnake rattling."

Lucy went on. " 'There are three guidin' principles: we must *create* government; *we* must control it; an' if we're not preparin' t'do these things, we're waitin' for someone else t'govern an' control *us*.' Signed, Bennett J. Williams, Editor, *The Postman*."

"I guess it's clear," I replied, feeling disgusted—although I shouldn't have been surprised—"whose side he's on."

"Not ours," Will said. He could be the master of brevity when he wanted. Probably helped a lot, living with two wives.

"If that's his philosophy," Clarissa said, looking away briefly from the road and giving me a cheap adrenaline rush, "why not just emigrate to one of the thousands of—."

" 'Cause there ain't no guarantee that he'd be the one in charge, dearie! That's the trouble with bein' a radical authoritarian: You're an authoritarian, but on the other hand, you're a radical. Most of the regimes he'd theoretically approve of would lock him up first time he opened his mouth. It's happened t'far better'n him!"

"I see," This time Clarissa didn't look away. "Thank you, Lucy."

"You're welcome, honey."

Confederates are neither stupid nor naive. That goes double for my lovely spouse. They're simply uninfected with the form of mental illness that results in a craving for power. It's hard, even for a Healer like Clarissa, to identify with those who have the disease. There are always exceptions, of course, like the Franklinites.

"GREETINGS, MY FRIENDS, salutations!"

It turned out that to find Bennett Williams, we had to look up his big brother Buckley first. I was surprised to discover that Bennett didn't reside at the enormous Williams family mansion.

Liam Griswold wasn't the only professional paranoid in LaPorte. Everything Bennett stood for (like starting a government in the Confederacy) was just unpopular and repulsive enough to snap somebody's ethical strings and get Bennett shot—or at least called out to a duel. Buckley's politics were just as unpopular and repulsive (they were exactly the same, in fact) but he carried them with better style.

So here we were, at the extreme north end of the city (at a point where the Cache La Poudre River emerges from a canyon of the same name and eventually runs out onto the prairie) about where historic Ted's Place used to stand in my world before it burned down. In this world, it was "Buckley's Place," a half-mile-tall edifice roughly resembling one of those old-fashioned nonautomated toasters like my mother used to have, with the pair of chrome-plated doors you could swing down about thirty seconds after the bread slices had been reduced to bad-smelling charcoal. At the top of the structure, visible through the glass penthouse ceiling over our heads, was an enormous mast at which Buckley moored his two-hundred-foot, lighter-than-air "yacht," christened (of course) the *Benjamin Franklin*.

"Would anyone care for a drink? How gratifying to see you, Mrs. Kropotkin! Captain Sanders, splendid to renew your acquaintance. Win, why haven't we gone yachting? And this must be the charming spouse I've heard you speak of so often." He switched what he carried from one hand to the other to take Clarissa's hand and kiss it. Only in the Confederacy—and maybe the Federated States of Texas—would somebody welcome guests into his office holding a long-barrelled, large-caliber autopistol in his mitt.

Despite first-class ventilation, the room smelled of nitro powder smoke, and there were empty cartridge cases scattered all over a carpet expensive enough to pay for a dozen little red

Neovas. What made it interesting was that they were American cases, .45 ACP—Automatic Colt Pistol—a choice considered just as quaint here as the .41 Magnum I preferred.

At the far end of the office, which was almost as spacious as my living room, a thick-walled titanium bullet-trap had been bolted to the floor of a stone fireplace big enough to roast rhinocerouses in. It was the life-sized, torso-target hanging in front of the trap that Buckley had been shooting at before our arrival.

"I beg your pardon," he told us as we entered, "I've made a new acquisition and was giving it a try." He pressed the release button at the root of the trigger guard, popped the magazine out, shucked the slide back and locked it, then courteously handed the weapon to Lucy.

Newcomers to the Confederacy are often perplexed by the way that everybody here takes notice of what everybody else carries as a personal sidearm. Of course it never bothers them to see the same thing happening with people's cars. They're used to that.

And just as they believe that a man's choice of pickup, econovan, SUV, or midlife crisis roadster reveals something of his character and situation in life, so, sometimes, does his choice of weapon. Mine, an American revolver says (I think) that I'm a simple, no-nonsense sort of guy who finds something that works and sticks with it.

Will's choice, at least in my world, of a big, silver ten-millimeter autopistol, says he's interested in keeping up with the times, but not so trendy that he falls for every new toy that comes along. His gun's about as powerful as mine, but carries twelve rounds in the magazine and one up the pipe.

Lucy's choice of the right-hand Gun of Navarone . . .

It only took a glance around his office to conclude that Buckley was an antique collector of a new kind, possible only in a

culture capable of what's ofen called "sideways time travel." His
"antiques"—an H&K P9S hanging on the wall behind his chair,
a Steyr GB over the fireplace, a Makarov serving as a paperweight
on his desk—came from cultures contemporary with his own,
but a little behind in their technology (cultures like the one I
grew up in) the way an American might collect a Zulu assagai.

Once the pistol had made the rounds of its presumptive ad-
mirers, Buckley declared, "Everybody behind the desk and put
your fingers in your ears!" He slammed in a fresh magazine, let
the slide down, raised the weapon—but only to belt level—and
fired. At his insistence, each of us tried it. Gotta admit, it was
effective and fun. His latest acquisition was a good old familiar
1911A1-pattern—the basic .45 auto—that my world could easily
have produced, except that it was made entirely of stainless steel
and had a barrel—and the extra length of slide to go with it—
two inches longer than the standard issue weapon John Moses
Browning had invented. The generic term is "longslide."

But what made it special from a collector's point of view (and
what fascinated me) was that the right grip panel—black plastic
like the left, the same familiar thickness and general profile any
.45 afficionado was used to—contained a miniscule laser molded
into a slight thickening at the top of the grip, ending in a tiny
lens. When I'd left the States there were laser sights for pistols—
the size of a shoebox. This one you'd be a long time noticing,
even once you picked the gun up and examined it. Along the
front edge of the same right grip was a narrow rubber pressure
switch. Squeeze the switch, the laser painted a brilliant red dot
on the target. Squeeze the trigger and, if everything was properly
adjusted, the bullet went to the spot the laser pointed at. My
guess was that most of the time you used this thing, you wouldn't
even have to pull the trigger. The other guy would see that bright

red spot on his tummy, wet his pants, and just give up. I know I certainly would.

Finally, it was me who said, "Well, Mr. Williams—Buckley—this has all been a lot of fun, but as Lucy would say, we're burning daylight, and we need to get down to business."

"Of course, Win," Buckley swiveled in his chair and tapped a stylus against his teeth. "In what way may I assist you?"

"We need to speak with your brother Bennett, in connection with an investigation we're conducting. Will here is concerned about the Old Endicott Building and tubeway explosions. I'm only trying to find out something about some recent interworld imports."

"Well I'm certain." Buckley answered, "that my brother knows nothing about the former matters that would interest you. I wouldn't know about the latter. But it surely couldn't hurt him to speak to you, now, would it?"

He used the stylus, wrote the address on a scrap of paper, and we were off, with thanks.

BENNETT—PROBABLY NOT by accident—lived about as far from Buckley and the rest of the extensive Williams clan as he could and still remain within the city, way down at the southern outskirts of LaPorte, about where Loveland, Colorado ends in my world. Buckley wasn't the only antique collector in the family. Bennet's house was at least a hundred years old, three-story, white frame, surrounded by a covered porch and two hundred acres of what once had been an onion farm. It had a modern Impervium roof, I noticed, and I was willing to bet that if anybody batted a baseball through one of its windows on a sunny summer day, the glass would have healed itself by morning.

I was more surprised to find that there weren't any servants in evidence. Bennett answered the door himself—we'd called him on the way over—invited us in and offered to take the coats and hats we either weren't wearing on a July afternoon or didn't feel like giving up. He didn't offer us a drink, unusual given Confederate customs, but I wouldn't have offered us a drink, either, if I was about to be grilled as a suspect.

As anticipated, he was a big, broad man who'd let his hair go to salt-and-pepper, a choice relatively rare here and now, but favored by those who had nothing else to base their moral authority on. His voice was low, velvety, and reminded me of Orson Welles. He conducted us into a big living-type-room, sort of New Englandy with a hardwood floor, white walls, and low ceiling, with Early Confederate furniture in which we were invited to sit.

"Now what," he inquired, complacent as a Canadian, crossing one leg over the other knee and straightening the crease in his trousers, "can I do for you folks?" Will and I had agreed to keep the physical evidence from the train wreck to ourselves. He didn't want an unknown opponent to know what we knew. I had a hunch some mysterious ally of ours might be in danger if the real villain got wise. Somebody had noticed Bennett's thumbprint on that coin and left it as an accusation.

Will told him, "We're looking into the two terrorist crimes that were committed this week, the Old Endicott Building disaster, and this morning's tube-train explosion. We have a long list of all sorts of people we've talked to about it or are planning to, and just now, we've gotten to you."

Bennett leaned back, folded his hands over his middle, and smiled tolerantly. "I'm surprised anyone in this soulless, ungoverned culture is investigating these atrocities. So you'll want to know where was I at such-and-such a time on such-and-such a date, and so on?"

"And so on," Will answered in his soulless, ungoverned way.

"Regrettably," Bennett sighed, "I have an . . . what's the word? *Alibi*—like in detective novels. I certainly never expected to use it in any other context. I have an alibi for this morning."

Will raised his eyebrows in polite inquiry but said nothing.

Languidly, Bennett droned on. "I happen to have been attending a political convention. In fact, I was addressing its attendees on the urgency of establishing a real government to prevent such disasters as these in the future. So the tube explosion made my point for me. The blast shook the hotel we occupied, nearly spilling the pitcher of water on the lectern. My address was covered on the Telecom, and there's a list of one hundred witnesses I can give you to substantiate my claim, if you promise not to use it for commercial purposes."

"I promise. How about the night of the Old Endicott explosion?" Will asked.

"That occurred during the convention's opening ceremonies. Very disturbing—and about the same number of witnesses."

"Excuse me." I had to butt in; the guy was making me mad. "Just my curiosity mind you; nothing to do with Captain Sanders's investigation. I'm a blueback, and governments are something I know pretty well. What kind of government could have *prevented* either of these attacks?"

Bennett swiveled and looked down his nose at me, reminding me of his brother. Any minute, I expected him to tap his front teeth with a pencil. "One that balances every manifestation of private, personal liberty with an equal and consistent measure of observation and . . ."

" 'A microphone in every bedroom' ", I suggested, "the way George Peppard put it in a movie on the subject? These days, he'd have insisted on a camera, too. So, unlike your illustrious older brother, you're an open advocate of right-wing authoritarian collectivism."

Something resembling fury swept over the man's features, but he regained control in an eyeblink. "My brother has no real political convictions, no ambition. He's a media personality, pure and simple. As for what I advocate, understand that, although there have been minor variations over six thousand years of history, there are basically only three ways that human beings can organize themselves."

"One guy tells ever'body what t'do, that's one." Lucy counted on her fingers. "Ever'body tells ever'body else what t'do. Or nobody tells anybody what t'do!"

Bennett nodded. "The last way is chaos . . . anarchy . . ."

"I believe the word you're groping for is freedom, Mr. Williams," Clarissa offered. "It's how people have chosen to organize themselves in the Confederacy for over two hundred years."

"And look at the result!" Bennett protested, speading his hands as if what he had to say was obvious.

I laughed. "Yeah, look at it: the most progressive, productive, wealthiest civilization in human history!"

"Two thousand dead," Bennett argued, "no official way to prevent it, or even find the culprits after the fact and punish them! Try the middle alternative and it leads to hopeless confusion and paralysis—the stupid, useless, dangerous babble of democracy—and eventually evolves into the first alternative. Which would be acceptable, except that we don't have *time* for evolution!"

He was right about one thing. Under democracy, you're a captive of the fears of the least courageous among you, the integrity of the least honorable, the brains of the least intelligent, and the weakness of the least strong. But finding some clown to order everybody around is a cure worse than the disease.

"So we all have to start goose-stepping to your drumbeat right away," I tried not to yell, "before people wake up and start thinking for themselves again."

Bennett seemed to be exerting equal effort. "Unlike Ludwig von Mises's observation—you're surprised I've read von Mises?—about socialists," he replied evenly, "I don't insist that the man everybody obeys be myself. I can't tell you how I long to pledge my personal fealty to someone—anyone—I can regard as worthy."

"Of bein' *king*," Lucy finished for him, although he probably thought he'd finished already. "In your heart of hearts, you're a monarchist. Which means that, for all your criticism of left-wing socialism, you're a *right-wing* socialist, yourself."

"Call it what you like, Mrs. Kropotkin. I confess I've recently—and reluctantly—begun to see merit in Dr. Slaughterbush's campaign against the private ownership of deadly weapons, if that's what you're referring to. They're an obstacle to accomplishing certain reasonable, commonsense political objectives."

Just as Bennett, here, was the closest thing in the Confederacy to a monarchist, Slaughterbush was the closest thing to a communist. Come to think of it, he fit the profile pretty well as a suspect, and there were probably a few others we ought to look up. I made a mental note to mention it to Will.

"They're *supposed* t'be!" This was Lucy's hot button. "Personal weapons prevent anybody from imposin' his idea of 'reasonable, commonsense objectives' on anybody else!"

Bennett snorted delicately. "Then you object to establishing a peaceful, orderly society?"

She shook her head. "I thought that's what we have. Unless by 'orderly,' you mean regulated t'death."

He sighed again. "Madam, I have *always* favored economic freedom."

"Even if you're a bit weak in areas like unimpeded market entry an' international trade. An' don't call me 'madam'!"

"I merely wish to protect my country."

"My country, right or wrong, is that it?"

"If you insist; there are worse philosophies." Bennett sat up straighter in his chair. It occurred to me that this might have been easier if I'd had a glass of scotch in my hand. "The plain fact," he lectured Lucy, "is that people are all a *little* evil and they must be watched. Anything else is mere Utopian foolishness. It overlooks all of mankind's baser qualities. It's dangerous, Mrs. Kropotkin, to let people labor under the impression that they own their own lives. If they're to become worthy of their own past glories—"

"However mythical—or do y'mean the Crusades, the Inquisition, the Thirty Years' War, the Hundred Years' War, an' all those other wonderful things that kings an' their ilk bestowed on an ungrateful humanity? Y'know, Bennie, lookin' backward all the time's a mighty fine way t'trip over your own feet!"

And she'd be the one to know. I still had trouble, sometimes, dealing with the idea that my little old former next-door neighbor had been born in 1851—1851!—and personally seen exactly two thirds of the history of this great civilization unfold. In Lucy's century and a half, she'd become a legend. Married more times than she could remember—with children scattered all over the System—she'd pioneered several continents including Antarctica, piloted a dirigible against the Kaiser in 1914, and fought the Czar in 1957. She'd been a miner, farmer, judge, nuclear engineer helping to develop colonies in the Asteroid Belt, adventure novelist, and exotic dancer. No wonder everywhere she goes, she seems to know everybody and everybody knows her. The late husband whose name she bore was a prince who, in many worlds, gave up his title to practice anarchism. In this world, he'd practiced it with Lucy.

Bennett ignored her. "They must be taught, instead, that their lives belong, not to themselves, but to their own families, to their civilization, to a divinely sanctioned state ultimately presided over by a Supreme Being—"

"As primitive and vicious as the government He presides over?" She loved this kind of argument and no doubt had missed it on the Great Frontier. "Why do people like you always wind up with a paternalistic, punitive attitude toward other folks, Bennie? With no more evidence to support it than Slaughterbush and his Majoritarians? Whippin' for the little ones, an' for the big ones— I don't expect there's ever been an execution you didn't like! I thought we'd given up on mysticism as the governin' epistemology for civilization."

He lifted his chin. "There is a difference, madam, between mysticism and religion!"

"Describe it in twenty-three words or less—an' don't call me 'madam'!"

WE WEREN'T IN that house another ten minutes. Then it was out on the porch and when we got back in Clarissa's van, it developed that Will was unhappy with Lucy and me.

"Goddamn it, Win, you're an ex-cop! An ex-homicide detective! You alienated the subject for no good reason and turned my investigation into a political argument!"

I'd been feeling guilty about that, although there was sympathy in Clarissa's eyes, possibly because she'd helped with the arguing. I opened my mouth to speak—without the faintest idea what I was going to say—but Lucy was there before me.

"It's been my experience that Winnie's invstigatory instincts are unerring, Willie! Kindly don't criticize an act of genius!"

"What?" Will cringed. He hated being wrong, and he hated it even worse when anybody called him Willie.

"What?" I asked before I could stop myself.

"Look," she explained, "Bennie's a classic dogwhistle! That makes him vulnerable. Push him hard enough, he'll crack, let his guard down, tell you what he really thinks! He may need another dose before he opens up, but Winnie has us headed in the right direction!"

Will nodded slowly. "You could be right."

Maybe I *was* a genius. "What's a dogwhistle?"

"You oughta know, both of you, it's from a movie made in both your worlds. *Strange Days*. A dogwhistle's somebody with an ass so tight that when he farts, only dogs can hear him!"

12: LAY THAT PISTOL DOWN

> Better the "Me" generation than the "Duh" generation.
> —*Memoirs of Lucille G. Kropotkin*

The sign over the entrance said:

MR. MEEP'S AT THE MALL

An American hears the word "mall" and envisions a huge structure, often multistoried, usually at the edge of town where it was built to avoid sales taxes mere seconds before the city got wise and annexed the land it stood on. He sees dozens, even hundreds of shops—not one of which sells a thing anybody needs to keep from dying—maybe a smattering of fast-food counters, even a genuine sit-down restaurant. I noticed once, in the biggest mall in Fort Collins, the town that's "coextant," as they say, with central LaPorte, that there wasn't any place to buy matches.

Not so the Jefferson Plaza Shoppes at the corner of Mencken and Spooner, about where Fort Collins' Rocky Mountain High (no, I'm not kidding about the name) would be if Confederates weren't so particular about how they use perfectly good real estate. Two of us were getting started on a little late afternoon lunch and I was reminding myself that I should call my clients to give them a no-progress report. The other two, Lucy and Clarissa, were finishing up a little late afternoon shopping.

I said "the corner of Mencken and Spooner." What I really meant was *under* Mencken and Spooner. Like most commerical development in LaPorte in the last century, it was built underneath the intersection. When the speed of city traffic hit seventy-five (don't think it can't happen to you—last time I was "back home," legal traffic in downtown Lubbock was doing sixty), it had suddenly appeared prudent to dig tunnels so pedestrians could get across safely. What would otherwise have been free-mugging zones became shoppers' paradises, when convenience stores of all kinds—whose owners had paid for the digging in the first place—began to light up the pedestrian tunnels.

Jefferson Plaza Shoppes was the same idea, squared and cubed. It had been constructed in several stages, under twenty-five or thirty intersections, involving several square miles, and went Chinaward five or six levels. Even so, it was hard to tell that you were underground, thanks to the mirrors, fiberoptics, and 'Com screens that gave shoppers (employees probably appreciated it, too) a pretty convincing illusion they were doing their meandering surrounded by a great big, landscaped, brightly sunlit space.

So far, Will and I had electronically ordered and received coffee for him—station-house black, if you please—and Coke for me. I was a happy man. The sling on my left arm was twice the size of the earlier one and strapped securely to my torso. That had called for a stop at home, where—retaining the Browning High Power on my right hip—I'd stuffed my .41 Magnum into the pocket afforded by the sling. My left hand stuck out far enough that reloading wouldn't be too much of a problem. It was like putting on warm flannels after going half naked for three days. With my .41 and a couple of speed loaders, the Browning and two spare fifteen-round magazines (now illegal in most versions of the good old U.S.A., thanks to an inexplicable failure on the part of Americans to drag enough judges, politicians, and news broadcasters out and hang them from the nearest lamp-post), and the Chris Reeve knife that had saved my life the very day I'd bought it, I felt well-equipped to face the world.

Will was complaining over his coffee. "If Williams hadn't been addressing that political convention, he'd still be my best bet! I'd love to have asked him about his thumbprint on that coin, but if I had, he'd know about it."

"A policeman's lot—" I started to quote Gilbert and Sullivan. He responded almost reflexively, "I'm *not* a policeman."

"Sure you are, ossifer," I argued, just to be difficult. "Aside from various private security outfits like Griswold's and Forsythe's, and a tough Civil Liberties Association that keeps an eye on them, the closest LaPorte has to local police is the Greater LaPorte Militia, ably captained by none other than yourself. It's just that, unlike the cops where you and I hail from, the GLPM, long may it wave, has plenty of competition—something on the order of fourteen militia companies, last time I heard, and several gaggles of armed firefighters, that tend to keep each other honest."

Will and I are both from Denver, Colorado, U.S.A., but—in a universe that offers infinite alternatives—not precisely the *same* Denver, Colorado, U.S.A. Fifteen years younger, twenty pounds lighter, and somewhat more intense most of the time, Will isn't exactly certain how he got to the Confederacy. Apparently he suffered some mortal stress Stateside, in connection with his personal life or his job as a Burglary Division detective, which he still can't or won't talk about. He'll only say he woke up one sunny morning in an alternate world. *This* alternate world. Scientists who invented the broach—Ooloorie, Deejay, a handful of others like Fred May—and familiar with the relevant physics, are reluctant to believe a man can cross the ineffable gulf between worlds "by sheer force of personality." Will's reaction is, "Pardon me for living." He found the gulf to be plenty effable, and he's disinclined to look a gift horse in the mouth. The culture he now calls home is as easygoing about marriage customs as it is about drugs, weapons, and immigration. By what he considers a second miracle, he now finds himself married to a pair of beautiful sisters—Mary-Beth and Frances Kendall—both of whom are pregnant at the moment, a circumstance that seems alternately to delight and embarrass him.

"And despite our brief, uncharacteristic moment of professional friction back at the Williams hacienda," I went on reminding him that he was still basically a cop, "I'm damned glad you're here. I have a case of my own—"

"The Gable–Lombard thing," he said with the disbelieving tone I expected. He didn't think it was important, but it was paying my bills, and I'd given my word.

"That's right. And, encumbered as I am by this cast on my poor, twice-broken arm . . ." (All embarrassment to that, and no delight at all.) ". . . I'm shorthanded in more ways than one."

He raised an eyebrow. "I don't know, you seem somehow to have enlisted Lucy's help."

I laughed. "You know, when I first met her back in 1987, she was 'retired,' recovering, in fact—with Clarissa's professional help—from a dose of radiation."

He looked a question at me. That kind of thing was rare in the Confederacy, which preferred fusion to the vastly messier fission.

"Acquired in the course of atomically nudging an asteroid to a more convenient location," I explained. "It damn near killed her, but it was a lucky break for me. Over the years, she's become something of an advocate for newcomers to the Confederacy, like me to start with, and, lately, the less-helpless inhabitants of the Zone like Max Parker-Frost and his wife."

"I see," he nodded.

"Lucy," I went on, "practically jumped at the chance to help me, her old friend Olongo Featherstone-Haugh, his pet storekeepers in the Zone, and immigrants in general, all at the same time. It's absolutely typical of her that she framed it in the context of wanting *my* help—and offering to pay me for it!"

Will laughed. "My favorite writer once characterized Texans as having an attitude that says, 'You paid for the drinks, I'll pay for the Cadillacs.' "

"I think he was my favorite writer, too. I'd say that Lucy Kropotkin is Texas personified."

"Somebody talkin' about me?" Clarissa right behind her, Lucy was headed for the table with boxes in her arms and sacks dangling from her fingers. "Don't you look at me that way, Win Bear! This is the first chance I've had to shop on Earth for months!"

I shook my head. "I wasn't looking at you any way, Lucy, honest. I was just curious about what you got."

They sat down. "Well, Winnie, I guess you wouldn't care to see hats, slacks, blouses, or dresses—although you're bound to enjoy some of the flimsier items Clarissa picked up." Across the table from me, my lovely wife actually blushed. Lucy began punching commands into the tabletop. "Let's order something rare an' drippin' an' we'll show you the real goodies!" I followed her example, ordering myself a steak sandwich.

Lucy shoved most of her bags into an unoccupied corner of the big, over-upholstered, horseshoe-shaped booth we occupied and opened one of the boxes, a pink one, apparently from some boutique called "Polite Society." She pulled out a fantastic object that bore a resemblance to one of those big, pneumatic "Master Blaster" water pistols kids have back in the States, with the cylinders of clashing, brightly colored plastic. This was smaller, breadbox-sized, probably made of titanium and chrome-plated.

"The latest!" she exclaimed. "A plasma gun, from a new outfit called Borchert and Graham!"

"Nifty!" Will agreed, reaching to fondle it. "But only forty watts?"

Lucy snorted. "It'll put a hole in a brick wall you could throw a dog through!"

"I'll remember that," he promised, "next time I want to throw a dog through a hole in a brick wall. So you're finally hanging up your old Gabbett-Fairfax?"

"Don't even joke about it, Willie! No, I'm takin' this plasma piece back with me to the Belt. Gonna use it for my car gun."

I laughed. Confederates in the Belt operate little spaceships that they think of as their cars. "And what did you get, dear?" Lucy was wrong, I not only enjoy looking at clothes Clarissa buys, I like to go shopping with her—a grievous violation of the Husband's Union Rules, I know.

"This," she said, opening another box from Polite Society. Inside lay a plain metal cylinder that looked suspiciously like what you're not supposed to call a pistol silencer. "It's an extender," she said, "for my Webley. More coils—it doubles the power and range. We're out in the country so much these days, I thought it might come in handy." She drew her pistol and began screwing the device onto the muzzle, effectively doubling the barrel length.

Suddenly we became aware of a heated discussion at the table closest to our booth. Apparently a middle-aged patron and his wife had summoned the owner/manager, my old friend Mr. Meep, himself.

A word about Meep: he's a chimpanzee nearly as old as Lucy, with what seems to be thousands of relatives whom he employs at restaurants of all kinds—Mexican, Chinese, Zulu—all over the Confederacy, the planet, and now, even on the asteroid Ceres. Before we know it, he'll be putting his restaurants on starships and boiling lobsters or flipping burgers all over the galaxy. Usually, Meep had his wrist voice synthesizer adjusted to mimic a foreign accent appropriate to whatever restaurant he was supervising. This afternoon, however, he was all business and the Queen's English.

"May I help you in some way, sir?" he said.

"This flagrant display of firearms is unthinkable!" wailed the patron. "Intolerable!" The man, obviously a recent immigrant, pointed at the four of us, his wife *hmmphing* along in all the right places.

"Especially," she volunteered, "in the light of all these recent senseless, violent tragedies!"

"My wife and I are deeply offended, and demand that you—"

"That I what?" the chimpanzee asked. "Tell them they can't show off purchases they've just made in this mall? Make a fool of myself ordering them to put their guns away? Ask them to leave—depriving myself of income—or even die, trying to take their guns away?"

"You could at least—"

"Mister, ma'am, there isn't a thing I'd do about it if I could. As for the 'recent tragedies,' their right to own and carry doesn't have anything to do with somebody else's crimes! Things may be different where you came from, but people here have rights that are inalienable! You might as well complain about their *smoking!*" He left them with a shrug of dismissal. At our table we politely refrained from falling on the floor and laughing ourselves into tears. The couple got up and moved to a table farther away from bad old us. We finished ordering our food in person from Mr. Meep, himself.

He wanted to see Lucy's new plasma gun, too.

I'D PUT IT off. Sooner or later, however, I knew there was no way to avoid it. I had to go to the bathroom. I excused myself and plodded across the table-filled room toward my destination, dreading having to fool with my fly and other related appurtenances with a cast on my arm. On the other hand, it wasn't anything I felt like asking for help with, even from Clarissa. A man's gotta go where a man's gotta go.

The door swung. Nobody else was in the room. The Muzak was playing "You Go to My Head." Confederate public facilities are usually pretty plush—three seashells, and everything that went with them—and there would be no exception at Mr. Meep's. But I had put it off, and now I had no time or inclination to appreciate the amenities. I found a urinal—they put them in stalls here—performed the necessary preparations feeling grateful that it was my left arm that didn't work, and waited for nature to take its course. A 'Com pad fastened to the wall above the porcelain was carrying a run-down of the lineup for today's Patriots game. I asked it to focus a little farther away for my middle-aged eyes—about a yard—and it obeyed. Good news: Roger "Killer" Culver, the Patriots batting star was—

Suddenly, I felt a shadow looming over me from behind. I guess I'd forgotten to latch the stall door. "Turn around slowly," hissed an appropriately sinister voice, "if you know what's good for you!"

Maybe I'm too old to get scared like I used to when I was younger—my adrenaline gland wearing out or something. Maybe it was the car nonaccident I'd survived today. In any case I was more pissed (no pun intended) than frightened. I said, "If I turn around, buckethead, I'll be peeing on your knees. What the hell do you want?" Ignoring what had now become old business, I let my hand creep toward my sling.

He hissed, "I want you to mind your own fucking business, Bear," neatly identifying himself as an immigrant. Confederates use sex-free swear words, like I said. In the not-quite-matte surface of the 'Com pad, I saw him raise an arm. "I'm here to give you a warning!"

Embarrassingly exposed or not, I whirled as I drew my .41, shoving it into his face as I thumbed the hammer back. "Drop that arm slowly, blueback, or I'll clear your nasal passages right through the back of your neck!"

To my surprise, it was the little old "lady" who'd taken a shot at me in the Zone, heavily veiled under a wide-brimmed hat, half a head taller than me, holding a fire extinguisher up around the ceiling. I heard "her" gulp at the sight of my big black revolver with its gaping muzzle. "She" took two steps back and lowered her weapon, setting it gently on the sink.

"Now take off the hat," I commanded, "and let's see who you are!"

At that exact moment, the jerk who'd complained about Lucy's new plasma gun pushed the door aside, took one look at the very tall lady I was with, the drawn revolver, and the object sticking out of my pants, and froze. Hell, I wouldn't have been able to figure out what was going on, either. Before he could overcome his shock and confusion, the "lady" pushed out past him and was gone.

Talk about a policeman's lot. I couldn't very well pursue "her" without lowering the sixgun's hammer, pushing the .41 back into my sling, rearranging certain private attachments, and zipping up, all with one arm in a cast. On top of everything else, I'd wet the front of my pants. Thank heavens for serapes.

"Goddamn it," I complained to the frozen guy as I struggled with my trousers, "a hundred times I've told her, Mother, don't follow me into the men's room!"

By the time I got back into the restaurant, of course, the "lady" had vanished.

"WINNIE," LUCY WAS telling me, having finished her white wine and calamari, "every political philosophy comes with its own unique set of reasonable-soundin' excuses for deprivin' individuals of their life, liberty, and property. That's what politics is about: acquirin' enough power t'coercively redistribute wealth from its creators to those who won't or can't earn it."

"Didn't we have this conversation nine years ago, Lucy?" I'd told them—with certain editorial omissions—all about my adventure in bathroomland. Will hadn't believed me, thinking it was some elaborate joke. I reminded him of the hole in my cloak. He reminded himself that he knew me. This wasn't my kind of joke. (I'm the "bag of poop on your doorstep, light the top, ring the bell, and run" type. Like I said, a simple, no-nonsense sort of guy who finds something that works and sticks with it.)

Naturally, they hadn't seen the "lady" in question. Well, it was a big restaurant. And I knew one couple who wouldn't be coming back—they were probably packing for their homeworld even now.

For my part, I was drinking my Coke, eating my steak sandwich, and gazing at my darling Clarissa who was gazing back at me over her oriental chicken salad, probably wondering how I managed to get into—and out of—these messes. I'd survived again, grateful I hadn't had to set off the .41 in a small, enclosed, tile-lined space. That meant I could still hear her. Things couldn't have been better—keeping the Bear Curse in mind—and I was reluctant to spoil them by going back to work prematurely.

My would-be client—who'd gotten into, and out of, plenty of messes herself over the years—insisted: "Politicos to the right of center justify their trespasses against privacy an' personal freedom in the name of 'decency' or 'national security.' Those to the left suppress individual economic self-determination an' the right to own and carry weapons in the name of 'public safety' or 'social justice,' but it's all a pack of lies meant to put a pretty face on thuggery an' armed robbery."

"All individual behavior is about getting laid." I finally offered the most cynical words I knew, impatiently. "And all group behavior is about eating."

"Where'd you hear that?" Lucy demanded. "Is it original?" She always had an ear for an aphorism.

I shrugged. "Just something I've been mulling over."

"We'll talk about it later. It may even mean something. But just now, let's examine what the stakes are—"

"Mine's medium rare," I said, enjoying the expression it put on her face. "I'd like to finish it while it's hot, if you don't mind."

"The danger is that there's gonna be enough of these artificial calamities that people'll start listenin' t'Williams an' anybody else who thinks we oughta have a government."

"It was the stated purpose of various leftist terror groups," Will observed around a bite of his cheeseburger, "in versions of Europe Win and I both know, to create spectacularly violent incidents that would force existing governments to clamp down, making life so miserable the average person would revolt—presumably in a Marxist direction."

I decided to make up for my initial flippancy. "It always works, too. Not just for the left, but for anybody interested in running the lives of others. That's how we wound up with the Brady Bill and metal detectors in high schools. All you have to do is arrange for enough telegenic shootings, and—"

"Then you're both aware from bitter experience," said Lucy, "that if a Continental Congress gets convened in the present circumstances, the 'duration of the emergency' that made it possible will likely last forever, an' the unrestricted liberty that makes life worth livin' in the Confederacy'll be lost, probably never t'be regained!"

"So what you're saying, Lucy," Will asked, "is, suspect anyone

who stands to gain by reducing or eliminating individual freedom."

"That's what I'm sayin', all right."

"And we've just had a visit with the first and foremost of the
breed," I added, mentally calculating whether Bennett had been
as big as the guy in the bathroom. Surreptitiously I felt to see if
my pants were dry. They were, but somebody was going to pay
a cleaning bill, anyway.

Lucy nodded. "Leavin' a pretty small handful of others."

"Native authoritarians, maybe. There can't be many of them.
But immigrants—you saw that bunch of stupes this morning in
the Hanging Judge . . ." I interrupted myself briefly to tell Will
about the Anti–Vending Machine Society. "Now, this couple
of . . . of . . ."

"Pisswits," Lucy supplied.

"Pisswits. Despite the humiliating circumstances, consider it
stolen. We may have *thousands* of pisswits to wade through before this is over, and I'm supposed to be—"

"Working on another case!" Both Lucy and Will finished for
me. Clarissa gave me a sympathetic look.

"Well, it's true!"

"An' it means," Lucy said, "you have an excuse t'wade through
some of those immigrant suspects you were tellin' us about,
doesn't it? While Willie, here, checks out the homegrown authoritarians."

"I'll help," Clarissa volunteered. She was the helpy type.

"We'll all help," Will responded. Win, I want you with me
when we confront Slaughterbush."

Lucy chirped, "Don't forget Jerse Fahel!"

"Believe me, I won't," he replied. "And I'll come along with
you and help you with your interviewees. With that arm, you
need some backup. Is it a deal?"

Like I said, I was shorthanded. "It's a deal." I sighed.

"Then 'All for one . . .' " Will quoted.

" 'An' One for all!' " responded Lucy.

" 'And every man for himself,' " I said. "Who's Jerse Fahel?"

13: THE JAVA JIVE

Men are from Mars. Women are from Venus. Government is from Uranus.

—Memoirs of Lucille G. Kropotkin

"Pass me another one of those sausage patties, will you?"

Under what historians will surely refer to as the Bear-Sanders Agreement of 220 A.L., it had been decided that Will would help me with my case and I would help him with his. It didn't seem like a particularly equal exchange to me. Will's case was about the cowardly, cold-blooded murders of more than two thousand innocent victims. Mine was about . . . well, the movies.

"Sure, Winnie—-y'want some more of this omelette, too?"

As an historical footnote, my lovely Clarissa and our old friend (and I do mean *old* friend) Lucy would help us both. Having a medical doctor along for the ride seemed like a good idea until I thought about the implications. So far, in three days, I'd managed to break my left arm twice, have my car blown up, get shot at, and be assaulted in a public bathroom. The only bright (if thoroughly humiliating) aspect was that it had been the same arm both times. Stumbling around with both arms immobilized would have been too much to take.

"Are there any more of those sliced peaches left?" Clarissa asked.

All in all, it'd been a very long day. Thinking back, it seemed more like several very long days. By the time we left the underground shopping mall, the sun was already down behind Pistol Sight Mountain (absurdly known where I came from as "Horsetooth"), giving us one of those boringly predictable glorious Rocky Mountain sunsets, with a few sparse clouds brilliantly underlit in red-gold, orange-scarlet, and azure-purple. Will answered, "There will be for the next few picoseconds. Please pass the cantelope juice, will you?"

Will had called his car, which met us in the parking structure. He took Lucy back to the Zone to the Hanging Judge, where she was staying in an apartment over the bar. Clarissa and I went home and—in what we both hoped would be a lifelong study—got to know each other a little better. Note: Merlot is Cabernet Sauvignon with the heartburn removed.

BRIGHT AND EARLY the next morning, the four of us detective types met briefly and deliciously at Max and Yolanda's place for breakfast and a strategy session. It was decided that we'd check out a couple of my leads before we checked out one of Will's native authoritarians. Conveniently enough, the place I wanted to go first was right across the street, in an almost United Statesian glass-windowed storefront. Getting up from the kind of breakfast the Wizard and his wife served was an exercise of character, and my reflexes were a bit slow getting across the street, so it was a good thing traffic was slower in the Zone. When I got to the other side, I saw a familiar sight.

"Excuse me, sir!" Damned if it wasn't the little old "lady" I'd encountered twice before, tall, broad, and stooped over, clutching a small wicker basket to her person and ostensibly collecting for the Spaceman's Fund. "She" even wore the same broad-brimmed hat and a dark veil. "Sir?"

The Model 58 was out and in "her" face before I was conscious that I'd drawn it.

All right, asshole!" I growled. "*Now* let's see what's under that mosquito netting!"

The "lady" protested, "I'm afraid I don't quite—"

"Drop the basket! Lose the hat and veil! *Now!*" I levered the revolver's hammer back to underline the point. Individuals walking past us gave us some very strange looks and I was beginning to worry that one or more of them might decide to come to the "lady's" defense. It certainly would have happened in an instant anyplace *outside* the Zone.

The basket droppd to the sidewalk, spilling coins. Gloved hands rose carefully to lift the hat and veil at the same time— and a cold chill traveled down my spine. This was definitely *not* the tough guy I'd drawn down on in Mr. Meep's bathroom. She looked a bit like Nancy Culp, or that little old lady Jonathan Higgins used to have tea with on *Magnum P.I.*

Magically, I made the revolver disappear, trying desperately to think of where to start an explanation and apology. By any decent definition, I was the criminal now, and I was *really* worried about helpful passersby.

She started the conversation for me. "I'm just collecting for the Spaceman's Fund," she complained as she stooped down to pick her coins up. I stooped with her and tried to help. "I wasn't exactly trying to hold you up, young man!"

I stood. "Lady, somebody dressed just like you took a shot at me not too long ago, and tried to mug me in a restaurant bathroom. I swear to you on my mother's—"

She scowled. "And you fought them off with that ridiculous toy you pointed at me?" She drew her own weapon, a brandnew Bussjaeger .04 Hypersonic, titanium purple, and shiny. "Don't bother swearing on your mother's *anything*, young man. Just be more careful in the future—and get yourself a gun that was designed and manufactured sometime in *this* century!"

Needless to say, the Spaceman's Fund did very well that morning. Having emptied my pockets (and come pretty close to emptying other things, I ducked my head, anxious to get out of public sight, and hurried into the store.

The sign had simply said:

NEWS FROM HOME

Not bad for an immigrant quarter, I thought, short and direct. I stepped into the store carefully, not exactly trying to be invisible, but reaching up and silencing the little hanging bell out of prudence of some kind. I'd convinced my overly eager associates to let me handle this first one alone.

The store's owner, one David Fitzdavid, was right after Karl "Papa" LeMat (late of British North America) on my list of bluebacks who made a living importing unusual items from various versions of the United States and other places people were coming into the Confederacy from. Research indicated that he dealt mostly in paperback books, dead-tree newspapers, and magazines from the Old Country of your choice. But he didn't limit himself. I was especially interested in something he sold here that they hadn't invented back where I came from, Hollywood movies recorded on little compact laser disks, in an electronic format called "DVD."

I moved quietly. I didn't want to question Fitzdavid in front of a customer who'd promptly go out and spread the joyous news of my advent throughout the next dozen square blocks of beautiful downtown LaPorte, blowing whatever cover my investigation had. While they were talking at the counter in the back, I stayed toward the front of the store pretending to examine the most current issues of *The Confederate Enquirer* and *Sapients* magazine, both local publications, cosmically speaking.

I HOPED DAGGETT the knifemonger had been exaggerating my celebrity status here in the Zone. I was supposed to be a *private* detective. Private detectives are supposed to be stealthy, or at the very least, inconspicuous. Maybe Lucy throve on being the belle of everybody's ball, but it was going to be a pain in the ass for me if I couldn't go here, there, and everywhere unrecognized. Maybe what I needed was a trenchcoat and some of those Groucho Marx nose-glasses, with the big, fuzzy mustache.

In the back, a whiny voice complained, "I tell you, Fitz, I don't even know how to do business here!"

It turned out that the guy I'd been mistaking for a customer was just another storekeeper, apparently from the next place over. The two of them were enjoying a nicotine and caffeine break together and—literally—talking shop. The guy from next door was waving his cigarette around and bitching: "A customer you don't know comes in and pays you with a personal check. Naturally, you ask him for his ID—and then he looks like he doesn't know what the hell you're talking about!"

"Or if he does know," Fitzdavid added in an understanding tone and a heavy Brooklyn accent, "he looks like he wants t'remove yer tonsils—wit' a choichkey?"

"That's what he does, all right!" The other guy shuddered, took a great big drag on his coffin nail, and tried to drown his sorrows with an even bigger gulp of java. Suddenly I wanted a cigarette, too—and another cup of coffee—but decided to remain in stealth mode as long as I could stand it.

The guy with the Brooklyn accent nodded from behind his counter and made a sort of an east coast spreading gesture with both of his hands. " 'Cause it ain't really a check, don'cha understand? It's more like . . . like . . . well, like a warehouse invoice, payable on demand in da precious metal of yer cherce."

He tapped the bottom of an inverted pack of filtered Gallatins in the way only Americans—of one stripe or another—have mastered, pulled out the single cigarette that had obediently emerged, put it between his lips, and lit it with one of his imported Bics, reflexively cupping his hands around the flame. His guest was about to reply, but the owner took the first satisfying drag on his cigarette, exhaled, and went on. "Lookie, Mac: dese people here take everyt'ing real poisonal-like. Dey don't do group-t'ink. Hell, dey don't do *group-do*! Y'tell yer customer y'wanna see his bona fides before you'll do business wit' him, y'ain't tellin' him y'been boined before, by udders. He wouldn't give a rat's ass about dat, anyway. What does dat have t'do wit' him? Nuttin'! He ain't udders, see? What yer tellin' him is dat y'don't trust *him*!"

"I know, Fitz, I know . . ." The other merchant sighed and shook his head resignedly. He ground his mostly unsmoked cigarette out in a big tray on the counter and accepted another. At least he hadn't lit it off the first.

"Anyway," interrupted his host and colleague, pausing for a drink of coffee, then stirring it around and peering into it suspiciously. "How many of yer customers wanna pay dat way, by check? One in fifty? One in a hundred? Everybody I deal wit' pays cash!"

"Yes, well that's another problem," his neighbor replied, taking a long drag on his second cigarette. "If it were real cash—paper currency—I might be able to deal with it. Believe it or not, I managed to bring my cash register with me from Oxnard! But no—it's always in big, thick, heavy coins! Now what the hell am I going to do with big, thick, heavy coins?"

I almost interrupted right then, jarred to the bone by the dumbest phrase I'd ever heard, "real cash—paper currency." But I bit my tongue, instead. It hurt.

"Be grateful, Mac, be grateful! What precious metal coins mean is no inflation, damn little counterfeitin', no taxes at all! Din'cha ever have the Nixon-Ford-Carter currency soiplus in yer woild?"

" 'Wimp Inflation Now!' " his neighbor deliberately misquoted.

They both laughed. "You got it, Mac! Distributors and jobbers was sendin' out new price sheets every udder day! An' dat was one of history's *milder* inflationary episodes! Lemme tell you somet'in', Mac, inflation's nuttin' but *government* counterfeitin'. An' hard money—especially private-issue coins like dey got here—makes it impossible!"

The neighbor was persistent. He waved his arms, spilling cigarette ash. "But with all that anonymous hard cash around, what if somebody decides to rob you?"

"When's da last time y'seen somet'in' like dat on da 'Com, Mac?" Pouring himself another cup of black coffee from the carafe on the counter, the storekeeper chuckled. "Ever notice how everybody here is packin'?"

"Packing?" the neighbor sounded perplexed.

"Carries a piece." Fitzdavid slapped the automatic pistol he was wearing low on his hip, over his apron. "Well, dere's a reason for dat. If some lowlife scumbag's stupid enough t'try an' rob 'em—an' it don't happen often—dey don't gotta wait no forty-five minutes for da cops to get dere."

The other guy delivered a sort of outraged gulp. "Even the women and the children?"

"*Especially* da women an' children, Mac! Da smaller an' weaker y'happen t'be, da more need y'got for a weapon, don'cha? Dat's what guns're for, t'protect da weak from da strong! Sheesh! It just makes sense."

"But women . . . children!" It was almost a wail of despair.

"Mac, lemme tellya da kinda woild you've come to: In da Nort' American Confederacy—fer reasons of religious conscience—da Amish will only carry *revolvers*!"

There was a long, quiet pause.

Then: "But I don't *want* to carry a gun, Fitz! I've got other, better things to do with my time. I don't want to spend every waking minute defending my life and property!"

His host laughed. "Y'got better t'ings t'do wit' your time dan eatin'? Sleepin'? Takin' a crap? How 'bout sex, Mac, y'wanna let somebody else take care a *dat* for youse?"

Mac cleared his throat. "What does that have to do with—?"

"Everyt'in'! It has t'do wit' everyt'in'!" He waggled his eyebrows at the carafe, got a nod for a reply, and freshened his neighbor's cup. "Seems t'me like y'want somet'in' for nuttin'. Self-defense is whatcha call yer individual bodily function. Y'can't palm it off on nobody else. Every time people try dat, everybody winds up payin' a price—oppressive government, brutal, corrupt cops, a violent crime rate da natives here always t'ink we're lyin' about." His neighbor opened his mouth to speak, but was interrupted.

"Besides, Mac, you don't gotta spend *every* wakin' minute defendin' yer life an' property. That's just the usual anti-freedom, anti-independence bullshit from the Old Country." He tapped the side of his nose knowingly. "You only gotta defend yourself when somebody tries t'take 'em!"

"MR. FITZDAVID?" HIS colleague had gone back to work, raking in all those nasty old thick, heavy, inflation-proof coins. I moved to the back of the store, and the counter. I'd never given the meaning of the word any thought before; it's where all those nasty old coins get counted. Even after all these years, my reflexes still wanted me to reach into my jacket pocket and pull out my badge flipper. I still had my detective's shield; I kept it in the gun case at home. Instead, I showed the storekeeper one of my cards.

"Lieutenant Win Bear!" Oh, great. I was famous. "I *t'ought* dat was youse I saw up front, an' I wunnert what you was up to. Are you investigatin' somet'in'? Am I a suspect?" He looked like it would make his day.

"I guess you could be, if you wanted to," I told him amiably. "I just wanted to ask you some questions about the movies you import from the States."

He nodded enthusiastically. "Which movies? Which States?"

"We'll get to that, I hope. According to my notes, you're David Fitzdavid, age thirty-four, an immigrant, owner and proprietor of 'News From Home', is that right?"

"Sure, as far as it goes. I was a salesman for a pharmaceutical company back home, an' a damned good one—my territory was da whole Caribbean basin. Hell, I still got an inclination to assume suit an' tie (or whatever its local equivalent may be) and go out amongst da natives oinin' a livin' just like they do. I miss da road, but I gotta support my family, an' this storefrint is woikin' for me fine just now."

"I see." For some reason, changing professions had never occurred to me when I arrived. Now I'd met two guys, Daggett and Fitzdavid, who'd managed the transition without blinking. I probably would have ended up as a cesspool cleaner. "Mind if I ask you what brought you to the Confederacy?"

"Well," he squinted at me, "I could say it was my convictions dat ended me up here. I *was* a card-carryin' member of da Liberty Party, made my donations an' licked envelopes. But I only became a refugee when da house I owned in da State of Cuba was invaded by militant homeless activists, and da aut'orities wanted t'prosecute *me* for harrassin' a protected class when I kicked deir worthless, smelly keisters outa my home!"

I laughed. "So how come you're here in LaPorte, instead of in jail Stateside?"

"Or executed," he replied. "Dat's da penalty, officially. I got

dis postcard, see? Tellin' me t'bring da wife and kids—one suit-
case apiece—t'such an' such a place at such an' such a time. Bay
of Pigs. It was from somet'in' called da Erisian Rescue Brigade.
We drove all night, an' for all I know, our poor little '91 Bolivar
is rustin' on da beach today."

"Good story," I told him. "Who played Rhett Butler in *Gone
with the Wind*?"

He blinked, then recovered. "Never hoid of it—oh, wait. A
movie about da War of Secession from woilds where da South
lost, right? Dey never filmed it where I'm from, see? British gun-
boats shelled New York an' Boston in supporta southern bellig-
erency, Lee took Washington, an' da war was over in six
months."

Another new one on me. There are a million naked cities in
this story, I thought. "So you've never sold copies of that movie.
How about *It Happened One Night*?"

"I'll hafta look dat one up. Who's in it?"

"It all depends," I said, "doesn't it?"

ACCORDING TO WHAT few records most people will tolerate here
and now, Dr. Howard Slaughterbush (Lucy said that if she had
a name like that, she'd trade it for an armadillo and shoot the
armadillo) was a bona fide native Confederate. His doctoral degree was in "comparative political economies."

Despite his being a native, and accustomed to the highest living standard anybody anywhere knows about, Slaughterbush's
offices were in the shabbiest district of the American Zone I'd
seen so far, on the walk-up second floor of a creaky office building older than Bennett Williams's farmhouse, several increasingly
grimy blocks from the Wizard and Yolanda's wonderful bar.
There was nothing wonderful about this place, however. It
smelled like several generations of monks had taken a vow of

incontinence on the stairs and in the hallway. I hadn't even *known* that there were places like this in the North American Confederacy.

"I bet it's all a fake!" Will whispered to me as we ascended the stairway to somewhere other than heaven. "Conspicuous poverty, mostly for immigrant consumption, I'd guess. Given Confederate technology—cleaning machinery and chemicals, dirt-resistant surfacing materials—you have to work to keep a place this . . . this . . ."

"Film noir?" I suggested, pulling my felt hat level with my eyes and shrugging my jacket shoulders up around my neck. I thumbed the corners of my mouth like Bogey.

"Yeah, that says it pretty well."

"Ugh!" Clarissa exclaimed in horror as she accidentally ran a hand along the bannister and examined the resulting crud on her fingers. In her way, she's the cleanest human being I've ever known.

"That says it pretty well, too!" declared Lucy.

Will was right. It was studied shabbiness, strictly artificial, but just like a trip back to my homeworld. The letters in peeling paint on the pebbled glass of the office door said:

MAJORITARIAN SOCIETY OF GREATER LAPORTE

HOWARD M. SLAUGHTERBUSH, PH.D.

ENTER

Obeying the last line of the sign, Will turned the tarnished brass doorknob and the three of us filed in behind him. The joint didn't smell quite as bad as the hall outside. It was a good deal cleaner and brighter, with two big eastern windows admitting summer morning light, a well-swept hardwood floor, and the noiseless air-conditioning of the Confederacy (fans here work like the militia's electric flying machine) keeping it from heating up the room too much.

Nobody seemed to be in at the moment, although we'd called ahead. This place reminded me strongly of someplace else I couldn't quite recall. Bennett's right-wing collectivist philosophy had boiled down, in the end, to monarchism—one guy telling everybody what to do. Now, around the three unwindowed walls (except for the door we'd come through and another), bookshelves and literature racks were filled with badly printed tracts extolling the virtues of a system in which everybody tells everybody else what to do. I took a mental inventory. There were imported works by Marx, Engels, Lenin, Lennon, Mao Tse Tung, Fidel Castro, Saul Alinski, Pol Pot, Oprah Winfrey, Rosie O'Donnell, and assorted other left-wing locksteppers—even the widely despised *Ted Turner Diaries*—most of whom had been discredited long ago in their own worlds.

Then I remembered where I'd seen this kind of cheery political hopelessness before: the Colorado Propertarian Party had run an office very much like this one, back in Denver, when I'd begun the homicide investigation that had ended with my being blasted from Fort Collins into the middle of Greater LaPorte. In that sorry time and place, the idea of individual freedom that more or less governs the Confederacy didn't stand a chance. Not one person in a hundred would even stand still long enough to listen to and disagree with it, let alone nurture and fund it.

There, the urine in the stairwell had been perfectly genuine.

Here, socialism got the same short shrift—more deservedly so, I think, considering its dismal and bloody failures back home and the success of freedom here—and stood the same chance of attracting flies, let alone the enthusiastic support of enough people to keep this office building clean.

Suddenly, a man came through the door with a gun in his hand. "Four intruders?" Howard Slaughterbush exclaimed delightedly. "Where do you want your bodies sent?"

14: THREE DOLLAR BILL

> Want a clear indication of what the welfare state is really
> all about? Note that the barest necessities of life—food,
> clothing, shelter, and transportation—are all *taxed*.
> —*Memoirs of Lucille G. Kropotkin*

"Relax, relax!"

The man with the gun in his hand slowly lowered the muzzle of his unfamiliar weapon until it pointed at the threadbare carpet. The 'Com had told me he was an attorney—native born and bred—the second one I'd met in the Confederacy in nine years. He looked about seventy, cleanshaven, and had longish, white hair, combed back and plastered down. He wore a surprisingly American-looking gray suit with a sporty, diagonally striped necktie and yellow- and gray-striped sweater-vest.

"I'm afraid I can't resist doing that to all of my guests," he chuckled condescendingly.

I realized I'd been expecting him to say, "Away put your weapons, I mean you no harm." I never liked Yoda.

"It's simply my way," he continued amiably, "of demonstrating the utter insanity of every Tom, Dick, and Harriet carrying deadly engines of destruction about on their persons all the time. It's dangerous and archaic. What kind of evil, mean-spirited, reactionary hate-monger insists upon such a crazy 'right'?"

He finished his rhetorical question with four fingers in the air to simulate quotation marks, a gesture that had snaked in with recent immigrants and apparently settled down to stay.

I answered his question with a question I'd always wanted to ask one of his type. "What kind of moral cripple would rather see a woman raped in an alley and strangled with her own pantyhose, than see her with a gun in her hand?"

He protested, "But can't you see, if I'd suddenly lost control of myself, I could have killed you all!"

"Unlikely." I saw his chuckle and raised him a mild snort. Of course the instant I'd seen his gun, I'd pivoted clockwise on the ball of my left foot, taking hold of the rounded rubber grip of my revolver where it lay nestled in the sling. Now I let the .41 Magnum's big, hungry muzzle peek out the back of the sling at Slaughterbush. "Most of your 'guests' here must be pretty fresh meat, right? Bluebacks? Immigrants?"

He gulped hard, nodding absently. Apparently a lot of the same thing had happened at once. Clarissa had cleared her newly extended Webley and centered it on our host's torso, its coaxial laser making a tiny red dot on his solar plexus (brother Buckley, with his latest acquisition would have approved). Will had his big, dull silver autopistol out (I'd meant for days to ask him what it was). Lucy was pointing her gigantic Gabbett-Fairfax and her brand-new shiny Borchert & Graham plasma doohickey at the man's knitted yellow belly. I hadn't realized she was carrying both weapons.

Good for Lucy. If Slaughterbush kept the same kind of company he was, there was probably more lethal hardware in this room at the moment than our host had ever seen in one place before. The man stood there, frozen, like a deer in the headlights.

"Also, Dr. Slaughterbush," Clarissa offered, sliding her elongated piece back where it came from, "real people don't just 'suddenly lose control' of themselves. Unless that's what they *want* to do. Of course if you live by whim instead of purpose, steer your life by your emotions rather than your thoughts, you never really know what you'll do next, do you? Holly Golightly or Jeffrey Daumer. That's your problem, not ours; we're not about to give our rights up over it." Clarissa doesn't usually sound like an Ayn Rand character, but she has her moments. I could tell from the way she'd pronounced "doctor" how much she hated sharing a title she'd earned, with a specimen like this one whose academic credentials, given the respect his ideology indicated for two centuries of Confederate law and custom, might as well have been in sociology or underwater basket-weaving.

On the wall behind him, a little placard read, PROPERTY IS THEFT—PROUDHON. "I believe she's sayin' don't judge others by your own weakness," Lucy added, putting her guns away. I still haven't figured out where she was carrying that Borchert & Graham. "You're worried about what y'might do with dynamite, then don't have dynamite. Simple as that. You're worried about what y'might do with an autopistol, then don't have an autopistol—although I gotta admit that sounds a mite obscene—an' leave everybody else t'worry about themselves!"

Will laughed. "I'm a lot more worried about what you might do with a law degree!"

I wasn't sure whether he was talking to Lucy or our host. Both were lawyers. And—typical of many of the leftists from my world—according to several infosites on the 'Com, Slaughter-bush was also one of the wealthiest slobs in the Confederacy. Poor people generally don't have much use for socialism; they just want to get rich.

Gradually stirring to life, Slaughterbush stared down at his own weapon and muttered, almost to himself, "Oh, well, then, I guess I won't be using this thing anymore." Slowly, very deliberately, the man curled his wrist, bent his elbow, brought the gun up, put the muzzle in his mouth—

—and bit the end off the gun! He'd been faking being frightened, trusting us not to splatter the woodwork with his insides!

"Licorice!" I exclaimed before I could stop myself, remembering an almost identical moment from Hepburn and Tracy's

Adam's Rib. "If it's one thing he's a sucker for, it's licorice!"

He shook his head, speaking with his mouth full. "Chocolate. Very dark chocolate. And you're right, madam, I don't have a weapon of my own, precisely because I don't know what I'd do with it. And neither do you, no matter what you claim. Now please remind me what it was you wanted to talk about."

I could see her scowl. Lucy hates being called "madam."

LEAFING ABSENTLY THROUGH an imported copy of Thomas Merton's *No Man Is an Island,* Will said, "So what you're telling us, Doctor, is that democracy is valid because two people are *smarter* than one person. I always thought the measure of the intelligence in a room was that of the most intelligent individual in the room."

In a minute, Slaughterbush had rounded up a mismatched and worn collection of creaky folding chairs, but that didn't help me relax. Sure, I'd agreed to help Will, but this investigation-by-committee business was beginning to get on my nerves. Private dicks are supposed to be lone wolves—or old married guys like William Powell who take their bright, pretty wives along with them. Of course I'd have to be a thinner man, wouldn't I?

A poster thumbtacked to a wall and bled to the margin with pretty pastel posies, butterflies, and Bambi-imposters, carried a typical majoritarian slogan (maybe even the title of Slaughterbush's favorite song) on a ribbony band of music notation, "To dream the Impossible Dream."

I didn't want to sit down, or stay in this crummy place any longer than I had to. Bad enough it smelled of urine out in the hall. In here it reeked of the hypocrisy and cynical lies I'd come to associate with the left. Why do socialists pretend to be so damned impoverished, when—in the worlds I'm familiar with, anyway—they're always the ones with the well-endowed institutions and wealthy benefactors? Next question: where else but in America can you amass a fortune writing and performing songs that denounce money?

Slaughterbush responded, "No, I'm not saying that at all, Captain Sanders. That's strictly your interpretation. Although in the long run, the greatest wisdom is always to be found in numbers . . ."

Will winced. "Isn't that what I just—"

"Didn't you just get done tellin' us," Lucy demanded, "that, unlike right-wingers who believe that other people are all a little evil and gotta be watched, you believe that other people are all a little stupid and gotta be 'helped'—whether they wanna be or not?"

The man spread his hands and calmly replied, "As I told Captain Sanders, Mrs. Kropotkin, that's strictly your interpretation. I never actually said those words you're putting in my mouth."

"Yet," offered Clarissa, "you adopt a maternalistic, suffocating, overly protective attitude toward others, based on an unspoken and unproven assertion that the individual is the property of his fellow beings (meaning you), or the State (meaning you, you wish), or both."

"Yeah," Will put in, "if you never actually said those words— or never actually meant them—doesn't that lack a bit of consistency?"

"Consistency?" Slaughterbush looked at both of them unbelievingly. "What's consistency?"

"A little tweeting bird?" I suggested. "A wreath of pretty flowers that smell bad?"

"That's logic," Will corrected me.

Slaughterbush chose to ignore the witty reparté. "I'll tell you what it is. Emerson was right: consistency is the hobgoblin of small minds. It's no more than a sick, stupid, middle-class obsession that always gets in the way of moral progress. It means nothing. I've never been able to see why other people make such a fuss about it."

I think it was Lucy who told me once that this type—socialists who call themselves liberals—are all a little blind to consistency, logic, or plain old consequences, because they're psychologically one-dimensional. They're unable to "bind time" the way other humans do. That's because they're present-oriented, as opposed to being past-oriented like the right-wing Williamses, or future-oriented like most Confederates. She also said they tend to operate from whatever irrational epistemology happens to be trendy at the moment, astrology, numerology, Ouija™ boards, the Tarot, or the I Ching. Epistemology? That's how you know what you know.

Our host sure hadn't convinced me otherwise. He excused himself and went into the back where he'd come from. Maybe he had to go to the little socialist's room. Maybe he was snorting up a line. If it was for another one of those chocolate roscoes, I hoped he'd be a *good* little socialist and share. It was getting to be lunchtime.

"I believe that was a *pragmasm* we were watching just now!" Lucy told us in a stage whisper.

"A pragmasm?" I mouthed the question silently. I realized that I wanted a cigar, but there were NO SMOKING signs up all over the place—as if a little tobacco smoke could make this dive smell any worse. I'd noticed that, too, about the left. They claim to champion personal liberty—except in unimportant little areas like weapons ownership, drugs, pornography, romance in the workplace, and recently, tobacco.

"Sure. Any violent, convulsive eruption in which a person's basic principles are suddenly expelled t'facilitate the pursuit of a goal, usually an unworthy or evil one. That Emerson quote's a classic, along with 'That was then, this is now,' 'The perfect is the enemy of the good,' an' 'You can't make an omelette without breakin' eggs.' "

" 'For the children.' " Clarissa laughed. Will remained stone-faced. He was taking this a bit more seriously than Lucy and Clarissa were.

"A pragmasm," I said. "I'll have to remember that."

"By all means." Slaughterbush was back. I think he'd been spying on us, to hear what we'd say in his absence. "It will help you put off reasonable, commonsense reforms long overdue in the Confederacy."

Will was disgusted. "Doctor, all we really want to know about your politics is, would they allow you to blow up a building full of people or a hypersonic train if you thought it was good for your cause?"

The man rolled his eyes. "How dare you accuse me of such a thing, when all I want—all I've ever wanted—is to protect my fellow beings from one another and their own weak, sick natures!"

"But don't let us put words in your mouth." Will sighed and shook his head. "You know, in the culture I left behind, I was a police officer. That means I set my individual conscience aside for money, to do the bidding of men and women who were less brave, less bright, and less decent than I was—and who for those very reasons had found their place *above* me in the political hierarchy."

"I'm sure this is all very interesting, Mr. Sanders, but—"

"That's *Captain* Sanders," Will cut him off. "This probably is the first honest job I've ever had; I insist on the title that goes with it. Where was I? Oh, yeah: I also set aside my nation's highest law (which I'd sworn a solemn oath to uphold and defend, and then been informed I was too stupid to understand

and interpret) so I could deprive the people I'd promised to watch over, of their rights, their property, and their lives. All for the sake of those who profitted politically and economically by holding my leash. And all of them, Doctor, said exactly what you just said, about protecting their fellow beings."

"Yeah," Lucy agreed, "out of everything they own!"

Slaughterbush ignored her. "But Captain Sanders, if no one takes command, if no one passes the laws that need passing, if no one enforces them, civilization will be overwhelmed! You can't trust the people to take the law into their own hands! You can't even trust them to govern their own lives! Consider drugs alone—"

"I used to enforce drug laws," Will told him. "Drug laws amount to nothing more than government price-supports that take a drab, mundane agricultural product worth less than a nickel an ounce, and raise the price to hundreds of dollars."

He must have been excited, or he'd have been speaking in terms of Confederate money.

"And because the drooling idiots who pass and enforce drug laws are products of public education—and therefore abysmally ignorant of elementary economics—every time they hear that the street price of drugs has risen, they stupidly imagine that they've won some kind of victory, when what they've accomplished is to make drugs even *more* profitable and attractive to manufacture and distribute than before."

Slaughterbush shook his head sadly. "Have you no feeling at all for the suffering millions of innocents who, through no fault of their own, find themselves hopelessly locked into a vile, life-destroying dependency forced on them by profiteers interested only in their money?"

"Sounds like," Lucy muttered, "we changed the subject t'welfare."

Clarissa leaned forward on her chair. "Dr. Slaughterbush, we live in a country, in a version of reality, where everybody who was likely to destroy himself with drugs already has, removing himself from civilization and his stupidity from the gene-pool. That's the closest anybody ever gets to a drug-free culture. The sooner other cultures repeal the prohibitions that *created* the traffic in illicit drugs, the sooner they'll be where we are."

Did I say Ayn Rand? Make it Charlene Darwin.

"So you just let them die?" Slaughterbush appeared incredulous.

"You just stand out of the way," Clarissa answered, "while they willfully, knowingly, deliberately kill themselves. You refrain from distorting and destroying your own culture in a futile attempt to save them from themselves."

"Look." Will wasn't finished. "Crime was a solved problem where I came from; solved more than a century before I was born. People 'took the law in their own hands'—along with two pounds of Hartford iron—and crime was a solved problem." He looked to me for confirmation and I nodded back. "There was so little that even today we remember the names of the last century's individual criminals."

"Sounds kinda like the Confederacy, don't it?" Lucy asked.

"But solved problems don't interest politicians," Will went on. "There's no power or profit in solved problems, no opportunity that a politician can take advantage of. Richard Nixon—a U.S. president who had to resign because he was a criminal, himself—admitted it: 'I'd go further than the Brady Bill,' he said. 'Guns are an abomination.' And he was perfectly right—for any politician who hates solved problems, they are!"

Slaughterbush caught his breath. "But surely, Captain Sanders, a little reasonable, commonsense gun control—"

"The accurate term is 'victim disarmament,' Dr. Slaughterbush, and I'd appreciate your using it from now on, or shut up. You can't have a little reasonable, commonsense victim disarmament, any more than you can have a little reasonable, commonsense cancer."

I believe the man uttered a genuine, bona fide *harumph*. "The vast majority of the people will disagree with you, sir, once we've had an opportunity to educate them. And we strive every day for a democratic revolution to accomplish exactly that. As I'm sure you and Lieutenant Bear already know, in other worlds, majoritarianism takes many forms, ranging from representative republicanism to communism. Of them all, only pure democracy guarantees the utilitarian objective of the greatest good for the greatest number."

"An' the Purple Shaft for anybody who has anything that everybody wants," Lucy replied. "I could be wrong. Maybe he's sayin' two people are more *virtuous* than one person, or that they have more *rights*. Smarter, more virtuous, more rights: those three idiot assumptions are what any form of left-wing collectivism is based on—especially democracy—whether its advocates admit it or not!"

"The Purple Shaft?" Slaughterbush didn't quite scratch his head. "But I *oppose* inequities in the distribution of goods and services. More than anything, I'm an advocate of *economic* democracy."

"Meaning" Will translated, "you're against any form of economic freedom, whatever. I don't know how much alternate history you're aware of, Dr. Slaughterbush, but the best-realized expression of that philosophy—although I'll bet you'd never acknowledge it, even to yourself—is the China of the Red Guard, who murdered fifty million "landlords," or Cambodia of the Khmer Rouge, who murdered half their countrymen."

So we were having another political argument with an interviewee, instead of asking him proper, detectively questions, and this time, it was Will who'd started it. I glanced at Clarissa. She grinned back, appreciating the joke.

"In any case," Will concluded, remembering what Bennett had said, "and at the very least, under the system you propose, everybody winds up telling everybody else what to do."

Slaughterbush assumed the same expression I do when my hemmorhoids are bothering me. He tried to wipe it off and argue back, but he was too slow.

My spouse said, "The most important assumption of majoritarianism—and one that's true, but which people like you, Dr. Slaughterbush, always do their best to conceal or euphemize— is that two people are *stronger* than one, and that the one had damned well better go along with the other two, because there are more of them, and they can beat him up or kill him if he doesn't. That's what elections are all about, aren't they, counting up the sides in advance, in hopes of avoiding a real fight?"

I believe that was the first time I ever heard my darling Clarissa swear, however mild the "damn." And every time she said "doctor," it sounded like she'd discovered a fat, slimy garden slug slithering up her tongue.

"My dear," the fat, slimy garden slug waved a deprecating hand toward her, "you misunderstand me. Shall we just agree to disagree, and revel in the free expression of divergent opinions among polite individuals?"

"This isn't just a misunderstanding, Dr. Slaughterbush, and our disagreement isn't just a matter of 'divergent opinions among polite individuals.' Your political agenda requires that I get mugged, beaten up, or murdered, simply for exercising my rights. Mine, such as it is, doesn't make any such requirement of you. So how come I get to be an evil, mean-spirited, reactionary hate-monger all of a sudden? How come I get to be crazy?"

Slaughterbush started to say something rude, caught himself, and just sat there for a moment, speechless, as if it were the first time his harebrained ideas had ever been challenged. He glanced at a big, pointy quartz crystal in an upright hardwood mounting on his desk, quivering to channel with it, pray to it, or whatever he did with pointy quartz crystals. Maybe he wanted to slam it through Clarissa's pretty head. Here was another benefactor of humanity who hadn't even offered us a cup of tea—although I don't think I'd have accepted any product of the self-conscious proletarianism I saw around me. I was sure, from the sticky feel of the chair seat beneath me, that I was going to have to have my trousers dry-cleaned. I was also sure now that the people he saw were mostly immigrants, homesick and longing for the comfortable confinement of the Nanny State. I remembered hearing about Stalin's daughter Svetlana having to flee America and go back to Mother Russia because there were too many choices to make at the grocery store and it was driving her crazy.

"Look, Doc," I said, "What we would really like to know—and it doesn't have anything to do with your politics and economics or ours—is whether you've heard anything or got any idea who blew up the Old Endicott Building or sabotaged the tube-train yesterday." (Had it really only been yesterday? I guess Lucy was right, after all, we *were* having an adventure. I always lose track of time when I'm having an adventure.)

"Lieutenant Bear, how dare you—"

"Hey, I'm not accusing you of anything at all, Doc. It's just that you—I mean, we all—hear a lot about what's going on under the surface, down here in the Zone. I just thought you might have heard something . . ."

A shrewd look slithered across his face, like that garden slug of Clarissa's. "Well . . ."

"Yes?" I said, encouragingly.

"It's just the merest of suspicions, mind you. I hate to admit that I agree with the Franklinite Faction about anything, Lieutenant Bear, but they're absolutely right about the need for establishing a real government here in the North American Confederacy, and I've found myself wondering if they aren't perhaps . . . well . . . helping the idea along a little bit."

I nodded. "We wondered about that, ourselves. That's why we talked with Bennett Williams, yesterday. He had just the merest of suspicions about you. Got anybody else in mind?"

Slaughterbush reddened at the implied accusation. "He— that—well . . ."

You just had to love this guy. "Yes?"

"There's always Jerse Fahel," he said finally, folding his arms across his chest.

Who the hell, I asked myself, not for the first time, *is Jerse Fahel?*

15: BACK HOME AGAIN

> Any point of view that fails to assume—and accept en-
> thusiastically—that males and females will inevitably per-
> ceive one another as "sex objects" is simply deranged.
> —*Memoirs of Lucille G. Kropotkin*

". . . 'legislative intent,' " I said. "That's the phrase I was hunting
for. If Alexis de Tocqueville didn't say it, maybe he should have."

The home that Will shared with his wives Fran and Mary-
Beth—the design was Moroccan Spanish with an off-white
stucco finish and a red tile roof—was a lot like Will himself.
From the outside, the place was like a little fortress—if you call
an eight or nine bedroom hacienda little—with a few narrow
windows around the second floor, and a story-and-a-half arched
passageway in the front, with big, heavy wooden-beamed doors
at either end, wide open most of the time, that led into a large,
lush inner courtyard.

Within the arch, the hardwood-framed glass double doors on
the righthand side led into the house. Those on the left opened
onto Will's militia offices. Inside the courtyard, a covered walk-
way ran around all four sides of the house—offering shade in
the summertime and protection from the snow in winter—with
a matching covered balcony above. There was even space on the
roof to watch a Rocky Mountain sunset or jog around in a big
squared circle. It was from here, I suspected, that Will had been
launching pop-bottle rockets on the Glorious Second.

In the middle of the big, impressive garden—Will had palm
trees and cacti and mimosas warmed by infrared lamps when the
weather was too cool for them—he'd built a fountain in the
shape of a mermaid and a decorative pool (full of funny-looking
Chinese fish) with his own hands, along with a brick grill big

enough to roast an ox, and an oven with a blackened iron door for the veggies to go with it. He'd also built a big round redwood picnic table that would have seated twenty if the need arose.

A more-than-competent gunsmith, Will was also a carpenter, a mason (no, not *that* kind, at least as far as I know), an electrician, and a pretty fair country architect. He was a good husband and was gonna make somebody a swell daddy.

" 'Legislative intent'?" Lucy asked. "What in old Ben Tucker's name do you mean by that?"

We'd all agreed, when we got to Will's place, to leave discussion of our respective investigations until after we'd eaten. Which meant, of course, that we were now skirting the edges of his case by talking politics, instead.

The barbecue smoke drifting past my nose was beginning to smell wonderful. Lucy was listening to me talk (for a change) as I examined Will's big silver-colored autopistol. It had turned out to be from the United States, as I'd suspected—*a* United States—and was, by North American Confederate standards, a trifle puny ballistically. But it was very different and interesting, at least to me.

"I finally realized that that's what it is this morning," I told her, taking a sip of the Coke I was drinking until I finished playing with Will's gun. Clarissa was sitting beside Lucy on the other side of the gigantic picnic table—way too far away to play footsies with, regrettably—and at her side was Will's older wife Mary-Beth, who smiled at me encouragingly. More than likely it was a professional reflex. Mary-Elizabeth Kendall Sanders was an elegant five-foot-nine, maybe thirty-two, with lots of shoulder-length curly brown hair. She was slender—"sinusoidal" I'd once heard someone say about her—long-legged, with slim, capable hands, sea-green eyes, and a perpetual secret kind of smile. Even pregnant, she was all well-oiled intelligence and willowy body. A consulting ethicist—somewhere between a judge and a shrink with a little rabbi thrown in—Mary-Beth was shrewd, calm, and deep, with a quick wit and a subtle sense of humor. Until recently, she'd also been the hot pilot in the Sanders family and showed every sign of being so again, once gestation time was over, racing sport hovercraft designed by her sister and hand-built by both of them. If you're like me and tend to judge the character of individuals by their choice of weapons, Mary-Beth carried a plain, non-nonsense .41 Whitney automatic. I'd once seen her hit a rattlesnake in the head with it at seventy-five yards.

"You finally realized what's what it is this morning?" Clarissa stopped, mentally reviewed what she'd said, blinked, shook her head, but didn't try again.

"Why I hate to go into the Zone," I answered. "Why I always end up with my ears down between my shoulders like I was expecting something big and heavy to drop on my head if I spend more than half an hour there. And best of all, why I *don't* feel that way anywhere else in LaPorte or the Confederacy."

I paused to look at the pistol again. To begin with, it was solid, as if it had been milled out of a single block of steel. I was almost surprised—once I pushed the keyhole-shaped button at the root of the trigger guard and let the big, black, heavy magazine slip into my hand—that the slide came back so easily. Until that moment, I think I'd unconsciously seen this piece of machinery more as an item of realistic sculpture than a practical weapon. Glad I hadn't had to bet my life on that erroneous perception, I let the chamber round pop through the ejection port into the palm of my left hand where it was wrapped around the slide. Then I let the slide down far enough so that two little dimples at the back lined up, pushed on the righthand side of the slides-top, and then pulled it off the frame from the left. The slide then came forward easily off the frame.

"So tell us, Winnie," Lucy was watching me field-strip the pistol with patient appreciation. She likes guns for their own sake and knew more about them than any other woman I could recall. "What do the Zoners have that we don't?"

Turning the slide upside-down, I pushed the recoil spring guide and spring forward a little, lifted them up and out of the slide, then tipped the barrel up and took it out of the slide, as well. That, as the manual says, completed the field-strip. I peered into the barrel, but it was spotless. So was the standing breech inside the slide. Will would iron his skivvies, if they weren't already wash and wear.

I took a breath and exhaled, groping for words. "It may be a little hard for you native Confederates to take in. Will can back me up. It's a psychological condition caused by democracy, which you Confederates wisely passed up in favor of actual freedom. Back home—where the Bill of Rights got run over by Alexander Hamilton's steamroller, we never got a Covenant of Unanimous Consent like you did, and people are accustomed to voting on everything—back home, everything's always up for grabs."

" 'Up for grabs,' " Mary-Beth repeated, genuinely puzzled. "For example?"

I sighed and shrugged. "For example: although it's clearly my own goddamned business what I do with my own goddamned lungs, they decided they had a right to vote my cigarettes illegal. So I had to buy them on the sneak from the black market—at twenty bucks a pack! And if I hadn't been a cop, it would have been just as illegal for me to carry—or even own—a weapon, because they voted on it. Despite the absolutely ironclad guarantees of the absolutely worthless Second Amendment!"

Mary-Beth gave me another quizzical look. "Who do you mean by 'they'?"

"We, the goddamned people."

"How long since you came to the Confederacy, Win?" That was Fran, sounding very much like her sister, the counsellor.

"Nine years," I told her.

"But you still say, 'back home,' " she observed. "And you're still so angry about what happened there you can hardly stand it. You should start living here, Win, in your heart, I mean. In your mind. Think of the past, in the States, as a nightmare that's over now. Wake up in the Confederacy and be home."

"That's what I did," Will said.

Clarissa shook her head. "That's what I tell him all the time, myself. It hasn't done any good so far."

She was right. It hadn't. I felt a lot better when I looked down at Will's gun again. In this place and time, folks appreciate firearms the way people used to like cars back home—before those more or less got outlawed, too. This one, in addition to its other virtues, was either a bead-blasted stainless steel or had been given a matte coating of chromium or nickel or something. The legend, just visible on the left side of the frame ahead of the slidestop, executed with extremely tasteful restraint, read:

WITNESS

EAA—COCOA—FLA

At the bottom of the comfortable rubber grip was a single word, TANFOGLIO, which meant the pistol had been imported from Italy to be marketed by an outfit in Florida. The trigger, hammer, slidestop, magazine release and and thumb safety were all a nice contrasting black, like the enormous fixed rear sight. All in all, it was a classy piece of work, and I approved of it.

The caliber, engraved on both the right side of the slide and the barrel-chamber area where it showed through the ejection port, was 10mm auto, one of the better offerings for autopistols in any version of the United States, generating energy in the middle 600 foot-pounds—considerably more efficacious than a .357 Magnum, but not quite into the larger magnum revolver range.

"I personally corroborate everything my colleague has just told you, no matter how unlikely." Will grinned at me from the end of the barbecue grill where he was preparing lunch. He'd invited us all back to his establishment for some kind of special barbecue "experiment" he wouldn't describe further. I'd accepted, partly because I was curious to see how Fran and Mary-Beth were getting along. Like many women—and unlike many others; the whole thing is very mysterious and unpredictable—they were even more beautiful, if that was possible, waddling around with big fat stomachs than they had been without them. Of course it helped that Clarissa was their midwife.

"Probably worst of all," Will said, "especially if you'd prefer to think well of your fellow human beings, there were always thousands—or maybe more like millions—of drooling morons eager to rubberstamp whatever new or improved taxes their masters down at City Hall or the county commision or the state capital could think up for them to pay. A nickel here, a dime there—when I finally left the United States, the average slave of democracy was forced to disgorge more than half of his income to one bunch of lying, vicious, larcenous, disgusting, parasitic . . ."

"Slugs?" I suggested, Howard Slaughterbush apparently still on my mind.

"Or another," he agreed.

"I suppose I'm just as bad as the drooling morons," I admitted to our listeners. I was almost finished reassembling Will's pistol, and was looking forward to a real drink. "I worked for the City and County of Denver—"

Will pointed his barbecue tongs at himself and silently mouthed the words, "Me, too."

I nodded. "I suppose some argument might be made, defense and so on, for national government. Not a very good one; in the twentieth century alone—that's since 124 A.L. to you—national governments have murdered as many of their own people in this century as have been killed in war. Something on the order of 110 million individuals or more."

"War's a government activity, too, Winnie."

"Point taken, Lucy. So the butcher's bill comes to a quarter of a billion people needlessly, uselessly dead. Proving that government is vastly worse than anything it pretends to protect us from. It's a disease masquerading as its own cure."

"Hear, hear!" Will agreed.

I said, "But not even the Franklinite Faction claims that there's any justification for government at the city level. I know, I've been there. Everything that cities do falls into two categories: things that can be done better, cheaper, and more safely by individuals; and things that shouldn't be done at all."

Will laughed. "The people who run city governments fall into two categories, too: those who use their political power to accumulate wealth, and those (usually they're insufferable do-gooders of one stripe or another) who live only to control the lives of others. You always find the two of them locked together, feeding off each other in an eternal sixty-nine position."

"And you always find," I added, "do-gooders on the outside—taxpayer groups, reformers, minilibertarians—who say they want to 'cut back' city government, expose 'waste,' or reduce the number of city employees. But their kind—people who run city governments—don't need to be 'cut back' or 'reduced in number,' they need to be rendered *extinct*."

"So what," Mary-Beth inquired, "does all that have to do with 'legislative intent'?"

"Oh." I'd forgotten what had started all this. I looked down at Will's pistol which I'd reassembled more or less unconsciously and reloaded. My big revolver was at the grill "end" of the big round table, within easy reach of my host. It was a pleasant Confederate custom: I'd temporarily deprived him of his weapon— his personal last resort in the face of adversity—by asking to examine it, so I'd provided him with a "loaner." Nothing had been said about it, it was simply a custom, and had simply been observed.

Now I handed him his piece, holstered my own, and reached into the table's built-in cooler for a frosty long-necked bottle of Tres Equis.

"In a democracy," I repeated, "everything's always up for grabs. Without the absolute limits that were supposed to be imposed by the Bill of Rights, nobody knows how far it can be taken. Hell, they could just as well vote to confiscate your firstborn for lab experiments. But you can rest assured that somebody's always trying to take it further."

"Everybody," Will interjected, "has some kind of freedom he or she can't tolerate. Everybody has one little thing he or she wants to take your money for."

I nodded, "Exactly. So every conversation, no matter how trivial it may seem on the surface, becomes a political argument— openly or otherwise, consciously or otherwise—and every sentence ever spoken oozes with legislative intent."

" 'And no man's life, liberty, or property,' " Will quoted, " 'are safe when the legislature's in session.' "

Lucy said, "I see!"

"Maybe you do. You live like that all your life, with everything that you own or love constantly up for grabs, it's no damn wonder half the population's alcoholic or on Ritalin or Prozac. People who live in big cities can't stand the sight of one another—let alone the smell or the touch—because it's been pounded into them all their lives that they belong to one another, and at some level, they're all afraid someone's going to come along and collect!"

"What *is* a wonder, though," Will observed, "is that there aren't more poor fools up on rooftops with scoped, high-powered rifles, picking off random—"

"Voters!" Lucy exclaimed.

I clapped my hands. "You *do* get it!"

"Well, it's an interesting contrast," Fran observed. She'd been standing beside Will, supervising his culinary efforts. "As long as you don't have to live it."

"You can say that again!" he told her, turning with his hands full to give her a kiss. Frances Melanie Kendall Sanders—the younger half of the almost legendary Kendall sisters, had a voice best described as "silvery." Small and lithe, she'd had a somewhat boyish figure when I'd first met her (and probably would again), along with dark brown eyes and a freckled, tip-tilted nose. At five-three or four and twenty-five or twenty-six years of age, she had the most beautiful waist-length, buttery-blond hair I think I've ever seen, satiny skin, and enough energetic enthusiasm for a whole circus company.

She was a phenomenal shot with the Lawrence Shiva model plasma pistol that was always at her hip. For some years, she'd taught something called Intuitive Mechanics at LaPorte University, Ltd. Now she addressed me and her husband. "Let me see if I understand something here. If it's true, as you both assert, that the different political philosophies are really nothing more than competing lists of excuses for stealing from—"

"Or enslaving," suggested Will.

"Thank you, dear. Or enslaving productive individuals, then our view—the Confederate view that no one should be able to tell anyone else what to do—almost amounts to the *absence* of a political philosophy."

Lucy laughed heartily. "You can say that again with French horns! No 'almost' to it, dearie!"

"If you say so, Lucy. I believe I'll skip the French horns: the Confederate view that no one should be able to tell anyone else what to do amounts to the absence of a political philosophy."

"And that's the way it's been," said Lucy, "for a little over two centuries."

Mary-Beth held up an index finger. "Let's review, then, shall we? Confederates tend to be future-oriented, operating from a rational epistemology, rather than from organized religion like the right wing, or supermarket tabloid mysticism, like the left. We generally believe other people are neither inherently stupid nor inherently evil—the most frequently presented excuses for political oppression—and we try to exercise an adult, hands-off attitude toward others, stemming from our own assertion of absolute self-ownership. We endorse both personal liberty of a private nature, and unlimited economic freedom."

We all applauded. She put her finger into the nonexistent dimple in her chin and pretended to curtsey where she sat. "I confess I was primed," she explained. "I've been counselling unhappy immigrants in my spare time."

"Somethin' else worth mentionin'," Lucy added. "We may be the first *adult* culture in any universe. The official Confederate slogan—if we had official slogans—would be Admiral Heinlein's observation that, There ain't no such thing as a free lunch." Will and I looked at each other and grinned. In our respective worlds, the Old Man had been our favorite author. In the Confedracy, during the 1957 War against the Czar, he'd been the Hero of the Bering Straits, commanding a small but deadly fleet of hovercraft against the Imperial Russian Navy. In both situations, he'd been famous for that proverb and the acronym that went with it.

We all raised our glasses at once. "TANSTAAFL!"

"MASTADON?" I EXCLAIMED with my mouth full.

"No, mammoth," Will, Fran, Mary-Beth, and Lucy all corrected me at once. My darling Clarissa just sat there with a mouth of barbecued proto-elephant as full as mine, and a very strange expression on her face. There are a lot of things I love about her, but she is not particularly adventurous, foodwise.

She swallowed. "At least it doesn't taste like chicken," she observed. "I think I like it!"

I liked it too—I thought—but I'll eat a steel-belted radial tire if you put enough barbecue sauce on it. In fact, I was going to say that, but I realized it wouldn't be polite—and they don't have steel-belted radial tires here.

"Lucy very kindly brought the meat with her, in stasis, from the asteroids," Will explained, "and I concocted a special barbecue sauce for it. You know you can't just use a sauce that's meant for pork, say, or chicken or beef."

Lucy agreed, "An' you can't use it on mammoth, either!" Actually, she said "cain't," but you get used to Lucy's accent after a while, and besides, I've always suspected that she practices it at home, in front of a mirror.

"But . . ." I did like this barbecued mammoth, after all, and reached for the French bread and another several juicy slices to put on it. "Mammoth from Siberia, I understand—although fifty thousand years of freezer-burn sort of puts me off a little. What are mammoths doing out in the asteroids? Were they abducted by aliens or something?"

Lucy laughed. "They were cloned by scientists—mad scientists, if it makes y'feel any better, Winnie, because they're not gettin' near as much per pound for this stuff as they think they oughta—an' raised in the closed environment of a hollow asteroid I built for 'em. Makes y'think of Pellucidar! Y'gotta come out an' see it sometime!"

"In some other life," I replied. "I believe in *terra firma*. The more *firma*, the less 'terra'. I'll come out to the asteroids when they have a luxury hotel that flies there and back."

"I think it's time we got down to business," Will suggested.

Lucy agreed. "Yeah, we're burnin' daylight!"

I knew Clarisa disapproved of bringing business to the table—it's bad for those ulcers she cured me of nine years ago—but it looked like I didn't have any choice.

"Okay," I said. "Look at what we've got. One: somebody blew up the Old Endicott Building, killing one thousand, one hundred and ninety-eight people. Two: three days later, somebody sabotaged the tube-train and they still haven't figured out how many died in that one, but the estimate is eight hundred. Three: meanwhile, somebody tried to blow up the fusion dirigible *City of Calgary*. Four: somebody—maybe somebody else, maybe not—may have started poisoning stuff in grocery stores. Five: somebody *did* blow up my poor little Neova HoverSport, the only car I ever loved, with Lucy and me inside. And five and a half: somebody put that funny money out for you guys to find."

"That's a hell of a lot of somebodies," said Will, shaking his head. Like me, he was suspicious of coincidences. If the Confederacy was suddenly having a crime wave for the first time in two hundred years, we were both pretty certain it was the doing of one person or group.

I shrugged and said, "Maybe it is, maybe it isn't. Some of these somebodies have got to overlap. Oh yeah—and six: somebody's importing movies that Clark Gable and his wife don't like."

"Clark Gable?" Mary-Beth and Fran asked at the same time, their eyes as big as the appropriate cliché—now being scrubbed by an ultrasonic dishwasher in the house. "You're working for Clark Gable?"

"And his wife, Carole Lombard," I told them, trying to make it sound casual. "Think they'd like to try some of your barbecued mammoth, Will?"

16: TAKE ME OUT TO THE BALL GAME

> You say you never watch the 'Com like it was something
> to be proud of. Never look down your nose at the pop-
> ular culture, or self-righteously shun contact with it.
> How can you hope to change or preserve something you
> don't know anything about?
>
> —*Memoirs of Lucille G. Kropotkin*

The robo-umpire yelled, "Play ball!"

I began my usual mental inventory. All right, I've got my official colorfully printed LaPorte Patriots seatpad. (I've often wondered how the Patriots' batting star, Roger "Killer" Culver feels
about fifty thousand fans sitting on his face.) I've got my paratronic field glasses (they perched on your nose just like regular
spectacles). I've got the little radio built into my field glasses
(which double as shades) so I can follow the play-by-play on any
one of a dozen 'Com channels, including one based right here
in the ballpark. I've got my program—can't tell the players without a program—and I've got my tall, ice-cold, margarita. All I
was missing was—

"Craw*DADS*! Getcha red hot craw*DADS*!"

That was it. I nudged Lucy, who was sitting closer to the aisle
than I was, to signal the crawdad guy. She nodded back and
grinned. No baseball game—no Confederate baseball game, anyway—is complete without a flimsy paper tray of freshly steamed
crawdads disintegrating slowly in your lap. "Y'wannem plain
(steamed over beer), Louisiana style, or barbecue?"

"Steamed over beer," I said. I wanted to talk with the crawdad
guy anyway. He was one of the reasons we were here, instead of
grubbing around down in the Zone again. Interestingly, two of
the people on my computer-generated list worked here at None

of the Above Park (don't ask, it's a long story) and ran little import businesses in their spare time.

"Y'know, Winnie," Lucy jogged my elbow, distracting me. "I think they're tryin' t'walk Tommy Aurand!"

I peered down at the field. "I think you're right!" The truth is, you can follow the game a lot easier on the 'Com, but there's still nothing quite like being here, where the guy in the seat behind you can drop pickle relish down the back of your neck and the players look like ants.

Tompkins was pitching the first inning for the Patriots. Aurand was the other team's best batsman—the Patriots were in the third game of a four-game series with the Mexico City Aztecs (they'd won the first and the Aztecs had won the second)—and they'd better not be trying to walk Aurand. Confederate rules penalized an intentional walk by automatically turning it into a run, which is all right by me. I've always hated the bad sportsmanship of intentional walks. It was a rule I strongly approved of. I guess it goes without saying that no pitcher in his right mind *ever* hits a batter on purpose, in a civilization where they fight duels.

Just then Aurand smacked a ground ball into what suddenly seemed like a yawning chasm between shortstop and third. They scrambled wildly for it, but by the time the Patriots in the outfield got their act together, Aurand was standing on second, stripping off his batting gloves and waggling his eyebrows jauntily at the pitcher, who glowered back at him.

"Looks like it's gonna be one of those days for the home team, Winnie!" Lucy hollered over the general noise. I agreed with her. The Aztecs were tough, but I was pretty sure the rumor about their using obsidian knives to carve out the hearts of teams they'd defeated was exaggeration.

I split open the tail of a crawdad, thumbed out the tender,

savory meat, dipped it into a little cup of horseradish and ketchup and devoured it. God, it was delicious! Bear one, crawdads nothing. Licking a little salt off the plastic rim before transferring my attention to the straw, I took a long drink of my margarita. How could it be any better than this?

Confederate baseball—although at first glance it looks exactly like the game I grew up mostly ignoring back in the States—is as different here as anything else is on this side of the brilliant blue circle of the probability broach, and just as similar, too. As Walt Whitman observed in several worlds, it's *our* game, and it has a lot to tell about us as a civilization, for those who are willing to pay attention.

What makes the North American pastime different from baseball in the U.S.A.? Well for starters, there's the happy fact that artificial playing surfaces and the designated hitter are completely unknown. (Attention Kevin Costner, they don't allow pinch runners, either.) They've never heard of metal bats; the big controversy is between those that are turned on a lathe and those that are grown in a field and picked like canteloupe.

But the difference that makes a difference is that everybody does everything. Nobody specializes. It works like this: whoever pitches the first inning, catches in the second inning, plays first base in the third inning, second base in the fourth inning, and third base in the fifth inning. In the sixth inning the same guy plays shortstop—with the rest of the team rotating behind him exactly the way he did—and then proceeds to left field in the seventh inning, center field in the eighth inning, and right field in the ninth inning. If there happen to be extra innings, he pitches again in the tenth, then catches in the eleventh, then plays first base in the twelfth, and so on. Not much of a difference, you think? Well let me tell you it's a large enough difference to maintain my interest in a way that Major League Baseball never did at home. Instead of a multibillion dollar corporate exercise for a lot of overtrained, overpaid one-noters—including a stable full of infantile, nasty-tempered primadonna pitchers, almost invariably acquired at the expense of a respectable offensive lineup—it's a glorious romp for generalists where victory goes to the best all-round players. Believe me, there are still plenty of heroic catches and thrilling homers knocked clean out of the park. The double play is every bit as heartbreakingly beautiful here as it is in any universe. Everybody's strengths and weaknesses are displayed by turn, and there are no full-time catchers to bravely destroy their knees and grow old before their time.

The boys of this world's summer still wear knickers—and those cylindrical baseball caps with stripes around them. Pitching doesn't tend to be as high-speed or sleight-of-handy, so the scores would be higher—if they'd ever moved the pitcher's mound back, from forty-five feet to sixty feet six inches, which they never got around to here. (There's always talk of moving it to sixty-three feet, seven and two-thirds inches, the exact midpoint between home and second, but all it ever comes to is talk.) I guess you could say truthfully that Confederate baseball is a batter's game and that's all right by me, too. The best defense is a good offense, after all.

The second Aztec batter, former San Francisco Vigilante Mark Valverde, struck out ignominiously (three pitches, three swings, three strikes—sometimes you just have days like that; his average was .378) and Aurand had stolen third before I split my second crawdad open, steaming and fragrant in the noonday sun. The crawdad guy—wearing a name tag neatly inscribed E.C. and an impeccably tailored white coat—had promised to come talk with Lucy and me once he'd sold off the rest of what he was carrying. I asked him to save the last one for me.

Now the radio girls (yeah, that's how they do it here, and

always have; you can hear them more clearly and understand them better) were chattering about the third Aztec batter to come to the plate, Mike "Dugout" Dugger. A big, husky, prematurely gray fellow. Dugger swung the heaviest bat on his team—maybe in the league—and on days when Valverde had better luck at the plate, often swatted himself and a couple of other runners home. Personally, I'd always wondered why they didn't bat Dugger fourth, and get in an occasional grand slam. However, the reasoning processes of baseball managers are something that have never made very much sense to me. Twenty years ago, at a rare Denver Bears game, I told a friend that chimpanzees could probably do it better, but since I arrived in the Confederacy, I've discovered that they can't.

Dugger let the first pitch go by as the ballpark's invisible lasers scanned it from about fifty-seven different angles, measured its shape and speed and the direction it rotated, and called it a strike. The crowd sort of sighed and grew quieter. The batter settled down a little, hunched over, swung hard at the next one— a slider—and missed again. Strike two.

Lasers? Robo-umpires? Well, like everybody else, I hated the umpire, although I never thought much about it until I got here, where they don't have umpires anymore. People simply got tired of bad calls until in one game—Mexico versus Boise at Mexico— after six or seven stinkers in a row, the fans started sort of running in place where they sat (I've seen the video), making enough noise for an erupting volcano, and setting up vibrations that cracked the foundation of Montezuma Field from the nosebleed seats to the third sub-basement, and cost the owners several million gold ounces to repair. Umpires were replaced by electronics in the very next game.

Dugger suddenly raised a hand, stepped out of the batter's box, rubbed something on the bat, picked up some dirt and rubbed it on his hands, adjusted his antique cap and the crotch of his pants (baseball players' union rules require it, I believe), and finally stepped back into the box.

I was glad I wasn't down on the field. Some purists may not like hearing it, but I've never particularly enjoyed being hot, and I'd started going to games at None of the Above Park because— believe it or not—it's air-conditioned. Sure, it's wide open to the sky, but cold air tends to pool in any container, open-topped or not. It was replaced constantly in any event by a titanic bank of fusion reactors (Clarissa and I had taken the tour once) beneath the stadium. When the weather got cold—this is a civilization that heats its highways and streets to remove snow and ice—they managed to warm the place up, using radiant projectors, complicated air curtains, and electrically warmed seats, so that we got an extra six weeks in the two hundred-game season.

You can afford two hundred games when you aren't wearing out pitchers' arms or catchers' knees.

Now the crowd settled down even more. This kind of moment always reminds me of professional billiards or a golf tournament. I'm told it can be very different in other places—San Francisco, Chicago, Mexico City—but what I love most about the game in LaPorte is the quiet—or what the quiet means. It means the spectators are taking in the essence of the game, the awesome skill, the indomitable spirit, the . . . oh hell, I don't know. It means that they're all really paying attention—unlike a herd of brain-dead football fans making enough noise to raise Bob Dole.

Just then, the catcher called time and ran out to the mound to have one of those conversations catchers have with their pitchers. Speaking of pitchers, from the corner of my eye, I saw the margarita guy coming my way. Through my straw I made the traditional slurping sounds in the bottom of my tall plastic glass, then held it up for him to see. He turned out to be a different guy than the one who'd sold me my first margarita, and by happy coincidence, the other guy I wanted to see. As he bent across Lucy to hand me my drink and accept several somewhat fishy-smelling coins, I asked, "Jefferson 'Motherboard' Weller?" I suppose it was a stupid question, since his name tag said "M-board."

Heavily bearded, with longish, curly hair and wire-rimmed glasses, he glanced down at my companion: "Hi there, Lucy." Then at me: "Who wants to know?"

"Edward William Bear, private detective. I'd give you one of my cards, but ..." I held up my collapsing tray of crayfish and gave him an apologetic expression.

"That's okay," he told me. His voice was extraordinarily deep. "I know who you are: Lieutenant Edward William "Win" Bear, the first victim through the broach."

Win Bear, the not very private detective, apparently. I began to tell him that I wanted to have a talk with him when it was more convenient. Suddenly, he stood up to get out of our field of vision. He was just in time. Dugger had belted the horsehide hard and the damned thing was still rocketing upward and outward toward the left field corner. Of course Aurand was already beating feet on his way home, but nobody was watching him do it. The little white sphere that had everybody's attention rose into the flawlessly blue sky, rose and started to level off—*Booong!*

It hit the foul pole—which, rumor had it, had been especially constructed and tuned to make that noise. Dugger casually tossed his bat to one side and began jogging around the bases, with a surprising amount of away-game cheering to help him along. Fans in LaPorte are nothing if not generously appreciative of anybody's sportsmanlike skills, even when they're exhibited by the opposing team. I was a sucker that way for good defensive plays, and often find myself cheering for the other side—before I slap myself in the forehead and say, "Do'h!"

Three Aztec batters up, one out, and the score was already Mexico City two, LaPorte zip. Ah, well, back to work: I made arrangements with Motherboard to talk to him during the seventh inning, when he had a break. Now if only the Patriots could get one.

"YOU HAVE TO understand," said Motherboard, "I'm from a different world entirely."

He was reacting to something the crawdad guy had said. At age forty-six, Weller was an old acquaintance of the Wizard's. Both were engineers—he was software, Max was hardware—trying valiantly to catch up with the dauntingly advanced Confederacy. When I'd come here, the "science" of detecting was in its infancy, but I could see how the fact that it was fifty to a hundred years ahead in almost every other endeavor might be discouraging to somebody in a technical field. In the meantime, Motherboard wasn't too proud to sell margaritas to the crowd at None of the Above Park.

"My wife and I—" he said, "she was an Internet columnist and a self-defense instructor—we left the States more or less in disgust."

"Disgust?" I raised my eyebrows as I started on my second tray of crawdads.

He nodded. "That's right. When they rammed a Constitutional amendment through to permit an underage John F. Kennedy, Jr.'s election to the presidency, succeeding his father Jack, his uncle Robert, and his other uncle Edward."

"Oh, yuck!" both the crawdad guy and I exclaimed at the same time. Lucy looked a question at us.

"I'll explain later," I told her.

"I wanna hear that," the crawdad guy remarked.

We were at the top of the seventh inning, break time for both my subjects, and Derek Lile—a player they'd just brought over from some minor league in Wales, of all places—was pitching. The score was a humiliating five to nothing, Aztecs. I'd have turned my old fedora inside out and worn it on the pointy top of my head if I'd thought it would do any good.

The four of us had adjourned to the most interesting part of None of the Above Park, a big, airy concrete cave under the cheap seats, where folks could drink a beer and watch the game while leaning on a chest-high wall that looked out over the field. Or they could sit at a table, order a three-course meal, and watch the game on one of several 'Com screens hanging from the ceiling. Going to the park to watch the game on the 'Com: it had taken me a long time to learn that baseball in any world is a social event in which the game itself is the center, but not the whole.

"E. C." turned out to be Eads Carneval, forty-one, once the well-heeled, well-tailored chairman of something he called the Zeno Foundation, a quasi-freemarket Wall Street style think-tank financed by kelp-oil billionaire, Howard Hughes, Jr. Lucy was helping me interview these guys—in theory—but her attention tended to wander to the wall or the 'Com monitors.

"Permit me to be wholly candid with you about my past," Carneval offered. "I am a criminal. In a culture that *executed* Michael Millken, I faced life in prison for breaking a statute prohibiting 'undemocratic and discriminatory selection of personal investments for purposes of profit.' "

Weller's jaw dropped. The two had swapped their stocks-in-trade and were enjoying pond lobster and loony limeade, just like I was. Lucy didn't seem to have much appetite, for a change, and with the way the Patriots were playing today, who could blame her? "You mean you were supposed to deliberately choose *losing* securities?" Weller asked incredulously.

"Only a few," Carneval sneered. "Just to be 'fair.' Naturally, no one in or out of the S.E.C. ever defined "a few"—it seemed to change continually, depending on who it was they wanted to *get*. Given the opportunity offered me by your Investors Liberation Cadre—Millken's Marauders, they called themselves—I gratefully fled to this world, in preference to 'getting off lightly' in mine, with 'only' one hundred thousand hours of public service!"

Eleven years—provided he didn't stop to sleep.

Lucy wiggled my elbow, pointing to the 'Com. For the first time in the game, a Patriots pitcher had struck out the side. Zoughi, Chen, and Kearny had fallen to what tomorrow's sports sites were boringly certain to call "Lile's Wiles." Now it was the home team's turn at bat again, and like everybody here, I wondered—without expecting much—how they'd do.

Telling people how you got to the Confederacy was the small-talk that opened any conversation among immigrants. It reminded me of that song that Debbie Reynolds sang in *How the West Was Won*, "What Was Your Name in the States?" Of course they both knew my story—E. C. told me he'd heard that they were going to make a miniseries about it on some 'Com channel or other. The first thing that went through my mind was that I was damned glad they didn't have laws to discourage duelling here.

"But what I really wanted to ask both of you," I told them as soon as my blood pressure had gotten back to normal, "is whether, in the import businesses you run, you've ever sold copies of motion pictures like *Gone with the Wind, It Happened One Night, Teacher's Pet, Mogambo*—"

"Say, isn't that the African one with Ava Gardner?" E. C. inquired appreciatively.

"And Grace Kelly, if you like 'em freeze-dried." Weller shook his head. "Personally, gentlemen, I prefer Bettie Page." That was right. She'd made a movie or two here with the Gable I knew— Hey, I knew Clark Gable! She'd also made movies with Mike Morrison and Archie Leach.

"Personally," I told them, "if I had to choose between Ava Gardner and Bettie Page, I'd shoot myself to avoid the stress— and I really prefer blonds." Bettie Page and Ava Gardner were the exceptions to my preference for blonds—and for that matter, so was Mathilda May, to whom vast armies of men, young and old alike, shall and must be forever grateful.

"I'll say he does!" Lucy told them. "Say, isn't that Jorge Aunon comin' up t'bat, Winnie?" Aunon was Cuban, as were many other baseball players in every version of reality I knew about. Here, Cuba had been a part of the Confederacy for a long time and Fidel Castro had been a major league player, in the mid-170s, instead of a crazy Third World dictator. He was still active, I'd heard, managing a farm team under an all-weather dome in Saskatoon, Saskatchewan.

"So how about it?" I insisted. At that precise moment, Aunon "belted one upstairs" as they say, giving him—and the Patriots— a solo homer and spoiling the Aztecs' chances of a shutout.

"Is that all this is about, Lieutenant?" E. C. asked, completely ignoring the wondrous event that had just transpired and looking disappointed. "Movies? I'd heard that you were investigating the tube-train wreck."

Weller disagreed, but shared his disappointment. "I'd heard it was the Old Endicott Building explosion."

"Sorry," I told them both. "Our very own Greater LaPorte militia is handling both of them. With me, it's just the movies."

Suddenly, Lucy's attention was distracted once again, by something at the end of the concrete cave away from the field. "Lookie there, Winnie! Who does that varmint remind you of?"

I looked at the varmint she was refraining from pointing at. "No 'remind' to it—that's Bennett Williams!" Except that the man's taste in clothing seemed to have deserted him. He was wearing a loose denim vest over a loose denim jacket, with baggy denim trousers and what can only be described as platform combat boots. He carried a folded denim parasol. Everything, even the boots, was covered with snapped, zippered, or Velcroed pockets. The boots—the most conservative items he had on— were fluorescent lime green.

While I stared, open-mouthed, at somebody who actually dressed worse than I do, Lucy was punching buttons on her personal 'Com. I peered over her shoulder as Carneval and Weller looked on with amused curiosity. Lucy's call, apparently, was to Williams's home. I stepped back out of range as the call was answered. "Hello," said an all-too-familiar voice. "Why, Mrs. Kropotkin, how nice to see you again. Are we going to have another political argument?"

"Not hardly, not this morning, anyway. I just hit the wrong autodial button an' I apologize deeply an' humbly for disturbin' you."

"That's all right, Mrs. Kropotkin. Thanks for including me on your autodial list. I look forward to hearing from you again soon."

They both hung up.

"Deeply and humbly?" I asked in astonishment.

"I was right!" Lucy punched me in the shoulder. It hurt. "There's *two* of him!"

I guess I shouldn't have been surprised. There are two of me.

> To be human is to live by means of the artifacts that
> humans devise. To build a home, and scorn a weapon is
> hypocrisy. It's also a good way to lose the home.
> —*Memoirs of Lucille G. Kropotkin*

"Who the hell," I demanded for what felt like the hundredth time, "is Jerse Fahel?"

Lucy and I were roaring across town to meet Will, after a triply frustrating collection of experiences at None of the Above Park. First, we'd been unable to catch up with the Bennett lookalike in the forty-seven different colors of denim—although we'd found his entire ensemble, apparently discarded in a trash can that had been on its way across the parking lot to empty itself near one of the stadium gates. Damn things always remind me of R2-D2.

I'd had no choice but to run along beside it—vainly hollering at it to stop—while I pulled out a shoe, a vest, another shoe, the pants, the jacket, and finally, the parasol. Lucy, following at a more sedate pace, picking up each item of the guy's abandoned clothing where I'd dropped it in an effort to get the next piece, was trying not to fall on her elderly prat, laughing at me.

Second, the LaPorte Patriots had lost to the Mexico City Aztecs eleven to one, making the series so far two for them and one for us. Third, thanks to Mr. Ugly Denim, we hadn't been there to see it.

You could add a fourth frustration: my car having recently been reduced to hazardous materials and air pollution, and Clarissa's being unavailable because she'd had an appointment with a client, and Will off trying to locate another of his native radical suspects, we were using Lucy's car. It was one of a matched pair of enormous, antiquated, steam-powered Thornycroft hover machines (a century and a quarter ago, Thornycroft had been the first manufacturer of such devices; I suspected this had been his experimental prototype) that had been custom painted green-and-yellow paisley to match her favorite dresses.

Come to think of it, she and this extra Bennett would probably enjoy swapping fashion tips.

"Who is Jerse Fahel?" Lucy shouted my question back at me over the thunderous roar of the enormous, obsolete propellor blades beneath us. "I guess the first thing you gotta understand, Winnie, is that the conventional left-right political spectrum you're used to—with all the idiots who wanna be mommies (or be mommied) on the left, an' all the morons who wanna be spanked (or give the spankin's) on the right—the conventional left-right political spectrum doesn't work anymore, as a description of all the political territory there is."

I leaned over so I could holler in her ear. It wasn't easy for a man of my substance. The Thornycroft had duplicate controls like an airplane, including a pair of steering wheels, three feet in diameter. I was feeling a bit cramped—and terrified by the way she drove.

"This," I inquired, "is responsive to my question?"

"Trust me, Winnie! The plain truth is, the right-left spectrum never did work. I've even heard of political science professors throwin' out the responses t'their surveys that didn't fit their preconceived model."

So had I, when I was doing nightschool to get my detective's shield. The main victims had been Randites and Georgists.

Lucy continued. "The whole thing's a sham that deliberately makes no provision for individuals who wanna deal with others—an' be dealt with—as autonomous adults. There's no real choice at all. F'rinstance, there's not a single point on the conventional spectrum where you don't get taxed!"

"Confederate political science professors?" I asked, not really believing it. As we shot down the street in a wake of angry honking from other drivers, I was trying to examine the clothing we'd recovered, hoping we hadn't recovered something irrelevant—and really nasty—sticking to it.

"Professors from worlds like yours," she answered. "Remember what Franny said, about all political 'philosophies' bein' nothin' more'n competin' sets of excuses for stealin' from productive individuals? Well, that's where the stealin' starts, Winnie, with a crooked map that leads nowhere but straight into the Swamp of Kleptocracy."

Damn, I knew I'd heard that term somewhere before. "Kleptocracy?"

She turned to me—I wished she hadn't. "Government by theft."

I gulped. "A redundancy. And this relates to Jerse Fahel how?"

Mercifully, she put her eyes back on the road. "Well, most folks, tryin' t'be 'reasonable', tend t'put themselves somewhere between the extremes. But far from representin' compromise or moderation, the middleground between right an' left's another ideological morass. A better map'd be a triangle, with majoritarians in the left corner, authoritarians in the right, an' individualists who want no part of either, in the corner at the top."

I visualized it: a big chalk triangle drawn on the ground (make it the outfield of None of the Above Park; the Patriots didn't seem to have much use for it) with Williams in the right corner, Slaughterbush in the left corner, and—of course!—Lucy herself in the top corner. It made sense, and I told her so.

"Yep, that'd deal with the concept accurately an' efficiently—every known variation fits inside that triangle somewhere—if it weren't for those who try t'compromise between right an' left, despite the danger an' stupidity it represents. They crowd themselves into the middle of the bottom line, tryin' t'select Item A from majoritarians an' Item B from authoritarians, thinkin' they can reject whatever they don't like an' take the best from both ends."

"Eclecticism." I finally had hold of one of the spectacularly colorful pieces of clothing we'd recovered and was trying to see if there were any labels. I wondered if the guy'd had anything on underneath, or was wandering around now—no laws against it, here—in his unmentionables. Provided that he wore unmentionables.

"Eclecticism's best left t' paintin' an' jazz," Lucy said. "Y'see, there isn't any 'best' at either end of the spectrum, an' the line connectin' 'em won't bear the weight of the contradiction. It slumps, metaphorically speakin', formin' a *bottom* corner, turnin' our triangle into a diamond, an' what you find down there, is *fascism.*"

I frowned. "You mean like the Nazis?"

"Jackboots an' swastikas were only window dressin' for one brand of fascism, Winnie. I mean suit-an'-tie fascism, the kind you left your world to avoid. Look: majoritarians tend t'favor personal liberty—who y'go t'bed with an' what y'do with 'em—at the expense of economic freedom: acts of capitalism between consentin' adults. Authoritarians're the other way around—buy an' sell whatever y'like at whatever price y'like, but no unauthorized hanky-panky!"

"Yeah, I'd noticed that, myself." I'd also found a clothing label.

"Those in the bottom corner can't tolerate personal liberty *or* economic freedom. They're compromisers. Their takes on every issue are driven an' defined, not by themselves, but by somebody else—by advocates at the opposite ends of the bottom line. Left an' right define the 'reasonable' middle. An' because the compromisers sense, at some level, that they don't control their own opinions, they're more belligerent, more aggressive, an' more militant t'make up for it."

"Be 'reasonable' with us," I suggested, "or die. So who," I persisted, "is Jerse Fa—Aha! Lucy, I'll swear on a stack of *The Seat of All Virtues* that I am *not* surprised to find in the very first garment I grabbed, the following:"

MAYER CO. CLOTHIERS

5830 SOUTH SHERWOOD BLVD.

BATON ROUGE

FEDERATED STATES OF TEXAS

"This is fine gentlemen's fashion in that universe. There are tags like it in every item but the boots—they're from the Canary Islands—and the parasol, which came from El Paso."

"I guess y'found a clue, Winnie!" Actually, they spell it "clew" here. Lucy cornered by jerking her wheel, causing the Thornycroft to pivot on its center disconcertingly before it recovered and roared off in the desired direction. It's very interesting, anthropologically, to observe that Confederate drivers use the middle finger, too. What did surprise me was to find a little .14 caliber Muhgi, the size of the palm of my hand. It was a common kid's gun and could be found in any schoolyard or playground—if you asked nicely. The twenty-shot magazine was loaded, but there was no round in the chamber.

"He's obviously a blueback," I informed Lucy. "Somebody who thinks an unloaded piece is safer than a loaded one." When

I'd arrived here, I'd been astonished to discover that unlike the pistols where I came from, the safeties on guns here display a big red dot when they're *engaged*, that is, when the weapon can't be fired. To a Confederate, this conveys, "Warning! This weapon is temporarily useless for self-defense!"

"And Lucy?" I closed my eyes as she passed the equivalent of a semi tractor-trailer on the right.

"Yeah?" she said, as if she didn't realize how many years she'd aged me in five seconds.

"I think I've just figured out who the hell Jerse Fahel is."

She grinned. "Oh you have, have you?"

I opened my eyes again, carefully. "I have—he's what's in the bottom corner of the diamond."

"THERE HE IS!" In a bizarre feat of accidental coordination we probably couldn't have duplicated if we'd tried, Lucy and I in her giant, obnoxious, paisley Thornycroft, and Will in his old, battered, copper-colored Rockford, arrived at the subject's home at precisely the same moment he did.

Lucy had finished "briefing" me on the way over. According to her, Jerse Fahel was a prolific opinion columnist on the 'Com. To her, the writings she'd waded through indicated that he was "a bastard child of compromise," a centrist-collectivist of a variety often mistakenly labeled "populist." Striving to occupy the "militant middle" on every issue, he wound up combining the worst features of left and right, majoritarianism and authoritarianism. Under the system that resulted, one man would have the power to tell everybody what to do—but only in the name of everybody else. Lucy guessed Fahel believed that *he* should be that man.

He was also a mystic, with a screwball twist more characteristic of the trendy-beliefs of majoritarians than the grave pomposities of the authoritarians. (I thought about the stories I'd read of Hitler's obsession with artifacts and art associated with the Norse gods.) Fahel, like Bennett Williams, was fixated on a mythic past, but so much so that his mental processes would be limited, in Lucy's opinion, to short-term, range-of-the-moment reactions to improperly anticipated crises. I'd never realized that Lucy was a shrink and I suspected that she hadn't, either. I supposed we'd find out about her theories in a few minutes.

I don't know what I'd expected—Keyser Soze, maybe—but after all of the shuddery whispering about Jerse Fahel, reality was a real letdown. He was a slightly built fellow, graying at the sides with a boyish cowlick in the front, walking briskly along the sidewalk beside his private drive in a plain gray business tunic and trousers. Will had found his personal 'Com number (Fahel had been in the middle of a carefully timed exercise walk he took every afternoon) and given us a call once he'd arranged this meeting.

"Come in, neighbors," the man invited us in a mild, almost timid voice. It was three steps up from the drive, a stoop with a wrought-iron rail leading to an eight-paned door trimmed in white. The house was red brick with white accents, surprisingly modest for this part of town, although it was surrounded, like most of the homes here were, by several grassy acres; in Fahel's case, cropped level until you could play pool on it.

Inside, Fahel went to a closet, took off his street tunic, hanging it up carefully, pulled out a shapeless gray poncho, put it on, then stooped, untied his shoes, took them off, and replaced them with soft, comfortable-looking moccasins.

"There." He grinned up at the three of us with satisfaction. "It was a beautiful day for my constitutional, but now it's time for other things. I'm Jerse Fahel, and I'll bet you're Captain Sanders." He thrust out a hand.

I shook my head and tilted a thumb toward Will.

"My mistake." He took Will's hand and shook it. Then he turned to Lucy and took her hand, bowing slightly over it to kiss it. "My dear Mrs. Kropotkin. I'm very surprised to see you here, but nevertheless delighted."

Will said, "This is my neighbor, Win Bear."

He took my hand. I hoped he wouldn't kiss it. He smelled pretty strongly of mothballs. "The very first person through the broach. I'd like to think of you as my neighbor, too, Win. Wouldn't you like to be my neighbor?" He looked at all of us together. "Would you all care for some milk and cookies?"

Unanimously, we said thanks but no thanks.

"Then I hope you'll excuse the mess." Fahel led us from the foyer through a broad arch into a larger, brighter, immaculately clean and tidy room with snow white walls, beautiful, deeply polished hardwood floors, and big bay windows on either side, admitting almost as much light as if we were outdoors. It had been a dining room to begin with. Furniture, mostly white fold-ing chairs with canvas backs and seats, was scattered about. In the center, under a big, domed, vaguely Jeffersonian skylight, was a desk with three 'Com pads lying on it and several unfamiliar-looking instruments. In front of it was an enormous drawing board. I got a brief glance not at floorplans, cartoons, or home-made cheesecake, but graphs, pies, and flowcharts. Here I'd been thinking this was the age of computer-aided draftsmanship.

"The mess?" Will asked, rhetorically. We all accepted his offer of a seat, as he took his place behind his desk.

"I'm afraid so." Fahel looked genuinely distressed. "You see, I've been displaced from my offices by the Old Endicott Building disaster. I have no prospect of returning, as the building has been written off and will likely be demolished altogether. This is my home, and I'm having difficulty getting my business reorganized here." A door opened at the back left of the office and eight clean and tidy children, ranging from about eight to about twelve, trooped out in two columns, side by side. They were dressed in nearly identical gray pullovers, gray slacks for the boys, gray skirts for the girls. As the rest kept their eyes straight ahead, the oldest acknowledged Fahel with a respectful nod as they all marched softly through the room to the arch we'd entered and vanished through a door into the foyer.

"You see what I mean?" Fahel squirmed in his swivel chair. "How can I operate my business with the children rampaging through it all the time like a battalion of wild Hessians?"

"Your business?" Will sounded just like Jack Webb. He tended to react that way to weirdness.

Fahel opened his mouth, but just then, from a door at the other side of the office, there emerged a small, thin woman in a gray dress, about the same age as Fahel. She timidly approached and waited for him to notice her. When he did, she whispered something in his ear.

He rolled his eyes. "Another distaction! Very well, tell him I said yes, but only three thousand terabytes."

She nodded wordlessly and left like a little gray mouse by the way she'd come. "Your wife?" I asked.

"Please forgive me." He shook his head and added, "*Children!*" He sort of shook himself where he sat and went on. "You asked about my business. I'm self-employed as a time-motion analyst, mostly for corporations, although—"

"An efficiency expert," I said.

Fahel blinked. "If you must call it that, sir. My highest ambition is simply to apply what I've studied and practiced for more than twenty-five years to society as a whole."

"Whether society as a whole is interested in participatin' or not," said Lucy. She didn't make it a question.

He shrugged. "As you wish, madam. I am a scientist; you cannot offend me when it comes to conclusions I've reached by scientific means. In perfect candor, as a time-motion analyst and observer of all human behavior, I'm vehemently opposed to any and all manifestations of the uncontrolled expression of individual liberty or of the unsupervised exercise of economic freedom."

Lucy turned and gave me that look that says, "I told you so." Being the honest type, I signaled back with my eyebrows that indeed, she had told me so.

Fahel noticed none of this. "But I assure you all that if society were run with proper efficiency, no one would ever notice that they weren't free. They'd be guided by their leader to do only those things that are best for them, and would therefore make them happiest."

"But the trains *already* run on time." I couldn't help myself. I could think of lots of things that made me happy that weren't good for me at all.

"Lieutenant Bear, like you, I agree that liberty is precious. And like Lenin, I believe it is so precious that it must be *rationed!*"

Was that a sudden fit of temper I'd seen behind those mild eyes? A streak of violence? Frankly, I'd regarded the fact that he had offices in the Old Endicott Building as suspicious, rather than otherwise. Now it seemed significant, but I didn't have a way to tell Will and Lucy.

I shook my head. "So in your worst of all possible worlds, Mr. Fahel, other people are evil *and* stupid and must be controlled."

"If they aren't liquidated altogether," Lucy finished for me. I could still hear her saying what she'd told me in the car: "Watch him, Winnie. He may sling a lotta maternalistic, protective lingo around if it serves his purpose, but he'll be better at punitive paternalism."

"Which is why," I observed, only half aware that I was saying it out loud, "however incorrectly, you're frequently associated with authoritarians like Bennett Williams."

"You dare to associate *me* with Bennett Williams?" His eyes flashed. Now *there* was the temper I'd been looking for. Although I admit, after that particular remark, that I'd have thrown us all out on our bad-mannered keisters.

Good detective work, however, is seldom a matter of good manners. I'd gotten what I wanted, a little peek inside the man. Will stepped in. "Mr. Fahel, calm yourself. What Win said was, '*incorrectly* associated.' Nobody's implying you're like Williams, or anybody else."

Fahel blinked a few times and cleared his throat in an effort to regain control. "I'm happy to hear you say that, Captain Sanders. 'Incorrectly' is correct. For, unlike Williams or his brother—those overinflated, mealy gummed nibblers about the edges of the status quo—I am nothing more, myself, than a lowly and humble servant of Incomprehensible and Irresistible Forces of History, which sometimes choose, for reasons even I cannot fathom, to speak through me."

I guess that was a little more peek than I wanted. "Do they ever choose to *act* through you, Mr. Fahel?" I asked. (Mealy gummed nibblers; I had to remember that one.) "Never mind, tell me instead, if your forces *were* comprehensible and resistible, could you describe them?" He peered at me suspiciously, trying to decide if the question had been serious. If you can't blind 'em with your brilliance, Lucy always says, then bamboozle 'em with your bullshit.

He opted for serious. "You could say they're an amalgam of God, society, and family, for which I speak—all those entities with an undeniable claim upon the life and efforts of mere individuals. Inevitably, of course, the best institution to tend upon the interests of those entities would be a large, and unanswerably powerful State."

"Unanswerably powerful," I repeated. "With you at its head."

"Who else?" He raised his arms and turned to indicate the tools of his profession. "I am, as you put it, the only 'efficiency expert' in the North American Confederacy. Only I have the means at my disposal to determine what's best for everyone."

The door in the foyer that the children had gone through opened suddenly. Holding the knob, sticking her head through, an extremely large woman with a bun in her steel gray hair and a nose you could open cans with hollered, "Jerse!"

Fahel gulped and looked at us like a trapped animal, as if he wanted to be rescued and didn't know how to ask. Appeared to me like there was more than one unanswerable power around here. "Yes, Mother?"

"You remember what I told you this morning?"

He gulped again. "Yes, Mother."

"Don't you forget it!" She pulled her head in and closed the door.

There was a long silence. Then Will replied, "We really appeciate your straightforwardness, Mr. Fahel. I suppose you realize that by the standards of the culture you live in, you're a villain. Most villains aren't quite this forthcoming."

Trying to recover, Fahel smiled tolerantly. "Captain Sanders, you want to know who blew up the Old Endicott Building . . ."

"And wrecked the tube-train at Gonzales," Lucy told him.

"And put the bomb aboard the—" I stopped. I wasn't supposed to tell anyone about that.

"The *City of Calgary*?" Fahel asked. "Don't feel bad, Lieutenant. Why do you expect a trained animal like Olongo Featherstone-Haugh to keep a secret, let alone run even the shabby little enterprise that passes for government here."

"On top of everything else, you're a racist?" Lucy asked.

"A speciesist, Mrs. Kropotkin, technically speaking, and, as Captain Sanders has had the goodness to state plainly, a villain—at least from your point of view.

"But not the villain you're looking for." He stood, straightening his poncho. "I'll gladly swear to that in any terms you choose, submit to bodily response tests, or undergo hypnosis or truth drugs if it's under bonded supervision."

"Swear to what, specifically?" I asked him.

"That I had absolutely nothing to do with any of those events, whatever."

18: THANK GOD AND GREYHOUND YOU'RE GONE

Beware of geeks bearing GIFs.
—*Memoirs of Lucille G. Kropotkin*

The headline on the news vending machine standing just outside the Hanging Judge read:

SHOW THEM THE DOOR

Reluctantly, I inserted a small copper coin—vastly more than it was worth, as it turned out—and retrieved the dead-tree printout that had been custom-made for me. The paper's lead editorial was demanding, right out in the open, that every last otherworld immigrant who had ever escaped to the North American Confederacy (including yours truly, I assumed, although they didn't have the decency to mention me by name or give my business 'Com number) be rounded up and shoved back through the probability broach to wherever it was he or she had come from or wherever the machinery happened to be tuned for.

It didn't matter which.

The most disturbing fact was that it was NewHaps making such a demand, Greater LaPorte's newest, third largest, and fastest-rising events and comments service. They were locked, just presently, in a postively Darwinian struggle to make themselves Greater LaPorte's second largest events and comments service, and eventually Greater LaPorte's first. And another fact, that nobody had the power to do what NewHaps demanded, was comforting only as long as you didn't think about the effort being expended to create a government that *would* specifically have power like that. The only answer, Will and I believed (and Lucy and Clarissa agreed), was to ferret out who was really doing all this dirty work—and do them dirty. At this particular point in North American Confederate history, Dr. Howard Slaughterbush, Mr. Bennett Williams, and What-ever-you-call-it Jerse Fahel, were the principal—indeed, almost the *only*—native advocates of something other than the absolute individual liberty that characterized this civilization. Thus, we reasoned, they were the only ones who might wish to restrict that liberty in order to create what they would regard as a real government.

And yet we'd gone as far with each of them as we could at the moment. Will's militia people, with the help of about forty insurance companies, were still collecting physical evidence at the tube-train wreck, the Old Endicott Building, and, presumably, aboard the *City of Calgary*. So here we were, back—Will for his own reasons, me for mine—poking around among the various and assorted inhabitants and denizens of the American Zone.

Resisting a powerful urge to kick over the news vending machine and stuff the printout up its scuzzy port, I pushed through the double doors of the bar and grill I was part owner of, closely followed by Lucy and Will. Inside, in the same booth I'd helped occupy earlier in the investigation, my darling Clarissa rose and waved. Finished with her client for the day, she'd called me, saying she wanted to rejoin the manhunt. I squeezed in next to Clarissa, probably a little bit closer than geometry strictly required. She took my hand and squeezed back. "So how'd it go with the patient?" I asked.

She shook her head. "You know, dear, I've always wondered about that word, patient. Mrs. Higgenbotham isn't patient at all. She's almost beside herself, extremely eager to get on with life. But to answer your question, it's going wonderfully fine with my *client*, she's responding beautifully to the therapy."

Lucy asked, "What therapy, honey? Or does that violate client confidentiality?" She extracted a tiny silver pipe from somewhere on her person, stuffed its little bowl full of tobacco or something, and lit it with her plasma pistol, adjusted to an extremely low setting.

Her physician didn't even flinch. I love the Confederacy. "No, it doesn't, not at all, since you don't know who she is. It's sort of a new idea, Lucy—"

"Which Clarissa thought up, herself," I said, pulling out a nice Belizian Jolly Roger of my own and borrowing Lucy's pistol to light it. Me, I wasn't willing to bet Lucy didn't know Mrs. Higgenbotham. "Somebody notify the Nobel committee."

Clarissa actually blushed. "It's true, it was my idea. I wrote a paper on it last year, talked it over with a few of my colleagues who read it, and now, with Mrs. Higgenbotham's cooperation, we're giving it a field trial."

Don't tell the FDA, they'd soil themselves. Lucy said nothing, but waggled her eyebrows articulately. She'd likely had the same thought. By now, Will had heard enough to intrigue him, too. He'd taken care of ordering our drinks and sandwiches from the Wizard and his wife. The trouble with eating crawdads is that only three hours later, you're hungry all over again.

"Well, you may not know it," my spouse explained, "but of all the women who are basically given up on by fertility specialists, over eighty percent will get pregnant anyway, if they just gain as little as five pounds."

Lucy slapped the table. "So you're fattenin' her up, then?"

"No, Lucy," Clarissa shook her head. "She's a young, attractive, newly married young woman with a serious heart condition that I'm trying to clear up—and an unfortunate life-threatening metabolic reaction to most of the birth-control drugs we know about. She's certainly no invalid, and she wants a normal relationship with her husband—although he gallantly swears that he's willing to abstain if it's to save her life."

"Good for him." That was Lan speaking. Her husband Max the Wizard was standing beside her. Clarissa was beginning to attract something of an audience—*Tales from the Medical Crypt.* "What the hell is wrong with him?"

"Oh, he's all right." Clarissa grinned. "Although I wondered the same thing, myself. What I've done is isolate the endocrine activity that, in an excessively thin woman, 'decides' that she's experiencing a period of famine in which it would be dangerous to have a baby, and doesn't let her conceive."

"I see," Will told her. He had a growing personal interest in subjects like this I'm willing to bet he'd never even dreamed about having before. "And so you give her that—the hormone, would it be?—instead of birth control?"

Clarissa shook her head again. "No, that's still untested and potentially dangerous. What I do, instead, through a process of very deep hypnosis and other therapies of that kind is try to convince the body to send out those famine signals by itself, even though my client happens to be in the ninety-eighth percentile of the weight range for her age and height."

"And it works?" Will looked doubtful.

She nodded happily. "It's worked for six months, so far."

"And?" That was from somebody I didn't recognize, a grizzled old orangutan standing on a chair behind Lan and the Wizard. I learned later he was a fry cook and Mike Morrison fan who had adopted the name Hop Sing from one of Morrison's movies. Lan and Max had hired him with the idea of advertising: "Our Food Untouched by Human Hands." I could have told them Mr. Meep had thought of that almost a decade ago.

"I need another two months," Clarissa told him. "Then it won't matter—her heart will be repaired and she can have a dozen babies, if that's what she wants."

"Nifty!" That was me—and I'd already heard the story at least twice. I couldn't count the number of times Clarissa's ministrations had kept my tired old body alive—and I'm only talking about professionally. I like the approach they take to medicine in the Confederacy.

"Okay, then," Will said, "back to the detective business. I'd say Howard Slaughterbush is the closest thing this civilization offers to a left-wing ambulance-chaser, wouldn't you? We've discovered that he administers several socialist front groups out of the closest thing this civilization offers to low-rent storefronts, down here in the Zone. He barely scrapes out a living at it, according to him. Other sources say otherwise, with oak leaf clusters."

"He an' a low-rent, ambulance-chasin' son-in-law of his own three quarters of the spaceport parkin' structures in the North American Confederacy," Lucy volunteered, making little keyboard wiggles with her fingertips on the tabletop. "No doubt they feel socialist guilt all the way to the bank."

"In any case," Will continued, "he's still an active suspect, as far as I'm concerned."

I nodded. "While on the other side, what Bennett Williams wants, basically, is to displace his big brother as leader of the Franklinite Faction. I've done some cyberchecking, too—on the 'Com in Lucy's car. Their publication *The Postman* is heavily subsidized by Williams family wealth, doled out by brother Buckley. Until recently, it was neither widely read nor considered a very good place to advertise. Apparently, the current 'emergency'—and the Franklinites' public reaction to it—is changing all that."

"Fahel—" Will started.

"If it weren't for the fact," I interrupted, "that we found Williams's thumbprint on that coin, Fahel would be my choice as Suspect of the Month. He's certainly the creepiest of the three. You suppose he found a way to get Williams to—"

"I wish he did," said Lucy, "but I checked with Bennie while you two were sayin' your good-byes t'Fahel. We're gettin' t'be real 'Com pals. He swears he's never even seen Fahel in person or talked t'him on the 'Com or anything. If he has some reason t'lie about that, I can't figure it out."

"Cain't figger it out," is what she'd really said. Neither could I. I still had my list of people to interview in the Zone on behalf of my clients. Maybe we'd stumble across something that way— as soon as I had one of Yolanda's famous barbecue sandwiches. And that wouldn't happen until I did something else. I levered myself up from the table, excused myself, and headed for the little detective's room, located at the end of a short hall, opposite the little sidekick's room. I had my right hand on the door, ready to push it, when I heard a voice. "Lieutenant Win Bear?"

The hand slipped, all by itself, into the sling on my left arm, and wrapped around the rubber grip of my big revolver. I turned to see a tall, thin guy with a narrow face, wire-rimmed glasses, and curly reddish blond hair. "Yeah, who are you and what can I do for you?" I was a little impatient. I've always had a smallish bladder and it was at 105 percent capacity at the moment.

"My name is Lockhart," he said, in a pleasant voice. "I'm an immigrant like you and damned happy to be here, even though it's going to take me years to catch up on my programming skills. But that's not important right now. A heavyset gray-haired man out on the sidewalk a few minutes ago paid me a silver ounce to give you a message—and make sure nobody else was around when I did it. To tell the truth, I've been waiting twenty minutes for you to go to the bathroom."

"Okay, thanks," I told him, feeling funny sensations dancing up and down my spine. "What's the message?"

"He said you and Captain Sanders should meet him at nine o'clock tonight exactly where you saw him earlier today—and he asked me to give you this."

He held out his hand. It was a small piece of fluorescent orange denim.

As THE CLOSEST thing this place had to cops, Will and I had begun occasionally to feel more like Lucy's sidekicks than the other way around. When I got back from the bathroom, she was catching Clarissa up on the day's adventures, spending more time on the disastrous Patriots-Aztecs game than the investigation we were supposed to be conducting. That may actually have been appropriate, given how little we'd accomplished so far. She was also laying out plans she'd cooked up when I wasn't looking, to get to the bottom of this unprecedented crime wave.

"... an' then we'll go through all their trash cans an' see what we can find out about 'em that way!"

It wasn't a bad plan, actually. Government and private agencies thought pretty well of it where I was born, and we would get to it if we had to. It was just horribly messy, especially for a guy with a cast on his arm. In the North American Confederacy, it was probably actionable, too. Just because there aren't any laws doesn't mean you can't get your ass sued off for violating somebody's privacy. I let her finish—by now the spectators had departed and it was just the four of us again—before I told them about the brief, enigmatic message I'd just received.

"I know Lockhart." Will nodded, idly examining the small

swatch of outrageously colored denim. "He's a friend of Max's and good man—does some programming for the GLPM. Pretty fair shot, too."

" 'Deep Throat,' " Lucy said suddenly, snapping her fingers. "That's what we should call the gray-haired guy who sent the message. Wasn't that the name of the man down in the parking garage who gave Woody an' Buzz all the dirt on Jimmy Carter?"

"Nixon," Will told her, laughing. He picked up a french fry and waved it to underline his point befoe plunging it into the ketchup on his plate. "It was Woodward and Bernstein, Lucy, getting the dirt on Nixon."

"There wasn't any dirt on Carter," I added without looking up. "He was just the most impossibly stupid presidents we ever had."

"Better living through democracy." Clarissa was intent on her lunch—a specialty of the house Lan called "barbecue soup"— and didn't look up. These extraordinary therapy sessions were hard on her and left her hungry and tired.

Looking up from my sandwich this time, I spoke again. "Anyway, 'Deep Throat' has been done. Twice if you count the *X-Files*. Three times if you count the original porno movie—and you definitely should. On the other hand, from now on, I believe I'll refer to our unknown correspondent as 'High Colonic.' "

"Moved and seconded." Will laughed again. He seemed to be doing a lot of that lately. Could it have been the prospect of fatherhood, or just the fact that he was living in a free country? He took another bite of his own sandwich.

"An' unanimously passed," Lucy agreed. "If you'll pardon the expression in the present context. So whatta we do now?"

I shrugged. "I thought you had that all figured out for us, Lucy. I'll tell you one thing, though: I'm not going through any garbage cans tonight, and I don't plan to wait around until nine o'clock to go back to work. I came down here to the Zone again to talk to some people."

"Then," Lucy answered, "that's the plan! Before or after I have another sandwich?"

"Oh, *after*, by all means." Lucy could put more food away than any three men I knew. I suspected it was the secret to her longevity. "And I'll have a second one, too, with parsnip fries and an extra dill pickle. How about you, Will?"

THE OLD MAN lifted a knobby, wrinkled hand and greeted us. "If it isn't Will Sanders and Win Bear—the Husky and Starch of the North American Confederacy!" He laughed heartily at his own joke. He'd probably been waiting to make it since we'd called him to set up this appointment.

I didn't laugh. It was way too late in the day, and I wouldn't be finished living through it until well after nine. Will said, "R. A. Paulchinsky? We'd like to have a word with you, if we might, sir."

"So you said. Don't you 'sir' me, sonny. Come right on in! It's good to put a voice to all these stories I've been hearing lately. Knew your faces from the 'Com before you called. And it's good to know somebody's investigating all these hideously criminal acts that are being blamed on us bluebacks!"

Technically, he was a "bluefinger." Sixty-eight-year-old former "Congressbeing," R. A. Paulchinsky (Demopublican, E. Montana) called himself a "Constitutionalist of the Ancient Right," according to the 'Com. We'd been directed here by people who had a lot to say about the old man, mostly good, and some of it pretty funny.

When we saw him first, he was sitting in the open door of his rather narrow and antiquated garage (this was the Zone, after all), using a laser pen to burn serial numbers into the plastic backside of a small figure he'd just finished painting or dyeing in a coffee can—hence the blue fingers. It was a relatively strange thing to do, I thought, but I assumed he had his reasons. When he'd finished, he put the figure into a carton that already held several dozen other figures like it.

But not identical, which, it turned out, was the point.

A bit like Papa Karl LeMat, Paulchinsky was considered something of a social leader in the American Zone. One source referred to him as an "elder statelessman." At one time, in the world he'd come from, he'd even been a presidential candidate, or so we were told, for the now-defunct Fascio-Conservative Party. It had been one of the top two at the time.

"That's right," Paulchinsky confirmed the story when we asked him about it. "Damned stupid name for a political party, but we were stuck with it from the 1930s—that's the 150s, here—when fascism was all the rage. Sometimes a tradition can be carried too far."

He was sitting in a badly worn straight-backed kitchen chair— vinyl plastic and chromed tubing—behind a worktable made from a pair of sawhorses and a paint-splashed sheet of plywood. He picked up another little doll by a hank of acrylic hair sprouting from its head. The hair was almost as long as the doll itself. "I got thirty-five percent of the vote—at least that's what was publicly reported. Our exit polls said something else altogether. Something that sounded a lot like, 'Hail to the Chief.' " Holding it by the hair, he dipped the doll in a different can, brown this time. "Say, wouldn't you boys like to sit down and have a glass of lemonade?" He raised his voice. "Agnes! Would you please bring these boys some lemonade?" "

In a couple minutes Agnes appeared, a plain, plump, careworn woman about the congressbeing's age. She looked a lot like Mary

Lincoln to me. She set the glasses on the table, looked at Will and me as if she'd found us in her garden—under a rock—and went back into the house without a word.

"Don't mind Agnes," Paulchinsky said. "She doesn't like it here, and probably never will. She doesn't understand or care what makes it so desirable to live in a free country. She thought she was going to be the First Lady."

Will nodded, doing his Jack Webb number again. I suppose I really should have been the one asking the questions, but it had worked out this way and you have to respect that, sometimes. Lucy and Clarissa had stayed in the car, punching 'Com buttons, seeing what they could find out about our other prospects.

My partner cleared his throat. He hadn't lifted his glass or sat down—there were two other beat-up kitchen chairs in the garage, bearing no resemblance to each other or the one Paulchinsky occupied. I'd chosen the cleaner of the two and picked up a glass of lemonade. "Sir," Will said, "we were told kind of a strange story about the reason you left your version of America . . ."

"And now you're embarrassed to repeat it? Well, I don't blame you, son—sit down, will you? You're giving my neck a cramp! That's another reason Agnes is mad at me. We had to refugee out on account of trumped-up charges of 'animal sexual abuse.' "

"What?" We said it at the same time; I couldn't help myself.

"Sure." He laughed. "Somebody thoughtfully manufactured messages from me on alt.sex.bestiality.hamsters.ducttape. It's exactly like backing the wrong prayerbook during the reign of Cromwell. Or patting the wrong fannies in the universes you boys came from: Tailhook, Bob Packwood, John Tower—I do my homework, too, you know."

"I guess you do." Somehow, we'd all managed, lately, to absorb the histories of a thousand different worlds. It was probably good for us, but it hurt our heads sometimes.

Paulchinsky laughed again. Here was a guy who could obviously appreciate a joke, even one on himself. It probably helped a lot that he was here, instead of wherever it was he came from. "Understand, gents, that 'animal sexual abuse' is currently the most convenient transgression in my culture to accuse your political enemies of. Used to be children before they formed their own union. Nobody really gives a damn about the animals, mind you, any more than they gave a damn about the patted fannies or the prayerbooks. The criminal charges were brought by my antagonists, the Socio-Liberal Party, as soon as the election was over. Hell, most of them keep sheep and other barnyard critters around, themselves, for purposes I always found suspicious. But they didn't want any questions asked about the outcome of the election."

"I see," I said. I didn't know if I'd ever get used to being recognized this way. "And your wife is mad because—"

"Oh, hell, Agnes knows perfectly well that I didn't do it. For one thing, I'm allergic to wool. And for another, I had a personal problem back there and then that couldn't be cured because Viagra was illegal. Not to mention the fact that we lived in an apartment in the capital city—Philadelphia—and didn't have room for a goldfish, let alone a sheep or a llama. She's just mad because I got accused, is all, and on account of that, she never got to cut the ribbon on a bridge or break a bottle of champagne across the bow of a ship. I figure she'll get over it in a couple of decades."

"I'm glad to hear it," Will said. "So what's with all these little figurines?" I could tell from his voice that he thought they could be a lot weirder than making love to a llama.

Paulchinsky laughed again. "Man's gotta earn a living, Captain.

Could be you're too young, or from the wrong world. You remember the craze, back in the sixties—the late one hundred and eighties—over these little plastic dolls with hair they called trolls?"

It clicked in my head. "Sure I do! About the same time you could buy greeting cards and posters of sad little orphan kids with tears in their gigantic eyes!"

"There y'go, Lieutenant, you've got a Keane memory on you! Well, I managed t'stumble onto a whole warehouse full of these damned things and broached 'em over here. Nobody ever saw 'em here before, so they're fresh and popular as hell. I dye their hair, braid it or sprinkle sparkles in it, paint 'em different colors, put stars or hearts or circles around their little plastic bellybuttons—I keep careful track of all the combinations so I won't repeat 'em—burn serial numbers into their little asses, and sell 'em for a thousand times what they cost me!"

And here I'd wasted all this time becoming a private detective. Oh, well.

19: IT'S SISTER JENNIE'S TURN TO THROW THE BOMB

> If the backside pockets of your jeans are your "hip"
> pockets, does that make the ones in front "un-hip"?
> Then why is it that it's the ones in back that are *square*?
> —*Memoirs of Lucille G. Kropotkin*

It started as we headed down the walk from Paulchinsky's house.
All he'd ever imported were the little plastic trolls. If we'd been
after him for the other thing, all the deadly sabotage, he'd have
had the best alibi of anybody so far. He was being treated by a
Healer friend of Clarissa's for severe arthritis in his hips and
lower back and wouldn't be able to get up from the chair he was
sitting in, without grudging help from Agnes, for another several
months.

Back home, he could have been expected to die that way. I
wondered how they'd managed to get him here.

Even in this relatively impecunious neighborhood, homes were
large by Stateside standards I was used to, if not in number of
rooms, then in size. The yards in front of them were huge and
it was a long walk to the street. Halfway between Paulchinsky's
open garage door and Lucy's Thornycroft, I suddenly heard
something whizz by me, amazingly like the big "bumblebee" in
Peril at End House. I'd been shot at before, more than once, and
I knew that sound. So did Will.

"Down!" we advised each other at the top of our lungs, as
two more high-velocity bullets whizzed by overhead, and at the
same time, a finger-sized smoking hole suddenly appeared in the
trunk of a juniper tree beside me. The first thing that crossed
my mind, perversely, was how good it smelled: Xmas in July,
whaddya know! Somebody was using a laser on us, and a re-

spectably powerful one, at that. By the time I hit the ground I had my sixgun out and Will had his big silver Witness in his hand, looking for somebody to shoot back at. We were both trying to hide behind the same two-foot plaster garden gnome—probably Paulchinsky's way of advertising—looking for whoever was shooting at us.

"*Fffffft!*" This time both of us saw the brilliant flash of what had to be a suppressor-equipped weapon. My .41 Magnum slapped me hard in the palm as it bellowed and went off, a basketball-sized cloud of blue-pink flame dazzling me for an instant, even in broad daylight. It's a damned difficult gun to shoot one-handed—painful, too.

At the same time, I heard a sharp double crack as Will sent a pair of his 175-grain, 10-millimeter Winchester Silvertips in the same direction, at a big gray Studebaker RoadCruiser parked at the end of the block.

At the moment I fired, I heard glass-shattering noises as the RoadCruiser's side windows disappeared in a glittery shower. They'd be a while growing those back. No screaming or anything, though. How disappointing. The enormous road machine rose slowly on its skirt and began crab-walking toward us gradually, more gunfire coming from just over the bottom edges of its side windows. Abruptly, the gnome's plaster head exploded as something hit it, I don't know what, bullet or laser. Somehow, I managed to keep the shower of gravel out of my eyes, but I knew I'd be spitting sand the rest of the week.

I fired again, and so did Will, at the car doors behind which the shooters had to be crouching. My big .41 went *Boom!*, destroying the Studebaker's left headlight. Will's 10 millimeter went *Bamm!*, tearing a ragged furrow across its roof. We both needed to relax and shoot straighter.

KABOMMMMM! I jumped three feet, nearly getting plugged

by the jokers in the Studebaker in the process. Bullets fizzed and whistled all around me. The ungodly noise had come from Paulchinsky's garage workshop, where, thanks no doubt to recoil, he was now pointing an enormous, smoking revolver at the ceiling.

"Four-fifty-four Cassull!" the former congressbeing shouted at us, clearly enjoying himself, "Sorry!"

Will responded, "Shit!"

By now, there was gunfire coming from Lucy's car, too, as she and Clarissa got into the act, big booms from the Gabbett-Fairfax, sound-barrier shattering cracks from the .11 Webley. We all kept firing and the Studebaker kept coming, slowly, until its skirt bumped against another car parked at the curb. Both its sideways-forward motion and the gunfire coming from it had stopped.

Nevertheless, I counted a careful ten. Then Will and I stood up, my knees making noises like breaking a handful of celery stalks. We approached the RoadCruiser carefully, from behind as much cover as we could manage. Climbing onto the skirt, we found lots of blood inside, all over the seats, floor, and windows, and four injured individuals, a chimpanzee, a gorilla, and two humans. The gorilla had been driving. He wasn't only merely dead, as the song goes, he was really quite sincerely dead. A heavy .41 Magnum slug from ear to ear through the skull is bound to have that effect. The endangered species crazies back home would have had a conniption fit.

Slumped in the backseat, one of the humans was in pretty much the same condition as the gorilla, with a hole in his torso you could have thrown a hadrosaur through. You couldn't just see daylight through it, you could read the newspaper. The former congressbeing's contribution to the fracas, I figured. Even Lucy's antique handcannon couldn't do something like that.

The other human stirred and moaned. It was hard to see how

badly he was injured; he was covered with the gorilla's blood and brains. I reached through the front window to take a big enameled weapon from his hand. It was a White-Westinghouse WRT21GRB LaserMatic, according to the label. The conventional silenced autopistol used to start the fight lay on the rear seat floor where the chimpanzee had apparently dropped it. He was conscious, but not feeling very well.

"Toldja!" The human in the front seat was apparently addressing the chimpanzee. "Toldja!"

"You . . . *blagzerk!* . . . told me . . . *frumpiltch!?*" Either the chimpanzee's wrist synthesizer had taken some damage, or his wrist had.

"Oh, it's you, dickhead," sighed the human, disappointed. "It was my partner Smedley I told. We usta hit banks together in the Alaskan S.S.R., see? I told him stuff like that was too risky here. Back home the cops have rules they gotta follow—but here, the civilians'll fucking kill you!"

"Damn straight!" Will agreed with some enthusiasm. "Look at this!" He was sitting with me on the top of the Studebaker's skirt. Clarissa and Lucy were running toward us from the Thornycroft, the former with her little black bag in hand. Will lifted up his cowboy-booted left foot and showed me a half-inch hole burned from one side of the rebated riding heel to the other. Burned leather smells horrible.

"WELL," THE MAN said, "I think we're just about done, here."

There were two of them, a husband and a wife. They had nylon badge flippers hanging from their tunic pockets, but they weren't wearing uniforms and they weren't cops. They had no power of any kind to detain anybody for anything—but it was a pretty good idea to stick around until they said you could go. It was their job to see that things had been done according to long-established Confederate custom and the Covenant of Unanimous Consent—and to make sure the right person or persons had gotten themselves shot.

They were the Civil Liberties Association of Greater LaPorte. Long may they wave.

He was tall and thin, with a pair of electric needle-shooters like Clarissa's at his waist, carried butt-forward like Wild Bill Hickcock. I couldn't tell whether his hair was blond or white. He wore glasses—the mark of a newcomer, since vision problems are dealt with here using drugs, gene therapy, and particle-beam surgery—and had a voice that would have worked well on the radio. She called him, "Van." He called her, "Dear." She was shorter, a shapely redhead with a pageboy hairdo and a constantly quizzical expression. Her voice was surprisingly deep. She wore a plasma pistol just like Lucy's, in a shoulder holster, and a slim dagger in one of her boots.

"Then we can go?" I asked, trying to get Will's attention. He was calling his wives, letting them know what had happend, before our friends in the so-called news media got it all wrong and sent them both into premature labor.

The bodies, living and otherwise, were about to be hauled off, the latter to Griswold's, which had pretty good cold storage facilities, the former to one of the many small infirmaries that people in the Confederacy support instead of hospitals, the general view being that hospitals are great places to catch diseases that you'd never even hear of, otherwise. The surviving human and his simian coconspirator would do their recuperating in handcuffs and leg-irons at the Badguy Motel (which they would pay for themselves), until they were deemed fit, not to face criminal trial, but to get their bald and furry asses sued off, respectively, by any and all of those who felt they'd been damaged by this botched-up little raid. Paulchinsky would probably get a new gnome out of it, and a tree surgeon to take a look through the peephole in his juniper.

The CLA people both nodded. "I've talked with two dozen neighbors who saw the whole thing go down," said the CLA man. "It's perfectly clear what happened here—the first drive-by in Confederate history—and I intend to say so in my report. The only question that remains is why they did it, and that's outside my proper area of concern. You must have made somebody pretty mad, Lieutenant."

"Just talented." I shrugged. "And it's the second drive-by. The first one was nine years ago."

He went on. "The gorilla and the chimpanzee have criminal records that go back almost to the Gallatin Administration, and Forsythe's Security says they've had their eye on the other two since they came through the broach a month or two ago."

The CLA woman told me, "I guess the only thing you have to do now, Lieutenant Bear, is to accept these." In ten thousand other cultures, she would have added, "and sign for them." Or never made the offer at all, of course. In one hand she held out a black mesh bag full of weapons. Pretty good muscles for a girl. I was impressed.

Counting extra magazines for the ordinary powder-burners, and spare power cells for the laser, the damned thing probably weighed thirty pounds. Whenever you win a duel in the North American Confederacy—and I guess they were saying that this qualified—you're expected to take the other guy's toys. It's the custom. Matter of fact, that's how I'd wound up carrying that federal agent's Browning High Power and keeping Tricky Dick Milhouse's Rezin in a showcase at home.

"Remember, now," she said, giving me a big smile, "you're

supposed to share with your little friends." The tradition was that anyone who'd participated in a gunfight—on what was later declared to be the goodguy side—was supposed to receive some token of the victory of niceness over nastiness. Or a cut of the booty, if you want to look at it that way.

In her other hand she held out a stack of small plastic zipper bags, that innovation in evidence-gathering I believe I'm responsible for. Inside each bag lay a big, thick, heavy, two-ounce platinum coin, smeared with human, chimpanze, and gorilla blood and embossed deeply with the easily recognizable likeness of H. L. Mencken, the martyred former president of the Confederacy. Old Henry had fought a duel with his own vice president and won—then been assassinated by the vice president's mother.

I love this place.

"The Studebaker is yours, too, Lieutenant, if you want it," said the CLA woman. "So are these, to be divided, like the car and weapons, five ways I believe." With a look, she indicated the garage door—closed now, and locked, I suspected—of our most recent interviewee. I grinned, wondering how Congressbeing Paulchinsky's discontented wife Agnes would feel about living in the Confederacy once she'd received a fifth of the value of a big, expensive, and only slightly bullet-riddled hovercar and four platinum coins worth a little less apiece than a kilobuck back home. Here, where money went a hell of a lot further, they were worth a hell of a lot more.

I'd been through something like this once before. I knew what it was. I knew what it meant. And I didn't like it one bit. Badguys are few and far between in the North American Confedracy, so there isn't much of a criminal labor pool available for designer dirtywork. Nevertheless, somebody who didn't wish to soil his very own dainty little fingers had enlisted these goons, these gross incompetents—because there simply wasn't anybody else to hire—and paid them each the equivalent of three or four month's salary, to kill us as dead as they could.

"We'll take the car," I told her suddenly, "for about ten minutes. Then maybe the congressbeing can find a use for it. Help me look for something, will you? Hey, Will! Lucy! Let's check out the trunk of this thing, I just had an idea."

"Did it hurt?" Lucy winked at me.

It wasn't easy getting the trunk open. From the number and variety of bullet holes in it, I began to suspect that some of those two dozen neighbors the CLA man had mentioned had done a trifle more than watch the gunfight. If you've ever tried to shoot a door open (admittedly not too common an experience), then you know that more often than not, what you actually accomplish is to shoot it closed—and locked. Captain Ramius of the *Red October* said it to Jack Ryan: bullets are hard on machinery. In the end, we used the big White-Westinghouse laser to cut around the lock. It took all of us to force the lid upward on its damaged hinges. And I wasn't surprised by what I saw when we finally got it open.

"What in the abominated name of whiskey taxation is that?" Lucy exclaimed, pointing with her Gabbett-Fairfax to indicate a long green fiberglass tube with lettering stenciled on its surface in a typeface I've always thought of as "G. I. Joe." At the same time, my darling Clarissa waved to me from the back of an orange ambulance that had just arrived. She was taking off with the patients she'd just helped us to create. Sometimes being a Healer in this culture could be a lot like having one of those Roosevelt New Deal government jobs where you dig holes and then immediately fill them in again.

I replied, trying not to sound smug, "That, my dear friends, happens to be the field case for a Stinger missile where I come from, almost certainly the Stinger that was used against us on the Greenway. I don't know where these guys were hiding at the time, but they're consistent: they're terrible shots."

Suddenly, I heard an all-too familiar voice behind me. "Pardon me, sir!" It was the Spaceman's Fund lady again, with her big hat and veil and her basket of change. She was certainly nothing if not persistent. I stood up suddenly and cracked my head painfully on the underside of the trunk lid, but the look on her face when she recognized me was almost worth it.

"I believe," I grinned at her, holding the top of my now throbbing melon, "that I gave at the office."

SOMETIMES THERE'S MIDNIGHT baseball in Greater LaPorte— it's one of the most beautiful experiences you can have out of bed—but not tonight. There are heavily armed security guards at None of the Above Park all night (of course they're heavily armed in the daytime, too, when they're shopping with their wives and kiddies in the mall), but I was an old friend of their boss, the grim and grizzled chimpanzee who'd guarded my body when it had first arrived, full of submachine-gun perforations and leaking messily on Ed Bear's driveway at 626 Geñet Place, nine years ago. Sitting now, in a shadowed corner of the gigantic parking lot in Will's battered old 211 Rockford, I raised Captain Forsythe on my personal 'Com and gave him the *Readers' Digest* version of what the fearless leader of the Greater LaPorte Militia—and little old I—were up to.

"Please! Please don't tell me any more, Win," he demanded. "I don't want to know. You two miscreants promise not to burn down the ballpark or steal all the seats?"

I wanted to tell him I was more of a creant, than a miscreant. But the fierce old guy really meant it in his own way, although he was trying to be nice, and both of us promised solemnly.

Forsythe punched up a three-way conversation and told the employee at the nearest gate—his people *do* wear uniforms; you haven't lived until you've seen a fully grown orangutan in a military kilt—to unlock it, look the other way when we came by, and pass the word to the other guards that they couldn't see us, either.

"Come to think of it," I told Will once our business with Forsythe and his Assorted Anthropoids was over, "I have no idea how High Colonic's going to get in." Will yawned, drew his big silver pistol, and pulled the slide back a quarter of an inch to reassure himself that the chamber was still loaded. I don't know who the hell he thought could have sneaked into his holster and unloaded it. "Not our problem, partner. It's 8:52—let's go."

All right, so I dragged the .41 from my sling and rolled the cylinder to make sure there were six fat cartridges occupying the cylinder. So what.

Naturally, all of the elevators and escalators had been turned off, so Will and I got to climb six flights of metal stairs in the dark to get to the beer garden where High Colonic had said he'd meet us. Will seemed okay—he is younger than I am, after all—but by the time I'd finally clawed my way to the top, I'd decided to take some of that hyperbaric oxygen therapy Clarissa had been trying to sell me on.

I probably wouldn't want another cigar for a month.

I hated cloak-and-dagger stuff like this with a passion. Sneaking around and being sneaked at. Now that I was all the way up here, I'd much rather simply gaze out through the openwork of the most beautiful athletic arena I'd ever seen, and enjoy the multicolored lights of the most beautiful city I'd ever seen, scattered across the darkened land to an invisible horizon that—in terms of peace, freedom, progress, and prosperity, anyway—was truly limitless.

Unless the badguys won this thing.

I might even get to watch a real live spaceship taking off. They did that here, right from the tops of skyscrapers at the very heart of the city (wherever the hell that is), employing technology identical to that at work in the GLPM's electrostatic aerocraft. It was quite a pretty sight, with all their running lights twinkling and an eerie glow emanating from their several thousand high-voltage electrodes. Once aloft—at around one hundred thousand feet or so—they'd fire up their main fusion-driven engines, and that was quite a pretty sight, as well.

Even in high summer, it was more than a little frosty, six stories up, fairly late at night, in an openwork construction of steel beams, brick columns, and zero walls. That's the High Plains for you. The air curtains weren't running any more than the elevators were, and a Rocky Mountain chill had begun seeping into my kidneys and shoulderblades. I felt around for the control lump sewn into the seam of my cloak and turned up the temperature, hoping that whoever our unknown enemies were, they wouldn't have had time to hire a replacement for the four stooges—like somebody who had an infrared rifle scope.

Nine o'clock came and went.

Ten o'clock came and went.

By eleven o'clock, I couldn't feel my toes anymore (note to self: buy some electric shoes), and there were no messages, on any of our communications systems, indicating what, if anything, had gone wrong. High Colonic simply hadn't shown up and now I felt like an idiot for ever believing that he would. Fortunately, it hadn't been some kind of deadly trap, either. Nobody had taken a shot at us or tried to push us over the railing. Call it even for the night, I guess. Go home. Visit with Clarissa. Go to bed. Usually she warmed her cold feet up on me. Tonight, she was going to get a surprise.

Slower than we'd climbed up, Will and I climbed down the six cold flights of metal stairs. At each step my toes felt like they were going to break off, like glass, and my kneecaps were going to flip across the parking lot like Tiddlywinks. We asked the guard if he'd seen anybody (he hadn't, and checked with his colleagues for us), told him good night, and headed for Will's car. "Wait a minute, Will!" I hollered at him, just before he grabbed the door handle to lift it up. For a long minute he stood there with his hand outstretched, looking like a curbside jockey. "Who's to say somebody didn't sneak in down here while we were up there and put a bomb in your car?"

Will got an exasperated look on his face, and said, "Win, believe me. If anybody had even breathed hard in the direction of this car, it would have set up a shrieking that would have awakened every corpse in every graveyard in this city."

I gave it some thought. "Unless they knew how to cheat around your security system. You could do it, couldn't you?" When other arguments fail, try flattery.

He bit. "There's always that, I suppose. Say—"

I've tried. There isn't any way to accurately simulate the sound that interrupted him. In that moment something happened that I had previously thought could only happen in cartoons. An object fell out of the clear black sky. It was a car, about twice the size of Will's old Rockford. It crashed onto the surface of the parking lot, almost exactly sixteen inches from my left big toe.

I may never hear correctly in that ear again.

Overhead, just visibly underlit by reflected city light, I saw the long, ghostly silver oval form of a dirigible without running lights. I drew my revolver and considered shooting at it, but any of the big 240-grain slugs that failed to stop in the airship—which is mostly empty space, wrapped in plastic and filled with helium—

and came down again had to hit somewhere. At this angle, they might even hurt somebody.

"Okay," Will asked, once the dust had settled. The parking lot lights had come on by themselves, and there were dozens of guards from Forsythe's rushing toward us from the stadium. "Was that a trap or only a coincidence?"

"I don't know," I replied, suddenly distracted by the thought of all the wondrous things that are sold in vending machines in the Confederacy. "Do you suppose they'd let me back in to change my underwear?"

20: THAT'S ENTERTAINMENT

> Ever notice that the "Golden Age" of television was
> when commercial sponsors had the strongest control
> over program content?
>
> —*Memoirs of Lucille G. Kropotkin*

You'd think I'd have learned by now.

Will dropped me off at my front doorstep, still feeling like I
was frozen to the bone. It was like one of those Chicago drive-
bys where they roll the body out the door, onto the sidewalk,
and put the pedal to the floor. I no sooner got the door down
on the Rockford than he sped off, down the drive and across the
street, anxious to see his brace of pregnant brides.

I shuffled through my trouser pockets, an awkward task for a
man with his arm in a sling, and turned toward the door. I could
have had some kind of automated door thingummy, I suppose,
that would recognize my voiceprint, or the pore pattern on the
end of my schnozz, but I like real locks with real keys. For that
matter, I could have simply rung the doorbell, or even called
Clarissa on my pocket 'Com, but the girl works hard and I didn't
want to wake her up if she was asleep.

With my good hand busy with the key in the lock, and my
attention focused on maybe waking Clarissa up after all, I didn't
see or hear my assailant until he put his hand on my shoulder.
There were two of them. They'd been waiting in the bushes at
the front of the house.

The first one swung a big fist at my head. I saw the buttery
glint of brass knuckles, ducked, and stepped into him, letting go
of the key, getting a hand on my revolver as my elbow hit his
solar plexus. He smacked the doorpost, bruising the housepaint

and his knuckles, then danced up and down, cursing as the other one came at me.

They were wearing nylon stocking masks. By now my gun was out and I drew a fast bead on the second guy's midsection. I started pulling the trigger, but only got the hammer halfway back, when the first guy, accidentally or deliberately, crashed into me from behind. By reflex, I pulled the trigger the rest of the way through and heard an anguished bellow as I fell forward on my knees. Almost at once, somebody stepped on my gun hand, grinding down hard and crushing it painfully between pistol and pavement. I thought I felt my trigger finger break where it passed through the guard and was bent forward toward the muzzle. I couldn't support myself with my other arm, because it was in the sling.

Somebody else, or it could have been the same guy, kicked me as hard as he could in the ribs. He should have used the brass knuckles. I'd been kicked that way before, in a Federal Boulevard bar check that went sour back in my uniform days. It wasn't pleasant, but I rolled with it almost gratefully, and that saved me another vicious kick, this time in the head, from the other guy, who kicked his partner in the shin, instead.

It also let me take aim and fire from where I lay on my back—guess the finger wasn't broken after all—hitting the first kicker in the right thigh and tearing away at least two pounds of meat. I never heard the noise or felt the recoil, but I sure as hell heard him scream, and so did a lot of other folks from Oklahoma to Montana. The second kicker tried to rush me—the rule (and most of the time it makes good sense) being, "Run from a knife, attack a gun." I lifted the Model 58's muzzle in his general direction and pulled the trigger. The bullet took him underneath the jaw and seemed to lift him three feet into the air. He came down right on top of me, literally dead meat.

"Stand down, Win!" That was my brave and beautiful wife, standing on the doorstep in her pretty pink nightgown, Webley Electric in hand. The first guy I'd shot was unconscious, having leaked rather profusely on my driveway.

"Don't worry, honey, I won't shoot you." She took only a cursory glance at my attackers, threw herself onto her knees beside me, and began taking inventory. As her fingers moved professionally over my body, I felt hot, very unprofessional tears falling on my chest, but he didn't make a sound. I could have told her I was okay. The only damage I'd sustained were the stomped fingers and the kick to the belly that had probably saved my life. I climbed to my feet, feeling so stiff it almost brought tears to my eyes, but not wanting to show it to my child bride. "Let's see who these clowns are."

One was still breathing. Clarissa produced shears from somewhere and got his pantyhose mask off. To say that we couldn't believe who it was only understated the matter by a couple orders of magnitude.

Getting the dead guy's mask off—he'd taken one through the right upper arm, as well—was no joke, as accustomed as we both were—she the Healer, me the homicide dick—to that sort of thing, but the results were even more unbelievable, and horrifying. In the end, we stood together, arms around each other, staring down at two guys, one badly wounded, one very dead.

Both of them were Bennett Williams.

THE PRETTY LITTLE girl stood on tiptoes as the bespectacled proprietor behind the counter rang up her order.

"Now let's see here, Mary-Lou," said the man with the white apron. "You've got the CZ-61 Skorpion submachinegun, 500 rounds of high-velocity .32 ACP hollowpoint ammunition, and—what's this?"

The little girl was typically American. She couldn't have been older than eleven, maybe younger, to judge by the missing tooth in front. She wore a frilly gingham dress, white bobby socks, and saddle-shoes. Her shiny dark brown hair had been carefully braided into a pair of pigtails with ribbons in the ends that matched her dress, and she had freckles across both pink cheeks and the bridge of her upturned nose.

She was puzzled. "Why, that's morphine, Mr. Suprynowicz. It's for my mom."

He shook his head. "Now you just take that right back to the shelf where you got it, Mary-Lou, and look a little harder next time. Our store brand is a lot cheaper, and it happens to be on sale this week."

"Thank you, Mr. Suprynowicz!" When she returned, the storekeeper counted out her change, bagged her purchases, and she skipped out of the store, happy as a little freckled lark.

If I cringed, I guess it was because I'm still a blueback. It was also a leftover from the ugly place where I'd been born. I tried not to show it. My darling Clarissa didn't show it, either—because she hadn't even noticed the transaction, and if she had, she'd likely have thought nothing of it. She'd been born a Confederate and had probably gone to the store herself, for Mommy's narcotics and Daddy's ammo, once upon a time.

I was tired. I was seeing entirely too much of Mr. and Mrs. Civil Liberties Association, and they, in turn, were getting suspicious of me. I had to take them aside and explain exactly what kind of case I was helping with. I figured it was Will's case causing all the bloodshed, not my own.

They took the bodies away, one to the meatlocker, the other to an infirmary. We woke Bennett Williams up and confirmed my expectation that he wasn't either of the guys who'd attacked me. All they'd had with them, weaponwise, were the knuckles and a switchblade. Clearly amateur talent, from out of town.

Way out of town.

I tried to relax and sip my chocolated coffee. I still hurt all over from last night's adventures, but if there's anyplace in the American Zone that rivals the Hanging Judge as a place to catch up on gossip in a congenial atmosphere—and get a lesson on living in a free country—it's Suprynowicz's General Store next door to the Golden Apple Tea Room at the end of the 2300 block at the corner of Wilson and Shea.

Clarissa and I were here, on our own at last, to visit two more of the people on my list of possible importers of Gable and Lombard (not to mention Cummings and Davis) pictures. It was good to have her along; this was how I'd always wanted it to be, her Nora to my Nick.

Will was at home with his wives for the morning, dealing with some crisis, or so he'd claimed, involving paint colors for the nursery. It must not have been much of a crisis. He'd been humming cheerily to himself when he rang off. It was one of those stupid situations where I knew he was lying, he knew I knew he was lying, and I knew he knew that I knew, but the forms had to be followed nonetheless. Meanwhile, Lucy had grabbed an ultraspeed flight all the way down to Lubbock (twenty minutes' air time—they actually consume half their delta-V keeping the plane from going into orbit), believing she was in pursuit of another of Will's native radical suspects.

Somebody sitting near the front window leaned back, put his feet up on the table, and fingered a guitar.

> "Well I used to be an American,
> Where they told us we were free,
> But the only ones with rights were crooks,
> And the newsheads on TV—"

The little bell over the door jingled. Samuel T. Harkin IV had kept the appointment with us first. At forty-nine, according to my research, Harkin was a grim, perpetually impoverished in-the-cellar-with-a-candle-guttering-in-the-winebottle type anar-chist. Word was, he'd spent the last thirty years of his life Stateside laboriously writing, editing, printing, collating, and dis-tributing thousands upon thousands of smudgy political pam-phlets that nobody ever read. Until recently, when he'd emigrated to the Confederacy one leap ahead of the Immigration, Naturalization, and Condemnation Service's killer hounds, he'd been an illegal squatter—in the house that his parents had once owned—in southern California's "Earthquake Safety Clearance Area," one of those corrupt west coast government land grabs that stank across eleven thousand worlds. At least he'd fared better than Donald Scott, the California guy local governments had murdered for his ocean-front Malibu property.

It was said that Harkin had an odd knack for gathering about him artists and writers, mostly younger than he was, with genuine talent greatly exceeding his own.

Greeting a few of the regulars with a negligent wave—I no-ticed Daggett the knifemonger was here, having his first Diet Coke of the day—Harkin also nodded at Suprynowicz and looked around until he found us. He came to the card table Clarissa and I occupied, and seated himself without asking.

"I'm Harkin," he informed us. We knew, we'd seen his pic-ture. He was tall, but with a lot of belly under his black T-shirt and black jeans. (One report claimed that he wore black under-wear, as well.) Under a black beret straight out of a comic book, he also wore a big round face on which it looked like someone had pasted a fake moustache and goatee.

"I'm Bear," I replied, as deadpan as I could. "She's Bear,

too—but it's a free country." Clarissa stifled a giggle. I'd always wanted to say that.

No discernable sense of humor. Harkin pulled out a huge, well-used briar pipe from somewhere on his person, stuffed it full of some kind of vegetable matter—it may even have been tobacco—lit it, tamped it, and put his lighter away. "You wanted to ask me some questions?"

I lit a cigarette. For this particular setting, I'd reverted to American duds: my old gray working suit, white shirt, plain black zero-power necktie, comfortable brown oxfords, white socks, and the same felt hat I wear every day. Despite the fight I'd been in my still-mending left arm was supported now by a blue transparent plastic contraption that I could take off for bathing and dressing. It was still annoying, but an improvement.

At my suggestion, Clarissa had looked for American clothes, too, at the local equivalent of Goodwill: a very nice camel-colored suit without the least hint of sex-appeal, an off-white silk blouse, dark nylons, and what I call "Nazi nurse" shoes. The idea was to look serious and professional, not sexy or pretty. It didn't exactly work—she still looked sexy and pretty anyway—but it helped some. "We wanted to talk to you," she said, attempting to imitate Will imitating Jack Webb—which meant she sounded just like Dana Scully. "About what you import from the United States." I noticed for the first time in that instant that although there isn't any difference (not that I can hear, anyway) in the accents of Confederates and United Statesians, still, there's *something*. My lovely spouse was trying to sound American, but she sounded like somebody on the BBC trying to sound like somebody from Texas.

Harkin spotted her in a heartbeat, and stood up, not quite going for whatever it was he carried in his waistband. "Damn

Confederates anyway! What, are you planning to set me up for the train wreck or the Old Endicott explosion?"

You can never tell what's on people's minds. I stood up, too, put my good hand on the wrist that was reaching for his gun, and through gritted teeth, said, "Calm down, you idiot! I'm a blueback, just like you—Clarissa here is a Confederate native, my wife, and this happens to be her first case." Not exactly true, but it would do. I turned to her. "I'm sorry, kiddo, I guess I gave you bad advice. You should have remained your own sweet self." Back to Harkin. "We're trying to find out who's importing certain movies from various versions of the States, is all, not even dirty movies. I'd be glad to explain the whole thing, if you'll just sit down and relax."

He blinked. "Say, you're Win Bear," he informed me. I'd known that, of course, but didn't let on. "The first sucker through the blue hole. That's a pretty good shiner you've got there. Your secretary didn't tell me who you were when she called."

"Secretary?" I scratched my head. "Oh, *secretary*! I did ask her to call you, didn't I? I was confused because this is her day off, and she's gone shopping or something in Lubbock. Yes, well, I'm Win Bear, guilty as charged, and this is Clarissa MacDougall Olson-Bear."

Harkin sat down and nodded, giving Clarissa the once-over despite her getup. I offered him something to drink and he asked for beer. I went to the counter—this wasn't a restaurant, I'd been told, and it didn't have waiters—and ordered beer for Harkin, tea for Clarissa, and another mocha for me. By the time I got back, Harkin and Clarissa were chattering away, about movies, of all things.

"You know that in my world," he was telling her, "Bettie Page never got to be a movie star at all. She was a devoutly religious person who refused to sleep her way onto the bottom rung of the ladder, let alone to the top."

Clarissa answered, reminding me of conversations we'd had, "Yes, I know. Win says that her place—if we all have a place in the world—was taken by inferior talent blown way out of proportion by studio publicity departments. Just think, a world without comedy-mysteries like *The Striped Silk Chair*, *Daddy's Yacht*, or *The Two Leopards*. How very sad."

I put the small round tray of drinks on the table. Clarissa likes plain old Lipton's. Harkin had asked for Scheiner Bock, not quite a microbrew, but a pretty tolerable regional beer from Texas. I'd been surprised that Suprynowicz stocked it. "But she's a big star here," Harkin observed. "This version of her, anyway. I think my favorite movie is *The Blue Peekaboo*." A peekaboo is a tiny sliver of a two-piece swimsuit. They don't call them bikinis here, because there was never any thermonuclear explosion in the Pacific.

At that point the little bell over the door jangled again, and, leaning heavily on his cane, in clumped Ludfried von Haybard, Nobel Laureate and economist of the Austrian School. "Samuel, my boy!" The professor waved his cane dangerously and loudly addressed Harkin in what sounded to me like a stage-German accent. I learned later that all Austrians sound like Donald Duck's other uncle, Ludwig von Drake. "How pleasant to see you! Suprynowicz, still practicing practical economics, I see! And this must be the famous shamus Win Bear—somewhat worse for the wear, I see, like any good hardboiled detective—and his lovely companion to whom I have most rudely not been introduced!"

Harkin grinned. "I'll be glad to introduce you rudely, if that's what you really want, Doc. Don't be surprised if the detective shoots me for it, though. This is another kind of doc, Healer Clarissa MacDougall Olson-Bear."

Shifting his cane to the other hand, he took Clarissa's, bowed low over it, and kissed it. People in other parts of the store cheered, whistled, and applauded. They were all pretty easily entertained, I thought. I found him a chair. "I am delighted, my dear, to make your acquaintance. You know that at the age of seventy-two, I think of myself as political *zweiback*, the twice-baked bread of the wonderful world of refugees."

"More likely," Harkin muttered, "refried beans." I'd been thinking half-baked bread, myself.

"My boy, we'll settle this later, with wet noodles at fifty paces." Back to Clarissa: "You see (he actually said, "you zee"), I was originally a refugee *to* the United States—*a* United States—which, in my version of reality, reached a diplomatic understanding with a Japan unaligned with Germany, and never entered World War Two. I tell you, I was astounded—and deeply saddened—to hear the way the whole thing went in so many other worlds: Pearl Harbor, Hiroshima, Nagasaki, Beaverton."

"Beaverton?" Harkin and I both said at once.

But Von Haybard had the eyes and ears of what he had every reason to believe—and so do I—was a lovely young girl, and went on without us. "I had fled Austria to avoid the Nazis. I wasn't Jewish, there was no point in going to New Israel in Tasmania, so I chose the United States. Now I found that I was exiled permanently from my homeland, from all of Europe for that matter, with the passing of a prematurely aged Adolf Hitler—from Parkinson's Disease, and it couldn't have happened to a nicer guy—and the establishment of the Anglo-German Eurofascist Commonwealth."

"No, kidding!" I said. How many different versions of World War Two were there, anyway?

"What a mouthful, not?" he laughed. "And they always accuse us German-speakers of liking compound words."

"And now you're here," Clarissa coached him.

"And now I'm here. And now I find myself a refugee once again, owing to a book I wrote, unwisely criticizing America's ruling 'One Nation Under God Party.'"

Clarissa said, "I'd like to see that, sometime."

The old man laughed with delight. "I laboriously carried a single precious copy with me through the broach, my dear. It's available on the 'Com now, but I'd be happy to let you see the original." *Come up and look at my etchings, little girl.* I barely resisted inspecting his cane for notches.

It was time to take this investigation back in hand—although my lovely Clarissa had certainly softened them up nicely and gotten a lot of background.

I charged in: "What we called you here for, Clarissa and I, was to ask you if you know anything about imported copies of movies like *Gone with the Wind* or *It Happened One Night* from the States."

"*Gone with the Wind*," mused the professor (he actually said, "Gone vit' ze Vint"), "*Gone with the Wind.* An exceedingly long film from the 1930s about the Second American Revolution, was it not, with Robert Cummings and Betty Davis? And a real stinker!"

Actually, he'd said "Und a rrreal schtinker," but I was suddenly too excited to give a damn. I leaned toward him, almost into his face. "So who's importing it, Doctor Von Haybard? You got any idea?"

He shook his head sadly. "I haven't any idea at all. My wife— my dear, departed Hilda—loved movies like that, and she made me go to them with her. I haven't seen it, probably since 1939. Samuel, how many A.L.s is that, anyway?"

Harkin said, "A hundred and sixty-three."

"How time flies," Von Haybard remarked, leaning on the cane between his knees. "Mr. Bear, we will both ask around for you and your lovely Clarissa, after this *Gone with the Wind* movie, if you will do a small thing for us."

I squinted at him suspiciously. "And that would be?"

He glanced around from side to side, as if worried about being overheard. "First, you must promise to tell no one of this. It could be worth millions of . . . of . . ."

"Gold ounces," Harkin supplied.

"Yes, gold ounces. You see, my friend Samuel here and I have had an idea, and we are looking for financial backers."

Clarissa asked, "Financial backers for what?"

Von Haybard leaned toward us and whispered, "Governmentland!"

Harkin chuckled with moronic glee.

"What?" I said.

"Governmentland—what we shall call an *abusement* park! It is a brilliant idea, even if I say so myself, and certain to make everybody associated with it wealthy beyond the dreams of avarice!"

"How do you figure that?"

"You have probably noticed, as we have, how Confederate natives never believe it when you tell them how it was. They will want to come and see what living under a government is like, especially with the Franklinite Faction demanding that one be established here. We'll divide it into sections! Sun Temple Slaveland, Inquisitionland, Robespierreland, Stalinland, Great Leap Forward Land, Third Reichland, and New World Orderland!"

What it sounded like to me was a typical Old Freedom Movement idea, like the Minerva Atoll Landfill Project or any number of other harebrained schemes that had never come to anything back in the States. Von Haybard appeared obsessed with it in a way I recognized, and he didn't seem to notice what a terrible idea everybody else thought it was. I looked around: Governmentland was no secret here. People in the store seemed to be cringing with embarrassment as they heard him going on about it, probably for the millionth time. By contrast, when the Indiana Jones movies finally made their way to the Confederacy, some clever entrepreneur put together a *Raiders of the Lost Ark* brace of handguns, consisting of a P35 Browning High Power autopistol like mine and a large-caliber 4" N-frame revolver—followed as soon as possible by a commemorative Webley Mark VI. Now there was a commercial promotion to make the chicken-livered, lace-pantied, hypocritical Californians who produced those pictures swoon with the vapors. "Why not Plagueland, then?" I asked, "or Inflamed Appendixland?

21: TEA FOR TWO

> Those who sell their liberty for security are understandable, if pitiable, creatures. Those who sell the liberty of *others* for wealth, power, or even a moment's respite, deserve only the end of a rope.
>
> —*Memoirs of Lucille G. Kropotkin*

"What was my name in the States?" The woman looked at me down her long, straight nose. She had enough eye makeup on for a whole herd of 1960s go-go ponies.

I laughed. I'd just been thinking about that song the other day, and told her so.

"So that's what you're asking me?" the woman replied, utterly without visible emotion or even much facial expression. Keely Smith, that's who she reminded me of, deadpanned band singer and main squeeze to Louis Prima.

"I guess it is," said Clarissa. "Isn't it, Win?"

"I guess it is," I answered.

More Jack Webb. The woman reached a long, pale arm and what seemed like an even longer cigarette holder toward an ashtray. "Well, it was the same there and then as it is here and now. You see before you Andrea Galarynd, age thirty-five or thereabout, proprietor of the Golden Apple Tea Room."

I started to speak again, but she beat me to it. She'd started taciturn, but one of us, Clarissa or me, had finally pushed a button, although I didn't know who or how. Whatever it was, it had taken us half an hour.

She said, "I was a best-selling Gothic romance novelist where I came from, Lieutenant Bear. Unfortunately, that sort of thing doesn't seem to sell very well here. They like *westerns*, of all things!" she complained. "*Old westerns*, written by people like Louis L'Amour or Ted van Roosevelt!"

I shrugged, but didn't say anything.

"I was also a popular philosopher of some note—some would say 'self-styled'—and a health-food activist." She delivered it all in monotone, with a stone face. "They called me a 'cultist' at my trial. It's true that I'm a natural nonconformist, I suppose. If I hadn't become a radical individualist, I might have become a nudist, instead."

I laughed again. I couldn't help myself. I was surprised as hell to discover that I liked this extremely strange woman with her severe Walk-Like-an-Egyptian hairstyle and her buzzy, slightly accented voice. Assuming that she meant to be funny, Galarynd had a sense of humor I could appreciate, wry and self-deprecating. Even better, Clarissa and I had only had to walk about twenty feet from Suprynowicz's General Store to get here.

Speaking of Clarissa, she had another cup of tea steaming in front of her, this time some rare variety of clover blossom, atop an almost useless table about the size of my hat, covered with an elaborate lace tablecloth. Me, I was abstaining, and thinking about my bladder more than I should.

"I fled the Glorious People's Republic of California," Galarynd was serious, now, and apparently unaware that anybody had ever uttered those words as a joke, "when the vitamins, amino acids, and other dietary supplements I'd sold by mail order for ten years were suddenly asserted by the Food and Drug Enforcement Administration to be controlled substances—and unauthorized sale or possession made a 'L.I.P. Service' offense."

"L.I.P. Service?" Clarissa asked. It was interesting to watch my darling learning from somebody besides me just how perversely people with uniforms and funny hats and briefcases could treat one another in places like I'd come from—and what a difference simply arming everybody could make.

Galarynd ground out her cigarette, pulled the butt from the holder, and immediately replaced it with a fresh cigarette, which I lit for her. "Life-Indenture to the People."

I shuddered. Somehow, it sounded worse than Carneval's one hundred thousand hours of public service. Clarissa said something about reinstituting slavery.

"Perhaps so, but it was also a L.I.P. Service offense to call it that." Our hostess observed the shock on Clarissa's face. "My dear, you think that's bad? My husband—he's from a different world than I am altogether; I met him here in the Zone—he was compelled to flee for his very life during his world's beastly Edward M. Kennedy Administration."

I raised my eyebrows. "Because?" She flicked an ash into the ashtray. "Because he was a TV standup comedian who created the popular catchphrase—generically describing any lost cause or foregone conclusion—'Dead before she hit the water.'" I started laughing again, while Clarissa looked at me as if I'd grown an extra nose. Part of it was remembering a wonderful fake Volkswagen ad that *National Lampoon* had printed in the seventies—and been forced by the car company to withdraw—pointing out that if Teddy Kennedy had been driving a Beetle, which floats, he'd be in the White House today. I excused myself and told Galarynd about the ad. Apparently she thought it was funny, too, which made me think about Jessica Rabbit.

"What does he do?" I asked. "Your husband, I mean. Now."

She took another long drag on her cigarette. I pulled one out myself and lit it, not knowing how well cigars and tea rooms might go together. "Why, he runs Salmoneus & Quark over on Suter Street." She pointed a thumb over her shoulder. "'Acts of Capitalism between Consenting Adults.'"

"I think I've heard that slogan somewhere before. You import tea, I assume. What does your husband import?"

She released smoke, uninhaled, from her mouth and breathed it in again through her nose—French inhaling, I think it's called. "I import much more than tea: teapots, teacups, tea cozies, samovars, espresso machines—"

"And your husband?" I insisted.

"Anything that comes to hand, from microscopic test weights for scientific scales to—well, he imported an entire English Channel hovercraft once."

"Hardware," I asserted. "Any movies?"

"Movies? Yes. Would you care for any more tea, Clarissa?"

Clarissa shook her head. "No, thank you. Movies like *Gone with the Wind*?"

"Yes, that's a good one!" Galarynd brightened at the memory. "It always makes me cry. Do you suppose that Rhett eventually went back to Scarlett?"

I said, "Frankly, my dear, I don't give a damn. Does your husband the comedian ever sell or rent movies like *Gone with the Wind* to 'Com channels?"

A puzzled look. "Why, yes, he does. Why? Surely there's no law against it. I'll have you know that we both worked in Confederate sweatshops, four hours a day, three days a week, saving copper coins to get where we are, and—"

"Thank you! Thank you!" I wanted to kiss her, or jump up and shout "Shazam!," but Clarissa was there, nobody seems to remember Captain Marvel anymore, and I certainly didn't want anybody to think I remembered Gomer Pyle.

When we got back out to Clarissa's medical van, parked at the curb in front of Suprynowicz's General Store, there was a note lying on the passenger seat.

TOO DANGEROUS LAST NIGHT

DIDN'T DROP CAR—THEY DID

TONIGHT 10 O'CLOCK

CORNER TRENCHARD & GORDON

Handprinted in the center of the sheet, nice and symmetrical. I don't know what High Colonic would have done if I hadn't left the window open a crack. Windshield wiper? Except for certain old-timers like Lucy's Thornycrofts, which have big round glass centrifugal window disks like an oceangoing ship, the windshield-wiping systems on most hovercraft are electrostatic, with no moving parts you can slip a piece of paper under.

SALMONEUS & QUARK'S on Suter Street turned out to be right around the block behind the Golden Apple. If they'd wanted to, Galarynd and her husband could have stepped out for a smoke together in the alley—although there's nobody to say you can't smoke indoors in the Confederacy. By the time we got there and found a parking place, I'd faxed High Colonic's note to Will—more civilized than phoning him, I thought—and C-mailed Lucy's 'Com account, which she could access wherever she happened to be, from down below the Lubbock caprock to Tombaugh Station on Pluto.

We walked in on an argument.

"And I say you can't tell the Roosevelt generation anything at all!" somebody shouted. "They lived through every bit of it, the Great Depression, World War Two, Korea, the Cold War, and never understood a single goddamned minute! Back in the 1930s they all got together and decided to carve themselves a great big, thick, quivering, juicy slice of *us* to feed on in their old age! They sold their liberty—and ours right along with it—at garage-sale prices, for the illusion of security!"

That from the guy standing behind the counter, a slim, wiry, blond-crewcutted individual between forty-five and fifty. He looked familiar, somehow. For a moment he made me think of Crocodile Dundee. The other guy, presumably attempting to be a customer, raised both his hands in self-defense. "Don't have an epiphany, man! I only said that our parents' and grandparents' generations made a lot of sacrifices so that—"

"Yeah," said the proprietor, "and *we're* the sacrifices they made! I say to hell with them! I say let's repudiate the national debt. And I say let the vicious old bastards freeze in the dark like they deserve!"

So it was Standard Politico-Economic Argument Number 27-A. I'd heard a lot of this kind of stuff down here in the Zone. These guys all reminded me of Civil War buffs—make that War between the States buffs, or even War of Northern Aggression buffs—arguing themselves hoarse over battles that had been finished, and the grass grown back, more than a century before they were born. This particular pair of individuals was safe here in the North American Confederacy now, where none of that stuff mattered anymore. Who gave a rat's ass about the national debt?

Clarissa looked at me quizzically, probably wondering if this was another thing like the Volkswagen ad. I shrugged and bellied up to the counter.

"You rent movies, here?" I asked.

He looked me over. "I don't rent 'em, friend, I sell 'em. Eight millimeter celluloid, sixteen millimeter, seventy millimeter, VHS, DVD, Beta, Framnold, Acquiz, High-eight, Mpeg, or Laser-Disc?"

"Framnold?" I shrugged. "Have you got *Gone with the Wind?*"

"That all depends on what you want," the guy said. "You

looking for Clark Gable, Errol Flynn, Robert Cummings, Jeremy Hartshorn, or Nigel Wallenburg?"

I laughed. "Nigel Wallenburg? Jeremy Hartshorn? Never heard of either of them. I may take you up on the Errol Flynn version, though, sometime." I showed him one of my cards. "What I really want to know is where you get these things from. I mean, who drags them through the broach. Nobody's in any trouble, I just have a couple of clients who want to know."

He folded his arms. "Well you have got a hell of a nerve, haven't you? Look at it from my point of view. If I told everybody where I got my stock in trade, then anybody could get them, and then where would I be? Answer me that!"

"Where would you be?" I repeated. "Well, I guess you could be getting your ass sued by people who have an intellectual property right involved."

"I thought you said," he leaned forward on the counter, "that nobody's in any trouble."

"I lied. Look: I'll tell you the truth—"

He raised his eyebrows and widened his eyes in mock astonishment. "That would be refreshing."

"Okay, I deserved that." I tried reasonable. "The fact is, nobody wants to go to court about this if they don't have to. The process isn't any pleasanter here than it is back at home."

He laughed. "You're tellin' me—back home, they stake the loser out over a fire-anthill."

I frowned. "You made that up."

"Yeah, I did." He laughed again. "Now we're even."

I'd forgotten that this guy had been a standup comic on TV. I hadn't mentioned anything that his wife had told me, because I didn't want a domestic disturbance on my conscience. Now I wished I'd let Clarissa start this one.

Apparently, she'd read my mind. "Excuse me, mister—"

"Yosemite—Sam Yosemite. And don't say a word, it's a damned coincidence I didn't know about until I got here. See, where I come from, all forms of animation are illegal. It's called the Bambi Law, and from what I've heard about other universes since I got here, I almost approve of it."

He turned a hand over, indicating the man he'd been arguing with, a tall, husky, tanned fellow of about forty, prematurely gray, with about a week's beard showing. "This is my good friend, Tomas Godinez," Yosemite told us. I started to offer my hand and my name, but Yosemite pressed on before I could.

"Tom here was a famous personal weapons expert, and the author of many books and hundreds of articles and columns for shooting and hunting magazines. He even had his own reloading show, on satellite TV. But then he went and exiled himself from something called the North American Union, by writing an article for *Modern Machineguns* calling the statuatory infallibility of the Supreme Court into question."

Tom lifted his eyebrows and grinned modestly at us. "It's true, it's all true. I wanted to call them perverts in black dresses, too, but my editor wouldn't let me."

"I suppose my wife's already told you how I got here," Sam went on. "Just like Andy to preempt a good story. Now what were you going to say, lady?"

Clarissa sighed and shrugged. "The people we're working for feel, well, belittled or diminished by some of the movies being shown on the 'Com, movies that have otherworld versions of themselves in them, in roles that embarrass them."

"Or that they didn't get paid for," Sam responded. "Tell me about it! I was watching the 'Com the other day and saw a version of myself—different name, though, altogether—in a ridiculous thing called *Space Precinct*. Fake aliens with enormous buggy eyes. The writing was surprisingly not bad, though. I wonder what the guy was getting for—"

I knew I'd seen him—or someone like him—before.

"Excuse me, Mr. Yosemite," Clarissa cleared her throat. I could tell she was annoyed. She was a big *Space Precinct* fan. She must have recognized him from the moment we entered the store. "We need to know where these movies come from. Maybe we could work things out so all parties are satisfied."

"Believe me, lady, all parties are *never* satisfied," he told her, writing something on the card I'd handed him. "However, because you're both gainfully employed elsewhere—I recognize Win Bear when I see him, Lieutenant, and his good-looking wife, Clarissa the Healer—and just possibly to avoid getting my ass sued off, here's where I get most of my new stuff. Just don't tell 'em I was the one who told you, okay?"

"Mum's the word," I said. The address was farther into the Zone than I'd ever been before. I was suposd to talk to someone called Mickey Stonesoup.

" 'Shuddup' would be a lot more like it, friend," Yosemite replied amiably.

I grinned, thanked him, and left with Clarissa. There were two messages waiting for us when we got to the car. The first was from Lucy, a C-mail saying that she'd gotten the message I'd sent her, had her hands full where she was, and wouldn't be home in time for the appointment.

The second message was a video recording of Mary-Beth Sanders, looking tear-stained and uncharacteristically rattled. "Win, Clarissa! I can't find your personal 'Com numbers! I hope this message gets to you right away! Will is . . . Will's been shot!" She looked frantically from side to side, then at the camera again. "Please come to the house as soon as you can!"

I glanced at my watch and the timestamp on the screen. She'd called three minutes ago.

"SUPPOSE THE BADGUYS think they've killed you?" I asked. I stood on tiptoe, looking past and over Mary-Beth, Fran, and Clarissa, all elbows and decorative backsides, wielding bandages and sponges and surgical instruments and electronic goodies, while Will—fully as conscious as I was, albeit crankier—tried to have a conversation with me.

When Clarissa and I had roared up to the front at 625 Geñet Place, across the street from our own home, the pair of big wooden doors at each end of the arched entryway had been shut. Although I'd never truly gotten used to it, LaPorte, the whole Confederacy, in fact, was one of those rare, wonderful places— sort of like Trinidad when my mother was growing up—where you could leave your doors unlocked all day and all night. I'd always hoped to keep it that way here, so this was a dismaying surprise. Two very pregnant young women had greeted us with a four-barrel salute, a pistol of some kind in each hand. Will we'd found upstairs where they'd reluctantly left him, flat on his back in bed, sealed up with emergency plastic sheeting, and complaining to his wives, and anybody else who would listen, that he had work to do and wasn't hurt that badly.

"She came right to the door," he explained, as Clarissa, working under a pain-suppression field, extracted the first bullet. It clinked melodically in the enameled pan that Fran was holding. Mary-Beth just stood there looking worried. "Collecting for the Spaceman's Fund," Will went on. "When I reached into my pocket, she shot me. Several times, I think—it was a little hard to keep track. A little old lady with—"

"With a hat and a shawl and a basket, tra la," I finished for him. This was getting to be ridiculous, I thought, imagining how we'd deal with this in the States—a city-wide roundup of little old ladies with big hats and shawls. "I assume she got away while you were busy bleeding on your doorstep. So how come you're still alive to tell us about it?"

"Kevlar," he explained. "After last night's merriment, probably about the same time Clarissa was out shopping for her Marlene Dietrich outfit, I was down in the Zone myself, looking for Kevlar. You know it's absolutely amazing what some people manage to bring with them through the broach."

"And even more amazing," I agreed, "what they think is important."

I examined the battered vest. It looked like it had been worked over with a small caliber submachinegun—we could always put an APB out on little Mary-Lou, I supposed—or a 12-gauge shotgun spewing #4 buckshot. The damned thing brought back memories I hadn't realized were horrible until now.

"You know, I hate this piece of crap," I informed him, meaning the vest. "Don't get me wrong, my friend. I'm overjoyed that it worked for you, but this thing wouldn't have protected you from that plummeting Hupmobile or whatever it was, any more than it will protect you from an electric pistol like Clarissa's, or a laser. Besides, I've always thought that we were a lot nicer— we cops—before we started wearing the stuff."

Will winced a little as the second bullet came out—Clarissa immediately did something to the pain suppressor—but he managed to snort an old familiar snort. "Was the point to be nice, or to enforce the law?"

"It was to keep the peace, my friend," I said. "How can you even pretend to protect people once making them afraid of you becomes part of the job?"

Will tried to sit up, but his wives and doctor hollered at him and managed to push him back down again. "But our lives were on the line, Win, and—"

"Oh, please, Will, don't give me any of that." I was surprising myself how strongly I felt about this. I hadn't thought about it for a long time. "We're both adults, and neither of us would be here if we believed it."

"And the truth, according to Edward William Bear, is?" he asked sarcastically.

"The truth is that there *is* no 'thin blue line.' There's only a deep red stream—those who are forced to pay our salaries—a deep red stream that cops and crooks wade through alike, without any thought or care to the lives, liberties, or property they happen to be destroying in the process."

"Quite a speech." He sighed. "I'd beg to differ with you, but I'm too tired just now, and I'm unwilling to embarrass myself by telling anyone why I'm compelled to agree with you. Are you planning to make that meeting tonight at Trenchard and Gordon?"

I shrugged. "I don't know." I glanced at Clarissa. She gave me a particular look, to say that Will had had enough. "I think we want to talk to Lucy, first."

"You do that, partner, and let me know how it turns out. I think I'll just lie here for a while."

Clarissa turned another knob, and he was sound asleep.

22: ROLL ME OVER IN THE CLOVER

> The late-twentieth century Left fawns obsessively over animals because an animal has no intellect, is therefore incapable of challenging their ridiculous ideas, and can't say, "Leave me the hell alone and get a life, you geek!"
> —*Memoirs of Lucille G. Kropotkin*

"Whoop! Yipee!" I hadn't known I was capable of making a noise like that. "What a ride!"

Although she'd departed LaPorte in a conventional way—from an SST pad atop the Spooner Building earlier that morning—Lucy asked us to join her by extremely unconventional means, here at the Armadillo Interworld Terminal. I could see why, now, although it had taken me a minute back in LaPorte to understand exactly what I was expected to do.

Clarissa and I had stepped into the blindingly blue circle that was the locus of a probability broach, at LaPorte Interworld, then out of a blindingly blue circle exactly like it, into a transparent booth, and out onto the concourse. Waiting, as excited as I've ever seen her, was Lucy, who gave Clarissa a big hug and the same to me as if she hadn't seen us for months. "How'dya like that?" She grinned. "LaPorte t'Lubbock in a fraction of a second!" Glancing back, I could still see LaPorte Interworld, like looking through a window.

I looked down the long line of transparent booths exactly like the one Clarissa and I had just come from, and a few that were different, probably for freight. It was just the same at home—in Laporte, that was. This would have been a noisy place back in the States, full of hustle, bustle, and victims having their bodily orifices probed by uniformed perverts. I wonder why it never seems to have occurred to anyone that a "cavity search" is rape.

Competent design and plenty of air curtains kept the noise abated here. We'd merely come from eight hundred miles to the north by northwest. But now, in both directions as far as the eye could see (two miles each way in this titanic underground complex), people were stepping from one world—and in most cases, from one life—into another in which such violations of dignity and personal privacy aren't allowed to happen.

Not to people who followed Thomas Jefferson's advice and carried a weapon everywhere they went.

Some of the booths did have guards—denied any orifice-probing powers—posted around them as a measure of prudence. In an infinite sheaf of universes where anything possible was probable, it might be badguys coming through the broach, or would-be conquering aliens, or herds of stampeding dinosaurs, or giant mosquitos, instead of refugees. Or it might be precious cargo—diamonds or emeralds or sunstones that needed protecting. Thousands of companies were mining hundreds of versions of Earth that had never developed a sapient population. Since these companies already knew where all the big finds had been made in hundreds of inhabited worlds, they always struck the mother lode in any new place they explored.

Some booths just had families, waiting to be reunited.

And there were a few where operatives—I was one of them myself, from time to time—were headed the other way, looking for people to be rescued, or brutalitarian assholes who heeded their whole day ruined or their tickets punched.

"This is something like what happened to J. J. Madison, isn't it?" Clarissa asked us both. I realized suddenly that my wife had never been through a broach before. She looked a little frightened by what we'd just done, and she had good reason. Permit the toe of a shoe, or a trailing coattail to intersect the bright blue border of the broach; say good-bye to toe or tail. The end of a stick, cut by that boundary, will have a shiny, polished look. Naturally, any interworld terminal worth the name will design its debarking platforms to prevent that sort of thing.

But it gets worse. Cut the power and let the broach close down on something solid protruding through it, *Kaboom!* Or make that, *Kaboom* squared!, at both ends of the operation. The Hamiltonians who'd gunned me down nine years ago had been finished off when I'd sabotaged an experimental setup sort of ancestral to this one. Clarissa and I had been seriously injured in the resulting explosion. She'd lost a lot of her lovely hair, and I'd lost an eye, but she'd found a new one for me.

Used to belong to somebody named Abby—Abby Normal.

"Yep," Lucy answered proudly. "It's just exactly what you thought it was, a sure-enough genuine double broach! Beam me up, Winnie! It's the wave of the future! An' you two are among the first one hundred customers t'try it out! Instantaneous transportation!"

I peered at her suspiciously. "Does this thing work the way I think it does?"

"The first broach, in LaPorte," she answered, "goes t'someplace secure in another world—an undiscovered Egyptian tomb or a lost city that managed t'stay lost. The second broach, set up facing it a thousandth of an inch from the first, leads here."

"Ain't science wonderful?" my mate said graciously, not entirely believing it, herself. I could see her thinking that she wished she'd brought an overnight case.

I said, "Well, what'll they think of next?" a phrase that seems to have vanished from the vocabulary of worlds less blessed by freedom—and the peace, progress, and prosperity it invariably engenders—than the Confederacy.

I kept looking around until I saw a brightly lit sign that read, ALL EXITS. "Okay," I asked Lucy, "where do we go from here—and why?"

"Well," she said, "after we talked t'Slaughterbush, Williams, an' Fahel, I got t'thinkin'. I was kinda surprised, given what you boys've told me about your homeworlds, that we hadn't run into any native Confederate greenies."

"Greenies?" Clarissa asked. We followed Lucy to the sign I'd seen. People were getting into what looked like an elevator, except that above the door, where there should have been numbers, it read, AVENUE A & 34TH. People got in, the door shut, then reopened again and the car was empty. Lucy got in and punched a panel where you'd expect to see buttons. At the top, the address changed to EAST 50TH.

"Well, c'mon," she urged us. "We're burnin' daylight!"

The door closed, the goddamned thing lurched sideways, and we were gone.

"TREE-HUGGERS!" LUCY TOOK a long pull of her mint julep, a drink built on the same basic principle as a good martini, but with bourbon and various imaginary additives instead of gin or vodka and the same. I was sure that her Texican accent had thickened, now that she was in her native country again.

"Dirt-worshippers," she went on. "Animal fanatics. Toad lickers. See, where Winnie comes from, every last form of collectivism's been thoroughly discredited for a long time. That doesn't mean they're on their last legs, though—not as long as they've still got all the 'lawyers, guns, an' money.' "

We were relaxing at the lavish lakeside estate of yet another old friend of Lucy's. When we'd emerged from Armadillo Interworld into the hot, dry air on East 50th, Lucy had a car there—a brand-new purple Lenda J.—and we'd roared off due east along the same street until all of the buildings went away and it became a country road. Six miles east of the city, she'd taken a sharp right and frightened me out of ten years' growth.

This part of Texas is so flat that it makes Kansas look like the Himalayas. I'd never seen such a featureless landscape in my life, yellow-gray, bone-dry, and dusty, straight out to the horizon in any direction you couldn't avoid looking. It was a good land, though, full of friendly, hardworking people. It had taken us fifteen minutes to get from the elevator to the waiting car, one hundred yards away, because the strangers we met on the street all asked us how we-all were, and really wanted to know.

What had scared me out of ten years' growth, after passing dozens of what would have been hard-luck farms back home— here they were razor-edged islands of pure emerald surrounded by desert—and emu ranches, and forty-foot piles of industrial cottonseed you could see two miles away, was that, having driven south, away from the highway a few hundred yards, the Lenda J. suddenly plunged into a yawning hole I hadn't noticed, and we disappeared—well, if not from the face of the Earth, then at least from the top of what people around there call the "cap-rock."

A hundred feet below, after seven or eight hairpin turns—far more thrilling in a hovercraft than on wheels—we might as well have been on a different planet. The rocks and soil down here had turned red, the vegetation had gone to palmetto and yucca and prickly pear—a big fat raccoon waddled across the residential street we found ourselves on—and it looked and smelled a whole lot more like New Mexico than Texas. At the bottom of this fabulous Lost World lay a cool, blue, refreshing lake.

"Welcome t'Ransom Canyon!" Lucy told us. "When I was just a little bitty thing, this here was all dry, an' the Comancheros useta come down here t'buy back white children from the Comanches who'd stolen 'em. I was one of those children, Winnie. Now they got this little dam at the east end, an' the white folks an' the Comanches all go water-skiin' t'gether."

The trouble with thinking that Lucy was a liar was that she always turned out to be telling the truth. "Captured by the Indians," I told my wife, "her suffering was in tents."

Lucy gave me an evil glare—and then burst out laughing.

Five minutes later we'd driven across the little dam, up to an enormous Spanish-style home on South Lakeshore Drive with a huge front yard, walled off by a low brick fence, and full of sagebrush and yucca and other southwesterny vegetables. Huge birds with long, stiff wings circled overhead. As we got out of the car, a fox ran across the driveway.

A mere ten minutes after that, Clarissa and Lucy were reclining on redwood chaise longues, sipping something therapeutically alcoholic. I didn't want to ask them what it was. It didn't *quite* have a little umbrella sticking out of it.

For the benefit of our host, my lovely wife was recapitulating our earlier conversation about environmentalists. "So if I understand it correctly, the simpleminded manifesto of Lucy's 'dirt-worshippers' goes, 'Four legs good, two legs bad. Two wheels good, four wheels bad.' "

Our host made rueful clucking noises. "If accurately rendered, the self-loathing those prejudices reveal sends the imagination of any sane person reeling in shock, disgust, and pity."

Lucy had been struggling to explain the political deathgrip that environmentalists had on the worlds Will and I had come from. "Not to mention the corruption of the round-heeled press," I added, "who make sure it stays that way."

Lucy nodded. "But nobody actually *believes* any of it anymore, right, left, or center. Marx is dead, Rachel Carson is dead, an' Paul Ehrlich is feelin' puny. All any of 'em has left is brute force an' lies. That's why a logical argument never works with their proponents. They don't care t'hear about the facts, what's right or wrong, correct or incorrect. They're after somethin' entirely different from what they claim they want."

"Of course the Slaughterbush types are only getting started here," I cut in, sipping my rum and Coke and enjoying it thoroughly. For a person who never drank alcohol, our host certainly had a well-stocked bar and a generous . . . well, flipper. "First they'll try militant safetyism. That usually works pretty well as a justification for running roughshod over everybody's rights. Or they may try the ever-popular 'For the children . . .' "

"The only 'safety' I'm concerned with," Lucy remarked, "is the safety of liberty. An' what I want most 'for' the children' is a free country for 'em to grow up in!"

"Admirably stated," proclaimed our host, his gray-domed head, long nose, and perpetual grin bobbing atop the edge of a swimming pool constructed so that his head was level with ours, where we sat at a wrought aluminum outdoor table at the side of the high-walled pool. "So why does no one ever say this in the world of your calving, landling?"

"Because," I told him, "anybody who did would never be allowed on television—the 'Com—and any newspaper stories about him that failed to portray him as a thoroughgoing lunatic would be spiked with extreme prejudice." I looked into the mild brown eyes of Aalaalaa Ickickloo T'wheel, Lucy's finny friend and the longtime political editor for the *West Texas Whiskey Rebel*, the biggest online news publication in what used to be its own country until 1896. Or make that 120 A.L. We were here at Aalaalaa's Ransom Canyon hacienda because he just happened to be personally acquainted with a rare phenomenon: a genuine Confederate environmentalist.

"Well, you can tell it to Birdie when she gets here," Aalaalaa said. "The Great Deep knows I've tried to tell her this sort of thing often enough, myself. She always says the salt water in this pool or in my house might seep into the lake and spoil the ecology—meaning it might kill all of the trout our Homeowners' Association has stocked in our artificial lake."

General laughter, from me, Lucy, Clarissa, Aalaalaa, and the two other porpoises in the pool beside him. They'd been introduced to us as Uuruulii Ackorkick S'wheen, and Eereeree Ockockock F'wheem, Aalaalaa's wives. I've never figured cetacean names out, but I knew that Will Sanders and his family would be comfortable here. I made a mental note to call him later on this evening.

"The fact is," Aalaalaa said, "no rational individual willingly damages his own property. That—not the bayonet—is the solution to maintaining an acceptable environment. I myself have caused to be constructed a carefully valved tunnel between this pool and the lake so that, like my neighbors, I may go fishing there from time to time. They use hooks and lines, whereas I use more traditional methods. I must also wear a protective suit, as fresh water and fishhooks are rather hard on my skin."

I laughed. "Well, keep an eye on this pet environmentalist of yours, Aalaalaa. Handle her right, and maybe we'll find out what her priorities really are. Safety Nazism and 'for the children' work most of the time, but the left will turn to environmentalism whenever it looks like they might be losing control. That's when you see the watermelons out in force. I sure hope we won't be picking on a good friend of yours."

"Be assured, landling," Aalaalaa told me, "that she is no true friend, but rather a pest. She borrowed our lawn mower six months ago—with the handy attachment that kills rattlesnakes—and she hasn't brought it back."

"She probably melted it down to make a snake memorial,"

Clarissa told him. Pretty cynical. I wasn't sure I liked what this experience was doing to her.

"Watermelons?" Uuruulii Ackorkick S'wheen shook her head as if the conversation were making less and less sense to her. On the other hand, I was having a political discussion with a bunch of porpoises, so what the hell.

"Sure, honey," Lucy told her. "Watermelons: green on the outside, an' red on the inside."

"Red," Aalaalaa explained, "is the chosen livery of communism, I believe, the crown jewel in the diadem of collectivism, to switch metaphors in the middle of the thermocline. And collectivism is what these people are all advancing one way or another, whether they admit it or not."

"Maybe even whether they know it or not," I added. "Like Joseph Goebbels or Franklin Roosevelt or somebody said, there are a lot of useful idiots out there."

"It was Lenin, Edward William Bear. And I know all about the Reds, friend Lucy," Uuruulii told her. "Are you saying then that these environmentalists are all communists?"

"One name for a product sold under lotsa labels," she replied. "They're all workin' for it, one way or another. But there's more to it than that. There's that psychopathological component Clarissa mentioned. Y'don't hafta listen long before y'begin t'hear a 'subtext' in the pronouncements of environmentalists, a pathetic wail, straight outa John Milton, of absolute, churnin', acidic self-loathin'."

"A subtext." Uuruulii seemed to feel a chill and cuddled closer to her husband at the edge of the pool. I'd never seen a porpoise do that before. Eereeree, too, drifted closer to him.

"And because they hate themselves so venomously," said Aalaalaa, looking from one of his females to the other, a gesture I was sure he picked up from humans, "and by extension, every other member of their own species or anything remotely like it—"

"They hate and fear what's best for sapients of every kind," Uuruulii concluded. "It's a kind of political death wish. The less a given policy is likely to work, the more misery and disaster it's likely to cause, the more energetically they'll advocate it."

Eereeree's only comment was, "Sick! How did such sick people end up running so many nation-states?"

"Democracy!" everybody with two legs said at once.

Lucy said, "At the same time, they hate what works best: free enterprise an' individual liberty. They'll do anythin'—use any excuse—to destroy 'em. If it weren't global warmin', it'd be global coolin', and if that weren't handy, then they'd complain that world temperatures are stayin' the same all the time."

"And blame it on individualistic greed and selfish capitalism," Clarissa finished for her.

EITHER THE INTERVIEW was not going very well, or it was going perfectly.

"But don't you see, all of you, that we owe a debt of love to our Mother Gaea . . ." the woman had begun. She'd been going on like this since we'd been introduced.

I sighed, although I'd tried bravely not to. Clarissa bent her head wearily and covered her eyes for a moment. The ever-smiling expressions of our cetacean host and hostesses were as unreadable as that of any porpoise.

"You tree-huggers all gimme a pain in the patoot!" Lucy barely kept herself from shouting. She was embarrassed, I think, that this woman was a native Confederate and not some kind of immigrant. "Your precious Earth, your warm, nurturin', lovely Mother Gaea, is nothin' but a giant ball of *rock*, thinly smeared with three billion years' accumulation of *wormshit*!"

Not for the first time this afternoon—nor would it be the last—the woman was shocked. "But how can you . . . ?"

Lucy continued, "Earth is a great place to be *from*, that's all, a great place to be *from*!"

She'd already nearly given Aalaalaa's neighbor, Birdie, a coronary by quoting Robert Heinlein, more or less: "Well, this planet's just about used up, it's time to move on." I don't think I've ever seen eyes pop out quite that far.

People dress a lot of different ways in the Confederacy, just like they do practically everywhere in cultures you'd consider modern—except even more so. It's said that a person covered from head to toe in heavy furs, like an Eskimo, can encounter someone on the streets of Greater LaPorte, someone who's completely naked, and the first thought of neither will be about clothing.

This woman, however, was unusual. And not in a nice way. She wore a ratty old sweater over a threadbare jersey dress two sizes too big for her. She wore synthetic stockings of some kind that bagged around her ankles, and old-fashioned black-and-white tennis shoes. Her long, thick auburn hair looked like it hadn't been washed or combed out for months, probably in a conscientious effort to conserve water. It certainly wasn't poverty or she wouldn't have been living down here by the lake. Her neighbors told us she'd inherited about a hundred times her weight in platinum.

Never leave money to your kids if you can help it. You're not doing them any favor. I've never known a trust baby who wasn't stupid, evil, or just plain nuts.

Birdie was one of those people, like Hillary Clinton, who once trembled on the brink. If her face and her body had been driven by anything even remotely resembling a benign spirit, she'd almost have been pretty, say about thirty pounds ago. Instead, you could see that she was motivated by some malignant element in her personality so profound—Aalaalaa had said it was self-hatred—that she had come, in her mere thirty-five years or so of life, to look like whatever she was on the inside.

Whatever it was, it wasn't pretty.

"So what?" Birdie argued. "That doesn't give humanity—or any other species—the right to pollute our air and water, to ravage and destroy the land!"

Lucy shook her head. "Whaddya mean, 'pollute'? Whaddya mean, 'ravage an' destroy'? You mean we *changed* the environment?"

"Well." Birdie's lower lip was starting to tremble and she'd only been talking to Lucy for fifteen minutes. I'd seen others hold out for at least sixteen. Clarissa and I and our finny host and hostesses had pretty much stayed out of it. I still wasn't entirely certain why Lucy had dragged us down here. "Yes."

Lucy was in good form. "You bet your overly cosseted backside we changed it, girlie! The environment out here *sucked* when we got it! People died of cold an' starvation in the winter. They died of heat an' thirst in the summer. They were attacked by bugs an' snakes an' they got eaten up by bears an' wolves."

"Just as unnatural intruders should be!" Pretty good, although she said it in a quavery voice.

Lucy was undaunted. "Anybody that doesn't change an environment like that, pronto, an' change it *radically*, they gotta be . . . well, they gotta be at *least* as halfwitted as anybody who'd choose t'be an environmental activist in Lubbock, of all places, where there *is* no environment t'speak of, at least not above the caprock!"

"Aalaalaa!" Birdie protested, "are you going to let this woman insult me like this?"

The porpoise looked her in the eye. "I'd surely hoped that she would, Birdie. Now, are you going to bring my lawn mower back, or shall I sic Lucy on you again?"

"I can't," Birdie sobbed. "I had it melted down to make a snake memorial!"

23: MONEY FOR NOTHING

> There is some justice in the universe. Simply say, "I'm not a crook," enough times, and everybody will start believing that's exactly what you are.
>
> —*Memoirs of Lucille G. Kropotkin*

Back to LaPorte. Clarissa hadn't worried this time about the dangers of travel by broach, but if we'd been paying customers instead of Friends of Lucy, it would have cost us about the same as a hypersonic suborbital around the world. It would get cheaper. And better. That's the way a free economy works.

Our conversation with the only environmental activist in the North American Confederacy (or in northern Texas, anyway) was a success only because it became clear right away that if Birdie had the brains to build the bomb that took down the Old Endicott Building, to sabotage the tube-train, or to drop a car on us from a dirigible, she was the best actress I'd ever seen. I've opened cans of sardines that were brighter.

Birdie had ended up pulling out all the stops—global warming, acid rain, ozone depletion—pseudoscience imported from my world or others like it. Lucy had countered with a low blow: "You got this from government scientists? In worlds where they haven't even cured cancer or Alzheimer's?"

"Well . . . yes."

"How did we cure cancer?" Lucy demanded. "The same way we put people on the Moon a generation before those people did. And left a permanent colony there. We *didn't* turn it over to government scientists!" Not the best debating form, I suppose, but it sent Birdie away sobbing. Of course Aalaalaa knew now that he would never get his lawn mower back, which was probably okay. A dolphin needs a lawn mower like a fish needs a bicycle.

NIGHT IN THE city.

The American Zone is the only place I know where you can find what the Brits call "bomb sites," a generic term left over from World War II, meaning any building that's been reduced to kibbles and bits and left that way.

At the corner of Trenchard and Gordon, the basic structure still stood—it had been a four-story office complex—but the southwest corner of it, where there had been some kind of store, was nothing but a scoured-out concrete pad with a lone column supporting the rest of the building. Back in the dangerous-looking shadows, lay a little pile of brush and other rubble.

Not wanting another car dropped on my head, I stood just inside, close to the column, waiting for High Colonic to appear. Will was two city blocks away; I could see him parked in front of the bar, listening to whatever the 'Com in my tunic pocket could hear. Suffering mostly from what's commonly called "blunt trauma" (the bullets hadn't gone in more than a quarter of an inch, as it turned out, no matter how dramatic they'd sounded, hitting the pan) he'd been given a clean bill of health by Clarissa, almost at the same hour she'd finally cut the plastic off my arm. So we were both "operating within normal parameters."

Meanwhile, Clarissa, Fran, and Mary-Beth were parked in her van about the same distance away that Will was, but in the opposite direction, on the crossing street. I didn't even want to think about the fight the three Sanderses must have had over two pregnant women on a stakeout. It wasn't quite as cold down here as it had been six floors up at None of the Above Park, but it was dismal, overcast and damp, without a star in the sky. I was suddenly aware how much activity went on, day or night, in the rest of LaPorte. Ten o'clock came and went.

Eleven o'clock came and went.

At midnight precisely, Will whisked by. A gun in each hand and my eyes on the sky, I jumped into the Rockford, which was rolling again before I got the door down. I laid the Browning in my lap, wiggled the Model 58 back into its shoulder holster (I'd like to say it was good to be wearing that contrivance again, but I'd be lying), and then shoved the Browning into the holster on my right hip and fastened my seat belt.

Maybe this was just another trap that didn't come off this time. Maybe the guy was fearful and that was why he kept putting off meeting with us. Who cared.

So much for High Colonic. Up his, so to speak.

The five of us rendezvoused at the 600 block of Geñet Place, only because both the Bears and Sanders happened to live there, on opposite sides of the street. Everybody went to bed—or at least Clarissa and I did. We had a long day ahead of us.

MORNING. I WAS so sick of the Zone we didn't even stop for breakfast at the Hanging Judge. Clarissa was off somewhere laboring over a pair of hot tonsils. Lucy was on some errand of her own. The Kendall sisters were busy being pregnant.

Will glanced at the card in my hand, with Sam Yosemite's penciled notation, "Baje Wooley—Byzantine Pope—Talk to Mickey Stonesoup." He'd added a street address and 'Com number. We'd discovered now that we'd been directed to the Riverdam Hotel, an ancient moldering pile of plaster with its ratty backside hanging out over the Cache la Poudre River, tucked into the farthest, shabbiest recess of the American Zone. It took us ten minutes to get there. Somehow, the place reminded me of the Hotel California, the one where you can check out any time you want, but you can never leave.

A hand-lettered cardboard sign taped to the inside of the front door, visible behind a cracked pane of dirty glass said: PRIVATE RESIDENCE. There wasn't any bell or buzzer. Knocking, we were greeted by a tall, balding, middle-aged man in an American sport coat and slacks. He was wearing glasses, a western bolo tie, and no gun that I could see.

"What can I do for you gentlemen?" he asked, opening the door about six inches and peering out at us. He blinked as if the outdoor light bothered his eyes. His voice sounded exactly like that of Bullwinkle J. Moose.

"Win Bear," I told him, offering a card. "I'm a private detective. In fact, I'm *the* private detective. This is my associate, Captain Will Sanders of the Greater LaPorte Militia. I called earlier and talked to Mickey Stonesoup."

"Nobody ever tells me anything around here." He shook his head sadly and sighed in his cartoon voice. "Come in, I guess. I'm N. D. Forrest. Everybody calls me Endie."

Inside, the place still looked like a hotel lobby. There was even one of those big, round, overstuffed sofas with a conical backrest in the middle, although the maroon velvet it was covered in was more than a little threadbare. The place seemed earthy and damp, like a dungeon, partly because it smelled of mildew and old urinal cakes. Twenty-foot drapes, of the same material as the sofa and other furniture scattered about, had been drawn across the high windows, making it as dim as a dungeon, too.

Where a bit of light shone between the drapes, the windows were as dirty as the glass in the front doors. Dust motes danced in the feeble rays that made it through. Half the bulbs in the huge chandelier, high above the ancient carpet, had burned out.

On the front desk, where guests had once checked in and out, the current residents had put a big Telecom box, an unusual object in the Confederacy, where people usually preferred to use whole walls of their homes for communications and entertainment. This was an *old* building. The box was presently showing a soap opera with chimpanzees in the starring roles. It was being watched by a dozen or so drab, gray, middle-aged individuals who made me think of ghosts. Some of them were snoring.

I wouldn't have been surprised if Forrest had told us, "Walk this way," like a comical movie butler. Instead, he led Will and me through the dozing residents, across the spooky lobby, past the front desks—a little gray mouse squeaked angrily before scurrying out of our way—and into another big chamber that must have been for dances once, or banquets. Now, for all intents and purposes, it was a throne room.

It was also a big room, and we walked some more. I thought about my talk with Yosemite, about Mickey Stonesoup. "You remember Paladin?" he'd asked me as he wrote down where he'd gotten *Gone with the Wind* and the other movies.

I nodded. "Back in the 1950s. Black and white. Richard Boone. The hired gun with a heart of gold in the old TV show *Have Gun Will Travel.*"

"You got it," Yosemite said. "You remember that Paladin's calling card had a chess knight on it?"

The memory took me back a long way. "Sure I do. My mom had some made for me just like them, as a joke, when I graduated from the police academy."

"Well this Stonesoup," Yosemite had declared, "his card should have a *rook!*"

At the other end of the vast, dimly lit ballroom—what did these guys have against light, anyway?—stood a six-inch raised platform, originally for a live band, I assumed. Now it had been covered with a fringe-bordered carpet, no doubt snatched from some other room in the hotel. (What would the Bridal Suite be like with naked wooden floors; I wondered.) It was backed up with another carpet just like it, being used as a wall hanging. Apparently the Presidential Suite had been deprived, as well.

Here and there, sitting around in scattered folding chairs, or standing near the walls, were more gray ghosts just as lively as those in the lobby—maybe fifty or sixty men and women, none of them younger than forty, attired in workclothes, in suits and ties, even in pajamas and nightgowns. They weren't watching, they were waiting, there with their leader. I wondered if they knew for what.

Centered at the back of the dais, instead of the big armchair I'd expected, we found a luxurious sofa. Draped along its length was one of the oddest human figures I'd ever seen. This had to be Baje Wooley, known throughout the American Zone as the "Byzantine Pope." He seemed to me like little more than a living prop. He was waxy-complexioned, grotesquely tall, and inhumanly thin. His body language was like that of an Audio-Animatronics figure at Disneyland.

The man extended a pale, long-fingered hand at me, palm down, the fingers languidly curved.

"Kiss the ring! Kiss the ring!" a voice whispered hoarsely behind me. I turned to see a small, urgent, neatly dressed man—blue blazer, brass buttons, gray trousers, red tie, light-blue pin-striped button-down shirt—fidgeting back and forth at my elbow. "Kiss the ring!"

"Kiss my ass." I turned to the tall guy. "You Baje Wooley?"

"Yes," the man said in a funereal tone, slowly lowering his hand, "I am. And you are?"

"Win Bear," the nervous little man on my left said for me. "He's a *detective*, Baje." The word "detective" must have had some special significance for them. "And this is Captain Will Sanders, Commander of the Greater LaPorte Militia."

"Greater LaPorte Militia," Wooley repeated in the same lugubrious manner, but with a slight intonation of distaste, as if he'd just found a dog hair on his tongue.

"That's right." Will turned to the little guy at my elbow who was beginning to make me nervous. "And you would be?"

"Michael C. Stonesoup." He took a quick half-step to the left, then another half-step to the right, back to where he'd been. "Special advisor to Mr. Wooley." I looked around at the semiconscious figures occupying the room. Except for one well-dressed suit standing by a heavily draped window and visibly moving from time to time, they all might as well have been corpses. Forrest had disappeared without a trace, just like a proper servant, which was a little strange, I thought. None of these folks seemed well off enough for a valet. Wooley's several dozen yards of chalk-striped navy blue suit needed dry cleaning, I noticed, and the tips of Stonesoup's shirt collar were frayed.

I was impressed. Poverty like that was a hard thing to accomplish in the Confederacy.

Stonesoup blinked suddenly and shifted position again, as if he'd been pushed by an invisible hand. "But we're being ungracious, aren't we, Baje?"

"Ungracious," Wooley repeated mournfully. "We are?"

"Endie!" Stonesoup shouted abruptly. "Bring chairs right away! Bring—would you gentlemen like something to drink? Of course you would. Coke be all right, or would you—Endie! Bring Cokes in here right away!"

All that spoken at twice the rate of a Top-40 DJ, while he danced around like a bantam-weight boxer, never standing in the same spot or the same position for more than a fraction of a second. It must have been a psychological confession, I thought.

Maybe Stonesoup realized, at some level, that a moving target is harder to hit. At the same time that Forrest, huffing and puffing, hurried to do his master's bidding, Stonesoup demanded, "You're not armed, are you? Baje won't have a gun in his house."

After talking with Sam Yosemite, Clarissa and I had done a little research of our own, elbow to elbow and shoulder to shoulder. Back in the world he came from, Wooley had been the author of a bestseller—ghostwritten for him over a generation earlier—offering a variety of rationalizations and clever techniques for avoiding inconvenient personal responsibilities. He'd also been the perennial candidate for his country's National Chief Executive, standing for office on the "Freedom-Loving Party" ticket. Apparently he and his party of freedom-lovers were selective about which freedoms they loved.

"Of course not," I lied without a twinge. Maybe it was Wooley's house, but inside my clothes it was *my* territory. I knew that Will felt the same way. He didn't bat an eye. Of course Stonesoup knew we were lying. At least I hoped he did.

Seated on the rickety, straightbacked chairs we'd been offered—Will's with one leg casually repaired with a length of wire, mine with a duct-taped seat cushion—we accepted room-temperature Coca-Cola in mismatched teacups from Forrest, mine specially adorned with a long brown crack running from the rim to the bottom. With five dozen eerie figures watching us from the shadows, it was like being on a late-night cable talk show.

For vampires.

Will got down to business. "Mr. Wooley, Lieutenant Bear and I are investigating a couple of different matters, possibly related. Both of them are very serious, matters of life and death for thousands of people. We'd both like to ask you a few questions in connection with them, if you don't mind."

Wooley stirred as if from a dream, and blinked. "I don't mind, do I, Mickey?"

Hot damn, I thought, a whole sentence! Now we *were* getting somewhere!

"You seem to be disliked by your fellow immigrants," Will went on without waiting for Stonesoup's nod. "Many of them gave everything up to escape from countless tyrannies and come to a free world. Frankly, I've heard from some of them that you and your friends here are the only newcomers ever to be rounded up by their own government, hauled to the nearest probability broach, and *pushed* through. Is that really what happened?"

Gasps from the "audience." Wooley blinked in slow motion. I'd never seen that done before. "Why, Captain Sanders, I'm surprised you'd ask me a question like that."

Will laughed. "Yeah, but it did happen?"

Stonesoup took over at that point, and it became perfectly clear, if it hadn't been before, that he was the real brains, heart, and soul of the Byzantine Pope's little "court." For the life of me, I can't remember a goddamned thing he said—I've tried— but if there were five positions that could be taken on any given issue, he appeared capable of advocating each and every one of them in the same sentence, almost in the same breath, without upsetting a single listener on any side. What he said (I tried afterward to reconstruct the form, if not the actual content) went something like this: "Believe me my dear and good friends I can personally assure you on the basis of firsthand knowledge that the sun will definitely rise in the east tomorrow morning, have I ever lied to you, and we'll all enjoy watching it rise in the west so much when it rises, absolutely, you can trust me on this and take it to the bank, in the north and south and of course it won't come up at all."

My guess was that his usual victims—gullible idiots anxious

to have their own beliefs validated by him—never even noticed his remarkable talent. Here was a guy who could have given lessons to Bill Clinton.

Will ignored Stonesoup and pressed on. "To be perfectly truthful, Mr. Wooley, whenever Win or I or any of our associates ask around about you and your, er . . ."

"Hangers-on?" I offered to resentful muttering out in shadow-land.

Will glared at me; I convinced myself he didn't mean it. "You're invariably compared to 'gypsy roofers' in the worlds we all fled, who come around each spring to separate suggestable people from hundreds of dollars to 'tar' their roofs or 'repave' their driveways with cheap recycled fuel oil—and then disappear before they can be arrested on bunco charges."

I could see that Stonesoup was trying very hard not to get mad. He was a con-man, all right. We'd heard he'd given up a promising career doing kitchen appliance infomercials for politics. If it'd been me, with nothing to sell, I'd simply have cold-cocked Will. Instead, Stonesoup kept up that nervous, perpetual-motion game-show host manner of his. He took a deep breath. "What Baje did, Captain Sanders, in the ungrateful world we were all forcibly exiled from, was to offer himself generously, unselfishly, indeed, self-sacrificingly, to a nation that desperately needed him as Chief Executive, a nation that coldly rejected him and the Freedom-Loving Party because they were the ignorant products of the public education system who didn't understand what was best for them."

"Well I'm certainly glad to have that cleared up, because I heard differently." Will stubbornly addressed Wooley instead of Stonesoup. "I heard that what you and your friends did, back in the States, was to pretend to run for Chief Executive, when in fact none of you have any real convictions. You extracted millions from poor saps who only wanted to live in a free country, for political campaigns that somehow never quite solidified. And then you doled it out to yourselves as 'consulting fees.' "

"Legitimate expenses!" So Wooley had hot-buttons, after all.

Will said, "I gotta tell you, Mr. Wooley, the most amazing thing to me is that your Freedom-Loving Party rank and file appears to have consisted entirely of suckers on whom the same old tired con worked year after year."

"No doubt," I observed, unable to stay out of it any longer, "if you hadn't stumbled upon such a lucrative modus operandi, you'd still be back in our own continuum, working the Badger Game, the Spanish Prisoner, or the Pigeon Drop on an entirely different gaggle of hapless marks."

"Stop it! Stop it! Stop it!" shrieked a voice from behind. We turned. Forrest stood between us and the door with a long-barrelled stainless steel revolver in his hand. "You can't say that kind of thing and just walk out of here!"

"Pay no attention to Endie." Stonesoup turned his back on the man and made yawning gestures. "He's completely harmless. Endie was the original founder of the Freedom-Lover's Party, did you know that? He's a bit less than happy about being exiled with us. Somewhere along the line, in one last pathetic attempt to bring his tiny, insignificant third party out of the utter obscurity which is all it achieved after thirty years of struggle, he chose to shut his eyes to what you clearly regard as our shortcomings and let us take the party over, in exchange for a salaried position as its figurehead-in-chief."

Will nodded. "That's consistent with my understanding. He took his country's last, best hope for liberty and let you guys, Stonesoup and Wooley and their flunkies, deliberately corrupt and destroy it. Now everything he created has turned to garbage, in which he's forced to wallow every day."

"The irony is that he never got a chance to collect that salary." Stonesoup shrugged negligently, as if he hadn't heard what Will had said about him. "He's a gofer, the court jester. We call him 'Endie' because he's the butt of everybody's jokes around here. Isn't that right, Endie? Put that thing down immediately, and come here! All this man did was *say* things. If you shoot him, you'll be initiating force against him."

Forrest's shoulders slumped. He shoved the sixgun in his waistband and came to the foot of the dais.

"That's Endie," Stonesoup said mockingly. "An absolute sucker for the Nonaggression Principle."

Wooley stirred again. "An undesirable litmus test."

Forrest shrieked incoherently, pulled his revolver out, levelled it at Wooley, and before anybody could reach him, pulled the trigger six times.

The noise was horrific; .357 Magnum, at a guess. Suddenly, the air was filled with the odor of double-based nitro powder. Wooley, totally unhurt, looked confused. Eight feet to his right, one of his followers I'd noticed before—a tall, dignified, attorneyesqe, vaguely Irish individual with short gray hair—slumped to the dirty carpet and expired in a pool of blood.

Meanwhile Stonesoup, standing beside me, was trying to conceal a big, wet, rapidly spreading dark spot across the front of his gray preppie trousers.

24: THERE'LL NEVER BE ANOTHER YOU

The most dangerous and successful conspiracies usually take place in public, in plain sight, under the clear, bright light of day—often with cameras focused on them.

—Memoirs of Lucille G. Kropotkin

For some reason, hockey players and figure skaters don't seem to like watching each other work. I suppose that's why there was a big, thick partition—about sixty feet from side to side—between the two oversized sheets of cold, wet, slippery stuff at the Confederation Ice and Pool Esplanade on (where else?) Confederation Boulevard, a mile or so south of Laporte University, Ltd.

Within that wall were a score of locker rooms, a fully equipped weight room, a first-aid station with its own surgery and CAT scanner, and a pro-shop full of colorful jerseys and frilly dresses hanging side by side along the walls. There were also steel and titanium blades (with and without toepicks), helmets, sticks, hip and butt pads, three weights of pucks, unmounted boots of both denominations, and at least a carload and a half of assorted painkillers, blister pads, tape for several different purposes, plastic splints, air-casts, and bandages.

Surprisingly, figures skaters buy their full, fair share of the medical stuff.

Atop the partition was a restaurant and bar, which made being here very pleasant in and of itself. Back in the States, in the seventies, I'd once arrested a would-be child kidnapper at South Suburban ice rink in Littleton. I hadn't seen ice skating of either kind since then, not for twenty years. I hadn't even known that they played hockey here in the Confederacy. But it had developed that Clarissa had a client—a pretty little prodigy of an eight-year-old girl—with cruel bone spurs growing out of both feet that almost appeared to be a natural hazard in this particular environment.

On one side of the partition, the ice was kept relatively soft and the air inside was almost balmy. The place had a breathtaking skylight high overhead, spanning the entire building, and mirrors on every surface where there weren't enormous floor-to-ceiling windows. The restaurant and bar were divided in half by a transparent partition only half an inch thick. I happened to be on the figure-skating side at the moment, filling my lungs with the clean, cool air, looking down at half a hundred little girls as they swirled and twirled around.

I'd already contacted the Gables. Now that we knew the source of the movies they disliked so much, it was up to their lawyers to make the next move. I knew and they knew—I could see it in their eyes over the 'Com—that there probably wasn't much that could be done. It was still a free country and I was now free to help Will Sanders keep it that way.

The good news (one of those ill wind things) was that the single individual most responsible for the video researching and importing on behalf of the Byzantine Pope and his menagerie was the same individual we'd left lying in a pool of surprise, with Civil Liberties Association birddogs (not the same couple we'd met at Paulchinsky's) sniffing around him. It appeared that poor Endie had slowed the flow of otherworldly entertainment in his own way, and helped to solve the Gables' problem, at least for a little while. The CLA folks had gently escorted him to a place where, according to Napoleon XVII, anyway, life is beautiful all the time.

The Gables had said that the check was in the mail; I'd said that I believed them. Pappy had said they were pleased it had only taken a few days to "solve" their case. Janie invited me to visit the set of their current project, a nifty little murder mystery (so she said) involving reincarnation. I told her I'd bring Clarissa with me. She'd be absolutely thrilled. And it would be wealthier around the Bear estate for a while, too. Always a good feeling.

So who would be my next celebrity client, Bettie Page?

One could only hope.

For our little get-together this afternoon, I'd originally thought that we might have a picnic over in the park—what the hell was its name?—a few blocks north of here, where I'd first landed on my head in the Confederacy.

"Nah," Will had said. "It's too hot—besides, the way our luck is going, we'd get lost." He hadn't solved his case yet, and he was feeling cranky about it.

"No we wouldn't," Clarissa had told him. "We'd simply follow the advice first set forth by the estimable Brothers Grimm, and leave a trail of breadcrumbs."

Lucy had shaken her head. "Say, don'cha remember the rest of that story, dearie? Birds'd eat the breadcrumbs an' then we'd be lost worse'n ever!"

"Then what you want to do, of course, is drop *poisoned* breadcrumbs," Fran had answered her, grinning villainously, "and follow the trail of dead birds!

"ARE YOU COMING, darling?" Clarissa was standing in the transparent doorway, waiting for me to come to the table we'd reserved over on the hockey side, where her small client, armored like a fireplug-sized samurai, was trying the new skates her Healer had designed for her. On that side it was ten degrees colder, and the air smelled not very faintly of ammonia from the jerseys the players took a perverse pride in not washing until the season was over.

Some things aren't necessarily better in the Confederacy.

I lit a cigar by way of self-defense and made the trek across the restaurant, mostly empty at this relatively early hour, to join my lovely and talented spouse and our good friends. We were having a meeting of sorts, trying to figure out what to do next about Will's case. Clarissa and Lucy had come with me. Will had brought Mary-Beth and Fran.

The carpet—and the escalator treads we'd ridden to get up here—were a softer rubber than the sidewalks outside, so that skaters from both rinks could come up to the restaurant for a meal or a snack without having to unlace their accoutrements. "I'll have a scotch and scotch," I told the waiter before I sat down, "with a little extra scotch for flavor."

The waiter, a young chimpanzee who'd informed us proudly that he played hockey here on the weekends for the Rocky Mountain Oysters' farm club—the Boulevard Barnacles—started reading me a whole long list of different whiskies the restaurant offered. I interrupted, "A single malt, if you please. Glenfiddich will do nicely, or even Glenlivet." I wasn't being trendy; I'd been drinking Laphroaig for than thirty years.

The chimpanzee nodded his approval, and with the remainder of our party's order, went back to wherever it is that waiters go. I sat down next to my lovely Clarissa and listened to her as— keeping an eye on her young Rockette Richard some forty or fifty feet below us—she communicated with the kid by 'Com, the little girl's tranceiver being a part of her helmet.

Step by step, Clarissa put her through her paces—right and left crossovers in forward and reverse, slapshots made on the fly, T-stops and hockey stops, and even showstops ordinarily done by figure skaters, and finally a spectacular jump where the little girl did a three-sixty in mid-air. At last Clarissa folded up her 'Com. "Well, I think that new boot liner's going to work!" She beamed. "Now we'll just let the bone spurs dissolve by themselves."

"Yech," I told her, not for the first time. It's amazing what the human body is capable of doing, to and for itself. Bones, especially those of kids, are a hell of a lot less rigid and fixed than most people think. They're not even really solid, they're just the thickest part of the soup. "Do you have something to drink?"

She was about to answer me when an all-too familiar figure came shambling toward us across the rubbery restaurant carpet. It was the little old lady with the great big hat again, collecting for the Spaceman's Fund.

The question was, *which* little old lady.

Fran and Mary-Beth were on their feet in an instant, their hands on the grips of their pistols. From the corner of my eye, I watched as Clarissa drew her weapon underneath the table. Will sat where he was, but I knew he was fast when he needed to be, and I knew that Lucy was even faster.

As she reached our table, my heart was pounding and my right hand found its way to the worn rubber handle of my .41 Magnum. But she held her own hand out, toward me, and her fist was too small to conceal any kind of weapon.

"Lieutenant Bear," she said in a horrible, quavery voice, "you were exceptionally generous the other day."

"Well," I answered, grinning up at her and swallowing a little, "I hope it helped the spacemen." I'd been feeling pretty stupid— and confused—about this woman all week long. Was she the one who'd shot at me, attacked me in the bathroom, and put holes in my partner? Or was she the one who'd lectured me on the size (how very embarrassing) of my gun? "Two whole ounces of silver." Her voice was like fingernails on a blackboard—ten stainless steel fingernails, on a diamond blackboard a mile long. "I wanted to thank you, young man—and to bring you your change."

"But I don't want—"

She put her gloved hand over mine and dropped something, round and cold and very heavy, into my palm. It was another of the thick golden coins with an engraved picture of Sam Houston on one side. The old lady's painfully cracked, ancient voice immediately gave way to a smooth, ominously familiar-sounding male baritone. "To be perfectly truthful, I don't *know* any spacemen, but I've been trying to get this to you, for days!"

"She" lifted her broad-brimmed hat and heavy veil, and I was looking straight into the face—only one of them, as it turned out—of Bennett Williams. The unmistakable sound of half a dozen pistol hammers being thumbed back simultaneously to full cock was a lot like steel ball bearings rattling down a flight of metal stairs. You could also hear an ominous hum as an equal number of energy weapons came up to full power. I looked down and found my hands full of sixgun and autopistol. The poor guy was surrounded by about one hundred thousand foot-pounds of potential *schrecklichheit*.

To give him credit, he didn't flinch. "Dr. Benjamin Wilhelmsohn at your service, dear ladies, Captain, Lieutenant, late of the philosophy department on the scenic Baton Rouge campus of the Texas University of Agriculture and Mechanics, where I held the George F. Will Chair in Sophistry."

UNLIKE ANY BENNETT Williams I knew so far, Benjamin Wilhelmsohn had spoken in a southern accent about as thick and sweet as molasses. The professor lowered his ladylike veil again and looked all around as if he were afraid that somebody might decide to drop a car on him. It was a possibility. The ceiling overhead was perfectly transparent, a vast, arching, unbroken pane of that remarkable stuff Confederates call glass.

"I strongly suggest that if Clarissa is finished with her patient—pardon me, her client—we take this colloquium somewhere a little less public," Will said, thinking the same paranoid thoughts that I was, as he rose from the table and patted the holstered automatic on his hip.

Clarissa nodded, and stood up, as well. "Stick me with a fork, I'm done!" She loved that expression.

Lucy said, "The manager here's an old friend of mine, an' I think I can arrange somethin' for us."

Of course.

The manager, a limber-limbed gibbon who'd once played forward for the Atlanta Atlatls was more than happy to oblige his old friend Lucy, who, astonishingly, had managed the team for some length of time. In less than five minutes—with the enthusiastic assistance of the star goalie of the Boulevard Barnacles—we'd been comfortably reinstalled in one of the several party rooms downstairs that were a part of the section that divided hockey territory from figure skating country. These rooms were at rink level, and had big windows that looked out directly onto the ice. "Hockey or figure skating?" Will had asked me what side of the CIPE building we should be on for the meal and meeting that was about to follow.

"By all means, figure skating," I'd replied without hesitation. "I'm sure Professor Wilhelmsohn has a great deal to tell us, and we have a lot of skull-sweating to do. That should be less distracting than trying to talk about this case and watch a game at the same time, shouldn't it?"

So here we were, with our drinks, sitting around a table again, waiting for food to come. I'd forced myself to order crayfish, in honor of our guest.

But I'd been wrong about the distraction factor. Almost unable to look away, I watched in awe as a tiny, pixie-faced girl-child in an electric blue velvet dress and her straight golden hair in a ponytail, did something complicated and dangerous that involved skating very fast around the rink, then jumping at least four feet off the ice, turning two or three times in the air, and landing gracefully on only one skate, with the other leg extended and her arms upraised. I'd seen stuff like that on the 'Com, but never in person, and never by anybody under sixteen.

"I managed to avoid involvement in the first bombing," Wilhelmsohn was telling us. I forced myself to pay attention. "I had just arrived in the Confederacy and they didn't trust me. In a way, I don't think they ever did."

He poured himself a half-glass of the red wine that Clarissa was drinking, took a sip, then a gulp, and poured himself another glass, full this time.

He sighed. "As well, it pains me to confess that I was . . . well, I suppose in kindness you could call it 'socially disoriented' for a good, long while. Just imagine my surprise! Chimpanzees? Gorillas? Porpoises? Eleven thousand worlds like mine but different? One of the Bennetts told me that he'd escaped from a bizarre universe where the people without any pigmentation at all form a political elite—they call it 'albinocracy.' "

That was another new one on me.

"Regrettably, I was present when they wrecked that underground train, although I swear that I didn't know what they were doing until it'd been done. From where I sat, in the back of one of these wheelless cars of yours, it looked like they were drilling for some reason in the highway median—I had no idea there was a tunnel in it—and left the drill in."

"So that's how it was done. You left that money from your version of Texas?" Will asked.

304 • L. NEIL SMITH

Wilhelmsohn nodded. "I left it to communicate with whoever would be investigating these atrocities. I know it wasn't much of a clue, but it was all I had."

"How about their other crimes?" I asked. "And who the hell are 'they,' for that matter?"

"Well, I wasn't aboard the *City of Calgary*. I almost wish I had been—I've never flown on a dirigible before. I did help them drop that car on you the other night, but I managed to 'slip' at the last moment, and made sure it didn't hit you. They were angry at me, but I talked my way out of it."

"How about the grocery store poisonings?" Mary-Beth asked. So Will had revealed a state secret to his wives. I would have done—and did—exactly the same thing.

He shook his head. "I don't know anything about any grocery store poisonings—how very strange—do you suppose that might have been somebody else?"

"What about the guy at None of the Above Park," I asked, feeling the small pistol he'd abandoned in my left front pocket. "In that denim clown suit?"

He shrugged. "I'd wondered where those clothes went. I'll have you know that they're the height of gentlemen's fashion in East Texas just now. I was always known on the faculty for my sartorial refinement. I'd no idea what had become of them. But I think you should know that I risked escaping from Bennett Williams's house because the next thing they're planning to blow up is the dam at something called Pistol Sight Mountain."

"Pistol Sight Mountain!" several of us exclaimed at once.

"Swell!" Will was suddenly angry. He slammed a fist on the table. "Another regrettable tragedy for west central LaPorte—only this time *hundreds* of thousands will die—and we'll all end up with a goddamned government crammed down our throats whether any of us want a government or not!"

"Now hold your horses!" Lucy declared, fingering Wilhelmsohn's coin. "Before this goes on another nanosecond, how did New Orleans wind up part of Texas?"

Wilhelmsohn chuckled. In the relative security of this room, he'd taken off his hat and veil, also his gloves and jersey dress. Under it, he'd been wearing sweats. The Japanese running shoes on his feet (he'd shucked out of his high heeled ladies' shoes immediately) when they'd been hanging by their laces around his neck, had given him his girlish figure.

I'd noticed that his accent sounded substantially different from Lucy's, softer, and at the same time, thicker somehow. She was from San Antonio. Later, I tried to write down what his explanation to her sounded like to me.

"You must undahstand, ma'am, that the Texas in which I was bohn was nevah a paht of the Yewnited States. We nevah even came close. Durin' the Wah between the States, the Nawth offahed us any South'n land we wanted, up t'the Mississippi Rivah, if Texas would othahwise stay outa the conflict. Need I say, we accepted. At that point, I b'lieve most of the folks in the states we took wah simply grateful to be out of the wah, and what ouah "conquest" consisted of, in the main, was sendin' out . . . well, a species of Welcome Wagon, y'might say. The only real fightin' the Texas Ahmy had t'do was against Nathan Bedford Forrest at the Battle of Cape Girardeau."

You get the idea.

"But what you all have to understand," he went on in the same accent, "what I despaired of telling you, is of the vile conspiracy that's underway in your otherwise wonderful continuum. Not only are people going to die—why, this place we're in would be washed away!—but the survivors will all end up in chains, if you don't do something soon!"

• • •

IT SEEMED THAT Will and I had been on the right track, after all, and that we'd already spoken at length with the evil-doer behind all of the atrocities.

At least one of him, anyway.

Benjamin Wilhelmsohn told us the story, at least as much as he knew of it. On a fateful day two years before the Sanders-Bear investigation had been forced into existence, an outworld political refugee named Arlington Panghurst discovered a hologram of himself staring back at him from the online pages of *The Postman*, the opinion magazine of the Franklinite Faction of the Gallatinist Party. It was accompanied by a cutline claiming that it was a picture of the magazine's longtime editor, Bennett Williams.

Naturally curious—and with the sketchy beginnings of a truly evil idea already simmering in his head—Panghurst had looked Bennett up.

The two men had discovered that they were otherworld counterparts down to their very fingerprints. They also dicovered that they had virtually identical opinions on the issues of the day, and more importantly, identical ambitions. Neither of them aspired to be a great leader. Each preferred that some "worthier" individual be groomed to take up the scepter—and the high political profile that went with it.

Much closer than identical twins—for they were virtually the same individual—they both wanted to be the "man behind the throne," to enjoy all of the prerogatives of great power, while taking none of the attendant risks. Also, the "original" Bennett wanted out from under his brother Buckley's thumb.

By now, it had occurred to each of them independently that North American Confederate science was overlooking an unprecedented—and breathtakingly limitless—source of power.

Together, they began to cook up a thoroughly ethically deficient scheme designed to correct this oversight. And since each of them was the only individual in existence that the other felt he could trust, their first agenda item was obvious.

They'd acquire more of themselves!

> She never said a word to him during labor, but four and
> a half years later, as they stood in their daughter's bed-
> room, hip-deep in toys and trying to clean the place up,
> his wife glared at him and said, "You did this to me,
> you sonofabitch!"
>
> —*Memoirs of Lucille G. Kropotkin*

Bennett Williams and Arlington Panghurst's first move (Wilhelmsohn continued as I ate my creole—and watched skaters
doing things I'd have thought impossible in a one-gravity field)
was to lease their very own probability broach.

Only a few years previously, that wouldn't have been possible.
The one the Hamiltonians had tried to use had been cobbled
together out of stolen parts. Even now the devices were hideously
expensive to obtain, and worse to operate. Any of the booths at
LaPorte Interworld used enough power to land the Great Pyramid on the Moon and bring it back. The best the two conspirators could afford was a small academic survey device, rented
from a scientific supply company, barely capable of creating an
interworld orifice only about an inch in diameter. Williams and
Panghurst told each other gleefully and repeatedly that it was
through this aperture—however tiny—that whole worlds were
about to be changed beyond all recognition.

Panghurst, it developed, was the unique individual Wilhelmsohn had already mentioned, the one who'd escaped from a continuum where, for as long as anybody could remember, the
pursuit and maintenance of power had been the exclusive pur-
view of a hereditary ruling class of pure albinos. Political activity
of any kind was absolutely forbidden to pigmented commoners,
be they yellow, brown, black, or pink. As a consequence, unlike

his Confederate counterpart, he'd chosen to pursue a technical career. Now, with a wide-angle lens, fiberoptic cables, and computer image-enhancing software, Panghurst and Williams began to set a record as the ultimate Peeping Toms, exploring as many other worlds of alternative probability as they could, peering over the shoulders of unsuspecting individuals reading newspapers, watching local television and movies, "listening" with the aid of a computer program capable of reading lips (their cut-rate system wasn't capable of conveying sound), observing various phenomena occur sometimes with milkmen, little blond secretaries, Senate pages, or farm animals—that nobody else was ever meant to see. Later on, they planned to make some highly profitable uses of the secrets they'd learned this way. It could all be done at a cosmic arm's length, by remote control. What blackmail victim actually needed to know that his blackmailer lived on another "plane of existence"?

But for now, the plan was simpler.

Money was the problem.

The two "Bennetts" had only an inch of broach diameter to work through, although they could put their aperture anywhere they wanted, including the most tightly secured vault in any universe. But what should they take? Diamonds, emeralds, rubies, sunstones, sapphires—otherwise the obvious target for interworld pilferage—were of no particular value to them, being easily synthesized here in the Confederacy. Paper money was laughably out of the question as anything but a bathroom novelty. Platinum, gold, and silver, monetary metals in general, were usually stringently controlled (and therefore only available in bars too large to get throught the broach) or out of circulation altogether in most of the worlds they reached, although there were occasional exceptions.

In one version of the United States, however, they got lucky and stumbled onto "subcompact disks." A little smaller than a quarter, but otherwise identical to laser disks or DVDs in other worlds, they carried on their quasimetallic surfaces samples of that culture's amusements—plays, motion pictures—some going back more than a century. Many even featured otherworld versions of Confederate stars like Marion "Mike" Morrison, Archie Leach, Bettie Page, Clark Gable, and Carole Lombard.

"NOW HOLD ON just a damned minute!" As interesting as it had been, I interrupted Wilhelmsohn's story with a sinking feeling in the pit of my crawdad-filled stomach. "Do you mean to tell me that we *haven't* found the source of the Gables' cinematic grievances and stopped it up for them, even temporarily?"

Will had exactly the same pained expression on his face that I felt on my own, while Lucy pretended to try valiantly not to gloat. She'd warned me—just before I'd called my clients—that the *Gone with the Wind* case might not quite be closed completely. Naturally, I'd argued with her. Now, she leaned my way and simply whispered, "It's good to be Queen."

"You're absolutely right." I waggled my cigar and tried to look at her as blandly as I could. "Freddy Mercury thought well of it."

I tend to forget, from day to day and moment to moment, that as similar as we seem sometimes in outlook and approach to our work, Will comes, nevertheless, from a slightly different continuum than I do. Slightly, but different. "Who the hell is Freddy Mercury?" he asked.

"Was." It was Clarissa who spoke. "He was one of the first people in Win's world to die of AZT poisoning."

Wilhelmsohn shook his head, and I realized that he didn't have a clue what we were talking about. No "slightly different" to it with him. Earlier, he'd told us that he came from a place where, legend had it, Davy Crockett had eighty-sixed General Santa Anna with a six-hundred-yard Kentucky rifle shot. So I explained, as briefly as I could, about the Clark Gable and Carole Lombard who lived here and what they'd hired me to accomplish.

"Sir Robert Cummings is an actor?" The expression of shock on Wilhelmson's face was incredulous. "In my homeworld, Sir Robert is a great aviator and inventor—he headed the effort that put Charlie Lindbergh, Junior, on the Moon—and almost as famous as Thomas Edison or Henry Ford or Hedy Lamar!"

I had to bite my tongue to keep from shouting, " 'Hedley!' "

ALTERNATIVE CULTURES OF every kind were all the rage just now in the Confederacy. With the aid of a long pair of paratronically insulated tweezers (to avoid the high-energy slicery and dicery that occurs at the margin of the broach locus) and a computer program to scan and rerecord the microscopic pits in the tiny disks onto media more familiar in the Confederacy, Williams and Panghurst began peddling previously unseen entertainments to a hungry worldwide audience through several dummy corporations, free at last of what Bennett perceived as his brother Buckley's fiscal tyranny.

At the same time, they continued combing the sands of infinity for other Bennett Williamses—by whatever name they were called—and to their surprise, this proved even easier than finding an independent source of income.

They started by writing newspaper advertisements (or their local technological equivalent), accompanied by a flat-printed duplicate of the hologram that had attracted Panghurst's attention to Williams in the first place. They popped this material through their one-inch broach when nobody was around to see it arriving—for example, straight into the IN basket of that great metropolitan newspaper, the Las Vegas *Review-Journal*'s classified advertising office in the middle of the night.

Payment for the ad space was invariably made in cash—invariably appropriated with the same pair of insulated tweezers—invariably from the locked cash drawer of the same great metropolitan newspaper's classified advertising office. Nobody ever seemed to notice that (or connect it with the ad submission), or that it never appeared to be necessary to deliver the replies:

DO YOU KNOW THIS MAN?

DO YOU HAPPEN TO *LOOK* LIKE HIM?

REPLY DIRECT TO THIS NEWSPAPER, BOX 2323A

UNIMAGINABLE REWARDS!!

Williams and Panghurst knew that their advertising would prove effective—they were trying to communicate wih an extremely narrow segment of the newspaper-reading public—because it would have worked on them.

More often than not the reply they received from their counterpart in that portion of reality was the same that Han Solo had given to Luke Skywalker: "Unimaginable rewards? I don't know—I can *imagine* quite a lot."

The whole thing became routine.

Whenever they discovered a likely prospect, they stopped dealing with the newspaper immediately and steered a hovertruck with their rented probability broach in the back directly to the spot "coextant" with his home. The hovertruck was necessary at their end, because, like larger apertures, "dirigible broaches"—those that could be directed anywhere from a stationary location—were presently beyond their means to command. They hoped to change that.

One of the sadder facts of human existence is that power will get you through times of no brains better than brains will get you through times of no power. They were out to conquer universes, but sometimes it looked more like they were searching for a third Stooge.

Once, pretending to be maintenance men, Panghurst and Williams had been forced to run their fiberoptic cable to the bottom of a swimming pool at a girl's school to reach the coextant basement apartment of another Bennett Williams who was interested in their proposition. He didn't appreciate the small but steady leak on his carpet. Slowly, they established contact with several counterparts in other universes, explained what was at stake, and issued certain instructions.

The rest was simple and required no further contribution on their part. For some time, there had been a lively "underground railroad," a well-established infrastructure for rescuing willing refugees from the otherworld tyranny. LaPorte boasted several respectable organizations, like the Erisian Rescue Brigade and the Gallatinite Rescue Society, to do the work, and there was plenty of financial support available for such a humane, charitable, politically attractive undertaking. Williams and Panghurst, unable to afford a man-sized probability broach of their own, instead anonymously transmitted the coordinates of their potential new partners to the charitable groups who operated through the LaPorte Interworld Terminal and waited for their latest associate to appear.

Always, the newcomer was instructed to disguise himself, and to give a false name, so that no one at LaPorte Interworld would notice the arrival of so many "repeaters." (Wilhelmsohn, for example, had arrived in the dress and floppy hat that now lay discarded on an unused chair in the rinkside party room and had claimed to be Miss Bessie May Mucho.) It might not have raised suspicions—and the hackers among their number usually managed to clear the computer records afterward in any case—but the two original conspirators were unwilling to take chances.

Always, the newcomer was instructed to bring whatever real wealth he could lay his hands on, regardless of the source: gold, silver, platinum, portable antiques, such as watches and miniature paintings—and especially any films, tapes, full-size, compact, or subcompact disks he could beg, borrow, steal, or otherwise acquire that might prove salable in the novelty-hungry North American Confederacy.

One of the "Bennetts" had come through the broach and immediately collapsed, his luggage and clothing bulging. Nobody at this end cared—there can't be any smuggling if there aren't any "customs." He'd checked out a sizeable fraction of the fiction of several local libraries in his homeworld, and would return— if he was ever that stupid—to a king's ransom in fines and late fees. Another brave soul had swallowed half his weight in highly polished iridium spheres a centimeter in diameter.

"YOU KNOW," MARY-BETH observed shrewdly, "If they'd left it at that, they could have established one of the Confederacy's great fortunes. Think of it, free choice of an infinty of motion picture masterpieces—yes, and smaller pictures and music—with little or no production costs."

"Overlooking the fact that they're all stolen from somebody else," her sister said. "Clarissa, would you please pass the chocolate? Anybody want more coffee?"

They both looked to Will, and it wasn't about the coffee. He knew that, and shrugged. "Hey, whatever crimes are being committed here—setting aside a couple of thousand cold-blooded murders—they're all *way* out of my jurisdiction. Besides, I've told you all a hundred times, I'm not a cop!"

Five voices sang out at once, "Yeah, right!"

"So now," Fran told us, "even if we defeat these Bennetts, the

North American Confederacy will become a pirate culture, plundering all the other worlds for their art and literature and movies and music. And there'll be lots of interests here who won't be limited to an inch. They'll steal everything out there that isn't nailed down, and half of what is! God, we'll be just like the British Empire!"

She sat down, threw her face into her hands, and actually started crying. I hadn't seen her so upset since her husband got shot. I glanced at Clarissa, to see if she was worried that Fran was going to start having her baby. Clarissa gave me a shake of her head that said there wasn't any danger.

"Tell y'what, honey..." Lucy put a hand on her shoulder. "I'll promise that I won't do any interworld plunderin' if you will. That's two, an' we can get more—*if* we whip the Bennetts."

Fran, ordinarily one of the toughest individuals I knew, raised a tearstained face to Lucy and said in an equally tearstained voice, Really?"

"Really—course I don't promise not t'offer 'em a handful of beads for what they got."

Fran laughed, took a tissue from Clarissa, a hug from her husband, and blew her nose. Maybe it wasn't so bad a thing that my wife had never been pregnant.

SOON, NO FEWER than eight Bennett Williamses—by various names, from various places—were living and working together in the big old antique farmhouse at the extreme southern edge of Greater LaPorte. They were shooting for an even dozen. They agreed (of course) that they would need all the help they could get, for their overall plan was ambitious and immense.

The next stage would depend on the unwitting—but 100 percent perfectly predictable—cooperation of the original Bennett's older brother Buckley, head of the Williams family, and of the

Franklinite Faction, which was all that still existed of the historic but outmoded Gallatinist Party. Perhaps Buckley himself had begun to grow a bit soft on excessive freedom over the years. He'd attempted to make friends with that immigrant policeman Bear, for example, after the Hamiltonian incident. But Buckley's followers, Allard Wayne, for example, could be counted on, Bennett knew, to shriek long and loud for greatly increased political control of the Confederate population—perhaps even for the formation of a permanent government, which was what he and his counterparts really wanted—if a sufficient number of sufficiently horrible crimes were to occur. Especially if they could be made to look sufficiently like crimes committed by the motley immigrant denizens of the drab and grimy American Zone.

It was therefore up to Bennett Williams—to all of the Bennett Williamses—to carry out these crimes, and this, too, would prove surprisingly easy. Except for the personal weapons everybody carried in the Confederacy, and which rendered them all but invulnerable to common street crimes like mugging or rape or home invasions, the people here were shockingly undefended—physically and mentally—against apparently random acts of cold-blooded mass violence. Such atrocities simply weren't within their worldview.

Yet.

Wilhelmsohn had been astonished and horrified to discover that the eight Bennetts employed a "Wheel of Crime" dartboard to determine the place and type of crime to be committed. Believing they could send a subliminal message to the public, they let the media do their timing for them: whenever the 'Com announced that a new record number of refugee immigrants had been admitted through the interworld terminals in LaPorte and other cities of the Confederacy, they struck within the next twenty-four hours. While one Bennett made himself publicly con-

spicuous to establish an alibi for them all—the original Bennett
at that convention, for example—and another Bennett wrote the
authoritarian ranting that would be used at press conferences or
appear subsequently in the Franklinite online magazine *The Postman*, the rest of the Bennetts would sabotage a train, blow up a
building, or plant a time bomb on the *City of Calgary*.

It seemed like child's play.

And what would Bennett—all of the Bennetts, of course—
stand to gain from all this vile chicanery? More than simply all
the wealth and power in the world. That was chump change,
perhaps suitable for minor conquerors like Alexander of Macedon, Hannibal Barca, Julius Caesar, Napoleon Bonaparte, Adolf
Hitler, or Lavrenti Beria. They would have more. They would
have all the wealth and power in a whole *infinity* of worlds!

If their plan succeeded, with older brother Buckley and his
cronies firmly established in power, and younger brother Bennett
irrevocably a part of that power establishment, it would be easy
to appropriate tax money—*Confederate* tax money, what a concept!—to look for alternate worlds especially susceptible to conquest. These pushover worlds would be made to look like a
threat to the Confederacy and all that it (no longer) stood for.
An emergency would be declared. Conscription would be insti-
tuted for the first time in Confederate history, and huge armies
of invasion raised. Later, forces would be recruited from otherworld subject populations less likely to resist the draft.

An infinity of worlds.

Together, the Bennetts shrewdly calculated that their scheme
might require as many as ten years to bear fruit worthy of the
picking. That was fine with them; they knew they had plenty of
time. To the surprise and delight of many in their company (and
the incomprehensible horror of others), for practical purposes,
advanced Confederate medical technology made them all im-

mortal. Thanks to their import "business," they were already rich, and rapidly getting richer. In the end, they'd possess a vast interworld empire, boggling every mind and beggaring any previous such accomplishment in human history.

And what of the hundreds of thousands of Confederate victims of the heinous crimes the Bennetts planned to commit? Or the tens of millions of victims of the interworld rape and pillage they were planning? As one of them joked—*Star Trek* being a cultural experience shared by many worlds—the only person who could make an omelette without breaking eggs was the transporter chief of the starship *Enterprise*.

But what none of the Bennett Williamses had counted on was a traitor in their midst.

26: STRANGER IN PARADISE

America's historic misfortune is that her people have seldom been equal to the ideals upon which their nation
was established.

—*Memoirs of Lucille G. Kropotkin*

"I confess, at first, that I was merely curious," Wilhelmsohn said
between bites of the blackbottom pie he'd ordered, expecting to
be disappointed, "when I first was shown the Bennetts' ad on
our university comnet:

DO YOU KNOW THIS MAN?

DO YOU HAPPEN TO *LOOK* LIKE HIM?

REPLY DIRECT TO THIS ACCOUNT

UNIMAGINABLE REWARDS!!

"I knew him all right. I saw him every morning in the bathroom mirror, when I shaved." Most of our dinner dishes had
been cleared away by now, although Lucy's friend the CIPE restaurant manager obligingly continued to keep us supplied with
water and assorted other liquids. Serious goings-on or not, watching Wilhelmsohn, I was considering what I might have for dessert, myself.

"Well, by the end of the day," our guest from another Texas
went on, "Old T. Walt—he's the Philosophy of Economics Fellow in the office next door—Murray Suruasolaphecychap in the
office on the other side, and no fewer than a dozen of my other
colleagues—not to mention about a hundred of my students—
had brought that peculiar online ad to my attention."

Mary-Beth took a sip of the coffee she wasn't supposed to be
drinking and looked at him curiously. "I take it you don't nor-

mally read your own . . . what do you call it in the Federated States of Texas, E-mail?"

"Normally . . ." Wilhelmsohn smiled a strange, private kind of smile. "No, ma'am, Miz Sanders, I wasn't looking at it, not at all. I had reasons of my own—and we call it C-mail, just like you folks here do."

Mary-Beth nodded, still looking at the man sort of speculatively. I'd noticed that Clarissa was starting to do it, too. I wondered what was up with them, or him, or all of the above. There wasn't any chance to ask right now.

"Anyway," Wilhelmsohn took a breath and shook off whatever was bothering him. "I was a philosophy professor, myself, holder of the George F. Will chair of Sophistry at the Baton Rouge campus of Texas A&M—or did I tell you that?"

He had, but everybody let it pass.

"I'd been raised in a world where what we sometimes call the Lone Star Republic had never annexed itself abjectly to the contemptible United States." (He said, "YEW-natted.") "And although I was extremely well-educated in the rich-textured and most glorious history of my own beloved country, it had never before occurred to me to imagine a world in which it had."

Had what? Oh, yeah: annexed itself abjectly to the contemptible yewnatted. This clown used more adverbs and subordinate clauses than a Civil War documentary festival, although the womenfolk seemed to enjoy listening to him.

"No kidding?" I asked. "You mean they don't have any concept like parallel histories or alternative probabilities in the science fiction where you come from? No Jack Williamson, Poul Anderson, or H. Beam Piper?"

"Harry Turtledove?" Will added, "Brad Linaweaver, S. M. Stirling, Michael Kurland?"

"Andre Norton?" Clarissa finished the list.

Wilhelmsohn slowly shook his head. "I'm afraid that I've never even heard of any of them, my friends. Mind you, that doesn't mean that nobody else in my homeworld never has, I just don't have much of a taste for science fiction, myself. Although now I seem to be living it, don't I?" He spread both hands out on the table, and paused for a long while, seeming to examine them. "It's absolutely astonishing, isn't it?"

About that time, the waiter came back and I knew what I wanted. I'm not the dessert guy that my manly figure might indicate. I do enjoy Chinese and Mexican food, and it was the latter that had gotten me into the habit of eating flan. If you're not familiar with the stuff, it's a Mexican egg custard made with cinnamon instead of nutmeg, drenched with a thin but delicious caramel sauce. If it's one thing I'm a sucker for, to misquote Spencer Tracy again, it's flan.

Ironically the best I ever had was in a Vietnamese restaurant that decided to start making it for some reason (I always meant to ask why, but never got around to it), where the waiters came around and asked if you wanted *frawn*.

Frawn it was. I told the waiter, who nodded and vanished.

Finally, an impatient Fran said, "Please go on with your story, Mr. Wilhelmsohn."

The man from Texas A&M looked up into her pretty face and blinked. "That's Benjamin to you, Miz Sanders, ma'am, and I do believe that I will." He inhaled and exhaled. "Almost from the first contact I made with my counterparts in this world, I felt alarmed—and increasingly confused. An opportunity to follow in the illustrious footsteps of Alexander, Caesar, Napoleon . . . it should have been exhilarating. Why, I kept asking myself over and over, couldn't I simply throw my lot in with my newfound 'brothers' and cheerfully help them conquer the known universe?"

Clarissa seemed startled. "You mean you actually considered it?"

He grinned that self-deprecating grin of his. "Not at all, Miz Bear, not at all. And that was what troubled me, you see? What would it have hurt? Who would it have hurt? From an historical viewpoint alone, this is a very technically advanced and ethically enlightened civilization you have here. Far more so, say, than the Romans or the British. Most of the worlds it came to dominate would probably benefit from it.

"Meanwhile," he closed his eyes and imagined it, "I'd be rich."

He sat up straight. "I'd be powerful."

"He'd get laid," Will suggested.

Wilhelmson looked down at his shoes. "I most humbly beg your pardon, ladies!"

Clarissa suppressed a grin and blushed. It never fails to surprise me she can do that, given her medical education and everything she knows about life, inside and out. So, surprisingly, did Lucy, who's been married so many times she can't keep track. Mary-Beth grinned, and Fran laughed out loud.

"Why couldn't I simply join my newfound 'brothers'?" he repeated rhetorically. "My friends, I didn't know—and the question haunted me. Perhaps it was because, however you may wish to glorify their names—Alexander of Macedon, Hannibal Barca, Julius Caesar, Napoleon Bonaparte, Adolf Hitler, Lavrenti Beria—they're nothing more than a lot of murderous bandits."

Nobody gave him any argument about that.

"Perhaps," he offered, "on the opposite side of the scale, it had more than a little to do with where I'd been born and grown up, in the Federated States of Texas, which I soon came to understand happened to be the closest political equivalent, so far discovered, to the North American Confederacy."

"Sounds pretty much like it," Will observed. "Tell me, what kind of taxes do you have there?"

He blinked like many Confederates often do, as if struggling to recall the meaning of that hated word. "Why, no taxes at all, Captain Sanders. Although the practice is alive and well in other countries, the United States, the Republic of California, and French Imperial Mexico. For the last century, our government— what little of it there is—has been given a monopoly on the collection and recycling of garbage."

Everybody laughed.

"But you were speaking," Mary-Beth said, "of why you couldn't be a villain."

"I suppose I was, at that, Miz Sanders," Wilhelmsohn replied in his courtly manner. "How downright Shakespearian of me. Well, one thing I discovered, shortly after arriving in the Confederacy, was that I seemed to be the only 'version of Bennett Williams' (and how I'd begun to loathe thinking of myself in those terms) who hadn't attended a Jesuit seminary."

Now there was *another* new one on me. This adventure was certainly turning out to be educational. I hadn't even known that there *were* Jesuit seminaries in the Confederacy. There are certainly plenty of religious folks here, but out of fear, I think, of the bitter, bloody conflicts that have plagued other people in other times and places, and to stay focused on the one thing— absolute individual liberty—that makes all other things possible, they tend to keep their religious beliefs and practices pretty much to themselves. I'd never seen a priest of any kind in LaPorte— not the guys who followed Ringo Starr around trying to cut his finger off, nor saffron-robed Buddhists with shaved heads, nor Greek Orthodox, nor even Roman Catholic. I wondered if they carried guns. But Wilhelmsohn was going on. "Perhaps it had something to do with a little couplet that Bennett had framed on the wall of his office, all stitched up with pretty embroidered flowers, like an old-fashioned sampler:

MEN ARE NOBLER WHEN THEY ARE FREE,
AND WOMEN, WHEN THEY ARE PROPERTY.

"Let me tell you, that thing offended me mightily. The fairer sex, you see, at one time constituted the rarest and most valuable presence imaginable, during the founding years of our Lone Star Republic. The respect that they garnered then—we couldn't have tamed that harsh frontier without them, and there wouldn't have been much point to it in any case, would there?—had extended itself well into the twentieth century."

Of course the women-folk cheered and clapped, even though to them this was only the third century. In my homeworld, something like this sentiment prevailed in Wyoming, which had imagined it was conferring an honor on women by being the first state in the union to give them the vote.

"I may have tipped my hand just a little," Wilhelmsohn told us, "in a conversation I had with one of the Bennetts—not the original, but from something called the Scientific Hegemony of North America, where your vote is weighted according to your Intelligence Quotient.

"It's instructive that he refugeed outa there," Lucy observed. "Think he failed the I.Q. test?"

Mary-Beth replied, "It's far more likely he was fleeing from the consequences of rule by intellectuals—who can screw more things up, far worse, and in less time, than any other category of individuals I know of."

"Ouch!" Professor Wilhelmsohn exclaimed, laughing so heartily he nearly dropped a forkful of his pie. "I don't know about all that, Miz Sanders—and aren't you some kind of academic, too?—the fellow was talking about his fiancé, whom he planned to bring over as soon as he could. He kept going on and on about her having 'saved herself' for after their wedding."

That ancient notion was regaining some ground in my homeworld, too. I won't say it was the reason I left, but it was another swell reason to stay away.

"I observed—" Wilhelmsohn went on, "quite casually, mind you, not making a point of it—that it had been my observation that girls who don't believe in premarital sex usually don't believe in sex *after* the wedding, either.

General laughter. This guy had missed his calling. He should have been a standup comedian. I made a mental note to introduce him to Sam Yosemite.

When the laughter died down, Wilhelmsohn went on, just like a pro. " 'Any act of intercourse,' the Hegemony fellow waggled his finger at me, 'outside of wedlock, or that cannot result in the conception of a child, is a Grievous Sin, as well as an Abomination in the Eyes of the Creator.' "

"Some religious people speak in tongues," Will observed, "and others in capital letters."

"How very right you are, Captain Sanders. 'That's interesting,' I told the fellow. 'And how do you know that?'

"Well, he looked at me incredulously, as if I'd asked how he knew the Earth was round—or maybe flat, in his case. 'Why, my good man, it is the Revealed Word of the Living God!'

" 'I see,' I told him. 'Was it notarized?' "

By now it was all any of us could do to keep from rolling on the floor, laughing. For my own part, despite the fact that we often disagree on matters like this, I tend to get along pretty well with religious individuals—the armed, self-contained, self-sufficient, home-canning, home-schooling kind, inclined to thump the Constitution as much as the Bible, and whom the government back home regards as a threat—right up to the point when they start telling me how to live my own life.

"When both of us were teenagers," Mary-Beth told Wilhelmsohn, "our father used to assign us what he would call 'mental muscle-building' exercises. It was always a lot of fun. Frannie and I used to stay up late, sometimes, making up perfectly sound left-wing arguments for gun ownership—"

"How else are you going to overthrow the government," her sister Fran interrupted, "or seize the means of production, or massacre the landlords?"

"—and right-wing arguments in favor of abortion." Mary-Beth concluded.

Fran grinned. "Just suppose that *gayness* could be detected *in utero.*"

"I get it," Wilhelmsohn said, "Just think what a cleaner, better place the world would be today, if only Rose Kennedy had believed in abortion."

After the general laughter had died down again, Wilhelmsohn took a deep breath. "I suppose it's also possible that I couldn't join the plotters because I was the only one of the 'Bennetts' who was dying, slowly—and very painfully if I may be permitted to say so—of cancer."

"What?" Clarissa looked up, startled, and I felt a pang, myself. If I hadn't come to the Confederacy in 1987, and met Clarissa, I'd have been dead by now of cancer, myself. I told him so, squeezing the hand of the woman who'd saved my life on more than one occasion, and from more than one cause. As for her, she was up in an instant with her little black bag open and electronic diagnosing devices running. With every year that passed this business seemed more to me like DeForest Kelly, pointing his empty salt-shakers at actors wearing red shirts.

Wilhelmsohn, tolerating Clarissa's ministrations in fair humor, nodded. "It is a strange thing indeed to resign oneself to death. I had by then, I assure you, and had made substantial progress clearing up my meager personal affairs. That's why I wasn't answering my C-mail. And then to discover that you're going to live? Somewhat perversely, you discover that you resent it just a little."

I hadn't known that I had cancer, but I'd been where he'd been. Wilhelmsohn went on. "Well, partly because of that—the simple fact that the Confederacy routinely cures cancer with a handful of pills—I pretended to go along with their vile enterprise. My heart was certainly no longer in my work at Baton Rouge (to the degree that it ever had been), I had nothing and nobody in particular back home, and lots of very nice Confederate folks were going to get hurt if these . . . gentlemen—my "evil twins" as I'd begun thinking of them—had their way.

"But maybe I could prevent it, now that I'd arrived. (My financial contribution to their 'cause' had been my own precious video recording of Scott Joplin and Richard Wagner's epic opera, *Die Alamo*.) But what to do? I couldn't just call a cop. In the first place, there didn't appear to be any."

"We got reasons for that," Lucy told him cheerfully.

27: RATTLESNAKE MOUNTAIN

> Always attack in *perpendicular* fashion, from an uncon-
> ventional and unexpected (but relevant) direction. The
> enemy will be unprepared; you can strike him with your
> full strength while he finds nothing to attack effectively.
> —*Memoirs of Lucille G. Kropotkin*

"I'm not complaining, ma'am. My people don't have all that much use for policemen, either. But I wasn't convinced that the various private security agencies I saw advertised on the Telecom would be interested in anything I had to tell them. Please understand, I had to be absolutely sure."

"And why was that?" asked Mary-Beth.

He shook his head. "Because I couldn't take any risks. You see, at that point, they were all gleefully discussing long range plans even more horrifying than what they'd done to the Old Endicott Building or the tube train."

The Commander of the Greater LaPorte Militia sat up straight. "Like what?"

Wilhelmsohn took a deep breath. "Like arranging for a collision between a pair of spacecraft—passenger vessels, I believe— in order to distract everybody's attention from the theft of yet a third ship, some heavy-lift utility machine, which they planned to use to divert a small, near-Earth asteroid, dropping it where it would kill millions."

Clarissa shook her head in disbelief. The process of dealing with this insanity was very hard on her. "And exactly what was that supposed to accomplish?"

"At best," Wilhelmsohn told her, "it would make the formation of a permanent world government seem absolutely, inarguably imperative."

"And at worst?" I don't think I've ever seen her more upset.

"Why, ma'am, they'd use the threat of dropping a second rock on the planet to impose their values and beliefs on everybody else, in perpetuity."

We all sat silently, trying to take the sheer enormity of it in. When Wilhelmsohn spoke again, it was almost like he'd abruptly changed the subject.

"I was grimly certain that I would only have one chance to try and get some help before my fellow Bennetts discovered my true sentiments and killed me outright."

"How soon are they planning to do this?" Will wanted to know.

Wilhelmsohn shrugged. "Not right away, Captain Sanders. It was just one of the many things they liked to talk about and impress each other with. I mentioned it just now because I wanted you to understand exactly how far they're willing to go to get their way, and how frightened I was about it."

"Well it sure woulda scared me shitless, spitless, and witless." Lucy grinned at him. "I guess it turned out that y'wanted t'live, after all, didn't you, Benjie?"

"I guess so, Miz Kropotkin. Anyway, I didn't have any idea what I was going to do about it. Then one day, I was working in the back of Bennett's house—in the editorial office of *The Postman*—where all of the Bennetts ordinarily kept themselves. When suddenly, I was overhearing the original Bennett Williams being questioned by this hard-eyed pair—" He pointed at me and Will. Will nodded acknowledgement. Recalling Mary-Beth the other day, I put a finger in my nonexistent chin dimple and pretended to curtsey. This time, *she* laughed out loud.

"—and a voluble little old lady with an enormous automatic pistol. Everybody carried a sidearm where I come from, too, unless they applied for a license not to. It's a requirement of citizenship, you see."

"And every bit as great an ethical travesty as forbidding weapons," Mary-Beth insisted.

"Well, I believe I conceded that the Federated States of Texas are *almost* as punctilious as the Confederacy," Wilhelmsohn told her. "That very point is often made in ethics and political science classes where I'm from."

"As it should be," she replied.

"Be that as it may, I immediately noted their names: Captain Will Sanders of the Greater LaPorte Militia—to me, that sounded like the Texas Rangers I was accustomed to—Win Bear, a tough-looking private detective. And Miz Lucy Kropotkin, a little old lady who looked more dangerous to me than the two men put together."

"Why, thank you, Benjie." Lucy beamed at him. She was forced to call him that, since she was already calling the "original" Williams "Bennie."

"Delighted, ma'am. Somehow—as carefully as porcupines making love—I knew I had to let you all know what was going on. I began to look for some way I could send you a message— Good heavens!" He glanced at his wristwatch, stood up, and began putting his dress back on. "I've been gone longer than I ever expected, and now they're going to miss me!"

I rose and put a hand on his shoulder. "Benjamin, you can't be seriously thinking of going back—"

"I *have* to go back, Win. I mainly wanted to tell you about the dirty work at Pistol Sight Mountain."

"What dirty work at Pistol Sight Mountain?" we all asked at once.

"You mean, after all that, I didn't tell you? It's happening at the reservoir, and it's happening tonight! At midnight exactly!

And I have to be there with them to sabotage it, somehow, in case you all don't make it!"

Will told him, "Oh, we'll make it all right. Count on it. Where will you be?"

"With them," Wilhelmson said. "The original Bennett and Panghurst and the others, right at the top of the structure, helping them lower a great big explosive charge into the water where it'll be set off right against the inside of the thing."

I said, "Damn."

SOMETIMES I FORGET what a swell view LaPorte has to the west. On a clear day, you can see several distinct layers of "purple mountains' majesty," going up, one behind the other, like ragged stairsteps to somewhere around fourteen thousand feet. Between them and the city lies a line of "hogbacks," where the earth was split by emerging mountains, upward and outward, so that their eastern faces stand at forty-five degrees. In almost every version of this geographical region that I'm aware of, where the earth split itself like the edges of a blob of mashed Play-doh, dams have been erected and a large reservoir created to provide water for alternatives to LaPorte ranging in population from twenty-five thousand to twenty-five million. The latter wasn't a nice place at all—and I'm a city boy at heart.

We were climbing one of those dams right now, just to the left, or south, of the geological feature known here as Pistol Sight Mountain . . . more of a rock-crested hill, really. At the moment, if I'd looked over my shoulder, I could have gazed down at the lights of over two million people twinkling in the high summer darkness, their owners blissfully unaware of the five-hundred-foot wave of destruction that was about to sweep away everything and everyone they loved—unless my friends and I could stop it. On the other hand, if I looked over my shoulder now, I'd prob-

332 • *L. NEIL SMITH*

ably have missed my next step and immediately fallen several
hundred diagonal, sharp-edged-boulder-strewn feet to where my
darling Clarissa was waiting morbidly in her medical van for that
very kind of accident to happen. Already, I had a fine collection
of thistles in my palms, despite the thick leather gloves I was
wearing. That was nothing compared to the prickly pear. Its
spines were in the worst possible place—well, almost the worst
possible place—they could be, the back of my heel. Nobody's
ever convinced me that the damned things don't leap at you if
you step close enough.

As if to make up for that, I could smell sagebrush all around
me as I climbed the face of the dam, and the late evening breeze
carried the scent of evergreen from across the lake. A dirigible
at least a mile long, lit from the inside like a vast moon, passed
overhead, the lights of smaller craft flying up to load or unload
passengers and freight surrounding her like fireflies. I could just
make out the illuminated nameplate on her hull bottom: *San
Francisco Palace*, the first airship I'd ever— Suddenly, a rock
slipped under my foot. I began sliding backward. Just as suddenly, a hand grabbed the seat of my pants and stopped my fall.
Regaining my footing, and embarrassed to be rescued that way,
I turned to Will. "Thanks," I whispered. "Again, how many
troops do you command?"

I couldn't see the expression on his face, but I didn't need to.
"Twelve hundred, give or take. About three times that number
in reserve. Why?"

"Close to five thousand heavily armed troopies," I whispered.
"Now tell me again how come they're not here, climbing this
fucking mountain with us in the dark?"

He chuckled. "Be pretty hard to justify, Win. We're only up
against eight badguys, and you know the old saying, 'One mob,
one militiaman.'"

I didn't, but in more than one version of Texas I was acquainted with, I'd heard the expression "One riot, one Ranger," a sentiment clearly obsolete in an age of cowardly, body-armored, ski-masked, Nazi-helmeted, tank-driving, jackbooted thugs. These days, it was more like, "One wino, six hundred SWAT."

In the end, we'd borrowed the CIPE manager's personal car, so our own wouldn't be recognized, and dropped Wilhelmsohn off, to save him precious time, out of sight, but within easy walking distance, of the Williams farmhouse. I still had plenty of misgivings about his plan to rejoin the conspirators, but it was his right, and he seemed to know what he was doing. We then waited until about nine o'clock, and now it seemed like we'd been climbing for most of my adult life, since the sun had started down behind the mountains, giving us some shadows to work with. I'd been thinking about that farmhouse of Bennett's a lot, ever since Wilhelmsohn had outlined the Bennets' scheme to blow up Pistol Sight Mountain dam and destroy the city with an enormous wave of released water.

Consulting online topography maps on the computer in the manager's car, I'd understood immediately. Between the dam and the farmhouse lay half a dozen big irrigating ditches, and a river that people in my world call the Big Thompson. In my world, eleven years before I got blown accidentally into the Confederacy, a sudden summer thunderstorm had parked itself above the Big Thompson canyon for most of one July 31st, ultimately generating a twenty-foot wave that had scoured the canyon out and killed 139 people. The next week, they'd found bodies as far as Greeley, thirty miles to the east.

Natural phenomena like thunderstorms didn't vary much from one world of alternate probability to another. The same storm and flood had happened here, but with fewer than a dozen deaths, thanks to some foresight on the part of the river's owners,

334 • L. NEIL SMITH

and superior technology. Afterward, they'd fixed the river so that nothing like that could ever happen again.

This was going to be vastly worse, the wave twenty-five times as high and several times wider. It would rush out onto the prairie and wouldn't stop until it hit the Cache la Poudre River. But the farmhouse stood on a rise, with all those irrigation ditches and the new-and-improved Big Thompson river to protect it. Millions were about to die horribly—with the perpetrators high and dry—unless we could do something to stop it.

Will was climbing on my right, and Lucy—Lucy!—was climbing on my left. My favorite little old lady wasn't talking very much, but I found that I was having a surprisingly hard time keeping up with her. I absolutely gotta find out what vitamins Lucy takes. This time, Fran and Mary-Beth had lost the argument about pregnant ladies in combat. Understand that there's a perfectly good road from the town below to the top of the dam, with about a dozen switchbacks to make up for the lack of climbing power that happens to be a hovercraft's only limitation, compared to cars with wheels. Me, I'm from Denver, about seventy miles south of this place, and I can't remember, but I think there are at least twice the number of hairpins in the Confederacy that are in my homeworld, where the town below is Fort Collins, Pop. 100,000, and both the dam and the reservoir, named for the mountain, are called "Horsetooth." Hell of a stupid name for a mountain that looks so much like something else. What could the Fort Collins city founders have been thinking of? The mountain looks exactly like the sight picture of an 1873 Colt Peacemaker.

Our tactic was to cut across the road, skipping the switchbacks, and climbing as straight up the face of the earthen dam—covered in rocks, gravel, and high plains vegetation, all of it stickery and hyperallergenic—as we could. Meanwhile, what I was hoping most was *not* to find one of the diamondback rattlesnakes that this area is infamous for. Abruptly, less than two inches from my clawed left hand—God, how I hate heights—something far worse than any rattlesnake began to happen.

Knitch! Pwing!

"Shit!" I whispered hoarsely to my comrades on either side. "Don't look now, but some asshole's up there shooting at us with a silenced weapon!"

"Suppressed," Will whispered back pedantically. "Not silenced."

28: TEN LITTLE INDIANS

> Understand from the minute the fight begins that you're
> going to take damage. Accept it. (You'll always suffer
> more from the idiots and cowards on your *own* side than
> from any enemy.) Keep your overall goal in mind above
> all. Those who swerve to avoid a few cuts and bruises
> defeat themselves.
>
> —*Memoirs of Lucille G. Kropotkin*

Knitch! Knitch! Paweeeeng!

That last of that pair, bouncing off a rock, had damn near
taken my head off. In the position I found myself in, barely holding on to the scrubby-covered damside, there was no way in hell
that I could draw either of my—

BLAMMM! Somehow, Will had gotten off a shot. *Knitch!*
Pwing! Another bullet struck within mere inches of my all-too-
prominent backside—why were they picking on me?—and ric-
ocheted off toward Wyoming.

BLAMMM! BLAMMM! Will's shots were followed by a hair-
curling scream that started somewhere near the top of the dam
and continued as its source tumbled past us, finally stopping
below us with an audible *gortsch!* Sneakiness had gotten us part-
way there. Now we had to rely on firepower and darkness. Shots
began to rain down on us from both sides of the dam. Abruptly,
or so it seemed, the slope pitched over and the ground was almost level. We'd made it! But there was a price: the vegetation
up here should have been a lot thicker, but it had just been
mowed back. A few dozen yards away was the paved road that
traversed the top of the dam. All of a sudden we three had zero
concealment and even less cover (the difference being that cover
is something that stops bullets).

Lucy found a rock only a little bigger than she was, huddled down behind it, and opened up on the badguys with her .50 Gabbett-Fairfax, the world's loudest handgun. Apparently she hadn't brought her new piece, the nuclear plasma thingie. At 145 years of age, I don't suppose she could be expected to scramble up a mountainlike object lugging *two* guns.

Flonk! So much for the cover of darkness. A dazzling floodlight on the other side of the road suddenly made us all sitting ducks. I leveled my trusty .41 Magnum and shot at the one thing I could see. The floodlight went out with a delightful noise of imploding glass. There was also an agonized shout, apparently from someone standing beside it. I rolled a couple of yards to my left so I wouldn't be in the last place they'd seen me.

Then we got a break. The moon had set around lunchtime, twelve hours ago, which was probably why they'd chosen this particular day and time. What they hadn't counted on was somebody on the other side of the lake, with a great big floodlight of their own—we learned later it was a pizza restaurant—curious about all the sound and fury coming from the dam.

Suddenly the light was there, perfectly silhouetting three losers who'd come to the edge of the road to try and look for us. As quickly as I could, I fired all five of my remaining .41 Magnums at the middle figure, relying on Lucy and Will to make life impossible for the bookenders. Nobody yelled, but all three figures disappeared. I rolled to the left again. My .41 really lit up the night. I opened the cylinder, hit the ejection rod and heard brass tinkling away down the rocky hillside—a very pretty sound— shucked in six more with a speed loader, and closed the cylinder. Reaching around behind my back, I drew the Browning with my left hand. With a gun in either mitt, I got up and charged with my head lowered, gaining sixty feet, bringing me within yards of the road.

I flopped again and recoiled—I was lying on something big and warm and wet!

And quiet—it must have been the guy I just shot.

Temporarily blinded by my own gunfire, I couldn't tell much more. There was just enough of that floodlight to see that it was Bennett Williams—one of them, anyway—still clutching a huge .440 Anderson & Arts almost as old-fashioned as Lucy's Gabbett-Fairfax. I tucked the captured pistol in my waistband— you never know—and crab-skittered a few yards closer to the road, hiding behind a big gimballed trash can.

"Ssssst!" On my right, I guessed that Will had advanced beside me. I almost whispered back to him but I stopped when I caught an errant whiff of something . . . what? . . . cloves? Wherever this guy came from, they smoked clove cigarettes.

"Ssssst! Where are you?" Now I could see the guy's blocky form, partially hidden where he squatted behind a three-foot creosoted post marking the edge of a parking shoulder. Both his arms were extended in front of his body, his weapon, whatever it was, searching for something to shoot. It wasn't a long shot. I took careful aim, squinted my eyes shut in the last fraction of a second—not a generally recommended combat tactic—and stroked the broad, easy, mirror-polished trigger of the Model 58.

My eyes were open again before the muzzle flash had faded. I even heard the big 240-grain slug slam into the other guy. I frog-leaped toward him—it's amazing what a person my age can do with enough adrenaline in his bloodstream—and only just in time. A huge racket shook the night, explosions, bangs, and booms of various sizes and timbres. The big steel garbage can disintegrated under the impact of what seemed like a thousand slugs.

I felt around carefully, wishing I had rubber gloves. Sure

enough, the guy by the creosoted post was as dead as Kelsey's nuts, whoever Kelsey was. One dumbass, one detective.

That was Will and Lucy's cue to fire at the source of the shots, then roll off somewhere that the opposition couldn't predict. I'd shot two so far, both of them Bennetts. Not counting friend Wilhelmsohn—probably up ahead, pretending to shoot at us (note to myself: don't roll *too* far out of the line of fire)—that left five of the eight we'd been told about. If Lucy and Will had hit their marks when this started—and they were both better shots than I was—that might leave only three. Suddenly, I heard what I could only describe as an urgent grunt to my right, followed by a *BAMMM!* I could just make out a low shed in the moonlight. Will was struggling to his knees in its shadow, wrenching something from around his neck. "What?" I whispered as I slithered up beside him.

Will was disgusted, probably with himself. "Sonofabitch sneaked up and got this around my neck!"

I examined the object as well as I could and keep most of my attention focused forward. I'll be damned if it wasn't an original Rush Limbaugh necktie. I noticed that Will was rubbing the right side of his head.

"Coal-miner's tattoo." He lifted his big matte-silver pistol beside his ear and pointed it backward, demonstrating what he'd done to get out of his predicament. It'd probably be a while before he could hear in that ear again. "Powderburn. Another Bennett. He said if I didn't do what he wanted, he'd kill me."

"Yeah," I replied, "and?"

"I *believed* him."

"What're you two palaverin' about in the middle of a gunfight?"

"Yeek!" I screamed as quietly as I could. Lucy had sneaked

up on us when neither of us was looking or listening. It gave me a horrible feeling. "Exchanging recipes. Did you kill the guy on the left when the moon came out?"

"You betcha. It was another one of the Bennetts, armed with this puny thing! It's an insult t'hafta fight 'im at all!" She held out a 92F Beretta nine millimeter, standard U.S. Army issue where I came from, and the choice of those police forces that don't issue Glocks.

"The nerve of the cad," I told her. "Will, is this the third guy from the road?"

I sensed him shake his head. "I don't know. For some reason he has a hole in his leg, in addition to the face he's missing now. So how many does that leave?

"Two or three," I guessed, "one of them being Wilhelmsohn. Whaddya wanna do now, Captain?"

He snorted. "Aside from going home and crawling under the bed? How about we slither on our bellies around this little building and see what we can see?"

I nodded, although that was kind of stupid in the dark. "Gotcha. I'll take the left side. Lucy?"

She didn't answer. I shuffled over beside her. It was as if she had fallen asleep. Feeling around, I found her pistol, her hand, her arm, her chest—sorry, Lucy—her middle. And a big warm, wet spot. "Lucy!" I whispered as loud as I dared. She still had a strong pulse in her neck. I took my jacket and shirt off, wadded the shirt up, and pressed it to her belly. "Hold this!" I whispered to Will, "Lucy's been shot!"

I extracted my 'Com from my jacket and hit the button that would get Clarissa. "We're under cover here. Lucy's shot and unconscious. I think the only thing to do is finish the fight while you get up here as quick as you can. Look for Lucy behind the toolshed."

Clarissa merely nodded and the conversation was over.

I put my jacket back on, wondering how I'd gotten my shirt off without removing my shoulder holster. With every misgiving, Will and I left Lucy where she was, determined to get this over with quickly. I don't know why Bennett—the original—hadn't set his goddamned bomb off already. Somehow, I managed to get around the little building on my belly, Browning reholstered, Magnum held in both hands. At the corner, I heard somebody speak.

"I wondered what was taking you so long!" Bennett—the original, I was pretty sure—stood by a knee-high concrete barrier at the reservoir edge of the dam, about seventy-five yards away. On the other side, there was probably a hundred-foot drop, straight to the water. The mountains—Pistol Sight on his left— rose from the dam on either side, about a quarter mile away.

He raised a hand. Fireworks went off, rose, and burst, flooding the road at the top of the dam with light. It was an electric flare— brilliantly burning chemicals held aloft for a few minutes by a short-lived electrostatic device similar to the militia's flying machine, but about the size of a baseball. Bennett stood by the barrier. At his feet lay a figure I was certain was Wilhelmsohn, tied up, wincing as Bennett ground the muzzle of a big autopistol into the flesh at his hairline.

"Give up, gentlemen!" Bennett said. "Or I'll lobotomize your traitorous spy!"

Yeah, right. It was a long shot in weird light. I lined up the rudimentary sights of my Magnum on his chest, as I was certain Will was doing on my right.

29: MY BLUE HEAVEN

Go straight to the heart of the enemy's greatest strength.
Break that and you break him. You can always mop up
the flanks and stragglers later, and they may even surrender, saving you a lot of effort.
— *Memoirs of Lucille G. Kropotkin*

Suddenly, the unmistakable roar of an electric flying machine
made Bennett whirl to see what was happening behind him.

Covered with swirling and twinkling lights of a dozen different
colors, the thing rose from the lake side of the dam, about twenty
yards to his right, exactly like an immense predatory insect that
was coming for him.

Out of shock and relief I was yelling at Will when a bright
crimson dot appeared precisely in the middle of Bennett's forehead, and before that registered entirely on anybody, there was
a big *boom!* and the top of his head disappeared in a scarlet
cloud of vaporized blood.

To our left, the headlights of a hovercraft labored to the top
of the switchbacks and the noise of its impellers died as its skirt
collapsed. That would be Clarissa. I forgot everything else and
ran back to Lucy.

"IT'S GOOD TO see you again, Buckley." Lame as hell, I know,
but exactly what do you say to a guy who's just been forced by
everything he knows is right to shoot his own little brother in
the head?

"The, uh, gratification is . . . by all means mutual, Win." Buckley stood beside me with his shoulders stooped, his head droop-
ing, and that enormous longnosed stainless-steel self-shucker
still smoking in his hand, the muzzle hanging down beside his

right calf. "Although the particular circumstances leave, er, some-thing . . . something to be desired."

Something, er, to be desired. He could say that again—in Swa-hili. Lucy was now lying, her liver well and truly perforated, in the back of Clarissa's medical van, absorbing vein-juice (and whatever else they give you for a hole in that part of you that goes well with fried onions) by the gallon from a big clutch of plastic baggies hanging up over her head. Apparently she would survive.

She was already making snotty remarks about people who shoot other people with measly nine-millimeter pistols. Mean-while, the all-but-decapitated remains of Bennett Williams, for-mer cyberspace editor, meatspace terrorist, and would-be Master of the Universe, had already been carted off by the Civil Liberties Association. They'd also interviewed us all and let Buckley know he wasn't in any trouble. Good riddance, I told myself. We don' need no stinkin' Dark Overlords.

Several of Will's militia people were clambering around the slope of Pistol Sight Mountain Dam, looking for the other Ben-netts—or parts thereof. I would have waited until morning. Now and again, one of them would bend down, pick something up, holler for attention, and then hold up whatever he or she had found. It turned out Arlington Panghurst—who'd more or less started this whole fire drill—was the guy who'd tried to strangle Will and gotten his head blown off for the effort. Will was trying on his colorful new necktie—with an epauletted tan workshirt? I don't think so, Will—which by some miracle or something had survived the recent fracas without a stain or scratch. He was also squatting on his cowboy-booted heels, conversing earnestly with his wives, who were sitting on the ground beside the now-inactive aerocraft that Fran had piloted up here with her big sister's help and encouragement.

344 • L. NEIL SMITH

Not that Fran had needed much encouragement. It seems that Will's two girls hadn't lost the argument, after all. They'd simply known when to shut up and wait until the cat was away. In hindsight, it was just plain stupid of anybody to think that the Kendall sisters—the daughters of Scipio Africanus Kendall—could be kept out of any fight, pregnant or not. For one thing, they loved their husband, and would be needing a father for their children. What else were they going to do? What they had done, having spoken with Clarissa on the 'Com while Lucy, Will, and I were making dam fools of ourselves, was appropriated a GLPM flying machine, picked up a couple of Very Important Passengers (one of whom had helped them get their hands on the machine in the first place), and hot-winged it to Pistol Sight Mountain as quickly as they could.

The passenger who'd helped them acquire the transportation was no less than the President of the Confederacy himself (and therefore the loneliest man, professionally speaking, since the Maytag repairman), Olongo Featherstone-Haugh, who was presently supervising as a couple of militia types tenderly hauled Bennett's bomb out of the deep water of the reservoir where a cetacean member of the team had located and disarmed it. It was a great big one, all right, and it certainly would have done the job.

Glub, glub, glub.

"Mind you, Bennett would never have set that thing off before he was clear," Wilhelmsohn was explaining to us. He was still rubbing his wrists from time to time. The marks where Bennett had tied him up were purple and horrible looking, like ruts in a muddy road. "He was in it purely for the money and the power it could buy him. What he could do was use the bomb for two purposes, the second as a trap for his antagonists."

"Meaning us," I said, extremely mindful that Buckley was

standing right beside us, and embarrassed that Wilhelmsohn had chosen this moment for a postmortem.

"That's right. I'm thoroughly chagrined to admit that he'd been onto me for a long time, apparently, and planned to use whatever arrangements I made with you at the ice rink as an opportunity to kill all of us." He paused to gaze over his shoulder in the direction of the aerocraft. "Say, you don't suppose Will's wives have another sister, do you?"

I grinned at Wilhelmsohn with understanding and sympathy—Will was about as lucky as it gets—but I still felt a great need to say something to Buckley. I laid a hand on his shoulder, as gently as I could. "You wouldn't like to lower the hammer on that thing, would you?"

He looked down at his hand, absently, and then up at me. "Oh, I do beg your pardon, Win. Would you mind doing it for me, I fear I'm a trifle abstracted."

Yeah, I'll bet he was, at that. Mary-Beth and Fran had let me know that Buckley had been horrified to be told by his old friendly enemy, Olongo Featherstone-Haugh, that his own brother Bennett was the evil intelligence behind all of these murderous and criminal acts that had managed to kill more than two thousand people and shake the very foundation of Confederate civilization. He'd immediately determined to do something about it.

Remind me never to get in Buckley's way when he's determined.

I took the gun from his hand and let the hammer down. This time I noticed markings on the right grip, a trademark in a round boss, that said, CTC. Suddenly, I found I'd pressed the rubber pressure switch that lit the laser. Wilhelmsohn yelped, jumping backward when the red dot appeared in the middle of his stomach. I eased up on the switch and shrugged apologetically. I started to shove the longslide into my waistband until it clanked

346 • L. NEIL SMITH

against the .440 A&A I'd forgotten was still there. Guess we were all still a little abstracted. Instead, I opened the left side of Buckley's jacket—he didn't seem to mind, or even realize that I was doing it—and slid the pistol into the shoulder holster I knew I'd find there.

I made a mental note (how many mental notes did that make so far?) to tell him later on that I hoped he'd carry that piece with pride, for the rest of his life. It was a hard thing he'd done, but the right thing to do.

"This is all United Statesian hardware, isn't it, the longslide and the laser designator?" I asked, I guess to cover my embarrassment about lasering Wilhelmsohn—but immediately regretted what may well have been the most inappropriate topic possible at the moment. This was the very device, after all, that Buckley had used to kill his own brother. "I'm sorry," I said. "That's a topic for another time and place."

"Not at all, Win," Buckley replied to my apology. "Life must go on. It's long been an interest of mine, all of this otherworld weaponry. The Lasergrip, as they call it, is from the Crimson Trace Corporation of Beaverton, Oregon. I am informed that the man to see about it is Clyde."

Beaverton, again. What the hell is it with Beaverton? Suddenly, Will was up and running. I'd thought Fran and Mary-Beth had looked uncharacteristic, sitting on the ground like that, but I'd had other things on my mind.

Will headed toward the medical van, shouting "Clarissa! Clarissa! Come quick!"

30: DIRTY LAUNDRY

> No process, event, or situation has ever improved under media scrutiny. The average media personality rises to his level of incompetence simply by getting out of bed in the morning.
>
> —*Memoirs of Lucille G. Kropotkin*

Unaware of what was happening, Buckley went on, "That's an original .41 caliber Model 58 Military and Police you're carrying, isn't it? And a nine-millimeter Browning P-35 High Power if I'm not entirely mistaken. Would you care to see my Broomhandle Mauser sometime?"

"It's a .375 wildcat," I told him. "And I'd love to see your Broomhandle, Buckley, only not just now—there are babies about to be born!"

Clarissa already had her van in gear and reversed it carefully toward the aerocraft—with Lucy shouting directions from the back—where Will's wives were doing their Lamaze thing, puffing and blowing, while they waited. Buckley helped Will and me lift the girls up into the vehicle.

Over many years of police work, I'd delivered quite a number of babies myself, and I was looking forward to doing it again. But to my astonished disappointment, I got rudely kicked out of the now-crowded van—Will, of course, got to stay—and left to cool my heels with Buckley.

Of course the news-media vultures were all over the place before you could say, "Charles Foster Kane." Dozens of them had shown up within minutes of the president's arrival. They were taking long, loving holos of bloodstained crabgrass and the shiny shell casings lying on the road, pointing their lights and shoving their microphones and camera lenses everywhere they didn't belong and would be most annoying and upsetting to the survivors. It was their job description, after all.

I had an idea where they could shove all that equipment, and I told them, too, but it was Buckley who had the best way of dealing with these vermin. I intend to remember it for future reference and spread it around as much as I can.

"How does it feel," one obnoxious jerk asked Buckley, breathing garlic halitosis in his face as the hololens closed in for the kill, "to murder your own brother?"

"I believe you're Arlen Hopkins, aren't you?" Buckley replied calmly. "The fellow who was sued successfully for a drunken hit-and-run on a helpless baby chimpanzee last month?"

Hopkins cleared his throat, glanced wildly around, saw somebody who looked more interesting to interview on the other side of the dam, grabbed his cameraman—a chimpanzee—by the elbow, and evaporated. I pitied the poor sonofabitch a little—he was going to interview Lucy.

I congratulated Buckley.

"Dirty laundry," he told me, winking. "That fellow over there is recovering from a gunshot wound; his wife shot him after he tried to beat her up. And that one sends money to arm Howard Slaughterbush's majoritarian rebels in Patagonia. Win, they all have their own dirty laundry."

BUCKLEY WAS RIGHT, of course—about life going on, I mean. And it's true that time heals all wounds—with a little help from one's friends. Permanently cured of cancer, Benjamin Wilhelmsohn was free to begin enjoying life in the North American Confederacy—although I doubted he'd find anyone willing to pay him to teach sophistry. My guess is that he'd be happy just being a waiter at Mr. Meep's. The simple truth is that we'd all be—if we could do it in a free country.

Olongo went back contentedly to being caretaker president. I understand that he's a contender for this year's Telecom solitaire championship.

Will and I went back to our wives—and he to his babies—and I proceeded to get to know my lovely spouse better, some more. It's a life-long study. The babies? A fine brace of daughters, normal size and healthy weight. One of them, Mary-Beth's, I believe, is as bald as an egg, the other, Fran's, is a flaming redhead like her illustrious grandpa. Fran is calling her little girl Elcie, for her initials, L. C., which stand for Lucille Clarissa. I have a feeling that this was all arranged far in advance. Mary-Beth's daughter is called Cielle, for C. L., or Clarissa Lucille.

Will is nothing but a big walking grin.

Buckley took control of his own magazine—changing the title back to *The North American Franklinite*—and wrote a story for the very next issue, explaining what his brother had done, and claiming that the incident just resolved, *proved*, that the Confederacy needs a government.

Benjamin Wilhelmsohn, who spends a great deal of time "yachting" with his newfound "brother" Buckley (Clarissa and I have accepted an invitation to go with them once or twice), passionately authored the very first letter-to-the-new-editor, arguing that Buckley had it all wrong.

Best of all (at any rate, it felt that way at the time) was what I found in the driveway the morning after the gunfight up on Pistol Sight Mountain: a brand-new, fusion-powered, candy-apple red Neova HoverSport. I had declined Lucy's offer to pay me, and this was her way of getting even. I was overjoyed—and without the faintest foreboding. I guess somewhere along the way I'd lost the Bear Curse, or it had lost me.

To my utter astonishment—and mortification—Government-land looks like it's going to be a big hit. It's a good thing that

Clarissa and Lucy quietly bought shares in such a stupid idea. On the other hand, if anything ever came of Deejay Thorens's isotope theory, I never heard anything about it.

Immigrants continue streaming in through probability broaches everywhere, their numbers about evenly matched by individuals leaving the Earth, headed out to the Asteroid Belt and other places in the Solar System.

I guess what it all proves, if it proves anything at all (and my darling Clarissa insists that it should or, she says, the whole effort was wasted), is that if you want to be free you really only have two choices. The first is to do what I did, which is to escape to the North American Confederacy—if you can find it—and help defend it with us.

The other is to make another Confederacy, where you are.

ABOUT THE AUTHOR

L. NEIL SMITH has won the Prometheus Award for Best Libertarian Fiction three times, for his first novel, *The Probability Broach*, for *Pallas*, and for *Forge of the Elders*. He is the author of two dozen novels, including *The Crystal Empire, The Lando Calrissian Adventures, The Wardove, Henry Martyn,* and *Bretta Martyn*. A life member of the National Rifle Association since 1974, founder and national coordinator of the Libertarian Second Amendment Caucus, and publisher of an online magazine, *The Libertarian Enterprise,* he has been active in the libertarian movement for thirty-nine years and is its most prolific and widely published living writer. He is also an essayist and radio commentator. Smith lives in Fort Collins, Colorado, with his wife, Cathy, and their daughter, Rylla, and can be reached via the "Webley Page" at http://www.webleyweb.com/lneil.